D1484572

THE GIRL
WITH THE
HICKORY HEART

LAUREN NICOLLE TAYLOR

OWL HOLLOW PRESS

Owl Hollow Press, LLC, Springville, UT 84663

The Girl with the Hickory Heart
Copyright © 2021 by Lauren Nicolle Taylor

Library of Congress Cataloging-in-Publication Data
The Girl with the Hickory Heart / L.N. Taylor. — First edition.

Summary:
In an island nation akin to a wooden Hong Kong, two Asian women from warring tribes, Lye, a powerful slave of the Emperor and Luna, a Char defying tradition, must put aside their pasts in order to move forward.

Cover Illustration: Le Vuong
Typography: Les Solot
Interior Illustrations: Lauren Nicolle Taylor

ISBN 978-1-945654-80-0 (paperback)
ISBN 978-1-945654-81-7 (e-book)

*For Nana, who never let me think being mixed was anything
Other than wonderful*

Char do not fear death.
It is our constant,
As sure as the salted winds that thread between the islands.

But I fear death.
The death of three.
To be left behind would be the loneliest torture.

1

CHAR LUNA

The soft, strangled squeal of a creature who knows it's in danger but doesn't know what kind.

Teck, teck, teck... A finger taps my temple impatiently. But I'm already awake. I heard the trotting hooves on the boardwalk competing with the slosh of the ocean.

A hiss through fangs, black and slimy as squid ink. Acid leaking from yellow lips. Curled claws drag, keeping time with lapping waves.

Someone tugs on my plait like it's a well rope. I sit up, elbows digging into the hard, salt-crusted planks of my bed.

"Sister!" I know it's serious when he calls me sister. "He did it again," Joka whispers witheringly.

Eldest brother Sun's broad shoulders cut stern shadows on the floor. The squint of his eyes matches the pointedness of the dagger at his side. "You hear that?" he asks, ears pricked. A wicked smile hooks his lips as his hand tightens around the hilt.

Perched on my ladder, I nod and pat Sun's tense wrist. "Wait." *With food this scarce, Ben Ni will suffer for this.*

Joka eases a thin shoulder against the bedroom door, issuing a muffled bark at our youngest brother. "Ai ya! Wake up, dreamer! You forgot to lock the gate... again!"

Ben Ni appears, befuddled, hair raked like a backwards wave. Joka looks to me and we roll our eyes. "The pig..." He slaps his face. "The pig!" Hopping from foot to foot, he moans, "Papa's gonna kill me! Kill. Me!" It's a familiar song and I groan as the melody repeats its single bar.

"And the beating he'll give you with that oak arm'll make your ears ring for weeks," Sun emphasizes with a vindictive chuckle, clutching the sides of his head. Ben Ni blanches.

Scrambling down, I land quietly on the floor. A breeze sneaks over the waves beneath our house and pushes between the floorboards, creeping up my cotton pant leg. I shudder. Our pig's wheezy squeal softens as it runs from our house and the midnight mauler stalking it.

Ben Ni reaches for the net he made hanging from a hook in the hallway. It's cleverly weighted on the edges to pin its prey. The stones warble as they clang against each other.

"Sh!" I hiss, one ear focused on the sleeping village about to be woken by my cloud-bound brother, and the other on my parents, who could stir at any second. Sun runs a hand through his short black hair, and it springs back into place. His dark eyes dart from side to side, mind already in the hunt.

"We're not heading into battle, Sun." For once I can be sure of those words. The treaty with our mainland enemy has spread relief over the nine Char islands like a sweet, spiced cloud. "We can do this quietly *and* without bloodshed." I puff out his candle. Tart smoke stings my nostrils as his flare with irritation. But he gives a small salute, like maybe he'll listen.

I tiptoe through our simple kitchen. Papa rolls over by the hearth. His long black moustache moves like a lazy worm as he snores, too tired to lift its head. Papa's hand is fair but brutal. Ben Ni watches him sleep with tear-prickling apprehension. I shake my head and take his net, slipping into the humid, insect-filled night. Hopefully it won't come to that.

I scan the boardwalk connecting the huts of our village, winding like a crooked spine along the base of the coal-colored mountains. The one pure white hindquarter of the jet-black midnight mauler several houses down stands out like a beacon. The tree cat slinks awkwardly away from us, claws curled under, body rocking from side to side like it has drunk too many plum wines. My mouth sours at the thought.

Swatting at midges licking salt from my ivory-toned skin, I search for our pig. I can't see it, but I *hear* it. Trotting, snuffling. An apathetic wheeze like the squash of a tattered accordion.

Sun bumps into my back, followed by Joka and Ben Ni. Three brothers awaiting instruction.

"You should be more careful," Joka groans. "You're such an empty-headed…" He pokes an accusing finger at Ben Ni's chest.

Ben Ni's sigh seems to scrape the base of his ribs, golden eyes on the swirling night sky. His hair is softer, browner like mine, and the wind picks on it, sweeping it over his brow and blocking his vision. "I'm sorry, brother, I was playing around with the feeder." He taps the air, invisible ideas competing in front of his eyes.

"Perhaps empty-headed is the wrong word." Joka softens his tone, patting Ben Ni's shoulder. "There are too many ideas in there, and not enough room for common sense. Let's just get the pig back before Papa knocks those ideas from your brain."

As we creep further along the boardwalk, Sun wraps an arm around Joka's bamboo neck and squeezes. The smooth timber tightens, sounding like a finger smudging glass. "Leave little brother alone. Besides…" He holds up his dagger. "This makes for good sport." His shrewd eyes focus, concentrating as he presses his balsawood foot into the decking. His square jaw sways slowly as he scans the dark. He stops. "There it is!" He rubs his hands together, then points his dagger at the small pink shape nosing dangerously close to the water.

Joka sighs. "Maybe I don't enjoy killing things as much as you."

Sun releases Joka, thumps his back, and Joka stumbles, clutching his shiny green neck.

I pause, waiting for a window to blossom with candlelight. When it doesn't, I steal forward, watching the waving white hindquarter of the midnight mauler as it nears the pig, who seems to forget what scared it from its pen in the first place. "Quiet! We're not spilling blood on this deck. We just need to catch the pig before Papa finds out."

Sun snorts.

I speed up, passing dark window after dark window, praying we don't wake a witness to our crime. The village is sleeping. Peaceful within the haphazard huts.

"Come on." I take Ben Ni's hand as we come within ten yards of the witless animal and its slowly closing hunter.

"Sun," I direct. "Arms wide on the water's edge. We don't want it falling in." I eye the knife in his hand, pointing to the moon. Our eyes connect. "Last resort?" He nods, but it seems disingenuous. Protectively, I usher Ben Ni behind me.

Joka hangs back, a coat on a hook. "What am I supposed to do?"

"When the mauler comes your way, chase it back to the mangroves." His eyes widen and I grin. "Or if you're feeling brave, you could kick it into the water," I whisper. He's not likely to kick it. That would require getting close, and Joka's hands are for turning pages, not wrestling jungle cats.

Ben Ni bounces eagerly. "And me?"

I tap my chin, trying to think of a safe task. "Err, make sure Joka actually does what I told him to. From, uh, over there." I point to the railing that hugs the mountain. He takes a few steps, not far enough, and I push him. "Right up there." Ben Ni huffs but hoists himself out of harm's way.

Claws scrape. Hooves clatter. The pig shrieks. The mauler is within clawing range of the pig, and now the pig knows it. Warm mist is disturbed, and midges ride the current. Moonlight adds sheen to the air as if we're walking through thinnest silk. *Silk that bites.*

Sun closes in on the two animals, broad shoulders and thick body moving like a shadow creeping across a sunny deck. The mauler freezes, hissing softly with a double-pronged tongue, eyes floating like two yellow wish lanterns as it looks back at us.

I make a wish: For a living pig and no injured brothers.

Spooked, the mauler breaks into a strange canter, heading for our pig.

I sprint, heart beating fast. Feet picking out every solid board and avoiding the rotted ones as salt spray peppers my pale cheeks. Ribbons of mist flow from its back as it pounces on the pig, which stands in the middle of the walkway, blinking. Its ribs, ridged like harp strings, rise and fall rapidly. It has barely enough meat on it to feed one man. But it's precious.

Foolishly, I throw the net. Capturing both creatures and creating a scrabbling, hissing mess.

I can't hesitate. Lifting the net, I grab at the mauler's coarse black fur, sharp as needles, and pull. It screeches, lashes out to scratch me, but its claws are retracted, and it feels more like a bristled punch.

The pig is released with a thud and a grunt.

My relief is as short-lived as the last slice of mooncake at our dinner table. I hear the whistle of a dagger as it sails through the wispy air and then a single *plop!* as the poor little pig stumbles backward off the boardwalk and into the sea. I rush to the rail in time to see it sink like a stale dumpling. Sun kneels, arm outstretched. His knife digs deep into the mauler's leg and it screeches. Blood drips down its white hindquarter, acid saliva spitting from its mouth, flying toward me.

Joka and Ben Ni start toward me, but it's too late. Saliva burns my face and our food is sinking to the sandy seabed.

Before they can protest, I take a deep breath, hold it, and jump.

SHIVERING, I place the wet, spluttering, and quite irritated pig back in its straw bed. I pat its back. "You're halfway to cured pork now," I say with a smirk. It responds with a wheeze and an offended snuffle. I lock the hutch when I leave.

Squeezing the salt water from my hair, I shoot a disparaging look at Sun, who grins sheepishly. He kicks the pen door with his wooden foot, wiggling his toes and his eyebrows at the same time. "No harm done, little Luna." The way the brass tendons on his foot slide and contract like tiny spy glasses pulls a minute smile from my chagrinned face.

I reach up and slap his forearm, his hard-as-stone muscles stinging my palm. "I thought you had better aim than that! You didn't even kill it. And now there's mauler blood all over the boardwalk."

Sun throws an arm over Ben Ni's broadening shoulders. His golden head is dipped low, although I doubt shame pulls it down. He's concocting something. "Ben Ni's going to scrub it off before anyone sees it." Sun throws him dark eyes, laced with affection. "Right?"

Ben Ni lifts a bucket from the straw-covered ground. "Right."

Joka wraps a blanket over my shoulders and hugs me as I shudder. "How's your face?" He uses the corner to rub my cheek.

I force a smile, because guilt tugs at Ben Ni's features. "It washed off in time. I'm fine." I catch his doubting eyes. "Really, I'm fine." Joka opens his mouth to chastise our youngest brother while Sun cleans his knife. I put my hand up to stop him. "The weighted net worked well, little brother."

His dreaming, honey eyes lift, hopeful, "You think?"

My jaw itches but I make myself leave it. "I do. I bet it'd be very useful for catching forest turkeys."

Joka can't help himself. "Yes, it would be if Sun could keep from throwing knives or shooting arrows without thought." He huffs. "You should have listened to Luna."

Sun grunts and stands taller. "You know, books won't save you if Shen break down the door, brother. When they light your insides with fire or freeze your blood."

Joka opens his mouth to retaliate, to quote the words of the recent treaty, but I place a hand on his shoulder. *Stop.* It not easy for Sun to let go of the constant press of danger. It will take us all a while to get used to the idea of peace.

Joka silences his lashing tongue.

"Yes, Sun should have listened to me. I'm the thankless, un-lucky sap who keeps you all alive and out of trouble." I gripe, but I don't really mean it. Everyone has their role in this family. Hide-saver is mine. "As punishment, you can help Ben Ni wash the blood from the deck before sunrise." Sun's chest expands but the protest deflates. He picks up a bucket. None of us want to see Ben Ni beaten.

"You are very good at your job, sister," Ben Ni says, warming my heart with a toothy smile.

Joka rolls his eyes again. "She does get daily practice."

We leave it there. We don't belittle him, crush the ideas that spill from his mouth, or add stones to his guilt. Ben Ni is the hope-ful one. He dreams. He's uncorrupted. And we need him this way. So that when the pigs shrink to hide on bones, when the charred side of the village grows blacker and bleaker, we will remember what we were fighting to protect.

I creep back inside, hoping to the pebble-pocked moon that our parents didn't hear any of it.

Shen Lye Li
I am everything and I am nothing.
I am the beginning of new life,
And the instrument by which it ends.

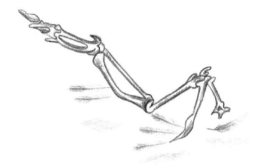

2
SHEN LYE LI

In the stony shadow of the rust-red palace with peak winds slapping his cheeks pink, the Shen boy kneels before me. I think "boy" because he can't be older than fifteen. I think "boy" because his eyes are rounder than a beggar's rice bowl and almost as empty. He's a vessel, ready to be trained, to be molded by our unforgiving *shifus*. A product of the emperor's long-term grooming of the mind, beginning the moment children enter the classroom. In the hands of these masters, the boy will fulfil his purpose. They will kink and curl him until he is seamless hate with terrible power.

I seek approval from the chancellor, second in command to the emperor, and he nods. Twisted mouth so sour, I'm sure he's eaten pickled lime for breakfast.

I cup the boy's ear and my thick gray sleeve slips over my scarred arm. His atmosphere reads forest fire and thick smoke. Full of animosity for a foe he's never met but has been taught to hate. It is our first lesson. Before reading and writing comes Hate. I wince at the ferocity, the effectiveness of his education. Mind and soul burning with it.

Something tugs at my conscience: Reluctance to send one more brain-washed child to war. To put power into someone so young and volatile. My hand breeds space between us. My eyes blink tears. The shadow of the palace grows darker and colder as I sink into my gilded chair.

Impatiently, the chancellor leans in and spits, "Fire, Water, Earth, Air, or Blood?" His voice has become the perfect torture. A cane hovering over my back.

My bald head hangs as I mutter, "The boy reads Fire."

So many have been Fire lately.

I glance at another boy training in one of many red-painted squares—my brother. His movements stilted because he's not concentrating. I know he can do better. He laughs when the trainer smacks his hand, a tell that he's frustrated. He wipes sweat from his brow and gives a brief wave before the trainer knocks his head with a bamboo pole wrapped in blue cloth. We share our mother's eyes, Ash and I. Changing blue like the sea. I smile so briefly it's like a blink. *I've never seen the sea.*

The chancellor's fingernails find the underside of my arm and pinch. His breath is foul with Black Feather Bone tea. The superstitious beverage of charred birds' wings won't give his slim frame strength and layers of muscle as he hopes. It will only stain his teeth. He's like me, willowy and bone thin. Our power comes from within.

"Get on with it, Keeper *girl*." His eyes land on the long line of selected new warriors running down the stairs and through the manicured garden. The sun cuts them into two. The men and women in shadow are too close to their grim destiny. Those in sun could still turn and run, wind their way back home through the precisely clipped trees and methodically trained branches. *Never allowed to grow the way they want to grow.*

But they march forward, slipping like amber beads through praying fingers and step under the curse of the blood-colored stone palace.

They want this. It's what they've been raised to want. This honor. This price.

They don't know any better.

I know better.

Shirking from the chancellor's pincer grip, I behold the young boy, his mouth set determinedly, struggling to hide the fear trapped behind it. *The uncertainty.* I lean forward, running both palms over the steamy air around his body. I'm searching for the place, different on each Shen, only I can see. Barely the size of a peppercorn, resting just where his jaw meets his neck, is his elemental Pulse. It flickers erratically like a flame seeking oxygen.

"Stay completely still, young Shen subject," I order with forced holiness. The boy nods, hands clasped and shaking like he's caught a cricket that's desperate to escape.

I place two fingers on his Pulse, breathe in and close my eyes. Flames drape my vision. Heat courses through my veins as Fire flows from my heart to the tips of those two fingers. I focus on the point our skin meets. *One, two, three,* I sigh, and push hard and fast. He gasps but doesn't pull away.

The erratic elemental Pulse slows and syncs with the boy's own heartbeat. I meet his eyes, now singed with orange, a growing heat inside him. He bows, dark, braided hair swinging like vines. *Or ropes to choke me.* He thanks me for something he may resent me for later. I have awakened the element of Fire in him. With training, he'll be able to use that power to burn Char soldiers from the inside. Climb their ribs like a ladder and press, sending ash clouds into their lungs, or molten lava over their eyes. The Shen Empire shaped his clay form and I fired him into a hardened, almost impossible to break weapon. I have created yet another instrument of death.

I bow in shame, although the chancellor will think it's in veneration.

The chancellor holds up parchment and I dip the pointed pewter thimble on my thumb in ink, scraping a mark on the page in the fire column. When he summons the next one, I quickly make a mark of my own. A quick cut and reminder, added to the others on my arm. Soon I'll have to mark my legs. *Soon I'll be a ghost.*

Beyond the terrace, blossoms are teased from cherry trees in a gust of wind and I breathe in long, desperate to smell the sweet fruit scent. Like the tree, parts of me are stripping away, but I won't grow new buds and flower. I'm becoming cracked and brittle, a shred of life. Good things can't slip under the imposition of the palace. It frowns down upon its subjects and its land, unsatisfied.

A small sigh; a bruisy sound. I remember when I looked upon this palace with awe and hope. When I swallowed everything the emperor fed us. My ignorance was truly bliss.

Palace workers scrub endlessly at the once pale sandstone. The ground the building sits upon is rich with iron ore. The rust colored mineral crawls up every tree trunk, every foundation stone, giving the appearance of weeping old blood. The sound mocks the emperor. It mocks me, because even if they remove the stain, it will always return.

My sigh is one of dashed hopes and crushed-to-dust exhaustion as I look down the line of eager young Shen desperate for their turn.

Young men and women ready to fight. Ready for the power I can give them. *Gift them.* They don't understand its burden.

But maybe they don't feel the weight the way I do. Maybe the burden is mine alone.

After all, it always begins with me.

3

CHAR LUNA

My brothers and I clutch the table like crabs to cage meat. Papa's dark eyes watch us shrewdly. In this game, no one can be first to look away.

"Go!" Papa's wooden fist with black-lacquered sap lines pounds the table. It's worn smooth in places, but the shine on the cogs and the brass hinges look as new as the day the Carvress presented it to him. The support stilts of our hut shift and shake. They plunge deep into the brine, nibbled by fish and rubbed by the wings of great rays. And one day, if he slams hard enough, the house will disconnect from its long legs and we'll float out to sea.

He spreads his oak hand over the oak table and creates the Call. Music that comes from touching one's wooden limb with its matching timber. I smile at the perfect sound. *Like bees harmonizing.* I gaze at my own hands, small but strong. Freckled and fairer than the others, wondering what my Call will sound like.

The setting sun spreads golden curls of light over the wall, piercing the window that faces out to sea.

I try to subtly sabotage my chances, eyes flicking to the wall. My brothers need to win more than me. My small body doesn't need as much fuel to grow.

"Ha! Little Luna looked away first. She loses!" Papa shouts, slapping my soft flesh with his hard oak hand.

Withdrawing my hand, I shake out the sting that feels like I've been clubbed with a bat and elbow Ben Ni in the side. I wink at the others. "I lost on purpose. We all know Joka needs fattening up if he's going to make it through Char training."

Sun loses focus, unable to resist joining in on the teasing. "One drumstick's not going to do much for those cherry twig arms." He pokes at Joka who turns his spiky haired head toward his older brother.

Papa chuckles. "Ha, again! All of you lose!" He points at his four children one by one. Gloating.

I grimace and shake my head. "You two are pitiful. Even when I hand you the victory, you let it slip through your fingers." Ben Ni is out of the running as well, probably dreaming about Joka with cherry twig arms, blossoms floating from his fingers.

When Papa goes to snatch the last chicken leg from the center of our tiny table, eldest brother Sun grabs his forearm. His newly gained muscles strain against Papa's long-developed physique. Oak contracts, brass winds up.

"If I'd known how useful an oak arm would be in the battle for the last drumstick, I would've chosen more wisely!" Sun announces as he tries to loosen Papa's grip on the last piece of chicken. The meat is stringy. The feet lack crunch. But it's a treasure.

Papa easily breaks from Sun's grasp and points the drumstick accusingly at his son. "Well, clearly a balsawood foot did not help you last night when you were chasing our pig down the boardwalk." A hint of sternness sharpens his voice.

We pause, anticipating punishment. He scans his children for expressions of guilt. "It was my fault," I announce.

"No, it was mine!" Joka says plainly.

Ben Ni blushes, looking as guilty as he is. "I left the gate open, Papa. Punish me."

We look to Sun, but he just shrugs, still trying to grab the chicken from Papa's hand.

Papa's jaw clenches, exchanging a look with Mama that could mean anything from *I'll beat them all* to *I'll let this go.* She gives a swift shake of her head and he grunts.

"All right, all right, I confess. I killed the mauler," Sun says proudly.

Papa strokes his chin, still easily fending off Sun's attempts to take him down. "Seems to me all you did was wound the creature, spilling blood all over the boardwalk."

Sun's eyes express a little regret, and the rest of us anxiously await our sentence.

"I shall think on what to do with the four of you… later."

Our punishment, it seems, is the cruel wait. The threat of a beating hanging over our heads.

Papa chuckles. "Now, where were we…" Punishment delayed. Game reinstated.

I ache to join this rare play with Sun. His heart and mind have turned to darker things in the last six months. I bite my lip, staring at the mama's back who will certainly disapprove. The weight of war pressed Sun into a straighter, broader man. *It's happening to all of us.* The treaty may be a pause in the fighting, but it does not unpick the deeply sewn threads of loss and fear woven into every Char. It's why we must revel in the deep bellowing sound of laughter, warm with love and breathed deep like air over coals coaxing flames.

I decide it's worth the risk and spring from my chair to swing from Papa's other arm. Using my slightness to my advantage, I work my feet into his ribs to unbalance him.

Second brother, Joka, narrows his dark, intelligent eyes at Sun and I. Chin in hand, he dips down to read, extremely disinterested in rough housing. His bamboo neck stretches and pangs, cracking from side to side.

"*Apa ini?*" *What is this?* A pot lid slams down, iron on iron. Mama clatters over to Sun, dangling from Papa's arm like a monkey, and me hanging from his other arm, more like the purple mango the monkey eats. She slaps the back of Sun's head. I try not to laugh at the hollow sound.

The disappointed stare she aims my way is enough to make me drop to the floor. Eyes downcast. Smile hidden beneath my long brown hair. I bow. "Sorry, Mama. I was just trying to help eldest brother to…" She humphs, and I stop talking. She wishes me to act like a Char woman: Dutiful and composed. Not a Yan boy.

Papa slaps my back like he would one of the boys. I stumble but keep my feet. "Ah, little Luna. You use your size well." He rubs at his ribcage where I dug my toes in. I grin proudly.

Mama waggles a finger. "Setsu," she warns her barrel-chested husband. "Don't encourage her. She is learning to be caretaker not to take no care." She doesn't understand I am a caretaker. Just not in the way she expects.

He bows his head low and apologetically. "Yes, wife."

Satisfied, Mama twists away from our chaos. Her cobalt eyes crinkle and she bends, right angled, toward the quiet, dreamy one, youngest brother Ben Ni, drawing patterns in the sauce with his finger. "I think Ben Ni gets the leg. He's the only one who has any manners." Sun complains but she raises one threatening finger and his mouth clamps shut.

Ben Ni licks the sauce from his finger and straightens. We settle back into our seats.

Light snakes across the floor as the sun sinks below the lapping water and I light a candle. A full ladle slops onto my plate. I lean my head against Mama's wiry arm. I know she stares down at my golden-brown hair, so different to her own, with puzzlement. I know she wonders if I'll ever reach her height. But I'm *Little Luna*. Mama tsks, pointing. "Here! Eat more taro." No matter how much food she heaps on my plate from her own, I may never gain another inch.

Three pairs of unhappy eyes watch Ben Ni take a victorious bite of the drumstick, smacking his lips tauntingly. The sound of wood and metal tightening belies Sun's tension. His jealousy. But it's light jealousy and soon his head is down, scooping up the last fragments of dinner, while Mama leans her cherrywood hip against the cooling stove. She tilts her head to the roof, tight bun slick as black sesame paste in the candlelight. The sigh she pushes up there is a contented one. I feel it too. A teetering-on-the-edge emotion. Happiness may slide away if the balance is slightly out.

We are in a brief breathing space. One we never expect to last.

"Mama." I offer her my seat, worrying over her sinewy structure. "Come eat." It's a dance we all take turns performing.

She shakes her head and waves me away. "I ate while I was cooking." We give her doubtful expressions.

If she ate, I didn't see it.

Ben Ni, the golden son with golden seams through his hair, slips a prized shred of chicken skin into my palm and knocks my shoulder, whispering, "Us fleshies have to stick together, eh?"

I smile secretly and lock it away. Because it won't be long. Soon I have to make *my* choice. Then Ben Ni will be last of the Yans to make the change. Twelve months and he'll be where I am now. Only his choices fan out before him like cards in a conjurer's deck. I only have a few cards in my pack, and they all read a similar destiny.

When Ben Ni's head returns to the clouds, his rice malt syrup irises unfocused, I tear the chicken skin in half and hand it to Joka and Sun beneath the table. They take it gratefully. Sun knocks my knee with his balsawood foot in thanks. Pride is a mask he must wear to save face.

FROM THE sea, Coalstone Village looks like a string of paper lanterns hung at the base of the crumbling mountain.

Dots of light puncture the darkness as families sit along the edge, dipping their feet in the warm water and watching their fathers blow smoke dragons into the sky. Calm conversations float over the sea. The village is settled, but in a way that's almost desperate. We cling to peaceful moments.

Sun and I pull off our slippers and dip our toes into the lapping salt water, while Joka leans against the hut, reading. We shudder even though it's warm as minute-old tea. Blood fish swarm around my legs, picking the dead skin from the soles of my petite feet. They seem to prefer my feet. Maybe it's the lack of hair. I giggle, watching the swirl of red. Blood colored and shaped like a droplet, they're harmless, cute even. But my face scrunches at those skeleton pantry days, when money went to battles and we had to scrape the meager flesh from blood fish bones. The terrible taste lurks in my memory with other unpleasant things, like washed up sun-warmed humming whale carcass, its harmonizing music fettered to its rotted tongue.

Sun wraps a toned arm around me and squeezes my bones roughly. "Little Luna!" he exclaims, pulling away like I hurt him with my pointed shoulder. "You're thin as a bamboo sprout. And you're shaking like you're about to be cut." He chuckles briefly. When I don't join him, a little weary of the "Luna's small" jokes, he nudges me carefully. "But you're strong in your own way. Small, but with a giant's heart."

He crosses one leg over the other, dipping his flesh foot in the water.

I pinch his arm, and he grimaces. "I'm far stronger than you think, older brother." Sun stands, rolling his shoulders, which click like cogs. His quiet lays blankets over the air as he stares out over the sea. I know he thinks of friends who have "sailed" away. *Wood scarred and blackened.*

Papa humphs, black diamond sparkle in his eyes. I shift closer, wanting to soak in his earthy warmth. Rib cage to rib cage, feeling his large chest fill with smoke. "A hoarder bear," I whisper, asking for a favorite of mine. He purses his lips and brings his inky brows together in concentration.

"A hoarder bear," he repeats after blowing a ball of illusion smoke into the air. The cloud forms four legs, a stubborn nose, and long spoon-shaped ears. It ambles away slowly, pausing to scratch at the earth. It turns and glares with round owl eyes, drawing me in.

Joka chuckles. I always choose hoarder bear.

The illusion dissipates and we sit in dusky light again. Papa deep in thought, me looking to the island of Black Sail City, speckled with golden light. It's the closest of the eight other Char islands to ours. Only a day's boat ride away. But it may as well be a million miles in distance.

The boardwalk slats creak under Sun's weight as he paces, practicing jabbing moves. Fighting an imaginary foe we fear will come real. I imagine my brother, face to face with a Shen warrior, only his balsawood foot to shield him and my *giant's* heart pumps wildly. My chin dips to the darker, deeper water. His future, as opaque as the open sea, frightens me.

Mama peers out the window, frowns unconvincingly, and disappears to clean the dinner dishes.

Sun slams down on the other side of Papa.

"So, my little Luna. Have you made a decision?" Papa rumbles.

Sun answers for me. "Teak legs will serve her well. She needs the height…" He nods to my pale legs swishing in the water, "and the color."

Papa glowers at Sun and his mouth zips. Papa's a man of few words because he doesn't need them. Words are like seeds flicked from his beard.

Joka, eyes not lifting from his text, a candle too close to the paper, breaks his story trance. "Leave her alone. The ability to stand in sunlight until your skin is damaged isn't a skill. Some might say the behavior lacks basic survival instincts. She'll make her decision when she's good and ready. She's got time, right, Papa?"

Sun's muscles tense, gripping the edge of the boardwalk. His spiky hair leaves a shadow like a red pineapple on the hut wall. His suggestion is in line with tradition. He's a traditional Char man, wanting nothing more than to protect his tribe and this family. *I know exactly how he feels.*

I let them discuss my future without protest. Not because I would heed any of their stupid suggestions, but because for right now, I'm happy to simply listen to their misguided but heartfelt concern.

Joka is right, I have time. But time seems rather pointless when the end result can only change by a fraction. My decision coasts over my head like a bird of prey. Any second now, it will dive and strike.

Papa nods, but there's a stiffness to it. To the water he mutters, "Not very much time." They wish a future of wifehood and fat grandchildren for their only daughter.

And me? I'm not sure what I wish, only that Mama and Papa's plan for me makes my stomach curl upon itself like the edges of burned paper.

Ben Ni emerges, wiping his dishwashing hands on his pants and sitting by my side. My ally. "So, what are we talking about?" he asks, though I'm sure he's aware.

I splash water at Sun, scattering the blood fish and landing a few drops on Joka's page. "We're tossing up which brother goes on the woodpile," I quip.

Ben Ni laughs, and it sounds like doves taking flight. All pure light and air. "Well, it's gotta be between Joka and Sun, right?"

Joka frowns finger running along a passage in his book and Sun slaps out at Ben Ni from above. "Ah!"

Papa rises, tucking his pipe in his waistband and placing a heavy hand on my shoulder. The coolness of the brass joints raises goosebumps on my skin. Patting me and coughing once, he says, "I'm going to bed." He casts a warning eye over his four children. "Do not disturb me. *Or* the neighbors."

Mama giggles when he enters, and we shift a good distance away. Past the last building to where the mangrove arms poke through the gaps in the boardwalk and whisper, *Shelter*. The boardwalk is at its lowest here and the sludgy sand begs us to bury our feet and shift sky crabs from their hiding places. Navy shells dotted with silver sparkle like the night sky. We sink into a halfway place between sea and land as we watch crabs swim gracelessly through shallow pools like they're trying to climb a ladder, not move through liquid.

Huddled together, my brothers wait patiently for me to speak.

Clasping my hands, I stare out at the large fish swirling around a baited cage in deeper water. Silver scales catch the moonlight, giving the sea its own dancing stars. I confess my heart. "What if I want an arm or a strong fighting hand? I want more than a steady marriage and a cherrywood hip to rest a laundry basket on. What if I want to train to be a soldier with you?" As soon as I say it, it becomes a steady flame in my chest.

Joka shakes his head slowly. "Think about it logically, Luna. You're too small. You may be strong, but you're a girl. It's extremely rare for a girl to join the army. And those women were formidable. They matched men's strength and endurance." His voice is strained because he doesn't want to extinguish those flames and leave me charcoal and drenched. "It would be so much harder for you." I bite my lip and Ben Ni threads his arm through mine. "Besides, the treaty means the war could be over. Our men are coming home. When *we* go to the barracks, it will only be for training. Then we'll come home and find wives, carve our boats, and—"

Sun chimes in, voice deep with responsibility. "Speak for yourself. I'm going to stay. Being a soldier like Papa is all I've ever wanted. But yes, I heard some are gathering at the barracks to collect their pay, and then there'll be an armada of ships sailing in celebration across the harbor in the morning."

We push past our curfew, talking of plans that seem close and yet unreal. We only choose to retire when a chain of yawning begins and can't be stopped.

I open the hut door and poke my head inside. My parents sleep on the bench by the hearth. Mama is happily locked beneath Papa's arm, snores coming from both of them. Theirs is a marriage to envy. But I'm not fool enough to think I will be so lucky. I breathe in and hold that pain inside for a moment, my lungs wishing to burst. *Would marriage feel like this? Air trapped with nowhere to go? Suffocation?*

I place a mask of sisterly mischief over my anxiety and sneak back out, giving the boys the all clear. One by one they filter through the door, kissing me on the cheek as they pass.

"Goodnight, little Luna," they whisper. Their blessings are like silver pins to my throat. A sharp unease sits there. Things are about to change for me and it's unwanted.

Ben Ni pauses in his doorway. Golden eyes warm, young. "Sister, wait."

The other door closes just as he disappears into the darkness of his room. He knocks my face with leaves and sticky branches. I step back. "What's this?"

"I made this for you." He presses a carved pot holding a plant into my hands. The leaves are diamond shaped and darkest purple, like a mysterious dream. The pot is beautiful. Smoke and willow trees. Clouds and heartbirds. "I know you haven't been sleeping well." A blush creeps up my neck. I don't like him to worry. I don't like any of them to worry… about me.

"How…" I had thought I was being stealthy.

His eyes drop to the floor. "I hear you."

My heart catches like I've swallowed a piece of coalstone. My nights have been peppered with nightmares. Men grabbing at my arms. Bartering, tugging at one of the only young, unmarried women left in the village. In them, I'm a doll, seams popping as they pull harder until I'm torn in two. I swallow. "Oh."

"The Anchu Anchu plant should help you rest." His earnestness, and his heart—the things I feel obligated to protect.

I press a leaf between my finger and thumb, releasing its mushroomy scent. My eyes crinkle like a paper fan and my heart opens like one. "Thank you, little brother."

He bows and retreats to his room.

I lock the front door, blow out the candle that has bloomed wax over the table, and pull the blanket over Mama's shoulders.

The house sighs with me as I climb the ladder to my loft, which is really an eked out six by three-foot platform in the crawlspace of the roof. I would be happier sleeping on the floor in Ben Ni's room but now I am *of age,* I must sleep separately to my brothers. Tied together for so many years, the day I turned sixteen began the slow and painful snipping of threads.

Until I am tied to another.

The boys snore and shift in their beds. The house is still.

4
SHEN LYE LI

It should have ended with me.

Even the brush of moonlight on my skin could cause me pain. I hold my pale, sliced wrists to the white light. Dried blood clings to the bandages.

The ink-stained, pointed thimble pressed in and I started joining together the small cuts that tallied my awakenings. And it felt like the first good thing I'd done in years. I opened my eyes wide and let the truth in. Shrugged off my denial like a heavy robe. What came next was a crumbling, endless tumble of weight.

I've heard that when you drop something into the ocean, deep pressure causes it to compress and eventually implode. I felt crushed to the size of a marble—nowhere to hide, no escape from my crimes.

I could be the Keeper no longer. I could not serve the emperor. I would not awaken one more element in one more Shen soldier.

My eyes closed and I sighed sluggishly. In the end, the guards got to me before I could end my life. Before I could finally pass over and rest. Now I lay my listless head on the stretcher bed. Rough fabric sanding my ear lobe.

The heavy door of the "safe room" flies open, banging carelessly against the wall. A brash, full-hearted boy, cheeks flushed, eyes alert and urgent, crashes into the room. He runs his ocean eyes over the ashen walls and finds my curled-up form. I am camouflaged gray robes on a gray wall, insubstantial yet heavy as stone.

I flap an airy wave and lay my hand by my mouth, mumbling, "Leave me. I do not wish you to be caught in my destruction."

Ash crashes to his knees and grips my elbow. "I am your brother. I am caught whether you wish it or not. Please, sister, there is another way," he whispers. I feel the flurry of his Water atmosphere, the telltale cloud of his mood, desperate like salmon pushing upstream. Surging toward life and, at the same time, their death. His hands are on mine, his eyes creased with exhaustion. "Lye." He tugs me to standing by my robe. "Listen to me. We must leave the palace."

I stare out the stone-lined window. The breeze teases like fingers pulling me outside. "Leave the palace," I repeat, scared at how wooden my voice is. It has grains running through it, knotholes and sap lines. I have a Char voice. *How ridiculous!* I laugh and Ash pauses, searching my eyes and trying to find his sister Lye Li, the girl inside the monster. I tap my neck. Actually, I have the voice of someone responsible for too many deaths. My throat scarred from shouting endless battle cries that spurred our soldiers to kill. I bow my head, wishing I still had long hair to shield me, not this razored scalp.

"I've seen your guilt these last few months, sister. The marks on your arms grow longer and deeper with every awakening, every battle. I do not know what tortures you so, but if you wanted to stop being the Keeper…" Ash pulls at my hands, causing scabs to fracture and leak. It's a deserved pain. His atmosphere has changed. It's more like leaves being washed to the corners by heavy rain, as he fears he's losing me. *If there's anything left to lose.* "Then there are ways other than suicide. Lye, I'm not letting you die here." There's soft determination in his voice. A shoulder heavy with the burden of my safety. *My sanity.*

I nod. Not sure if I care enough about my own life to flee. But I do care about Ash. So, I hook my heart to his, hoping it will be enough. "Very well, brother," I whisper.

We step over a guard shaking with induced chills on the floor, her brown Earth robe shuddering like a quake. Ash must have pressed on the guard's veins, sending winter ice through her blood. I lean down and touch the woman's throat, starting a small warming spark that will slowly fire her blood back to normal temperature.

Ash rolls his eyes but when the words "No more death" pass my cracked lips, he softens.

"Including your own," he whispers tersely as we run quietly through the palace, paintings of past emperors scowling at us from the walls. The smell of old blood and secrets leach from the ground.

"Wait!" I tug my brother's arm. He ignores me, pushing on. "Please. I need something. I cannot leave without it."

Grim and impatient, he halts and whispers, "What do you need?"

I don't answer but turn away from the exit.

I lead him down the elemental passageway. Sweeping tapestries depicting the elements rustle as we run. Air. Fire. Water. Earth and Blood. There's supposed to be balance between them, but the Shen order is tilted at a fiery angle. Our ways twisted over hundreds of years.

I stop at the Keeper's residence. *My* residence before I was moved to a more "secure" room for my own "well-being." Carved symbols of the five elements decorate the open door. Five elements I hold inside me. Five I can manipulate and use as weapons. One of five I can "gift" to Shen. I touch my heart, which feels spliced pentagonally. Gift is not the right word for what I do.

Bloodstained sheets are bundled for cleaning in the corner. Drawers are emptied on the floor. I fall to my knees and retrieve my pointed thimble, hidden inside the finger of a glove. I close my fist around it until the point pricks my palm.

When Ash steps in behind me, his eyes paint agony all over the walls. He sees a site of violence and desperation. He sees his sister seeking an end. "Ash, I'm sorry." The words are insubstantial, tumbling to the floor before he can take them.

Muffled sounds of soldiers stirring urge us on. I climb onto my mahogany desk and push open the window. We jump down and take flight. Our toes barely touch the ground as we race through the dead-of-night courtyard, jumping over red painted squares that we were trained to stay within. An invisible barrier. One toe over the line and a staff would come down on your head. I duck at the memory.

I allow myself a brief smile as the smell of star cherry blossom lays gently, fleetingly, across the bridge of my nose. The forest welcomes us with dark green jaws. Dangerous, full of yellow eyes and crusted, hungry fangs, and yet still more inviting than the palace. It has to be better than here. If it pulls me out from under the emperor's foot and jerks me free of the chancellor's grasp.

My cut wrists pulse wretchedly, and I touch my nose to them, creating a rustle of cool autumn air under my skin.

I don't look back. Soon they will come for me.

5
CHAR LUNA

"Luna, you awake?"

Not waiting for an answer, Ben Ni climbs the ladder and jabs me in the side with his finger. I eagerly take the candle, cards, and matches, shuffling over so he can sit on the platform beside me. He opens the flap above my head to let the candle smoke out and the starlight in.

He strikes the match and lights the crawlspace golden. His hazel eyes with sunflower edges, just like mine, are always half in a dream. Whereas I'm in the present. The future too complicated to contemplate.

"Whose deal is it tonight?" he asks. We haven't played since the pig incident a few days ago.

"Always mine." I snatch the pack and hand out cards. White as pure silk faces with red rose blush cheeks stare from the tattered paper. These mainland cards are painted with things we don't have. Gold robes, silver clasps. Lip paint and charcoal eyes. They're not things we crave either. When the Shen outnumber us ten to one, the only thing we crave feels out of reach: guaranteed safety.

"I don't trust you, little brother." I wink and he grins.

His chest expands. "Rightly so. Maybe this way you'll have a beggar's chance of winning."

I sigh, holding a poor hand. I try to bluff, smiling and narrowing my eyes. Ben Ni chuckles as I take a card, a man with a long white beard dressed in emerald greens. "I know you're bluffing. I can tell. All of a sudden, you've turned half blind, squinting at the cards like Joka at one of his dusty old philosophy books." He lifts his head to the stars. Great Char warriors stretch their bows or polish their swords up there. Watching and waiting.

I ignore his taunting and take a card from the deck. "Just play."

"Huh?"

I groan softly. "You know, if I weren't so honest, I could simply cheat while you're staring into space."

Ben Ni draws a line from the heart star to the winter planet, swirling his finger like he's mixing paint. "I see a woman."

I punch his arm and scoff. "Big surprise."

His laugh is muffled but full of golden wings just bursting to escape. Mine feel pinned to my sides. "No. She's mourning. Holding her heart and staring down at the sea. Maybe her husband was a sailor and he crashed on the knife edge rocks east of the island…"

Ben Ni. Head full of stories.

"Maybe you should stop staring at the stars and start playing," I chide, but I love his imagination. He sees things no one else sees. It's a gift worthy of wrapping and unwrapping every day.

We play two rounds and much to Ben Ni's delight, I lose both. He's in the middle of gloating when we hear clatter in the kitchen. I blow out the candle, and he shuffles into the corner as Mama walks down the hallway. Her cherrywood hips give her away, cracking like mangrove branches baking in the hot sun.

"Luna," she whispers. Her shadow graces the base of the ladder.

"Yes, Mama?" I swing my legs over the edge, putting my hand up to Ben Ni to be quiet.

"Come here for a moment. I want to talk to you." One long, stern finger beckons.

I climb down and sit on the bottom rung, looking up at my lithe but sturdy mother, hair plaited but scruffed up at the back. As if hearing my thoughts, she smooths it. She rocks nervously. Cracks pop between her hips and real bones.

"What is it, Mama? Are you all right?" I ask, concerned. I reach for her arm. Almost touch her and then pull back.

She nods. "I wish to counsel you on your upcoming ceremony and the choice you need to make." Her voice already sounds guarded, like she knows I'm going to oppose her. "You need to be sensible, Luna. Even though your brothers can be foolish at times, they are right that legs *are* a good choice. You will stand taller. Men will *see* you and then you will make a good match."

I bow my head, not sure I want to be "seen" yet. I like the ability to shrink below the level of the crowd. Dart between. Pull Ben Ni's shirt back before he tumbles into the water and nimbly tear Sun and Joka down by using my size as a skill.

"I suppose…"

"You suppose?" She places a finger under my chin and lifts it to connect with my eyes. Hers are almost black. Mine fail to be that perfect dark soy color Char women prize. They're diluted. She sighs, letting go of something. It escapes and flutters like a desperate moth trying to find outside.

"Luna, I want you to be happy. And I love that you are close to your brothers. Your bond is special. But you are not like them. You're not a man. If you choose to be like them and follow their path, your life will be so much harder." Her voice breaks as she whispers, "And possibly shorter. Do you understand?"

I set my lips. Wondering how much to say, choosing not to say much at all. "Yes, Mama. I understand." But *she* doesn't understand. I don't want to simply *follow* my brothers. I want to walk my own path. Not have it set out for me, straight and narrow and lined with unsuitable suitors.

Placated, she strokes my cheek lovingly. I know I'm not what she expected nor wanted. But she does love me. She loves all of us. Unconditionally. Even if I chose to try and march with men, keep my feet in time with a battle drum, she would love me still. She would hate it also.

I hang from the ladder, watching her swing away and back to Papa, until Ben Ni tugs on my hair. "C'mon, little Luna. I've still got a few more rounds in me."

When I reach the top, the candle flame lights Ben Ni's eyes all serious. I try to smile but it's pathetic and drips over the edge of my lips. "I know you're going to ask but don't. I have no answer for you."

He grabs my hand and squeezes. "Well, you know what we think."

"Do I?" We joke. We wrestle. We don't have serious conversations very often.

His earnestness hurts me when he says, "You are perfect just the way you are, big sister. No matter what you choose."

I roll my eyes to break the moment. "Oh, you're just saying that because you want me to introduce you to Ali Mah!"

He waggles his eyebrows, taking up my attempt to lighten the mood and juggling with it. "Can you blame me? She's the prettiest girl this side of the Coalstones."

I slap at his arm. "Just take your card already." He chuckles. "I know what you'll choose, youngest brother. Broad pine shoulders for posing on the boardwalk and attracting unsuspecting girls." I swing my slight shoulders from side to side and pout.

I regret saying it, because he probably thinks that's a great idea. His eyes grow distant as he pictures himself with wooden shoulders. At least he still has a year before he must choose. My date is approaching fast.

6

SHEN LYE LI

As the stonework of the emperor's compound deteriorates, giving way to jungle, so does my toothpick-thin resolve. Soon, I will hear men shouting. It will grow and grow until my ears are filled with their anger and disappointment, ringing like a hard-struck gong. The chancellor won't let the Keeper go free and live. Only one is born each cycle. Without me, Elemental powers will be lost in a generation. Without my death, it will be even longer.

There's a horrible silence, but it cannot last. I cannot last out here. *They* will not allow it.

We whip through the jungle, vines snagging our arms and legs. I strain for the sure sound of boots thudding over damp ground. But there's nothing.

Ash mashes my thin fingers together tightly like he's scared to release me. Like I'll turn around. I have no want to turn back. What *I* want is lost in a swirl of blood and damage. *I can't find it.* My hand goes to my pocket, the thimble a reminder of the Shen I've changed. The trust I lost in its purpose and in myself. My breath comes fast and tight and I touch my chest, halting. Even if I can't unearth my wants, I do wonder whether Ash would be better off without me. Safer. Because they will come for me. They need me. They don't need him.

Ash spins, smooth face moonlight pale, eyes stony and insistent. "Lye, we can't stop. Not here." He sweeps light brown hair that's escaped the knot from his forehead.

I ask the question, back pressed into a tree, wet moss staining my pale gray robes. *I'm turning the color of the dirty mats placed at the palace door.* "Why are we not pursued by a troop of Shen soldiers, brother? Where is everyone?" Dread pushes on my eyes like gradual blindness. Perhaps I have dropped down on the list of priorities in favor of a larger plan.

His shoulders pull up, a deep, dark sigh pushing from his lungs. Regret hovers around his face. Reluctance pushes at his teeth.

"You've been locked in that room for days—"

"Days?" I interrupt. Time lost meaning as meal trays stacked up in the corner, untouched. Light, dark, light, dark.

"And in those days, the Shen army mobilized." He shakes his head. "Battalion by battalion, section by section. I was on skeleton guard duty. They never told me why. They kept me in the dark because of my 'connection' to you, I suppose." His eyes drop. There's anger there as he feels the "connection" between us is broken. Because of what I did.

"What?" Things pound like fists against the inside of my chest. "That's not possible."

Ash pulls me along, picking over damp logs and parting thorny vines. "Once I realized they weren't returning, I seized the opportunity. There were fewer guards. Fewer everything. So, I did what I had to to get you out."

Sucking in a breath. I know why they left, but I dare not speak it. Speaking it implicates my part. My mind leaches away from even thinking it, but my heart beats out the sound of a war drum. The timeline has been moved up. The plan rolls out like a long, forbidden scroll. If they've been gone days, it will soon be too late.

My mind is pulled backward. *How many young men and women did I awaken? How many did I show the way to defeat the Char?* The answers line up like too many Mah Jong tiles spread endlessly over the floor. Faces. So many eager, hateful faces. My ribs seem to overlap, pulling tighter over my organs, and I gasp. My part in what is coming is too painful to acknowledge. *I won't. I won't. I won't.*

Ash shoves me gently. "We need to keep moving. You can wallow and torture yourself later." His words are reluctant barbs. "Right now, we must get you to a safe place."

I laugh hollowly at this. He doesn't know the half of it. "Where could I possibly go that would be safe?"

Ash forces a smirk. That overconfidence. That bloody earnestness shining like a small sun in the darkest galaxy. "We're heading into Char territory, sister. We're going to hide right amongst those dull, wooden puppets."

A single flaming torch lights up one small circle at the top of the hill. "That's crazy!"

He casts a wary eye on the approaching light, hand tightening on mine like a clam shell protecting its pearl. "Desperate times call for crazy measures, sister," he mutters.

My skin prickles. My stubbly head scratched by netted branches. "You just made that up."

He clucks his tongue and pushes my head under the arm of tree. "Just keep moving."

He would have been better off without me. But his choice to free the Keeper changes everything. His back has sprouted a target. With a silent groan, I stumble after him. I must stay alive to protect him.

7
CHAR LUNA

The word *fire* blooms in the background, spoken and screamed by multiple voices colliding like bells struck too close together, chiming over and over in different ways. Observant to dubious to panic. In my sleepy state, it takes time to crystalize in my mind.

Fire!

I nearly topple over the side of the landing as I roll. I sniff the air for smoke. I smell nothing but salty sea air and the faint yeasty smell of crystal buns rising in the kitchen. No one's stirred, and for a moment, I think I dreamed the word. But then the sound of wood smashing against wood brings me to my senses as Char villagers sprint along the boardwalk.

The hut rumbles like a small earthquake has traveled through our foundations.

Through the small round window at the end of our short hallway, I see our people gathering and pointing. I swallow drily, absorbing the growing panic. Bedraggled, sleep in their eyes, they stand in their red-and-black nightclothes and tasseled slippers.

Leaving a smear across the condensation, I pad fast down the hall, banging on doors to wake my brothers.

A blanket lies across the crumbling hearth, black with soot. I frown, wondering how my parents didn't set fire to themselves in the night. I rattle Mama's hip violently and shout, "Mama. Wake up!"

She jolts awake, her short, dark lashes shooting down like warning arrows to the earth. Confused, she mumbles and shakes her head. I rip the blanket from my parents, too anxious to avert my eyes. "Fire!"

My brothers stumble toward the kitchen as Mama and Papa dress. They rub their eyes, drag their feet. They don't feel the urgency and panic that's crowding the boardwalk. I throw coats over their shoulders, jumping up to reach. They file dopily outside.

Sun rakes a hand through his black hair and yawns. "Is this a joke, Luna? If it is, it's not very funny." But his arms tense, and he searches for a weapon.

Ben Ni tucks his hair behind his ears. "Luna wouldn't do that." His syrupy eyes squint as the rising sun pushes through mangrove branches.

I scowl disapprovingly at Sun, half naked, and slap his bare stomach. "Cover yourself." He growls but buttons his coat.

When my family sees the Char huddle, faces pointed out to sea as they squash themselves into the gathering point, they speed up.

I still can't smell smoke but as we round the curve of the mountain, I see it. Fire as orange as the sunrise breaks the sea into puddles of color. I draw in a disbelieving breath. Miles across a flat sea, Black Sail City is burning.

The crowd parts for Papa's hulking form, fanning out around the edges of the planked space. The boards are laid to resemble the Carvress's mark: A simple sun with strong spokes of light shining defiantly from its center. Papa leans dangerously close to the water, shields his eyes and grunts.

"Where's Bullseye?" he asks, calling for his friend and comrade, a Char scout.

Bullseye's lanky body slips through the crowd like a ribbon to Papa's side. He appraises me, his pinewood eye rolling and never landing on anything. He runs his tongue over sugar-rotted teeth, making me feel like a prize fish in a basket. He is in the market for a second wife. I look away.

Papa bows bluntly to Bullseye and points at the growing orange harbor across the channel. "What do you see?"

Bullseye covers his flesh eye. Sucking his lips against his gums, he sighs, fingers cracking nervously. He doesn't need to say it. He nods confirmation to Papa and my hope fades to mist.

We've seen this smoke before. Sometimes much closer to home.

"So much for the treaty." Papa's voice is rough with sadness, splintered with anger.

The Char of Coalstone Village look left to right, find their young sons and feel their hearts burrow deep in their chests. I look to my older brothers, Joka and Sun, faces stony, concealing leaping hearts.

If we're lucky, we'll have a few hours to say goodbye.

"I CAN'T find my ankle knife," Sun shouts, aggravated. "Ben Ni, if you've used it for your carvings again, I'll carve you a new…"

Fabric flies from roughhewn door to roughhewn door. A pile growing into a mountain blocking the hallway. Mama sips tea at the table as I wind her long hair into a curled bun, pinning it with her favorite silver clasps decorated with pearls Papa found diving from Ghost Lovers cliff. She pats them once they're in place and I take her shaking hands.

"It will be fine, Mama. Maybe they won't come. Maybe Bullseye was wrong." I desperately want to believe something I know is untrue.

She smiles thinly. Bullseye is never wrong. He saw flaming barracks, and our army taking serious losses. Men with arrows piercing their backs dove into the sea as flames ate their wooden parts and scarred their real flesh. A hollow feeling opens inside my heart. The bodies will float home. Knock against the boardwalk posts. I shiver involuntarily.

"Help your brothers," she urges, releasing my hand like unclasping a necklace. Prim mouth clamped over a cry she'll release later.

I open the kitchen drawer and pull out Sun's ankle dagger, gripping the handle so tightly it leaves an imprint in my skin. Already missing him. Mourning him.

Tucking it into his bag, I stare down at the mess. Sun is eighteen years old. He can accurately hit a forest turkey from fifty feet away. But he's always had Mama to fold his laundry, to tell him where to find his hunting pack. In this, he regresses to a child. I sigh hard and lift his bag onto the bed, pulling out the random assortment of weapons and sharpening tools.

"Will you hunt in your pajamas, big brother?" I whisper while dragging out the more practical items needed from his chest.

Sun appears next to me, kissing the top of my head fast, but it's like he laid a stone there. "Ah, you found it! What would I do without you, little Luna?" His sure voice falters. I know he wanted this. But the wanting and the getting are two different things. Home won't collapse into his pocket. He will miss us terribly.

I swipe at tears as I fold clothes into his bags. He thanks me wordlessly and carries them to the front of the house. Perhaps it's all for nothing. An overreaction. They might not come. Soon I'll have to unpack all these things and slap the tops their heads for getting into such a panic.

Please let it be so. I feel like a shell in the shallows, stripped away until all that's left is the spiral spine. I cannot shelter life.

Joka's bag is already by the door. He collides with the door frame as he enters with an armful of books. Startled, he pushes back strands of hair that have dared to fall out of place. He laughs awkwardly. "I guess I can't really take these with me, can I? There's probably not much time for reading on the battlefield."

Something akin to a fishbone is wedged in my throat. "Maybe just one book."

We push a book into his bag and button it closed. His hand stays flat against the rough canvas. "I'm not a soldier either, Luna." His desk, a couple of planks held up by stacks of books, is spotless save a half-written summary, squared neatly in its center. It's in direct opposition to Sun's half of the room. Chaos.

"You know why I chose a bamboo neck?" I know but I let him tell it to me one more time. "It was so I could read all day and never get sore from craning over a book. I could map the nine Char islands and their satellites hunched over a drafting table for hours and hours. I'm a scholar not a soldier," he repeats, voice shaky. It doesn't suit him. My brother Joka is always sure to the point of being obnoxious. Smart and thin as a pencil but solid. Now he looks down from his tall height, shoulders rounded and small.

He bows his head and I run a finger over his bamboo neck, tracing the dark rings that break up the almost-polished smoothness of the green wood. As he ages, it will yellow. "Did it hurt?" I ask.

He glances up from beneath sharp, pointed brows and begins to shake his head, then stops. "It hurts and it doesn't. It's like the hottest sunlight burning across your skin but it's almost pleasurable." He touches his throat with a thin, meant for writing and drafting, hand. I hang from his words like they're cliff holds. "Yes, it hurts but you know the pain is worth it because you're taking your place in the Char. You feel like it's… like it's meant to be."

I think about the Shen. They find the weak places on our bodies and expose them, sending storms and fire through our veins. The Carvress only has the power to protect one part of us, leaving the rest open to attack from the Shen's manipulating touch. I shudder, staring at the papers tacked to the wall of Joka's bedroom. Flapping like surrender flags. Hundreds of schematic drawings of our village, the islands, and the mountain behind us. While the mainland covers the north like a giant stain. The Char islands look like scattered crumbs. Dots in the ocean like one small constellation in the shadow of the sun.

He's not a soldier. Not yet. But he'll have to become one. He will learn to protect our people. He'll do what's necessary. It's part of what makes us Char. We fight. We have always fought.

I squeeze his hand and do what I must to prop him up, prepare him. "You are strong as well as smart, brother. Tall and lean. You have excellent aim. So… strong, smart, with an unbreakable neck." I tip my head to the side, pretending to inspect him. "Seems to me, you'll make a formidable foe." I punch his arm and am terrified when he rubs it like it hurt.

He kisses my cheek and I know he'll say it. It's as common as hello or goodbye in the Yan household. "What would I do without you, little Luna?"

A tear escapes and I bow in shame. He wipes it away with his thumb before throwing his bag out into the hallway with the other two. Making three.

Three? There shouldn't be three.

Ben Ni tries to slink around me, but I grab his shirt. Papa growls at me, but I growl back, baring my teeth. He steps away, hands up in surrender. "It's your brother's decision," Papa says, leaning against the kitchen table.

Mama lets out a small cry, soft as a starved baby bird.

He's only fifteen. Every single part of him is vulnerable.

I cannot let our baby brother walk into battle unarmed and unwatched.

If they need three, I should be the third.

8

SHEN LYE LI

Red murder birds wedge their sleek bodies in tree forks, feathers puffed and bursting with song. Their blue eyes judge us as they wait. Tail feathers scraping the bark like fingernails.

If I could reach, I could silence them. My fingers shake; my wrists burn. Those very feathers were the tools I used to open my veins when the thimble proved inadequate. Strong and sharp enough that servants used them as razorblades to shave my head. My skin tore easily, until blood soaked the sheets and I felt the ease of my life, *my burden*, draining away.

We've slid carefully down the mountainside, pressed to trees, ducking behind bushes, but the torch has steadily followed. The torch is attached to the arm of the guard Ash attacked.

Ash nudges me. "You'll be faster. I'll knock her down and you do what is needed."

The single guard stumbles through the forest heavily. Unstealthy and out of breath. Ash's touch only disabled her for minutes.

"I don't think I can." Perceptively, the murder birds open their blunted beaks. They love the smell of blood. But it has to be fresh. My wrists are not what they want. They're eyeing the cut above the guard's eye, the red running down her cheek, mixing with sweat. My skin prickles. "Looks like the birds might take care of her for us, poor woman."

Ash knows me. His blue eyes crinkle softly as he whispers, "She'll be fine." The birds hop down the branches as he speaks. "More will come." I shake my head. *No more death.*

Before he can stop me, I throw my hands up, scattering the birds. The guard looks straight at the origin of the squawking. We're shadows in this dawn, shrouded by heavy vines and fern curtains, but she finds me. She tumbles toward us, grunting and shouting. Her white robe gives her away as Air, as does the small wisp tattoo over her eye.

"Keeper Lye! Stop!"

Ash takes a deep breath, dips his head, and charges.

When he concentrates, my brother is agile. This guard is heavy on her feet and trips on every tree root and loose stone, while Ash flies over them, picking out the obstacles before he's upon them. They barrel at each other, atmospheres colliding as an electric storm brews around their bodies. Neither are thinking tactically. They're fighting commonly like peasants over the price of rice. Clawing, punching, pinning. They're not doing what they've been taught. Find an entry point and press. Manifest the version of your element you want, be it hot coals, icicles, choking sand, or a hurricane, and let it flow from your fingers under your opponent's skin.

I step forward, scared to start again. But there's little choice here. Ash calls to me, pulling the guards arms behind her head. The woman's eyes bulge with fear. I could kill her with a touch. My fingers ache like dying bruises to let lightning surge up her veins. The power; it *wants*. Sometimes, feeling like it has a life of its own.

"Lye!" Ash's muscles strain as he holds the tub of a woman down. "Just do it. Now!"

I kneel before the guard, reach out and then pull back. It's like releasing an arrow. But I must shoot this arrow at half strength. I can only pull the string back so far. "This will only hurt for a moment," I whisper.

Climbing my fingers up her arm, I find a small gap in the muscle. She pushes cold winter wind through me. I brace, my whole soul wanting fire and molten lava. But I breathe in and instead force warm, sleepy sun rays into my mind and press. Instantly, her body relaxes. She slumps, pulling Ash with her, lying face first in the mud. Snoring.

I help Ash roll her over. A seduced smile spreads over the guard's round face. I use my robe to clean the blood from beneath her eye. Hopefully this will keep the murder birds away.

Ash tugs me upright. "What happened to you, sister? The Keeper is usually so cool, so precise, so..." His brows pull together as he thinks words he doesn't want to say.

My eyes can barely meet his when I say, "I think the word you're searching for, brother, is cruel."

The woman kneels before me shoulders set proudly, almost arrogantly. Her eyes are tinted amber. She wears a necklace of the same around her neck. I recognize it now after nine months as the Keeper. She is from a family of Fire.

Her mouth opens to front teeth sharpened to points. This is a warrior. A Char killer to the core. I smile. She will serve us well.

Impatient as always, the chancellor cracks his fingers. A sound that both grates my ears and excites me. Because I know I earn favor every time I awaken an element in a Shen. "You are from a Fire family, I see," the chancellor says without emotion.

With unearned confidence, the woman bows sharply like she has already entered our ranks. "Yes, Chancellor. I come from a long line of Fire Shen."

The chancellor looks to me to begin.

"Hold still," I order. I hold my hand up, sensing her atmosphere. It is hot and furious. Powerful. Bubbling, boiling mud and sinkholes. Earthquakes and tumbling rocks. She is not Fire. "She reads of Earth."

The woman's pulse beats on the round of her shoulder. I reach for it, ready to awaken her power and she grabs my wrist. "I am Fire!" she insists. "Fire!"

Curiosity pushes the chancellor to lean forward in his chair. He does not need to protect me. "You are Earth." My voice is definitive. Unyielding.

She rises threateningly. "Check again!" She squeezes my wrist tightly and shakes my arm. Her eyes are watery. "My family... they will not accept this. Change it! Do it right!" She is too close. Far too close to the Keeper. My fingers heat with fury and flames.

"Release me." My voice is calm waters hiding sea monsters beneath.

Stomping her feet, she pinches my skin with her fingernails. Desperation and shame creating a storm she cannot escape. "Not until you change my read. Not until..."

I will not be questioned. I am the Keeper.

Softly, deliciously, I lay my palm across her forehead. "You are not Fire but you will die by it."

I relish the slow flames as I push them into the woman's head. I scorch and retreat. Scorch and retreat. It is more painful this way. More of a demonstration to the others behind her. She screams only once. The pain so intense she can't vocalize it.

Her eyes are last. Shriveling to black as I release her lifeless body.

I stand and address the others waiting for their turn. "Awakening an element is a gift. You do not choose." I point into the line, then at myself. "I choose."

The chancellor motions for the guards to remove the woman's body so the next can come. I watch them drag her feet first down the steps, detached. As her head bounces on the steps, I put a hand up. "Wait!" The guards pause, backs hunched in fear of my temper spreading. I rise from my chair to stand over the body, lean down and snatch the amber beads from around her neck. I wrap them around my wrist. "Shame to see nice jewelry go to waste." I return to my plush velvet chair. Sinking into its comfort.

"Good example, young Keeper. Best to rid the empire of these untrainable soldiers early," the chancellor says with a sly grin. The buzzing in my body feeds off his approval.

I nod. My heart pounding at the gift of a life taken. "Yes, Chancellor. Shall I take another to make sure they truly understand?"

He shrugs. "You could."

My smile stretches over my teeth like a wolf tiger ready to tear open its kill. I am ferocious, regal and powerful. The subjects should know this. And if they don't, I will demonstrate until they do. "Let's see whether this next one irritates me."

Our laughs mingle together. Terrible and taunting. Let us see who would dare challenge me now.

9
CHAR LUNA

We sit at the oak table, pocked and dented with family use. Once our legs swung from too high chairs, gangly arms threading like boat rope through the backs. Now the boys cram shoulder to shoulder in their good tunics and I shelter beneath them wrapped in scraps and leftovers. A green tunic of Sun's cinched at the waist, so it looks vaguely like a dress.

Teacups are set out like the hour marks of a clock.

We wait.

The afternoon sun heats the shingles on the roof, causing them to crack and whine. Mama looks at the ceiling trying to hold in welling tears. Papa lays his heavy hand on her shoulder, and she pulls it into her own. She traces the oak, brushing her fingers over the exquisitely carved joints. The brass has turned a little green and she clucks her tongue, fetching a cloth and oil to polish them.

There are only drips left in our cups. There are only minutes left to broken hearts.

I help Mama clear the dishes. I can't look at Ben Ni. He can't look at me either. Fury and jealously compete in my thoughts. *How can he go? How can I not go?*

I glance out the window. Fog rolls across the water but the vague shape of Black Sail City still presses through the clouds, a charred shadow, the smoke waning. *Maybe they got it under control. Maybe the losses weren't as bad as Bullseye thought.* I touch the glass. "I don't think they're coming," I say quietly, a wish more than an observation.

Joka looks hopeful. The other two, disappointed. Ben Ni's head sags and it's too much for me to tolerate. I reach over and slap the top of his head. Mama turns away, pretending to rewash the teacups.

"Ouch! What was that for?" He rubs his brown hair, flicking golden light from his shoulders, and glares at me.

Papa gives me a warning stare, but I'm too upset to care. "You should be happy they're not coming, you idiot!" My eyes scan the table but it's only Ben Ni I'm angry with. He's not ready for this. "You're *fifteen*! Why would you want to go when you have no protection against the Shen?"

Ben Ni appeals to Papa, who speaks in a voice as deep and decisive as a gavel. "Everyone is heard at this table."

"I don't want to be left behind. I want to fight alongside my brothers," Ben Ni says defiantly, and I feel his words deep in my heart. Truth like spears. Because that's what I want too. I'll always want it.

I shrug hard. "It doesn't matter. They're not coming."

Things break all the time in this house. There are six Yans and four seem to always be tousling in a scrappy ball. When a plate breaks, we just throw it in the water. I imagine the pile of broken dishes will soon breach the surface. But we'll want to keep this one.

Mama is frozen, holding two perfect halves of a teacup. Her eyes on the red-spined sails, stiff and foreboding like severed dragon's wings, cutting through the lapsing fog.

As we knew they would.

They have come.

THE CHAR army is welcomed and yet doors creak on their hinges, wanting to close at their presence. These men protect our homes. They deserve honor and respect. But they're here to take our children, and that deserves fear and a small pill of animosity.

With a practiced hand, a Char soldier throws a loop over the bollard. The sail folds down, crisp and definite, and three warriors step confidently into our village.

With Sun striding in front, we tap a rhythm over the boardwalk planks, hesitation and obligation. Heart and ready fists. The boys close around me, and I stand on the balls of my feet to see the visitors. My honey eyes take in a large crowd and two empty boats. I hug myself tightly as I notice one of the sailors prodding at a bloated body, washed up from the barracks. Oar thudding into the back of the facedown soldier, breaking the stems of five blood-slick arrows wedged between his ribs. Mama's eyes breeze over the corpse and then back to the soldiers. We would gasp if this were not an image we'd seen many times before. The sight of him is usual yet still rallying. Because we wish for nothing more than floating Char bodies to no longer be 'usual'.

The Ghost boat will round up this man and other dead after the recruitment.

Broad-shouldered men in dusted black cloth and brass-buckled leather vests stand at the landing platform. Legs wide, swords swishing at their sides.

In the center, a man strokes his dark, wooden jaw carved with sea swirls. Hinges move seamlessly. "Good afternoon, people of Coalstone. I am General Fah." His voice is smooth and calm. He sweeps an arm across the waiting people elegantly. "I wish I were here on a more pleasant errand, but as I'm sure you are aware, our barracks have been attacked by a small but effective troop of Shen."

A woman speaks out of turn, her voice hollow with unmet wishes. "But the treaty…"

The general's eyes swiftly pass over the woman. "There is no treaty." The Char barely react. Breath is held, fists tighten, but we half expected it. The respite could never last.

Fah pulls a scroll of paper from his shirt, sighing sadly as he unrolls it and hands it to the soldier beside him. "The Shen paid heavily for their crime, but so did we. Here is the list of the casualties so far. I am deeply sorry for those families who have lost a loved one. These men were brave soldiers. Many of them were also my friends." His lullaby tone is needed when we're about to lose more.

A soldier walks brusquely to our meeting hall and tacks the scroll on the wall. Half the crowd follows him. Carefully, apprehensively. They follow because their lives are tied to someone at the barracks. They fall to their knees as that tie is cruelly severed. Sharp cries rise like steam through splits in the earth. By the sound, our village has lost many men. Men we couldn't afford to lose. My heart beats fast and uneven as it reaches out to those grieving families. A woman drops behind me and I stoop to help her. Tears sting my eyes as my father's hand clamps over my shoulder. Mama's sniffing is just another murmur in a sea of almost-weeping women who are trying to stay composed.

Something twists in the general's face at this sudden outpouring of grief and he takes a step back from the crowd. "I know this is a difficult time, but we need to replenish what we have lost. We have come for your bravest, strongest young men as we plan and exercise justice upon the Shen." His eyes dance across faces and study each outraged young man in our village. "As the barracks have been destroyed, we shall be accommodated at Lin Lan monastery. You shall be given board, food, and excellent army training in return for your necessary service. This will be an intense course. Our plan is to strike fast and hard. They will not be expecting retaliation so soon after such heavy losses."

Sun steps forward and my heart sags like a lost soldier carrying a wounded man he cannot save. "I'm ready to fight!" he announces, fist clenched.

The general barely blinks, just nods. Joka falls in behind his brother, as I knew he would. Ben Ni moves, and I grab his shirt, jerking him backward. Through clenched teeth I whisper, "Please, brother. Don't do this."

But although Ben Ni is younger than me, he's far stronger and he removes my clutching claws easily. "I must," he whispers, voice tainted with youth. Something that will be flattened.

My feet vibrate with wishes, with the tear of separation and the lack of time. No time to catch up. No time to prepare. An intense training means it shall be peppered with holes. My brothers bow to my parents and head to the two flanking boats waiting to accept the breakaway parts of our families. Sun stalks purposefully onto the boat like it's made for him, but his eyes show twists of uncertainty in the way they glance out to sea and then back to his home. Joka is more apprehensive, but as soon as his brother throws an arm over his shoulders, he relaxes. A wary grin spreads over his serious features. I appeal to him, a glance and a tensing of my jaw, to be careful. Death is breathing on the back of his bamboo neck.

Joka's grin wavers, replaced with a steady stare. He nods.

When Ben Ni tries to embark, the general bars his way with a strong arm, examining him closely. He bends down to lift Ben Ni's pant legs, checking for the Carvress's mark. I release a nervous breath. Maybe they won't take him, knowing he's more vulnerable than the others. Arching an eyebrow, he turns Ben Ni to face the crowd of hopeful, hopeless faces. "Here is an example of true courage!" He dips his mouth to Ben Ni's ear. "How old are you, boy?"

He's too young. He's only fifteen, I want to shout. Papa's fingers clamp around my collarbone like a vice.

"Fifteen, sir," Ben Ni admits, puffing out a chest that still needs to thicken.

He pats my brother on the back and allows him to pass. "Very impressive! Who is the father of this brave young man?"

Papa coughs and raises his free hand. "Nice to see you again, Juni!" He laughs unconvincingly. "My sons..." He points to my brothers. "Are honored to train under you."

The general's wooden jaw creaks as it spreads into a grimacing smile. "Ah, Setsu. Should have known these boys were yours."

Papa looks him up and down. "I see you've been recently promoted. Congratulations."

General Fah raises his eyebrows. "Yes, well, the survivors of tragedy must bear the weight of the fallen."

Swallowing pride, Papa reaches out. "You'll take good care of my boys, won't you?"

I know Papa wants to join them by the way he rolls onto his toes and leans. But there are laws. Battle limits. It's one way the Char make sure there are still Char people left to protect. It is a miniscule mercy for our family.

Swiftly, the village is emptied of half its youth like sifting rice from husks. The boats float low, water testing the edges of black, barnacled wood. A coin bag of faces shine back at the ones left behind, the values of excitement, anxiousness, and pride.

Papa's grip on my shoulder relaxes and his hand goes to Mama's. Her body shakes with sadness.

My brothers lean over the bow, eyes on me except Ben Ni, who gazes past the village, up the Coalstones to where the Carvress does her work. Joka pensive. Sun is sure. Their words from this morning rise like the tide. *What would we do without you, little Luna?*

I push away from Mama and Papa and through the crowd to grab the general's tunic. He spins around as I shout right in his face, "Wait!"

General Fah snaps his tunic from my grasp and glares at me like I'm a cockroach in need of squashing. "Wait? For what?" He appraises me in the breadth of a second and finds me insubstantial. Inconsequential. But then something lights in his eyes that gives me hope. My heart leaping onto the boat like he's already said yes. "Oh. I see. Do you wish to say goodbye to your family, little girl?"

Papa clears his throat, a sound that taps me on the shoulder. I do not turn, do not want to see his eyes begging me not to shame him. Chin jutting out proudly, I say, "No, General, I wish to join my brothers. I wish to train with the Char army."

The general holds a weighted breath, readying an answer that will either encase my heart in gold or break it apart. He lifts his hand, eyes malevolent, and I brace myself for him to strike me.

Footsteps through the silenced crowd, and then Papa is next to me. General Fah's eyebrows draw down and his jaw lengthens, revealing two neat rows of wooden teeth. They crunch together and then he lets out a bellowing laugh, his square face rounding.

The hand I thought would strike me slaps his leg instead. He glances out to sea. "You're a girl. You've not the heart to be a soldier. No woman does. Look at you now—tears in your eyes that overflow with emotion." He shakes his head. "No. Your heart serves you well as a wife, a mother. Not a soldier."

"But there have been women warriors. I could be—"

He shakes his head once like a swinging axe. "Not in my army."

In one motion, the general turns his imposing figure away from me and pushes the boat from shore. My brothers bob away and are engulfed by mist. Gone. We are separated by tradition. All because of my...Stupid. Female. Heart.

My knees weaken and I wish to sink to the ground and weep while the whole village watches.

I cannot stand their eyes. Their shame.

I dive into the salt water. The idea that the ocean can cleanse my pain is a foolhardy one. But at least I can delay the scolding I will receive.

10
SHEN LYE LI

Ash scrambles down the mountain, leg over leg, hand over hand, sinking into the loose shale rock. I watch with endearment and fear. He's all heart and determination. Risk and responsibility.

He will do whatever it takes to protect me. He thinks he failed me. And now he will strive to not let it happen again.

He beckons me to follow.

Behind me, high and deep in the mountain, lies the palace. Staff will be frantic. Anxiously wondering how to tell the emperor as he wakes from a plush, silk sleep, concubines warming his sides, that the Keeper has deserted. Then word will be sent to the chancellor. I'm not sure who will be angrier. I have my own confessions to make but they strip what's left of my honor. I'm not ready for Ash's gaze on me to fall even lower.

Our way to escape the mainland, the sea, ruffles like a shook blanket in front of us. It is beautiful and desolate and nothing like I thought it would be. Beyond the shifting water sits the outlying islands of Char territory, pushing up like rows of budding baby teeth.

Somewhere behind them is Black Sail City. *In ruins? On fire?* I do not know. If the troops have mobilized, then the treaty must have been broken. If only that were the worst thing to follow.

I touch the earth. The stones make themselves known beneath my fingers. I reach my thoughts under the crust of flat, my expression smoothing to serenity. My awareness skates rocks and finds places where the loose gravel is not as deep. Moving in a zigzag pattern, I walk with much more ease than my brother down the incline. Grace inherent in every step.

Ash watches with awe. I wish he wouldn't. My way was born into my body. It is not skill. I shouldn't be envied. I should be pitied. *And oh, how I wish I was not listened to.*

I take a bow when I reach the shore. "You made that look so easy," he remarks, eyes landing on several boats tied to posts sticking out of the mud like drowning arms. They clunk against one another in the choppy bay.

A small smile. Barely worth mentioning. "You made that look unbearably difficult."

He chuckles, touching the nose of a rough, carved boat, pushing it down to test its buoyancy. It's bigger than the taxi boats we used to carry crops to the palace but I'm sure the premise is the same. "Remember when we used to be evenly matched?"

I roll my eyes. "No."

He nudges my shoulder, attempting to build steps to my heart. "You know, before you completely outshone me. Before you showed everyone your power." He steps onto the boat, wobbling at first, and offers his hand.

The water laps like a parched tongue against the sides. It tells me storms are a possibility. I blink eyes of water blue. The sky is whispering, *Rain.* I take Ash's hand and sit in the hull, pulling my thick hood over my cold head. "You mean before my power made me a slave to death."

Ash releases the oars and leans over, squeezing my arm, careful to avoid brushing my wrist wounds. "That wasn't your power, Lye. You cannot control what is done with Shen power after you gift it." His eyes are quick storms and silent seas. The worry hidden within doesn't know where to go. "You gave me my power also. Do you regret that?"

His chest swells with a deep breath and I feel him force his atmosphere to calm, like water over rocks in a stream.

"Of course not. But you use it wisely. Not everyone is like you. Not everyone can bend to the wind one moment and straighten against it the next. You are capable of changing." His expression is guarded, like he doesn't know what that change may be or even if he wants it. "Like I changed when I said no more death." *If I say it enough, maybe I will start to believe it.*

"You said *no more*." His mood slips to a small waterfall, boring a hole into a riverbed. There's something unsaid. "So now, we make a fresh start." He moves to lift the sails.

"I sense a storm, don't you?"

He cocks his head and closes his eyes, reaching out with his Water sense. "A little rain. Nothing to worry about."

Grimacing, I close my eyes also. "Wind is gathering, but not in the right direction."

He lets the sails fold down, trusting in my ability. "See," he challenges. "Together we'll be fine." He readies his oar. Our vessel pointing to a future which sits beyond the swell.

A fresh start seems a farfetched idea for me. How can someone with so many black marks against their name truly start over?

"Ash?" I say, my confession bubbling at my throat like blood from a sliced lung. I want to tell him the worst. The thing that pushed me over the edge.

But he lifts his eyes and they cut my words to ribbons. They believe in me. They see a sister, not a schemer. "Yes, sister."

I can't do it. "I know I'm injured but you'll still struggle to keep pace with me." I bury the emperor's dark plan deep in graveyard dirt. It sits on top of my vilest truth: That I'm the one who handed it to him.

We row out of the bay. Dark green lumps of earth brood over us. They know things are never simple. Ash knows it too.

Never.

UNINHABITED ISLANDS grow in size like a family order.

The sky is strokes of grey and blue. The sea an algae green. I pause in my rowing to place my hand in the water, jumping as a creature's head emerges, trailing in our water stream. "What is that?" I ask, alarmed, pointing at a large fish with purple eyes following our boat.

Ash squints, pursing his mouth. "Um… I think it's a dolphin." Noting my apprehension, his voice softens to mist on the mountain. "They're harmless."

I return my hand to the water and whisper, "A dolphin." One bobs its head under my palm, and I force myself to stay still. Its skin is smooth and warm, streaked with stripes of pink and orange like a sunset. It calls to its mate in a horn-like bellow and dives beneath the water.

There is beauty in this world.

Sometimes I need reminding.

After hours of paddling, the water feels like mud. "Do you know where you're going?" I ask gently.

Ash grimaces as he counts the islands. His shoulders pull up as he points and mutters. "Stepping stones. Each one bigger than the last. Climbing to the clouds." He counts again, finger pausing on the three islands in front.

"Ash!" I'm exhausted. But not so exhausted that I can't smack him with my oar.

He comes back to me. Smiling sheepishly. "Yes. I know where I'm going." He pauses. "I think…"

I groan.

The first drops of rain hit like buckets poured from the sky. Ash looks at me through dripping hair and I shake my head. Fresh water slowly fills the boat, soaking my slippers. I lift one soggy foot and then the other. "We have nothing to bail with," I shout through the screaming winds. "We need to get out of this rain before our boat sinks." I search the coastline; a dark gaping hole offers shelter and I point. "Over there."

He nods grimly. Shaking with cold, we pull our last strength from the marrow of our bones and row toward the cave.

11
CHAR LUNA

My hands cut the water in practiced movements. My small muscular body knows the sea like my own blood. I kick my feet, streamlined like a dolphin. The arc of my arm was shaped by my father. The straightness of my legs was locked by his rumbling, repetitious voice. Memories of the bubble and splash of my brothers as Papa taught us to swim swell in my ears. He was not always home but when he was, he ensured the time counted. And now, his time with his sons has run out like the tide.

His knee feels like a tree stump. When he bounces his leg, I feel like I'm hitting stone. But I'd never complain.

"And what happened next, Papa? Did you run him through?"

Holding his face in my hands, I press his cheeks together. Through smooshed lips he says, "There are many things you should know about the Shen, little Luna. But the first and most important thing is they are not easy to kill."

I run the bumps of my plait through my fingers. "It's coz they're magic, isn't it?"

He nods, dark eyes twinkling like flickering candlelight. "They are magic, and they are fast. You can't get close to a Shen. For if you get within reach, it's almost impossible to win. If they get their hands on your skin, you're done for."

I place a hand on his fish barrel chest, scarred inside and out. "But you did get close, didn't you? You got really close to a Shen."

The twinkle in his eyes shifts like the moon sinking. It dulls and he pulls me closer. "Yes, I did. I do not recommend it."

My hands ball and then I make them explode. "And it was like this, wasn't it? Like boom!"

I shake in my seat as his body shudders. "Yes, little Luna. He managed to get two fingers on the soft inside of my elbow. Where my oak arm ends and my flesh begins. He whispered one word. One word..."

"Lightning," I murmur, conjuring imaginary magic storms with my little fingers.

He coughs. The burn is still bright in his memory. "Yes, he whispered lightning. And I felt like my insides had been set alight. Like someone had lit the wick of a firecracker under my skin and it sped up my arm, heading for my heart. I've never wished for a wooden heart more in my life! I knew he had me. I knew my body would be scorched like the earth after fireworks if I didn't shake free."

Hanging on every precious word, I kick my legs out. "But you didn't give up, did you? Because that's when you thought of Mama and me and the boys. That's when you grabbed his hair and pulled."

Papa chuckles. "It was enough to break his concentration, my love. It was enough for me to get the upper hand and grab my dagger..." His oak hand wraps around an imaginary weapon.

Mama slaps the top of his head. "Ai ya! That's enough, she's only seven."

When Mama isn't looking, Papa demonstrates how he ran the Shen soldier through, cleaned off his dagger, and placed it back in his boot.

His laughter is a sound I could live in.

He is home again. He has fought his last battle. Our family is whole.

12

SHEN LYE LI

Rain pours over the entrance to the cave like a beaded curtain, filling the hull to my ankles. Gray light adds only a shadowy view of the inside. I pause, thinking about the boat growing heavy with water and sliding down to the sea floor. *How long before I would freeze? How long could I hold my breath?* The boat drops lower and I see Ash's distress. A tilt in his eyes that goes from blue to green. I cup my hands to bail out as much as I can. Ash searches for a place to land.

My nostrils flare at the smell as we row deeper inside. A strange smell. Neither sweet nor sour. Earthy and unfamiliar. *Living*.

We beach with a crushing sound like stepped on shells. Ash hops out and I help him drag the boat further up the small curved beach, securing the sails. The leaden light paints everything silvery. I twist back to the water. The froth looks out of place as there are no waves to speak of.

I scoop up the foam and my hands are stabbed with sharp spines. I gasp and drop a handful of feathers. Ash rushes to my side. "What is it?"

Disgusted, I move away as quick as possible, sure I will see the bodies of hundreds of dead birds washed up on the small shore. "Feathers," I answer, pointing to the large clumps bobbing in the waves.

Ash places his hand in the water before I can stop him. His Water blue sleeve dampening. "What on earth?" He picks through the handful. All cut neatly. All white. He shudders, eyes raised to the high, dark ceiling of the cavern. It glistens, reflecting the water.

I slap the dirty feathers from his hand, and a small spark of fire shoots from my fingers, running up the lifeline on his palm. "Ouch!" He withdraws sharply, blowing on his tanned skin.

Focusing on cooling, I ask for his hand. Reluctantly he gives it to me. "Sorry, brother. I wasn't concentrating. I forget myself sometimes." I place one pale finger on his palm and trace his life-line. The deep crevice that runs from index finger to wrist if you're lucky. The longer the line, the longer the life. Ash's runs long, but there's a break in the line near the top. I wish I knew what that meant.

His eyes connect with mine and his atmosphere is ice thickening over a pond as he closes over what he's thinking and feeling. "Forget it." He shakes his hand and holds it up for me to inspect. "Feels better already."

He ties the boat to a rock, and we climb away from the water.

CLAMBERING AND falling over sharp rocks, we look for a flat space to light a fire. Light is failing as night takes its turn. Ash hands me a bean cake from his pack. "I managed to steal some food from the kitchen. But it won't last us long." It's soggy but sugary and I devour it, licking the red paste from my fingers.

He brushes dust from his strong jaw. Sweeping strands of beach sand-colored hair behind his ear, he holds up a purse. It jingles promisingly and I gape.

"You stole gold?" I stop walking. "Ash, how could you? You know you'll never be able to return now, right?"

He shrugs and tucks it back in his waistband. "I wasn't going to stay there without you, Lye. With our parents gone, you're all I have."

My head falls. *What a sorry excuse for a family I turned out to be.* To his broadening back I say, "I know I dishonored you. Dishonored our family." I tuck my hands inside my robe, feeling small. Wanting to be smaller.

He stops. His torso straight and strong. His will, even more so. "I think I know why you did it. I do. I just wish you could have stopped and thought of me before you decided death was the only answer. I would have helped you, Lye. I would have done anything to help you."

I place a hand on his shoulder. It tenses but he doesn't jerk away. "I know. I'm sorry. I won't make that mistake again. I promise. I will always think of you before I act."

"I want to believe you, Lye, but to get to *that* place and make *that* decision... I, uh, I don't know if it goes away so easily." He reaches back and pats my hand quickly. I want to believe me too. I want him to be wrong. I press the point of the thimble into my finger, letting the pain settle there. Ghosts follow me. Call me. And I feel like I'm half in, half out of this life.

With his back to me he shrugs, a forced, tight action. "But never mind it all now. We're here together. Wet and miserable, but at least we're free, right?"

I straighten. Try to be what I used to be. Before Fire, Earth, Air, Water, Blood. Before I was called to be the Keeper, and Ash and I were just children. When I could find joy in the simplest pleasures. My hand in my brothers, threading our way through the gardens on ribbon day. Our mouths watering at the prospect of the Emperor's peasant banquet. A once a year invitation to dine at the palace. But the best part of those days was hopping from pillar to pillar and jumping up and down the hundreds of stairs with my little brother, a red ribbon in my long, dark hair. "Right."

Ash stomps the ground. "Here looks good." He drops his pack and we gather driftwood, throwing it in the dried-up rock pool.

Ash struggles with the damp flint. "I wish you could spark fire from your fingers onto wood as well as flesh," he mutters, irritated at his slow progress. Forehead crinkled, tongue poking out the corner of his mouth.

I laugh quietly. Though, it feels like I shouldn't. Like I'm not allowed to. "I can dry the wood a little." I put my hand to the straggly beach wood. It's difficult to warm it when I feel so out of control. I close my eyes and picture simple pleasures. A warm towel after a bath. The feel of a freshly laundered robe.

Finally, a flame catches and the fire grows, warming our bodies and drying our clothes. It reveals the walls of the cave as glossy black with chipped white streaks running in lines up and down the rock in an almost-pattern.

I put out my hands to soak in the heat. I can warm myself from within, but I can't dry my clothes as quickly as a real fire. And I don't trust myself to warm Ash without hurting him, not right now with my fingers sparking flame. I lean back against the rock. My body feels unpredictable. Too ruled by emotion. I take a deep breath and try to center my heart. Focus on its beating. Its strength.

"Are you all right?" he asks, catching my wrist wounds with his eyes and holding them close to his heart.

I nod. "Just a little cold," I whisper.

Ash reaches behind himself and grabs a branch rustling with dead leaves. He throws it on the fire, sending glowing embers up to the roof. The heat intensifies.

We watch the embers float up to the top of the cavern like orange fireflies.

Along with thousands of yellow eyes blinking open across the ceiling, twinkling like false stars.

The first screech is barely a warning.

The false stars fall from the sky. Stars with fangs, claws, and black, leathery wings.

13

CHAR LUNA

Soaking wet and pathetic, I cling to Dragon's Teeth Stack. Darkness is setting in, along with the cold. I have a long night ahead. I sit on one of the molars, listening to the water suck between the gaps in the teeth . Similarly, I feel like I've been vacuumed of all my happiness. Replaced with fear for my brothers' safety and shame. That is why it's preferable to spend the night on this wet, ragged rock formation than go home. I sniff, wipe my nose with my soaked sleeve. Pragmatism is shoving me from my position. Stubbornness locks my legs.

The sea has other ideas and swells to scrape me from the rock like a dying barnacle. I jump to the next tooth, the fang, higher and slipperier, arms and legs wrapped around the point.

Papa is probably searching for me in the family boat. Eyes scanning the blackness. Tired and worried. I have caused pain and embarrassment. And now panic. My feet struggle to find purchase and I slide down, my palms shredding on the rough black rock. After this, I'll be lucky if old man Ga Nah will take me as his third wife.

A wave crashes over my head and knocks me from my precarious perch. My back hits the water and I sink like a bird that has lost the will to fly. Cold and heat. Resignation and fight. I flap my arms. Fight wins. It always wins.

I break the surface, drawing a deep breath. The sound of fishing nets hitting the water grabs my attention. Further out to sea, the lanterns of a small boat shine temptingly. Surrounding me, numerous creatures cut through the water. Some hungry, some frightened.

I risk it. I have nothing left to lose.

Past the stacks the water is cold but calm, and my strokes are strong and even. I plow through, eyes on the light. Avoiding thoughts of what may be lurking beneath. Like my ever-narrowing future, whatever is out there feels beyond my control.

Something nudges my foot twenty yards from the boat. My heart cramps in my chest and I pick up the pace. Hands chopping the black water as fast as I can. If it's a drill shark I'm as good as dead. One puncture and I'll bleed dry before I can scream for help.

Ten yards. It bumps my foot again and its mouth closes over my toes. A loose grip but strong enough to pull me under. I kick out, trying to dislodge the creature, but it drags me under, bubbles streaming from my body as it whirls and spins, getting closer to the light.

I can't fight it. I can't...

The light brightens and I see the creature holding me, or is it... *helping me.* Round black eyes like marbles. Soft spotted fur. Four flippers churning the water. A windmill seal pup. It watches me with intelligent eyes. Being this close to a human is odd behavior for a mill seal. They're usually deathly shy of people, generally choosing to linger on the sea floor.

It releases my foot and nudges me with it head until I break the surface. Frightening the spirits out of the fisherman pulling in his net.

I grasp the net, pulling myself up. Wishing to thank the creature, I awkwardly twist around, but it's gone, startled by the men poking spears at it to protect their catch.

The first mate kneels down beside me and offers a rag from his pocket. I take it, almost dab my face but think better of it. "Why're you crying?"

I touch my heart. It beats strongly but it also heats and hurts with every breath. "My brothers left me." I dip my head and stare at my feet. As we travel over a wave, fish brine slops onto my shoulder. "I couldn't follow them. Because of this." I punch my chest with my fist. Once. Twice. The third time, he grabs my hand placing in my lap.

"Ah, little girl. Don't hurt your heart. You need it."

Knees to my chest, I sniff. "Do I? Sometimes I'm not so sure." All it does is get in my way.

He squats beside me, offering rice wine from a clay bottle. I sip it, grimacing at the sour taste before handing it back. He drinks it, licking his lips like it's sweeter than candy.

"Have you ever heard of the legend of Anh Roka?" he asks, taking another large swig. I shake my head. "Anh Roka, the man with a wooden heart."

A sharp beat in my chest as if my heart protests. "Wooden heart?" I tap my fingers over my sternum carefully.

"Mmhm. The most feared and formidable soldier the Char army has ever seen. More enemy kills than his whole regiment combined. But..."

Coalstone Island is approaching fast. Dark hills grow out of the water with a golden, dotted crown of candlelit windows. The bone white bow of the Ghost boat does its solemn business of pulling bodies from the water.

I stand, throwing a rope around this idea. "So, he could live with a wooden heart."

He stares up, thick black moustache moving as he talks. "Yes." Hands on hips, I let the air cleanse my lungs, breathing in slowly. "The legend tells of a battle so fierce and bloody that Anh Roka lost every man in his regiment. The Shen pushed him back until he was flat against a sheer rock wall. There was no way out. Other than to fight."

"Did he?" I picture Anh Roka as an immense Char man with a double sword, standing defiantly against dozens of Shen.

The first mate lowers his head and sighs. "He did. And when there was only one Shen left, begging for mercy, Anh Roka slit his throat without a second thought."

The boat nudges the boardwalk. I'm home. *I wish I were any-where but home.*

"Well, they killed his whole regiment. They did not deserve mercy."

A soft whistle blows through his lips. "But he'd already won. The battle was over. It's not the Char way to kill soldiers who surrender."

I step onto the boards and turn to the mate, his half-drunk eyes on me as the boat rocks. A channel of water grows between us. "What happened to him?"

The boat pulls away and the mate's voice grows softer. Two words float back to me: *hero* and *haunted*.

A wooden heart...

14

SHEN LYE LI

I think I'd rather hot burning stars were falling upon us than this shrieking, scratching avalanche. I scream, hoarse and hollow, as Ash is enveloped in a cloud of black wings studded with beads and buttons.

"Vanity bats!" he shouts as they claw at his head.

I try to scare them with a burning branch, lifting it like a torch. The fire illuminates thousands of nests built into the high rock walls. Colorful feathers, strands of hair, and odd trinkets hang from every carefully made cocoon. Distracted by a dangling gold chain and locket, I almost forget to duck as one swoops at my bald head, catching onto my clothing. It pulls at my plain gray robe but quickly gives up. Ash is their prize with his golden-brown hair and bright blue uniform.

Ash's hands are up over his head as the bats try to pull out his hair. My heart pounds like a hammer as I swipe with the flaming stick to no avail. Pushing my way through the clamor of wings and teeth, I find Ash's shoulder just as he shouts in pain. His face blanches an unnatural white, and blood drips from the center of his forehead. A bat flies upward with a long lock of hair gripped in its talons. Some follow it, fighting over the tresses so they can decorate their nests. Others keep at Ash.

I tear at their wings and kick their bodies across the sharp rocks. Reluctantly, I shoot Fire through them, but they just keep coming.

Ash's voice is muffled by the horrifying shrieks of the vanity bats. "Lye," he yells, slapping at the creatures with ice in his palms. His high-boned face is angled with pain and panic. "Run!"

They're going to kill my brother. Pick him clean of everything beautiful until there's nothing left.

Slinging his pack over my shoulders, I clench my fists and take an offensive stance. "Not without you, brother," I whisper.

Sweeping my arms in an arc, balls of lightning in my touch, I cut through the layer of gnawing bats attached to Ash's arms. They fall back flat, stunned with wings open, eyes vacant and greedy. I tug Ash closer, refusing to let go as I climb over the sharp rocks, cutting my knees, shredding my robe. He shouts out, "Look. Light," angling what little spare limb he has toward a small circle of light at the back of the cave.

We scramble. Focused solely on that light. The swarm of wings creates a gust of wind. The sound of a thousand bats screeching is like a hurricane lifting a house from its foundations.

Run. Run. Run.

Don't look back. Don't let go. Don't pay attention to the blood dripping into your hand. The lack of breath in your brother.

Just run.

The light is a window out of reach. A small circle only a few feet in diameter punched in the top of the cave. Confused, some of the bats fly straight for it and exit. But most still continue to strip my brother of his hair, his blue uniform and gold strapping. *His life.*

I kick and punch. Wicked, destructive things spark from my fingers. But I hold back, a flag at half-mast. I don't want to reach the peak of my abilities. When I do, I darken. The power becomes deliciously dangerous. Cruelty a hearty meal.

Climbing, climbing.

I force Ash up first. He fights me but I send a strong wind to his back.

The bright light can only be the moon, calling us to safety. "Climb. Keep climbing," I urge as Ash slows, blood blooming from deep claw marks on his back.

It's just surface wounds. Just the skin, I tell myself. He'll heal. Flesh wounds can heal.

The rock is wet and slimy. Ash pushes his foot too hard into the side and slips down on me. The bats scatter like a flock of birds from a cannon shot and a few are too spooked to return. He glances back at me. He is a mess of blood, with patches of hair missing, and one eye swollen closed. I draw in a sharp breath as my face contorts with worry. And he smiles.

I don't know how he manages to smile. But that's Ash. Like a small sun to my dying planet. "I look that good, huh?" he grunts through pain and blood, before more bats circle around for another go. He's scrambling upward again, while I push him on.

We're nearly there. Bats scrape on the edges of the entrance, banging their heads and screaming like children having a tantrum. "Get up, get out!" I manage.

A bat sinks its teeth into Ash's ear; he throws his head back and curses. I use my last strength to heave him over the edge and out of the cave.

The effort has me skidding back on the slippery rock, my arms grabbing, unable to grasp slick stone. I fall, landing on a ledge with a thump several yards below. My ribs scrape and my skin tears open.

Bats scatter, flapping black shapes against the sky.

Then a new sound amid the wingbeats. Feet thudding. The circle of light changes from pale white to golden. *Lanterns.*

I'm about to call out to Ash when words from a foreign mouth speak. "Are you alone?"

His voice breathless, pained. "I don't see anyone else, do you? Of course, I'm alone."

And then Ash is gone.

15
CHAR LUNA

Our house lies at the end of the boardwalk. Right where the mangroves dip their toes in the water. It looks so small. It *is* so small. And now it is empty.

My heart jellies in my chest.

The family boat is missing. I stare at my feet, feeling guilty for putting Papa through more worry.

Lightless and quiet, the window reflects the moonlight and nothing else. I slope to the door, so very exhausted, and reach for the handle. It's locked. My mouth pulls down. Wells of sadness pooling under my eyes.

I lift my fist, but it never connects. By now my brothers have reached the monastery. They'll be given supper and allocated a bed. They will meet recruited Char from the nine other islands. Young men with different homes, different stories to their own. But all with the same losses and the same goals.

When they are alone, they'll talk about me. They'll shake their heads in sympathy, embarrassment. My hand drops to my side. Most of all they'll miss me.

Sliding down to the ground, I curl my knees to my chest and rest my head on my arm. Water laps at the posts beneath our home. Fish jump safe in knowing no hook or net hangs below. I close my eyes and try to shut out the pain. *Why am I always on the wrong side of things?* I don't fit where they want me to fit.

Sleep comes to me in uncomfortable pieces, interrupted by buzzing elbows and my neck cracking.

THE SMOOTHNESS of long-polished timber grazes my cheek. "Luna. Little Luna. What are you doing out here? I've been looking for you all night."

The sun breaks my vision apart. I yawn and unroll, my sore body protesting. Yesterday comes back. Papa's large head blocks the light as he kneels down.

"Papa," I manage. "I'm so sorry." My voice is small, circular, searching for which particular thing it's sorry for.

He looks left to right and drags me over the threshold. "Sh. Sh. You are safe now. You are home. Come inside and talk to your father."

Mama sleeps in the corner, eyes puffy and red as guava skin. Papa motions to her and puts a finger to his lips. He moves around the kitchen carefully. An elephant squashed into a pantry. He warms a teapot and tucks two cups into his belt, beckoning me to Joka and Sun's room.

He sits heavily on one of the beds and I pull up Joka's stool, the leather worn from hours spent huddled over his desk, sketching and reading. I sigh sadly as I run my hand over the soft hide. Papa's dark eyes crinkle; he's better at this than me. But then he's had to let go so many times. The loss of his own brothers, his friends, are etched in lines on his face. Happy memories somehow pull the eyes down. Sad memories pull the mouth forward. I feel each one like they're my own. They bury under my skin for now and will rise like riverbed cracks as I age.

Papa pours tea and I cup my hands around the mug, enjoying the warmth. I inhale the jasmine scent and let myself smile. A brief comfort. Then I confess my need to join my brothers. My heartache at being dismissed simply for my female heart.

He chuckles once I'm finished. One eye squints, a dimple in his cheek. "You speak as if this is news to my old ears, daughter. I know you. I know your heart." He pokes me in my tiny sternum. Bird-sized but holding so much emotion.

I sip my tea. The glossy liquid coats my throat. "I know it is wrong to want such things. I know how hard it would be. I just don't care."

Papa leans back and stares at the ceiling. "No, Luna, you are not wrong exactly, but you need to understand what you ask is almost unheard of. You would need to prove yourself to be more."

"More?" I tilt my head.

"A woman must be more than typical and, most unfairly, *much* more than a man to enter the Char army."

I roll my eyes, and he catches my chin, bringing my gaze back to his. His dark eyes have seen beyond what I know.

"It was always going to be hard for you to enlist. Much harder than for your brothers. In one sentence, you needed to prove that you could be like them. That you would make a good soldier." He pats my head condescendingly. "You were never going to be able to do that. And especially not to someone like Juni Fah. Fah is unwaveringly traditional. Challenging his values in front of the whole village was only ever going to end one way."

With rejection.

I know this but I think I wanted him to lie. To tell me there was hope. "I want to stand alongside my brothers, Papa. We're a band, a unit. I don't know how to be without them. They don't know how to be without me. And now I've ruined everything."

Papa shakes his head. "It will be all right, little Luna. But you need to face the way things are. You could have a good life if you stopped fighting against the natural order." He places a hand on my heart. "This here is a good thing. Your heart is never full. It always has room for more love, more compassion. But…"

I chew on my lip. My long hair scrapes my forehead as the sea breeze picks up and pushes through Joka's always open window. "But what, Papa?"

He groans, looks down and scratches his chin with his oak hand. "A woman's heart, her empathy, is a wonderful thing. It makes for good mothers and wives, as Fah said." He takes my hand and I want to pull away, but I can't. His creased face tells me this is hard for him to say. That maybe he doesn't fully believe his words, but this is just the way things are. "And good mothers *raise* great soldiers. Good wives *care* for weary husbands, tired and shocked from battle. But they may not make good soldiers."

It doesn't really matter whether I believe him or not. This *is* the way things are. And I don't think I have the power to change them.

My heart stutters out a strange beat. *A reminder beat.*

Mama knocks sharply on the door, and it opens. "Ai ya!" She grasps at her chest, scrunching her shirt, then rushes to me, throwing her arms around my neck and pulling me close. "Luna, darling. You're home." Then she pulls back, cupping my face in her hands. "Where have you been all night?"

Papa shuffles past us with a look of amusement. "Just be happy your daughter is safe," he grumbles, knowing full well she's not going to let it land there.

I watch him go from between my mother's hugging arms, feeling the beat of my too full heart.

16
CHAR LUNA

Mama smooths her exquisitely designed ceremony dress out on the kitchen table. Brown silk embroidered with gold threaded tree rings. I yawn, dragging my feet over the cracked floor. "I've been to the village circle, Luna," she says, like it explains why her ceremony dress is out. "People are talking."

I nod. It's a small village. Of course, people are talking.

Staring at the empty seats, I wonder what my brothers are doing. Eating breakfast. Patrolling the woods. Training. My stupid heart aches for wooden training posts. Marked with Shen symbols and Char blood. It wishes for the sweep of Char army robes over stones and it almost breaks for the noise and knocking of three brothers.

My chest burns like someone poured boiling water over it. My flawed female heart almost revels in this pain.

I run a finger over the silk. "Mama. What do you know about Anh Roka?"

She pauses in her chores, black eyes twinkling with remembered starlight. "He was one of the bravest soldiers in Char history.

It's no ordinary man who can bear the burden of a wooden heart. But he made that sacrifice to protect our people."

I shove the dress to one side, crinkling the stiff silk, and Mama sighs with disappointment and a hint of unsurprise. "What happened to him?"

She holds the dress to my shoulders. "Ah. You're so tiny compared to your mama. I'm going to have to take it up *and* in." Pins between her teeth, she pulls the dress away.

"Anh Roka, Mama?"

She waves me away. "Oh, it was so long ago, Luna. I don't know exactly. Just that he was a brave, honorable man. A great soldier." She scurries around the kitchen searching for thread.

"Why are you rushing? My ceremony isn't until next month." I look left to right. "Where's Papa?"

Her cheeks color. Her cherrywood hip cracks as she tilts to one side. "Your papa went to visit the village elders to see about moving your ceremony up. We think it might be best to distract everyone from your... the..." She doesn't want to say it, so I do it for her.

"My shameful display of female emotion?" I stare at my feet. "Or is it my unwomanly desire to join the Char army?"

She pats my shoulder warmly, not answering either question. "It's for the best, little Luna. This way we can show you to men before rumor grows into truth and it becomes a thick coat you can't shed. If you choose your limb wisely, it may be enough to elevate you from embarrassment." Her mouth puckers at the sour shame.

My heart beats unsure. *Choose wisely. Choose marriage.* "What men? There are barely any in the village." What was left swept in on the tide, pierced with arrows, or floated away on overburdened boats to Black Sail City.

Mama rattles off the names of several much older villagers. Some only looking for second or third wives. The distraught look on my face causes her to soften. "Papa agrees this is best. If we don't find a match here, we'll try another island. Nothing's set in stone." Her black hair is perfectly pinned. I catch my reflection, lighter brown hair hanging in sleep tangled clumps. I run a hand through it, and it snags.

Nothing's set in stone, just wood. Everything is set in wood.

I scratch at a spot of dried soy sauce on the table, chasing away thoughts of wrinkled lips approaching my small but plump plum ones. Of first wife's resentment and cupboard-sized sleeping quarters. "So, when is my ceremony then?"

Needle darting in and out of the fabric at a cracking pace, Mama mutters without looking up, "Tomorrow."

My future dawns and sets before I can even take a breath. And it's dark, drudged, and horrifying.

Papa swings through the door with a simple red band clutched in his oak fist. "So, it's all set." His eyes connect with Mama's and they share a steadying look. I don't share that steadiness. The ground beneath me rocks and pitches from an unearthly storm. "At dawn, we shall walk the mountain path and you will have a new life."

I force a nod.

We sit at our lonely table. Three that should be six. The ghost of a shove. The tap of a balsa foot on my knee beneath the table. *Little sister. Little Luna. You'll be all right.* A plate pushed toward mine begging for an extra piece of pork. Proud cut chin, dream spoked eyes, knowing glances. My sigh is deep as the ocean. So deep there's sand in my throat.

Tea is poured. A usually comforting ritual. Papa wipes liquid from his moustache. "Luna. Only daughter. This will be good for you." He reaches for my chin, the wood warm on my skin. "You seem worried. Are you afraid of the change?"

I shake my head. "No. I'm not afraid Papa. I just wish…"

The joints in his oak hand creak as he strokes my cheek, catching saltwater on his finger. "Don't wish. The Char don't wish. A wish is a waste. Put your thoughts to the future."

The future. I picture myself standing on teak legs. Tall to reach the washing line. Long and thin, draped in a skirt. Children rapping at my knees. It doesn't fit. I don't think it will ever fit.

I remove Papa's hand from my face. It rests on the oak table, producing the Call, treating my ears to a beautiful, musical harmony. Papa knew exactly what he wanted when he met her. Maybe when I meet the Carvress in the morning, I'll just know what is right. It will come to me and so will the peace Joka talked of. The feeling of "meant to be." I tap my milky throat.

I gulp down my tea and stand. Papa rips the red band in half and ties a piece around both my calves.

Mama smiles but it's a wane smile. There's no life to it. We're living in last resorts, ditch efforts and desperate measures. This rush to marriage isn't what they wanted for me either.

I kiss his stubbly cheek. "Perhaps this is for the best, as you say, Papa." I sound like someone else. A girl who might be satisfied with caring for children, cooking, cleaning and polishing her husband's wooden part. Mama is happy. Many of the women in the village are happy. It's a good life. There's nothing wrong with that life.

I tell myself I'll get used to it.

I tell myself it is for the best, just like my parents say.

But my heart knows even though they say this, they don't believe it. Not completely. They follow tradition as everyone does. It's been this way for centuries. Years and years of women going one way and men going another. Meeting only in the home and in the bed. My legs tense at the idea of being that close to an unknown man. My trust is seeded deep. I'm not ready to hand it over.

I reach for my brothers. *Has Joka been beaten yet?* He holds back in a fight. They will punish him for it. *Has Sun got himself in trouble for leaping ahead of instruction? For acting before thinking?* And Ben Ni. Something cold passes through my body. He has no defense. How will they teach him to avoid Shen touch when he has no wooden limb to utilize? Especially when they plan to strike first. There's not enough time.

I CANNOT sleep. My head is restless. The watery quiet only intensifies my thoughts. This pressing need. I shrug on pants and a tunic and roll out of bed, climbing down the ladder. The silence of the usually snore-filled hallway adds lead to my already heavy heart.

My heart.

It beats slowly. It beats fast. It strains in pain. It flutters in excitement. It pushes at my chest in empathy, nudging my actions. In

Fah's eyes, it characterizes me as an emotional girl without control. My stupid, feeling heart.

Mama's, now my ceremony, dress hangs from the window, brought *in and up*. A flag for tradition. A curtain over change. No matter how she adjusts it, it will never fit.

A change. I need a big change.

I touch my chest and it dissents.

But if I am to prove myself...

Outside, my brothers haunt every board. They swing from the mangrove branches. Their feet disturb the water.

I walk through their ghost impressions and they scatter like smoke, my eyes on the charred part of our village.

Right where the boardwalk hooks around the corner is a re-minder of when the Shen scrambled stealthily down the shale mountainside. There was no warning war chant as they glided be-hind buildings, setting small fires, reaching into windows and touching sleeping villagers The senses of the sleeping townsfolk were blinded so they neither smelled nor felt the flames until it was too late.

That was over a hundred years ago and still we fight.

Mama cleans the wound on Papa's back carefully. Bandaging it with tight clean cloth. My tears flow freely when I see him gri-macing in pain. I kneel in front of him and take his flesh hand.

"Why did they do this to you Papa?" I cry. "Why must you always leave? Why do you have to fight?"

He grips my hand and presses it to his rough face. "I fight to protect you, little Luna. I fight to protect the Char islands from a greedy man."

I sniff. "The Shen emperor?"

He nods sadly. "We are so very different now. But we were once the same. Something happened a long time ago that split our worlds apart. One day maybe we can pull it back together."

I shake my little head. Still not understanding. "But if that happened hundreds of years ago, why do we still fight?"

His eyes change, drop in strength. "Sometimes I wonder if it's because it's all Shen and Char know how to do. Caught in a cycle we cannot break free of. Maybe one day, a Shen emperor will be born that can see past his fear and distrust of the Char. An emper-

or that can be happy with the vast, rich land in front of him. Maybe then there will be peace."

My hopeful eyes meet his doubtful ones.

Mama helps him with his shirt. "I don't think we'll live to see that day, Setsu."

He laughs grimly and pats my head. "Maybe not. But perhaps little Luna will."

This is what we do. What we have done for hundreds of years. Beat them back to the mainland. Tried to survive, preserve our ways and our culture despite the growing blackness. The Shen know we cannot rebuild over Char bodies. Ash mixes with ash until it's impossible to tell what is building and what is body. So, the ruins must remain untouched.

Kneeling at the point where the boards change from brown to black, I place my hand on the crumbling charcoal. It comes back sooty and wet.

The pain of the past leaks from the wood. It wafts around me, filling my heart with a hundred years worth of grief.

I turn toward the mountain path winding like a lifeline, up, up, up to the hidden home of the Carvress.

I remove the red bands that are stinging my calves and wrap them around one hand.

My feet lead to the sky. To a different future.

17
SHEN LYE LI

I'*m alone,* he said. Emphasis on alone.

The word was a warning. "Don't reveal yourself. Don't try to save me." But I should have tried. Shaking and pinned to the wall like sun-starved moss, I didn't move. I haven't moved. In how long? *I don't know.*

"How long has it been?" The exquisite, regal voice lays over me like a silk cape. My forehead presses to the floor. Golden light and golden purpose fill me. The emperor's mother exudes warmth and grace. I must please her.

"Thirteen years, your majesty. Thirteen long years since we have had a Keeper in the palace." This voice tries to be silk when its true origins are rough as canvas.

I am unsure and alone. My head aches against the cold hard tiles but I dare not move. I cannot do anything to harm our position in the palace.

Ash is not allowed to live with me but at least I know he is safe. They placed him with a servant family within the compound. He is close and cared for. I allow myself a breath of relief.

My chest expands and feet move in my vision.

This place is foreign and frightening. But I am meant to be here. It is my destiny. My room is too lavish. I cannot sleep for fear of being smothered by so many feather pillows. But I am honored. I am blessed. Everywhere I look the elements are represented in some form or other. Tapestry, painting, carving. So much work to honor me and those before me. It pressurizes an already tense feeling that I must not let anyone down.

My fingers curl, sparks of lightning and fronts of hail burning to be released.

"Stand," *the emperor's mother demands without needing to raise her voice. I do as I am told, and she beckons me closer with a long, painted fingernail.*

I approach, eyes down. A single nail, filed to a claw, digs into the soft underside of my chin. Pressing. Pressing. I swallow. "Thank you, your highness. You do me great…"

The nail jabs hard, a sharp and unexpected pain, and my eyes lift. Connecting with ebony elegance. Kohl and red lips. "Have you been hiding from us, young Keeper? Your people have been suffering, searching for thirteen years. And what have you been doing?" *She smiles with the sweetness of a crocodile plant. Sugar that entices, jaws that engulf.* "Playing in the swamp with your dirty sibling, I suppose."

I try to shake my head, tears springing from the corners of my eyes. "Please, forgive me. I did not know my calling."

Her grin stretches, wide and inviting. Her nail retracts and she cups my cheek. Brushing away the tears. Her expression is welcoming. Motherly. And I am pulled to it like an orphaned bird to a child's breast. "All is forgiven, child. You are part of our family now." *She pats my hand.* "We will make sure you live up to your duty."

I bow low. Thankful. "May I ask after my brother, Ash?" *It has been a day since I saw him last, the longest time we have been apart that I can remember.*

Spears hit the tiles and the emperor's mother directs her guards. "Take her to the baths. See what you can do about that hair."

Not answering, she turns her back on me, whispering in the emperor's ear. His concubines stand dutifully behind him. Painted eyes watching me with sparks of distaste and jealousy.

The walls of isolation and loneliness already begin to form around me. As is right for the Keeper.

Ash is gone. Snatched by the Char. Again, I failed to protect him.

Their accents were clear. Blunt and gravelly. Bellows deep within the chest.

A cold wind howls through the cave, carrying the sounds of the sea and the beating of wings like battered sails.

I can't stay here.

I look down. From this height, if I stepped off the precipice, I may only break a few bones. Not enough to kill me. Not enough.

My toes creep to the edge, rock teeth digging into my soles. But Ash's words are inside me. Pulsing with my heart and pushing sharp characters into the walls of my veins. I am *alone.*

But he's not alone. I'm here. I'll find him.

I roll the thimble between my thumb and forefinger, the ridges massaging my skin. Edging backward, I tighten the straps on the pack. I hoist myself up, bruises aching with every movement. Straggler bats whip past my face, but they have no interest in me. I'm plainly dressed, plain faced. I have nothing they want. Peeking from the hole, I check for Char. Wait a few minutes and pull myself out of the hole. Standing straight, I breathe in the smells of soft earth and greenery dripping with water.

Turning in a circle, I gasp.

Ash must have confused the islands—miscounted them. My eyes trail upward past thick jungle to a stone monastery sitting like a crown on the top of the mountain, lit and busy. An aura of golden light glows behind it, the mark of a large city. And the Char only have one: Black Sail City.

We are in the worst place possible if we wished to avoid discovery by the Shen.

I duck, scared of being spotted. Pulling my hood over, I slink across the earth, holding onto branches like a sun sloth, searching for a safe space to sleep. I follow the curve of the mountain, ridges cut into the side like wrinkles.

I lean against a tree while voices carry down the mountainside from the monastery. Char men laughing. Sparring. Men who would kill me without hesitation.

I swing the pack up and climb as high as the boughs will allow.

Don't worry brother. I'll be watching.

18
CHAR LUNA

Moisture soaks into my slippers as I stomp up the mountain, following red scratches on trees. Tiny claw marks only a Char would find, leading to the Carvress's cove. Noise doesn't matter. No one comes up here at night. The change always comes after dawn.

The stars blur. There's little time.

I hurry up the path. Counting the marks.

Two hundred and seven.

Then turn toward the sun.

Sink down below the horizon,

Light as a fish in water.

Let go and listen for the music.

A song we are sung from birth. Directions to the Carvress. Though, at the two hundredth and seventh mark, I spin in a circle, not sure what to do. The horizon is barely visible through the trees and I squat down to peer through a tree fork. The water sparkles silver, with no golden reflections of Black Sail City. This is the other side of our island. The wild side.

A smile spreads fiery across my lips. I like it.

A murder bird bobs its head above me, razing over my silk soft skin. It pauses on the red bands over my hand and I shake it. "It's not blood, bird. Just cloth." The bird flaps its wings and I crouch, afraid of its pecking beak and razorblade feathers. But it has no interest in me.

Crouched low, the horizon disappears from sight and I see what I'm meant to: A small carved hole in the rock. Just large enough for a man to fit through. I peer into darkness. *Sink down below the horizon, light as a fish in water.*

Holding my breath, I grip the sides of the entrance and swing in. My legs dangle, touching nothing. *Let go and listen for the music.*

My ribs expand. My heart beats anxiously.

My fingers grip the rock tightly.

"Let go, Luna," I say to myself. "Just let go."

I release my hands and fall, expecting a whoosh of air past my ears but it's only a three-foot drop.

Darkness is complete. I put my hands out, hoping I won't run into a hoarder bear with its giant black eyes and spoon-like ears. If I kick over a pile of bones I'll be in trouble. I shudder. They hate their bone sorting disturbed.

I step forward like a blind woman, sweeping my arms in small circles. "Hello?" I whisper. No one answers.

Part of me wants to turn around. This would be easier with Mama and Papa by my side. But then I think about my brothers. The danger they will face soon. Danger I should be facing with them and I inch forward.

The cave broadens as I go deeper, my hands no longer able to touch both sides. Sea wind calls. These mountains are honeycombed with passages that mostly lead out to sea. I picture stepping off the edge of a cliff and hug myself. For all I know, I have traveled down a wrong tunnel. But so many Char have touched these smooth walls. Have chosen the right direction. I stop.

I strain my ears. Slow my breath. Concentrate.

Listen for the music.

Wind chimes play straight ahead.

I gulp, following the crescendo of sound.

Rounding a bend, light glows and disappears. A creaky hum then a deafening rattle as a gust of wind surges through the tunnel. Closely hung, wooden chimes smack me in the face as I hurry through. Light swells, filling the space, and I take in the details. Every timber imaginable in varying sizes hang in display around me. Every color from blondest birch to darkest ebony.

They hum. They warble. They sing. They are one half of the Call as they are yet to be turned into limbs.

I fall to my knees, a power I don't understand pressing down and threatening to pull me apart. I stare at the dusty earth, my ears peeling open. Each chime seems to want something. *Choose me. Choose me,* they shriek as the music tries to pluck my ribs out one by one.

"Ah!" I scream, bowing low. Curling up like a slater bug.

Leather slippers with purple woven tongues shuffle under my eyes.

The Carvress's voice is rough as raw silk, sweet as lychee syrup. "You are early, Char Luna."

19

CHAR LUNA

I push against the sound to stand. The Carvress's stares with swirling wooden eyes. Alternating brown and sap honey rings like a tree. Her long, slender figure towers over me, draped in red and pink silk. I bow low and she laughs, grasping my elbow. "Come, come. I'm guessing we have much to do in very little time, eh?"

I gape as she ducks and weaves around the hundreds of hanging chimes. They louden as we pass, seeming to swing out of her way and bash into me. "I'm sorry I'm early..." I start but she clucks her tongue and silences me with those tree ring eyes.

"Don't mind the chimes. They just want to be chosen," she mutters as we near a heavy carved door. Then she turns her head and scowls. "But *they* know it's not up to them, don't they?" Her voice grows at the end. The chimes ring once and then still.

I grip the red cloth around my hand tighter.

No one told me what to expect. My brothers' lips were sewn shut when I asked about their ceremonies. And it's safe to say if they'd told me even a little of this, I wouldn't have believed them.

The Carvress opens the door. It drags across the stone floor, and she pulls me inside.

SHE SWEEPS her arm around the cave in graceful arcs pointing out teetering stacks of raw timber. Open drawers full of brass hinges and joints shine dully in lantern light. "Welcome, Char Luna," she announces like the room is full of people. Rough carved limbs hang from racks along the walls and they quiver at the sound of her voice.

She takes my hand in an iron grip, holding it up to a lantern to inspect. "I see you've changed your mind." She purses her beautiful wooden lips. "I guess I'll have to find someone else to take the teak legs I started. But yes, I can make a hand. Oak like your father…?"

Nervousness causes my hands to shake. A hand. I could take a hand. Then maybe I could throw a powerful punch. Stop a Shen from reaching my skin. *But would it be enough to convince the general?*

The Carvress presses down on my palm with fingertips as rough as sandpaper. She scrubs at it, reading my fortune. "Ah. There's a loop here, but not the usual illness or wounding." She glances up. Stooped over, she looks like a broken twig, sinewy bark holding her together. "No," she croons. "This is a pause. Almost like a long sleep. A coma…"

I clear my throat and claim back my hand. It wouldn't be enough. Not for General Fah. It must be something drastic. The biggest change. I press the cloth hard against my heart. It sputters and pumps. Fearful. Doubtful. I gulp and try to roll right over those feelings. I think of battle; Ben Ni running to the point of a spear or the devastating touch of a Shen. It tears shreds from my heart like it's being grated.

"No, Carvress. Not my hand." I push confidence into my voice. Try to pretend that I'm sure.

Her mouth winds into a strange smile. It whispers knowing and sympathy. "You wish for a wooden heart."

I bow. "Yes, Carvress."

In the center of a carved-from-rock workshop, the smells of sawdust and oil filling my nose, the Carvress scrutinizes me. "I haven't done a heart in a long, long time…" Her eyes roll to the roof. Then she bends down to my level, stares into my golden eyes. "Are you sure, Char Luna?"

Two words. All I need is two words and I'll be steps closer to joining my brothers. To making a way that's not been set out for me, no matter how lovingly, by my parents. By defying them, I draw a line in the sand they can't easily cross over. Not unless I bring many Shen scalps home to honor them.

My fingers itch at the chance to play my part.

This could be my fresh start.

This could be a huge mistake.

This could be the greatest thing to ever happen to me.

Still clutching the cloth to my chest. Clear thoughts and a clear voice. "I'm sure." I stamp the words to the floor, the walls, and the ceiling.

Hands on hips, she stares a while longer, making sure that what I say is what I mean. She brushes her sanded fingers over my cheeks, under my eyes, over my lips. Satisfied, she nods and stalks toward the bench that runs around the edge of the cave.

"Well then, Char Luna Yan, we have much work to do!"

20
SHEN LYE LI

I slide carefully between crowded trees toward the monastery. The low walls are not suited to barracks. The heady smoke of incense carries over the wind. It's indefensible. My head drops, hands curled into fists. Now I'm certain the chancellor has slid the first tile into place. The path to war I set has been staked out and lit with burning torches. The betrayal of the treaty will never be forgiven. I sense it in the five hundred or so Char men stalking with heavy purpose between buildings. Their atmospheres surrounded by dark clouds and crackles of electricity. Unrest. Unease. It is exactly what we wanted.

Hate. It is his currency. He may be a Water Shen but fostering hate is his true power.

The pronged tip of his staff pierces my hand. Pain shoots up my arm and wishes to fly from my fingertips. Blood trickles between my fingers, making strange patterns on the floor. A bad painting. Spilled red sauce.

"Get up!" the chancellor shouts, thin face stretched with forcefulness. "You think I care to make the Keeper bleed. I am helping you. The sooner you understand this, the better. You need

to embrace your power. Let it go and let it in. You don't realize how good it will feel. I am doing this for your benefit."

I want to believe him. I'm trying, but I have spent thirteen years hiding from my power. Letting it swarm through my body and shoot from my fingers feels the same as allowing my skin to split open and fall to the floor like a casing. His sharp gaze assesses me. I want him to find me worthy, more than sufficient.

I jump up, my bald head still stinging from the razor. I blink sea breeze eyes. The man before me grins. Sweat dripping over his long, sloped nose. He lashes out, slicing my leg. The pain fills me with the need to purge my pent-up fury. It builds inside, delicious and dangerous.

My shifu, Che Lu, steps forward, concerned. "Chancellor, she is young. Give her time to learn and harness her skills." I look upon my master with affection. He has taught me so much and with a gentle, encouraging hand. Although he has never breached into friendship, he has always treated me with respect. Giving me faith that we are working toward a great goal. Slowly convincing me that the Keeper means something to the Shen people.

The chancellor's neck snaps to the stocky Che. A tree stump dressed in white Air Shen robes.

Faster than thin ice breaking under a heavy foot, the chancellor spins upon Che and presses the pointed end of his staff to Che's neck. Che cannot even utter a word of protest. Blood pools around the points as he pushes harder. The chancellor's expression is even. Calculating. Each move he makes is to create a stronger, better Keeper.

Fire blasts in my chest. Raging flames that cause leaves to crackle, branches to break. I am brimful of power and anger at his threatening of my shifu. My shifu! My expression is stone, carved like ancient gods and heroes. I know he is manipulating me, but it works well. I feel all Keeper history and future roiling inside just looking for an outlet. The chancellor will be that outlet.

I pounce upon the chancellor and touch my fingers to his throat. My smile lengthening at the same time as his. I blast him with controlled fire. When he releases Che, I follow my fire with heavy rain, so he's not permanently injured. The elements surround me. I see earth soak up the rain. Hear creatures digging at *new growth. Feel wind carrying seeds, promising new life. All part of the elemental cycle. The cycle that lives in me and gives me power.*

The power balloons and bursts inside my blood. I feel everything. Every. Thing. And the chancellor is right, it feels good. Feels right.

He brings out my power like no other.

The chancellor stands, satisfied. I offer a hand to Che and he withdraws sharply when I accidently sting him with a tree snake bite.

The chancellor bows shallowly to both of us. "I think we are finally seeing the true Keeper and I am impressed."

I do not bow. I am the Keeper. I hold all the elements. They should bow to me.

"But you still have a long way to go. Mercy is your weakness." The chancellor glances at Che, standing to attention.

To reach my full potential and serve the emperor and the Shen, I will learn how to separate myself from my emotions. If mercy is weakness, I shall burn it to ash and send it on the wind to a place no one can find.

I breathe in too sharply and the wounds across my ribs stretch and break. I should be used to this pain, but in the last few years, as my power honed and developed, my training became less improvement and more upkeep. My skin softened.

Access to the best healers and medicines also helped.

Fingers scrape the moss-covered stones as I try to catch a glimpse of Ash. My eyes jump from giant incense pot to carved gods staring severely at a landscape they probably wouldn't recognize. A listless movement catches my eye. I spot his golden-brown head sagging. His arms tied behind his back and around a post. I sigh with relief. He's alive.

A Char soldier stomps towards Ash, placing a bowl of water at his feet. His strange wooden shoulders roil beneath a light tunic. My heart shrinks in my chest as Ash reaches for it and finds it just beyond his grasp. The Char man laughs cruelly.

My heart urges me to spring up, scatter the soldiers one by one with lightning and lava. But I force myself to remain still. My injured body will not carry me far.

A younger man—no, a boy—peeks out from behind a pillar. When the solider leaves, he pushes the bowl closer to Ash with his foot. I look for the Carvress's mark, but if the boy has a wooden limb, it's hidden.

Ash stares ahead blankly. Though he's not as resigned as they may think. He has that familiar look of planning and plotting.

I count the soldiers as they walk to breakfast but stop at two hundred. There are far too many for me to take on my own, especially in this state. They've tied him in the center of the monastery square, making a covert rescue impossible.

Slipping back into the jungle, wet leaves slap my face, I know my expression is less focused than Ash's. I lean into hopelessness as I struggle to find a way to help my brother. I feel weak with my side open to the air, my heart open to the sky. I was once fearsome and cruel. It took me a long time to find my mercy again. I cannot storm this place and lose what little I have gained. If I stoop that low, then I am no better than *him*.

21
CHAR LUNA

"What am I looking for?" I ask, bewildered, standing in swirls of sawdust, hands limp at my sides. The Carvress grips me with long, strong fingers and leads me around the benches, making me touch each lump of timber.

"Not looking. Listening…" Her words hiss on the tip of her carved lips as she cups her ear and leans down to the hunks of wood.

I sigh. "What am I listening for then?"

She grins with silky wooden teeth. "For a Call."

I tap various blocks of wood. Some dark as volcanic mud, others rusted red. A faint buzz emanates from them, but I don't hear a Call.

The sun must be shaving the waves outside. The threat of my parents winding their way up the mountain path approaches. When they wake and find me gone, I know they'll come here. I find a pile that's higher than the others, a light timber with a pleasant smell. Gravity pulls at my ears, stretching me down to the sound of music strung together like an unfinished, uncomplimentary necklace. Not quite harmony. Notes competing. My hand trails over the stack, magnetized to one particular piece. When I touch it, the sound is unearthly. Like a war horn and a woman's voice colliding. The song is conflicted. But it's the only one that calls to me.

"It's this one." My voice wavers, and my finger retracts. Power resides there. Power I hope I'm ready for.

The Carvress pulls it out in one swift movement, the other pieces teetering but not tumbling. "Bitternut hickory. Hmm." She frowns. A look of confusion crosses her face and is gone like the turn of a dancing heel. "Interesting choice." Eyebrows draw together.

Time is passing. I straighten, try to look sure. "Yes. Hickory. That's my choice."

She doesn't argue. The Char choose. The Carvress provides. That's how it's supposed to go. Her role and mine.

She takes the lump of hickory to the other side of the round room, walls carved with thick scratched lines like the inside of a walnut shell.

"You sit over there," she orders, pointing to a stool next to a small fireplace. "Lemon fin tea would be nice," she throws over her angular shoulder as she begins her work. I pull out a jar of dried yellow fish fins and lemon peel. As the hot water hits the fins, they fan out like a bird's wing. Spines so delicate, they look like feathers. I inhale deeply. The briny smell brings me home. I set the tea down for her.

The Carvress works lightning fast. Chiseling, chipping, inserting brass pieces. I crane to see her progress but am slapped away. "Ai ya, child! Give me room to work."

Each second she takes is a footstep up the hill. Each minute brings my parents closer to stopping me.

Finally, she sweeps the bench of sawdust and exhales loudly. "There."

I jump from my stool, desperate to see my hickory heart. The beginning of my new life. She holds it out and I frown.

It's ugly. And as big as the heart of a whale. It's not going to fit in my chest.

The Carvress cackles. "You look disappointed, Char Luna. But we're not done yet. No, not done at all."

She hands me the rough and heavy heart. My hands sink with its weight as it sings distantly. Cautiously. A breath outside actual music.

"Come, child." The Carvress beckons, eyes bright and ringed with amber. Grayish light spooked of morning beckons us from the workshop, the sea so close I taste salt.

"They're always disappointed," she mutters as she pulls me to the light. "They don't understand it's a process." She holds up her fingers, counting. "First there's music, then there's the bond."

I nod along, watching this woman, whose beauty is so defined it's as if an artist sculpted her, thread through passageways with bone deep knowledge of their twists and turns. Until finally she shoves me into the open air. I cover a scream, toes gripping a cliff ledge, the sea chanting below. The wind whips her strange wooden hair that moves as if it's real. My plait slaps my face. The sun peeks over the horizon like a hidden treasure yolk, ready to burst across the water.

The Carvress taps the ground with her foot. "Put your heart here."

I stare down at the crude lump. My *heart*. *My* heart.

It wobbles on the uneven stone floor when I set it down, rocked by the strong sea wind. Placing one hand on my chest and one hand on the hickory heart, the Carvress breathes in deeply. Suddenly scared, I put my hand on hers. "Wait! What's going to happen?" My eyes brim with expectant tears. Doubt clutches my shivering shoulders.

Her eyes land on mine, kindness pouring from their centers. Wrapping around my body, calm washes over me. "If you knew the answer to that question, Char daughter, I'd probably be out of a job. Now close your eyes and let the sun's rays bathe you. This is your new beginning. Today you take your place in the Char." Watching her anxiously for signs of uncertainty, I clench my teeth. The Carvress's chin tips toward the sea, the sun. "It always starts with dawn."

I close my eyes. The heat of her hand on my chest spreads like she holds the sun in her palm. Her voice is warm as fire as it builds from a heated coal to a flame. She sings in an old language of ancient magic and dark places. Of tradition and a history so deep, it can't be written. The music pierces me like a spear. My body stiffens. Her fingers feel caught in my ribs, creating spaces where there shouldn't be spaces. A small gasp of pain comes from my tight, tight throat. My heart beats wildly. As if it's fighting a battle and losing.

I'm losing.

I want to open my eyes, but I don't. I'm worried my chest is cracked open to the salt spray. My heart bloody and stammering, pressing against my back with no escape. Pain cuts at me. Tears my skin. I'm being turned inside out. Maybe my heart is fleeing. Working its way up my throat to get away from the Carvress's sandpaper fingers. The air I breathe feels like cement. I scratch at the ground, too terrified to touch my chest. Too scared to stop her in the middle.

I remember Joka's words. *It hurts and it doesn't. But the pain is worth it because you're taking your place in the Char. You feel like it's... It's meant to be.*

I'm taking my place. Soon I will stand with my brothers.

My heart slows, beating every other second as I drum my fingers listlessly on the floor. I await that feeling of peace. That feeling of *meant to be.* The bashing of waves against rocks becomes distant and echoing like I'm being swallowed by a big nothing.

Warm light kisses my face. My heart slows further. Inside, I am hardening. My flesh twisting and changing to fibers. To splinters.

My heart reduces to a single drum beat. One last thrum.

I force my eyes open and gasp for breath. What was once smooth, pale flesh over bone is now hickory with small brass rings attaching my sternum to my ribs.

I try to draw air but I'm choking.

My heart won't beat. I touch the timber and shiver, try again.

My heart won't beat.

The Carvress smiles, perfect face orange-tinted by the sunrise.

Her smile never falters as the cave walls close in and my head hits the ground.

22

CHAR LUNA

Thump.
Like a prisoner banging on the underside of a trapdoor.
Thump. Thump.

"Luna." Mama's voice is mountain peak high. *She shouldn't worry. There is nothing to worry about.* "What has she done? Setsu, what have you let our daughter do?"

Thump... Thump-thump. Slow then quick. Drum beats out of time.

I touch my chest. Hands lay over mine, long, thin, hard as crab claws. "You have to teach it how to beat, Char Luna. You have to remind it of its old life. Its first life."

Blinking, blurry images of my parents come into focus as my head sinks into plush feather pillows. They're concerned. I should feel regret, guilt, but I can't find them. Feelings locked behind a hunk of wood.

My heart beats naively. It knows what it should be doing. It's just not sure. *Sure.* I await that sense of peace. That feeling Joka described. *Meant to be.* I reach for it but it's like smoke blown over the water. Traveling too fast for me to catch. I shrug, ambivalent. Maybe that is learned also.

Papa strokes my cheek and I sit up on the Carvress's bed. There's pride in the way his square cheeks lift and the puff of his chest. *Do I see love?* Perhaps. It's inaccessible, stretched below glass. Buried beneath hickory sawdust.

"That was very brave, Luna. Foolish, but brave."

My brows pull together. "Was it?" I don't feel brave. *I feel... I'm not sure how I feel.*

Mama takes my shoulders and shakes. I slide over purple silk covers. "Why would you do this, Luna? You had a good future ahead of you. A *safe* future."

My brain reminds me of the why. What I wanted to achieve.

Elbows fold and prop. I educate my limbs, my body, to move how I want. I'm a newborn goat. Shaky but ready to run. "Yes Mama, but it wasn't *my* future. That was a future you set out for me. One you've traipsed along, clicking your wooden hips. It was never for me. You know that. Now..." I tap my chest. "I choose my own path."

The Carvress nods knowingly. Papa's chest expands with honored breath. "And what path do you choose, Char Luna?" she asks, voice like a melody, a song as old as our people.

I swing my legs to the edge of the bed. My heart strengthens. It pumps better. It's a machine. A machine at my will. "To fight alongside my brothers."

"YOU WILL feel an ache. Part missing, part physical adjustment, as your body accepts your heart. You will need to..."

The instructions are difficult to register above the loud, impatient beat of a learning heart.

Thump! Thu—ump!

The Carvress leans her head out the hole I jumped down not a few hours ago. A few hours ago, I was all flesh. Blood and warmth. Fear and vulnerability. Now something foreign beats in my chest. I trace the brass connectors attached to my ribs. The polished smooth

sternum bearing the Carvress's mark. I frown. I should feel more…
More something.

Sheltered by shadows, the Carvress repeats her words. "Char
Luna. You've made a significant change. One that could aid or destroy you. Remember to learn around your heart. Feelings will not
be easy to recognize. To feel." She presses a small lump of hickory
into my palm. "To remind you of your place."

I shove it in my pocket. *Feelings.* They're the reason I made
this decision in the first place. They're what stood between me and
joining my brothers. *Thump. Thump. Thump.* I talk to my heart.
"Steady. Slowly." Feelings need to be shelved *behind* my heart, not
encouraged around it.

Mama and Papa stand beside me on the tip of Coalstone Island, wind surging up from the sea and slapping our faces. Sun
spreads warmth over the black stones. Mama pinches my arm.

"Ouch!" Pain is still felt, that's for sure.

"Are you listening to the Carvress?" she hisses through
clenched, unhappy teeth.

I roll my eyes. "Yes, Mama. Learn around my heart," I repeat.

Like the sun is chasing her, the Carvress bids farewell. Sap-
colored eyes narrow in the light and she disappears. I jump from
the rock, a splintering twinge shooting up my throat. I grasp at it.
Breath vanishes like clouds in the wind.

Papa grips my arm, large body wedged between twisted tree
trunks. "Luna. What is it?"

I tap my heart, fingers light. Remind it to beat. The hickory is
hard and pushes against the softness inside me. This will take time.
Time I don't have.

I pat Papa's arm. He seems like he needs reassurance. *I think.*
Things I would have been sure of are not as clear. "It's nothing,
Papa. Just as the Carvress said—an ache."

He grunts, stroking his moustache. Mama huffs behind us,
hips creaking as we descend toward the village. Right now, I'm
grateful for my heart's lack of sensitivity. Because I know she's
upset with my choice. I *know* her heart must be blistering with disappointment. But knowing and caring are two different things and
I'm glad the pumping machine in my chest can't discern. It doesn't
care.

I SHOVE my belongings into Mama's maroon velvet sewing bag. I was never given a traveling pack of my own. I was never meant to go very far. Just from one home to the next, hopefully doors down.

"But why must she leave so soon? The boys had two weeks of adjustment before they even started doing chores."

I remember! Sun was the most intolerable. Lying in bed, foot elevated, ordering the rest of us around like servants.

I wait for that twist. The pang of missing them. My heart thumps come closer together, but it's confused. My brain plays the memory. Logic reminds me of why I must go. Why I must help.

I plunk my bag on a chair. My parents regard me suspiciously like they're waiting for my eyes to burn red, my voice to come out in a growl, but I merely sigh and listen.

Papa coughs rough and bark like, leaning back in a chair that barely holds him. It whines under the pressure, toothpicks trying to support a barrel. "Ah Ki Anah, she's made her decision and we must support it. If she is to train, she must hurry. You heard Fah, they intend to strike hard and fast. Besides, no man will want her for a wife now. Who would want a heartless mother for their children?"

Mama gasps and turns to me. There's an imprint behind my heart, a small glow whispering I should be offended or hurt by these comments, but my brain sees his point. Whether it makes sense or not, no man would want me now. I have forever marked myself unmarriageable. I shrug. *So be it.*

"Papa's right. But it's fine. I never wanted that life." I flick my hand like I'm shooing a bug. Or if I did want that life, it was so far in the future it might as well have been a dot on the horizon. "And I need to leave now so I can catch up on training. If they intend to move soon, I want to be ready to fight." I nod mechanically, mindlessly pulling my plait through my fingers.

Mama's tears are a dam broken. Her unpinned hair hangs wild and sorry about her shoulders. "You were supposed to stay here with me. Your brothers were always going to leave me, but you were meant to live down the boardwalk. Fat grandchildren were to run to my house when you scolded them. I was to teach you the ways of the home. The preparation of food, the way to…"

She crumples. Her dream scrunched like rice paper peeled from a pork bun. Her expression is tiered: exasperation, fear, and sadness. I tap my side. I should reach for her. Comfort her. Steady and slowly my heart beats *no*. My hand rests on my pants, a pair of Ben Ni's that drowns my ankles. I say what I need to.

"I'm sorry, Mama. I'm sorry you are so upset."

Papa rubs her shoulders. She tips to one side under the weight of his oak hand. "Wife. You will recover from this. You are shocked. Many will be. But this is a great honor for our family. Luna follows the fate of the legendary Anh Roka."

Mama grimaces. She doesn't care for honor in this way, and I know I cannot please her. Even if I'd taken teak legs and married a withered old man from the village, I would have been a disappointment. She places her hand over Papa's and lets him sooth her. There's so much love between them. I can't feel it, but I recognize it plain as whitecaps on waves.

Papa gestures to me. "Say goodbye to your mother, Luna."

I raise an eyebrow. "Just Mama?"

He tips his chin, sliding his military vest over his broad shoulders. "Just Mama. I shall accompany you to the monastery. I don't want Fah turning you away again."

Mama's hands grip me like hunterberry thorns. Fingers pressing between my ribs. Tears staining my shoulder. "Goodbye, Mama. I will miss you," I whisper, pushing feeling into my voice. There's a tapping inside my chest. A ghost of doubt. "Slowly. Steady."

She breathes hot air in my ear, whispering, "Learn around it. Don't forget what makes you Luna. Not Char Luna. Just Luna. My little Luna. My daughter who has the biggest heart in the village." *Had*. I *had* the biggest heart in the village.

I swallow. I can't promise. But I whisper a lie into her hair.

"Yes Mama. I promise." Lies are easier.

Papa ushers me out. "Give my love to the boys. And make sure you do what you have set out to do, Luna," she shouts, hiccupping on emotion. "Bring them home safe."

The weatherboard door shuts on her voice. The rush of the sea envelops us. Birds screech and fish nets drag.

Bring them home safe.

23
SHEN LYE LI

My tongue scrapes the roof of my mouth rough as sandstone. *I need water.* Grasping my bleeding side, I slip gently down the side of the mountain, listening for trickles, sniffing the air for damp. The pain from my wounds roars like a lava lion protecting his volcano. Lifting my shirt carefully, I drag in breaths made of slate. The gray cloth clings to the blood as I ease it up. The sight is devastating. It's far worse than I'd imagined. And I can imagine all manner of dark and horrible things. I'm the creator of many.

Masking the pain with my powers may have been a mistake. The wound is infected. It needs cleaning and it needs marrow root.

"It's porple," Ash shouts as we wade through the marshlands, watching out for the slit eyes of giant ghost geckos floating in the water. Translucent bodies able to fade into the muddiness. Toothless and tasteless, they grab your feet and pull you under, waiting for the water to rot your flesh so they can tear it easily with their gums.

Ash splashes loudly, lifting his legs high with every step. His long, golden-brown hair runs in streams behind him.

"Purple, Ash, they're purple, not porple," I correct him. He grins, teeth white save a black gap at the front.

He waves dismissively. "Purple, porple. Doesn't matter. I know what it looks like." He huffs.

I sweep my hands over the water's surface, unnerving electricity sparking at my fingertips. My feet press into the mud and I sense the way the earth will fall. I can avoid the dips and traps. A disturbance several feet away makes me pause. But I sense it's just a large coughing trout. Its wide mouth takes in water and bacteria, coughing out the un-nourishing parts. I feel its heart beating as it expels the bad water back into the river.

All of this is felt in a second. A moment that's over before it began. But it stays with me because I'm only supposed to feel an affinity for one element, not all five. And I know with sadness what this means.

Ash watches me, eyes narrowed, body turned. "What's wrong, sister? You look as if we've failed already. We've only been searching a few minutes."

I reach through the water. Sensing the way it curls around the plant I need to find. The current changes in these places and I feel it like my own heartbeat. "There." I point to the purple tips of marrow root, barely visible among the scratchy marsh grass.

Ash rushes in that direction, scaring fish, and hopefully geckos, as he goes. He cuts the plant with a knife, holding it up. "How did you spot it from all the way over there?" he asks. I know he suspects. He's seen the way I twist away from the world. Sense movement or change before it begins. He sees me shrink from my power.

I pull through the water, clothes swirling around me. "Just lucky, I guess."

He frowns, doesn't believe me, but lets it be. The longer we pretend I'm not showing signs of being the Keeper, the longer I can stay with my family. Or what's left of it. We pocket the marrow root and trudge out of the marshland. Mother sent for it as a distraction. Her infection is too deep and lasting to be cured. She's not long for this world. Soon her spirit will lift and join her element, Air.

Then it will just be Ash and me. The other one doesn't deserve to be counted. And I've ensured Ash doesn't remember him.

Yes. Soon, it will be just Ash and me. At least for a time.

Marrow root couldn't save my mother, but it should be enough to heal this surface infection. I pray.

I strap the memory of a time before the emperor found me to my back. Before I was called on to do unspeakable things and believed it was honor. "No more," I whisper.

Straightening, although it's painful to do so, I walk across the ridge of the mountain, reaching for cracks in the earth. For water to make itself known. I'm rewarded and almost plunge into the small rocky pool in relief. But I stop, cupping hands into the cool liquid and sipping it carefully. It tastes of dead leaves and rust, but is clean enough. Large creatures drag their bellies over loose pebbles on the pond floor.

Little toads with stars for eyes swim up to the surface to observe me curiously. Blinking strangely, their yellow and black hides shine bright in the sunlight. I pet one and recoil at the flash of pain it causes. Poison. My fingers turn white and numb. I wash them quickly and scare the frogs away with a stick. Being the Keeper may mean I have access to every element, but it also means every power is diluted. Stretched in five directions instead of one, I miss things.

The wound is a large, oozing red graze stretching from armpit to hip. I bite my lip and try to ignore the sting. It's as if a giant bear has torn my skin with its dirty paw. I dab my balled-up shirt over the skin gingerly.

I wring the rinsed shirt and pull my robe over my bare skin. I need to find marrow root. I climb around the edge of the pool, plunging my hands into the water to sense for rooted plants. I find nothing. Just poisonous toads, sediment, and an evasive lurker I can't quite wrap around.

I teeter on the edge, when I hear a rustle and a cough. A puff of smoke. "You need to breathe it deep into your lungs, brother." A Char man with a dark, serious voice allows himself to laugh and slaps the back of another.

"I'm not sure smoking is for me, Sun," the smaller one says, pushing the bigger one lightly.

"A soldier who doesn't know how to smoke! You best stay here and practice, little brother." The bigger one, Sun, knocks his brother's shoulder and marches away, wooden foot tapping over the brush, head swinging, hand at his hilt, alert for danger.

Holding a painful bubble of air in my chest, I hover over the boy from the high side of the rock pool. At his feet is a pack. I bet it has soldier's supplies, bandages, antiseptic, a blanket... He's close enough that all I would have to do is reach out and shock him. He wouldn't feel much pain. At least, not for very long.

Gripping a branch, I lean closer, aching to harm. Power clouding my senses. The boy sucks in a puff of smoke and coughs again. The branch snaps. I lose balance, sliding down the rocky incline to fall at his feet with a thud, robe open, broken body on display.

Shocked by my nakedness, the boy's cheeks flush red and he quickly turns away.

I was about to kill this boy and he's concerned for my modesty.

I try to speak but my mouth crackles with dryness. My heart hammers furiously. I close the robe and scramble to my feet, shoving a hand in my pocket. The thimble works its way into my palm; I push the point into my skin.

Slowly, the boy turns with hands up. "You're injured," he states, eyes landing briefly on where he saw my bare skin raging and red. They coast over the thimble marks and the scabby cuts on my wrists. His eyes are showered gold. Hopeful and heart full. "I promise I won't hurt you." His mouth sets in a thin smile, naively kind. It's obvious he's yet to experience the corruption of battle. He stands taller than me, but he's young. Too young to recognize who he's facing.

I step back as he reaches down to fetch his weapon. My feet spread, ready for a fight. But when he comes back up, it's with bandages and a pot of healing balm in his hand. Pushing it toward me, he whispers, "Here, take it." His eyes dart sideways anxiously. He may not recognize me as the Keeper, but he seems to know I'm Shen. "Quickly, before my brothers return."

Like a feral animal scared to eat from a generous palm, I snatch the supplies. "Thank you," I manage, meeting his gaze. His chest rises and falls quickly as he stares into my eyes. His are honey and hazelnut. Mine are calm seas.

Sticks break underfoot and his expression turns from wonder to alarm. "You shouldn't be here. Go!" He flaps his palms. "Go now!"

I scramble up to the rock pool, pulling behind some bushes just as more men arrive. They all slap the young boy affectionately.

"Ah Ben Ni, we're only joking." The man's laugh is scraped deep with love. "Come back to the monastery. It's unmanly, yes, but we don't care if you can't smoke," he teases.

The boy's eyes pierce the leaves in front of me. Searching.

Ben Ni. My fingers tap the name over my heart. *Your brothers don't realize you have proved yourself a man ten times over with your actions.*

24

CHAR LUNA

The carved Yan dragonhead of our family boat nods in agreement at my plan. Oars dip into calm water in a simple and easy rhythm, one my heart seems content to match. Papa watches me, eyebrow rising like the tiniest shrug, as I display the improved strength my mechanical heart has given me. He's still far stronger and tempers his strokes to mine.

Halfway across the channel, he lifts his oar and the boat spins in a wide, lazy circle. Crimson-chested heart birds pierce the clouds with their darting play. Always in pairs, always frolicking. Light as air.

My breath grows thin and I remind my heart to beat. Slow, steady. It's getting easier.

"Why did you stop?" I ask, though from his creased brow and pulled in shoulders, I know I'm about to get a talking to.

I run my hand over the carved curls of smoke flowing from the dragon's snout and all the way around the rim of the boat. The heart birds weave through the wind, delighting in their play and in each other. Against the clouds they look like shifting dots of blood. They come together and fall apart but never for long.

Papa squeezes my hand. If it's love, it's beneath the surface of the water. If it's concern, it's on the sky side of the clouds. I stop. Breathe. Think. I *know* he loves me. That knowledge doesn't just go away. I can't feel it but it's there.

"Are you sure you're prepared for what comes next, little Luna?" he asks. The boat bobs on the light swell. He rakes a hand through his thick black hair. His military vest is tighter than it used to be. His middle has turned comfortingly soft in these last few months home with us. *Us.* The us before we split down the middle.

"Papa, I know the dangers of war. I understand what it takes from a person." I'm unable to meet the eyes of the man who sacrificed so much to keep our family intact. Kept it laughing. Loving. I'm the last eyelet to be unhooked and now the sail flaps frighteningly untethered. I don't want him to think he failed us. "I've seen the way it's carved years from you. I see it in the charred remains of our village and the black spots in our people's eyes. You've prepared us well. This has always been our life. The Char life." It's sad but true. "I've never known any different." I sigh. "But really, can anyone truly be prepared for war?"

At this he grunts and shakes his head. "No, I suppose not. You can only train as hard as you can. Be smart. Be fast. Be strong. Live, daughter."

I smile. A shape I make fit. "That I can do."

He places an oar in my hand and takes up the other. "You'll have much to prove."

"I know." I dig the oar in, ready to pull the water and he grabs my hand, staring at the sky. Strands of clouds stream across the sea in search of a mountain to sit on. "What is it, Papa?"

His dark eyes coast the difference between us, finding the bridge made of blood and bone. "Little Luna." He sighs, constrained by his vest of leather and brass. "You've made a change. A *big* change. My advice, dear daughter, is this…" Our boat sweeps over a swell, the world tilting for a moment. "Make sure it was a change for the better."

I bow low and respectful. "I will, Papa."

25
CHAR LUNA

Papa doesn't wait for permission, banging loudly on General Fah's door. When there's no answer, I reach out to stop him, but he shrugs me off.

"We have come here for a purpose, daughter. No use being timid now."

I dip my chin. *He's right.* He continues thumping, and I pray his rank and relationship with Fah grants him that permission.

The pounding echoes down the long, open-air hallway. Stone arches catch Papa's impatience and throw it back. I am glad for my lack of feeling, as my brain tells me I should be very nervous right now. I stand on my tiptoes, wondering how I could disarm my father if he doesn't stop.

Fah's irritated voice finally answers. "I'm very busy. What do you need?" he asks as he opens the door. Eyes widening at the sight of Setsu Yan, in all his imposing broadness, filling his entryway. "Setsu!" he exclaims. His voice drops lower than a deep-sea anchor when he notices me. "And his daughter…"

Papa waltzes into the chamber. "May we come in?" He's not really asking. Fah steps back, clearly ruffled. I shuffle beside my father. Wishing to stand separate to his shadow but knowing it is necessary to show humbleness.

"Of course, of course. Though I don't know why you've come all this way, comrade. It won't change anything. Your daughter, lovely as she is…" This is said begrudgingly and only because my father could snap Fah over his knee. "Your daughter is not suitable for service. We need strong, focused young *men* willing to do what's necessary. Not girls who are weak with emotion and longing."

Papa makes himself comfortable by sitting on the edge of Fah's bed. The simple monk bedding is out of place with the drips and drops of gold and silk Fah must have brought with him. "Sounds to me like your mind is too closed. I'll admit it is unusual, but it has been done before. Rare, special women can make good soldiers. And you dismissed Luna without giving her a chance to prove herself. Do you fear she will show you up?"

Fah scoffs, walnut jaw jutting out in an almost pout. He feigns surprise, but in the face of Papa's unwavering stare, he falters. "Old friend, I am a traditional Char man. And as such, my duty is to protect the weaker sex, not send them into battle." I should cringe at his words. They are intended to make me feel small. But he cannot reach me.

He points a hard finger at us. "Besides, women show too much sympathy. They let it rule their actions. It is an amiable quality in many other vocations, but not in a soldier. Not the kind of soldier we need. And fear that she would show me up is, well…" His eyes run up and down my petite form. "Unlikely."

Papa strokes his chin with his wood-grained hand. "Hmm. Maybe so. Maybe so. But what if she could prove her emotional composure? Show you she has changed and is entirely committed."

It's like I'm not here. I press against the wall, bumping the end of a prayer scroll. It makes a hollow sound as the men argue over my future. Fah stalks to his dresser and pours a small glass of rice wine. "Impossible! She couldn't have changed from that weeping, red cheeked girl on the docks in such a short time." I bite my lip.

My father gives a sly smile. "She has certainly proved her bravery and commitment in *my* eyes."

Fah places the etched cup down precisely, squaring it off next to the others in the set. "She's your daughter, Setsu. Can she really do wrong in your eyes?"

Papa huffs and tries a different tact. "What are our numbers, Juni? We lost so many in the attack."

The general strokes his jaw, tapping a count over the walnut. "We lost half. But add the new recruits to the survivors and we can still mount a good offense."

"Seems to me you need every volunteer you can find."

Fah frowns. "One thousand is a good number, a workable number. One thousand and one makes little to no difference."

Papa rises, leaving a large dent in the straw bed, and beckons me. I approach and he moves behind me, placing heavy hands on my shoulders. I try to bear the weight evenly. Fah stares, not cruelly, but like I don't belong. An eel in a koi pond.

"Have you heard of Anh Roka?" Papa asks, voice muted and coercive.

"Yes, of course. It's a myth." Fah waves his hand dismissively. "A story meant to lift men's spirits."

My heart beats unfaltering and strong. Wooden doors open and close in the hard lump in my chest. *My only chance.* Papa pushes me forward a little. My heels dig in. If it could, my heart would beat fast from being this close to Fah's clenched jaw.

"It is no myth, my friend. Show him, Luna." Whispers of pride and pain. Though I have done nothing yet to deserve it.

Fah's eyes move to my chest. "Im... impossible," he utters with little conviction and an air of wonder. "A woman would not survive such a change."

My hand dances over my top button, the silk knot hard between my finger and thumb. My high collar is protection. A wall I must pull down. Brick by brick it reveals my strength and my vulnerability.

Papa nods. "Well, my daughter did."

I unbutton just low enough to reveal the Carvress's mark. The brass ray spokes in the wood. Fah gasps in shock and awe, as brief as a whale coming up for air. He narrows his eyes, doubtful. "How do I know the change was effective?" He scrutinizes my small frame. "She is very... female, in shape and manner. Most of all, her emotional behavior concerns me."

Fastening my collar, I stare straight up at the general, mouth set, hands relaxed at my sides. Papa prepares to answer, and I put up my hand. Now it is my turn to speak. "I can prove the change in me is real." General Fah crosses his arms over his chest, walnut jaw working, brows raised and framing bemused eyes as he entertains me. Leaning back against a rough desk spotted with ink stains, he opens his palm, releasing the metaphorical gag and allowing me to speak.

"Before my hickory heart, listening to two men discussing my future like I'm mute and incapable of rational thought would have made me furious. My mouth would be aching to snap at both of you for your rudeness and ridiculous assumptions." I cast even eyes over the men. Papa steps back, slightly embarrassed. I have Fah's attention. "But now, while I recognize your behavior is insulting and demeaning, I am able to hold my tongue. Your arrogance feels more like an irritating insect bite on the back of my neck rather than a raging fire in my chest." My voice is as level as bay water.

Papa chuckles and Fah blinks at my bluntness. Yet he's a little impressed.

Rather than acknowledge acceptance, Fah waves his hand. "You will need to work on your strength. I will not go easy on you because of your, er, disadvantage in size." He looks me up and down again. It takes a half second.

My toes press into the floor and push up. It's the closest I can get to elation. I smile, teeth actually showing. "Thank you, General." I bow, ready to skate out the door.

"Wait!" Fah's voice is the boom of a drum. "Despite this new heart, you're still a girl." He says the word distastefully. "Hun Nah!" he shouts to a guard passing by. "Show Luna Yan to the Silent Vow room."

Hun Nah, a shrinking man, thin and knobby as a diseased tree branch, salutes and questions, "With the...?"

Fah clears his throat. "Do you have a better idea? She can't bunk with the others. Or are you suggesting we tie them *all* up?"

Fah takes my arm and pulls me closer, gently but firmly. "And I think it's best you keep your heart a secret for now. I don't need the men getting unnecessarily riled up. You may not be here long enough to warrant it."

Papa shoves me out the door, worried Fah will change his mind. "Go litt... go Luna." Already things have changed between us, my old nickname no longer appropriate. "I have some catching up to do with my old friend. I'll see you in the morning."

And with that, I'm accepted into the Char army.

26
CHAR LUNA

The door whines on old iron hinges. Hun Nah exhales like he's expelling a crescent moon from his throat and mutters, "Breakfast is half after sunrise. If you're late, you don't eat."

I clutch my small bag to my chest and give him a disapproving stare. If this is the type of physical specimen I must compete with, I'm sure I'll be able to make my mark. "Can I see my brothers?" I ask. "Sun, Joka, and Ben Ni Yan."

Hun Nah snorts and taps his stomach, making a wooden noise. "Tomorrow."

Tomorrow.

He leaves with a knowing look and a laugh like bay leaves tossed in hot oil. My eyes follow his candlelight until I'm left in darkness.

Moonlight fills one small, high window. A tiny arch with close bars to keep the birds out. Constructed for deep contemplation, the Silent Vow room is plain and empty and dark. I search my bag for matches, coming across an unexpected texture, then pulling out my best silk dress. Mama must have stuffed it in the bottom while my back was turned. I huff and then freeze at the sound of metal dragging on stone.

"Who's there?" I whisper, fists tightening, heart doing nothing but beating steadily. Giving me no clue to fear.

A sigh, human and desolate, like parched village roofs waiting for the first rain of the season.

I strike a match, the room filling with dull yellow light. A woven grass mattress with a thin blanket sits in one corner near a narrow table. My eyes sweep to the other corner, to a young man ten feet away, leaning against the wall. Arms resting on his knees. Chains clapped around his grimy ankles.

Tilting my head gently, I feel new. My reactions different to what they would have once been. Where my heart would previously have beat faster with apprehension, it reacts as if this is perfectly normal. It allows my mind time to observe and deduce.

His golden-brown hair reaches his shoulders. It has come loose of its binding and is clean save a bald patch dirtied with dried blood. I scan his limbs, which are covered in scratches and what appear to be bite marks.

I arch an eyebrow. He bears no Carvress mark and when his eyes meet mine, I am sure. A small tattoo of a water droplet curls around his left eye. "You're a Shen," I announce, leaning in but making sure I'm still out of reach.

His blank expression rearranges to a frown and he jiggles his leg to make the chains rattle. "Your deductive powers are astonishing."

A Shen *in my room*. My mind clatters over the possibilities, over the ways in which this is a terrible situation. Patting my heart, I thank it. Panic is subdued. But I'm still uncomfortable, and I shift nervously about the small room while the Shen watches.

It's late. I must sleep well to be ready for tomorrow. I glance at the Shen's boyish cheeks but broad and defined body. A young soldier. His eyes are unblinking. "This must be some test of my strength, my, er, fortitude," I mutter, thumping my chest and trying to emulate Papa. His gaze drifts over every inch of my body, maybe sizing me up, wondering if he can take me. He can't. He *won't*. "You *must* turn around while I undress," I order, spinning my finger in a circle.

His smile is unnerving. Curved dark lips. Far too genuine for a Shen. "Where is it?" he asks.

My chin tips, my mouth feels dry as dust. "Where's what?" I step toward him.

He points up and down. "Your, you know, your limb? Where's the wooden part?" He leans his head in his hand, slightly mocking.

Remembering Fah's orders, I lie. "I don't have one yet."

Chains shift. His accent is strange. He speaks our shared language like the soft end of a struck gong. "So, you and I are more alike than I would have guessed," he muses, a quirk to his lip that pushes his cheek up.

"You and I, alike?" My hands knot and my legs lock.

He shuffles forward, half eager. "Yes. You're not a full Char yet and I'm, well, I'm…" His eyes crinkle closed in secret pain. His shoulders tighten. His mouth twists.

My mind drifts to the fire at Black Sail City. Men jumping into the sea. Orphans and widows made by a broken treaty. A broken promise. With as much anger as I can muster, which is sadly less than I'd like, I snap, "You and I are not alike. I have honor. I know what you are. Shen are parasites. Never satisfied. Always consuming."

He turns to face the wall. "You know nothing," he murmurs to the black stones.

If I could, I would hate him.

I will certainly try.

27
SHEN LYE LI

The healing cream has worked beautifully. I lie in the bough of the great fig tree and stare up at the stars. Kindness from a Char. It seems so unlikely. We have relentlessly pursued them for hundreds of years. Each emperor passing the mantel to the next. The obsession growing stronger with every cycle. In schools, they teach Shen to regard Char as rough, barely human creatures that hoard their magic so they can one day destroy us. It's a bitter meal fed to children with their rice porridge. We grow up believing Char are monsters. A scourge.

It was all I knew until the greedy truth tried to consume me. Until I almost let it.

They are not monsters. *We* are.

Our stories, our traditions, are like a hammer to every Shen child's head. I don't blame them. They are innocence twisted. The blame lies with the emperor, the chancellor.

And me.

I squeeze my middle, pushing on the wound just to feel the pain. Pain keeps me alert, alive. Pain reminds me of my sins, creeping up from dark places in my mind and blanketing all good thoughts. The world would be better off if I dropped from this tree and let the roaming hoarder bear drag me to his cave. Pick my bones and feather his nest. My eyes drop to the level of the monastery. They took him inside an hour ago. *Are they torturing you, Ash? Do you sleep? Can you sleep?*

Ash is special. He is not beyond untangling. I imagine he absorbs the Char's humanity. But it's doubtful they will do the same for him. He is Shen. And after everything we have done, it's only a matter of time before they kill him.

28
CHAR LUNA

Shackles snap open. The Shen winces in pain at the release, ankles raw and bleeding. I'm impressed with his stoicism. When the men taunt, kick, and shove him from my room, he merely blanks his expression and walks.

It's only when he pauses at the door and remarks, "See you tonight, Char girl," with a wink that he shows personality. Personality that's rewarded with a swift blow to the shoulder by a soldier with a chipped and dirty ironwood hand. All Char know it's the heaviest timber you can choose. I cringe at the sound of it crunching into the Shen's bones. Now the Shen boy knows its weight it too. I jut out my chin proudly as the boy passes. Letting him know he deserved the blow. Secretly wondering why he would be so foolish.

As soon as the door closes, I yawn wide as a possum trap. It wasn't easy to sleep with a Shen ten feet from my bed. I feel as if I've been held to the sun all night. Crackled and devoid of rest. I wonder how long this chamber sharing situation will last.

I button my shirt high, and sprint to the hall for breakfast with the heartbeat of someone walking heel to toe.

I'm nearly there when a hand grabs my shoulder and yanks me backward.

"Ai! Luna! When did you get here?" Ben Ni swings me around to face him. The immense relief I should feel is lukewarm. I throw my arms around his neck and embrace him. A small feeling swells in my chest as we connect. It moves around my heart. Clouds it for a moment. I step away. Push the feeling aside.

"Last night," I answer looking my brother up and down. He grins. "Papa helped me talk Fah into letting me train." It's part truth.

Ben Ni accepts this and looks around excitedly, golden eyes dancing. "Papa's here?"

He directs me to the dining hall. Sun and Joka join us at the door, and Papa's long arms wrap around everyone. It's the reunion I'd wanted. To take my place with my brothers. But somehow, knocking heads and caught in a typical Yan embrace, I feel like I'm on the outside. The lock on the box where my family are the treasures within.

I curl away, touching my heart and trying to mirror their joyful expressions. Joka catches my eyes, suspicion crossing his high-boned features. Sun lifts sparring fists to his chest and tries to land a punch on Papa.

Papa blocks and slaps the top of Sun's head. "Act like a soldier, son." Sun swallows and straightens, cool exterior returning. But Papa hardly means it. He's so full of pride it's dripping from his fingers.

Through large precisely balanced stone arches, I see the slumped Shen being tied to a post in the center square. Ben Ni seems interested in this also, and he waits with me as the others bustle into breakfast, nattering like morning birds waiting to peck the leftover seed from our stables.

When the dining hall door closes, Ben Ni climbs through the glassless walkway and approaches the prisoner.

Ben Ni pauses as the guards place a tray of food and water just out of reach. Once they leave, he quickly runs to the Shen boy and taps the plate with his foot. I think he's going to kick it over. It's what any self-respecting Char would do. Instead, he nudges it closer. The Shen grasps it desperately, gulping the water down fast.

My mouth hangs open as Ben Ni returns, eyes serious. There are secrets swirling in those irises. I slap his arm. "You're going to get yourself in trouble, little brother."

He shrugs, staring out at the jungle that cradles this place with mossy hands.

"A fight should be fair, at the very least. Don't you think?"

I nod in concession. *If only such idealistic notions were branded onto the heart of every soldier.*

I drag Ben Ni inside before someone notices what he did. "Come on. I'll need a good meal to prepare for what comes next."

He knocks my shoulder and I try not to stumble. "You'll need a great deal more than that, little Luna."

THE IMMENSE dining hall shows the results of the recruitment. Nearly five hundred young Char crammed shoulder to shoulder down long wooden benches. Monks shuffle between the rows, placing bowls of food on tables.

Surrounded by the scent of garlic oil omelets and sweet sticky rice, my brothers bombard me with advice.

Be strong. Be smart.

Be strong and *smart.*

Don't let them see you hurting.

Don't let them see you out of breath.

You will be better in hand to hand, you're swift.

You will be better in archery, it doesn't require brute strength.

I catch the words, and but for the sound of my brother's voices saying them, which I treasure, the advice is useless.

Papa interrupts the noise. "Boys, you need to let Luna find her own way." He looks at me, choosing his words carefully. "She needs to *learn* around the usual way of doing things. She's not as physically strong, so it will be by strategy and control that she'll find her place."

Sun and Ben Ni nod in agreement. Joka nods too but in a sly way, like he's bartering over the price of oranges and finds they're rotten beneath the first layer. He's not buying it. "How are you finding your roommate, Luna?" he asks shrewdly.

Papa's eyebrows rise, concerned.

I shoot the boys a silent warning. "You mean the monastery dog? Oh, just fine. You know me and animals…" His eyebrows fall just as fast and thankfully, Joka gets the hint. Papa would yank me down the mountain, past the grand black rock sails of the city, through the streets of rickety, bamboo pole-constructed buildings, and straight into a wedding dress if he knew I was sharing a room with a male Shen.

Papa taps each of his children on the head and wishes us well. He can't stay. It's not permitted. He fought his last battle. He trained his last soldier. He smiles, but there's somberness to it. We may laugh and joke, but we know a door is opening that will never close again. Taking our place in the Char also means letting in the horrors he tried so hard to protect us from. So, it's with heaviness and a proud heart that he turns and walks away, swinging to the side to fit through the narrow door made for starving monks, not great Char warriors. There's little hope of any of us living up to his legacy.

But it will be all right. At least I'm here now.

My brothers' expressions say it all. They're relieved to have me here. I complete the sliding puzzle. Everything is finally in its rightful place.

29
CHAR LUNA

I'm at the end of a very long line, in plain clothes because no uniform would fit. Just another way I stick out like a rat in a snake's nest. We're arranged in order of height and I'm behind a man who seems almost as wide as he is tall. My first sparring partner.

Sun's impressive physicality propels him to the head. He nods to his Yan siblings and steps in to fight a well-matched partner.

Fah looms on the edge of the circle, barking commands, which Sun follows well. He moves swiftly. A dance of avoidance and utilizing strengths. Fighting a Shen is a harrowing prospect when one touch can fill your lungs with mud or rake fire through your veins. You must strike fast, avoid skin to skin contact. Use your wooden part to your advantage.

When Sun ignores instructions to kick high, instead choosing a sweeping kick to throw his partner off balance, Fah strikes him with a bamboo pole.

I step from the line, a protest on the tip of my tongue. I hold it there. It tastes stodgy, like uncooked pudding.

"We have six weeks at best to prepare, and see what he did?" Fah shouts, making an example. "He opted for the quick disarm, but in doing so brought the Shen within reach of unprotected skin. We cannot make foolish mistakes!" He strikes Sun's flesh ankle hard. "Foolish mistakes will lead to needless pain." My brother clutches his foot, quietly suffering. I move closer and Fah's walnut jaw twists in my direction.

My heart is my friend in this moment because I don't feel the shame of everyone's gaze. I step to the edge of the sparring circle. Sun's eyes are edged with dismay. His partner bows and offers a shoulder. Sun refuses and stands, weight very much on his balsa foot and limps over the line. Keeping his honor.

Licking my lips, I swallow and shout loudly, "A sweeping kick could also work if the Char soldier shifts his weight back, ready to jump out of reach. Then a knife could be thrown into the Shen's..." Words dry and scatter like ash.

Fah's stare burns. "It seems our new recruit couldn't wait *her* turn."

I look back at the short, fat boy I'm to fight. Wooden knees almost buckling beneath his weight like an overburdened cart. I bow, palms flat against each other. "I'm happy to fight now, General Fah. I'm anxious to learn."

From the center square comes the Shen's bitter laugh.

Fah beckons a wooden shouldered, towering man with an expression of disdain to the head of the line.

"Lakh, enter the circle." Fah points sharply.

Sun starts to protest, but he's in enough trouble.

I take a deep breath and step inside the chalk drawn lines.

Lakh is hulking and slow to my small and fast. It's my *only* advantage. I cling to the edge, mirroring his movements as he lashes an arm out to slap me. I duck.

Our slippered feet scratch against the uneven stones.

The word "weeks" seems carved into the floor. Time. I need time.

Sun shouts, "Hands up, little sister."

I don't have time.

Hands up. Heart beats.

I raise my fists to my face, blowing a long strand of hair from my eyes. Soldiers laugh. Lakh lunges, creating too much distance between his back and front foot. I take the opportunity and kick out his front foot. He skids, stretching his groin painfully, but throws a desperate punch. It hits my neck, sending shock waves up to my head and down my shoulder. I make a sound akin to a bag of flour dropped on the floor. The noise seems to please Lakh. He shortens his stance and I draw away.

Minutes drag as I cling to the edge and Lakh pursues me. I duck and weave. Tiring him out.

Fah sighs impatiently and bored soldiers shift in line. My brothers watch anxiously. I shouldn't have turned to them. Lakh slaps my face hard and my jaw feels split in half, teeth out of place. Salty, copper-tasting blood pools in my cheek, and I spit it onto the stones. Dizziness wraps around me like the top of the mountain has detached and spins at a different rate to the rest of the world.

Keep your head. Your place. I will not fall.

Fah's ill-disguised voice hisses, "Grab her hair. Pull her down." Lakh twists to the side, acknowledging his teacher, eyebrows scrunched together. "Now, soldier! Grab her hair."

Lakh swipes at my long plait, hanging like a rope, tightens his paw, and pulls.

I shriek, scalp stinging.

I hit the stones hard and he's on top of me, pressing his forearm to my neck. I could squirm from his grip or kick him in the groin. His red face and deep, drawn breaths are signs he's tiring. There are options.

I'll...

"Stop!" Fah shouts, scaring blue-crested birds from their perch. Lakh's eyes soften in apology for fighting dirty. He relaxes his forearm. "I think *the girl* has had quite enough."

At the end of a spar, opponents get to their feet in their own time and bow to each other. The winner must wait as long as it takes for his foe to stand. I ease myself from the stones, ears ringing, but at least I got a few good shots in. In fact, given a few more minutes I may have beaten him.

Fah steps into the ring, offering his hand. "Here," he says, again as loud as thunder. "Let me *help* you."

This is not the way. But he's my superior. I take his rough, cool hand warily, squinting in confusion. Pulling me up, he makes a point of looking me over and brushing the dirt from my shoulders. I hang limp like a shirt on the line as he gently takes my jaw in his hand and tilts it to check the growing bruises. His touch is very unwelcome.

I sense a seed being planted. But what will grow?

His eyes, dark and malted. "Are you all right, Luna?" His voice is fringed at the edges. It could be simply kindness. My heart thumps steady, unsuspicious.

I bow to Lakh and clap my feet together. "Yes, General. Now please, tell me what I can do better next time so I might learn from this defeat."

There's a press to his lips, so brief it's like the metallic flash of a murder bird's wings. Then he smiles. "Yes, later, later. You look like you need rest."

I'm ordered to sit on the wall and observe. If we have such a short time to train, rest should be the last thing I need. And I begin to wonder, are his actions kindness or condescension?

30

CHAR LUNA

Over bowls of rice and dumplings, which are more cabbage and corn flour than meat, Ben Ni turns to me, head in hand and asks, "Tell me of the Shen in your room. What's he like?"

My brothers lean in, their whispers drowned out by hundreds of men talking. I shrug. "He's Shen. I know nothing about him, and I don't intend to."

Optimistically he says, "The general must trust you well to allow you to bunk with him, though, little sister. Perhaps he expects you to inform on the prisoner."

Ben Ni, always the fantasist, thinks only of grand gestures and dreams of destiny. I wave his words away. It feels less like trust and more like punishment. "He's just a boy really, no older than me and no great spy. Besides, I think the decision was more to do with lack of space rather than entrusting me with an important task."

Disappointed, Ben Ni huffs and returns to drawing lines between the stars.

To my older brothers showering me with protective gazes, I say, "He's chained to the wall. It's uncomfortable for him and me, but not unsafe." I think of last night, a catch buzzing in my throat. Turning my bare back to his unwavering regard, the cloth of my tunic slipping down over my shoulders. I never felt unsafe. But I felt watched.

Sun grunts. "What do we care of a Shen boy's comfort?"

I tip my chin and push my bowl of opened dumplings toward him. He snatches it eagerly, eyes lighting at the precious pork I have left. "We don't care," I state.

Ben Ni's sigh is a meaty thing that seems difficult to push from his lungs.

I'm about to ask what troubles him when Joka, like a bird holding fast to a bucking trout, pushes further. "What will happen with your ceremony? Will you go to the Carvress after training? Will there be time?"

I tap the table. "Postponed. If our little brother can face the Shen without protection, then so can I." It's a warning aimed at Ben Ni but he's not listening.

Joka opens his mouth to press, but I interrupt him with a loud yawn. Extending my arms and clipping the top of Ben Ni's head to disturb the clouds.

"Do you ever think about the Shen living as we do?" he whispers. Eyes earnest, a net open to catch any point of view. "With families. Hopes. Desires?"

These are dangerous words and I cut them to pieces. "No, brother, I only think of Uncle Katsu's insides cemented with cooled lava. His body turned hard as a rock, so that when we committed him to the sea, he sank like an anchor. Or Sun's best friend, Elah On, destined to drag his charcoal leg along the deck until he finally succumbed to rot. The moment they betrayed the treaty, there could be no room to think of them as anything other than *enemy*."

He blinks. Remembers. His expression torn. He places a hand over mine and I withdraw. "You're right, sister. I know you are."

I scruff his hair and try to act normal. "You think too much, little brother." I stretch. "I'm going to bed."

They begin to stand, to accompany me to my room but I give a threatening glare true as an arrow. It won't help to have my brothers crowding around me like bodyguards.

I turn and march to the door, Joka's curious eyes burning my back.

AT THE sulfurous spark of a match, the room fills with dull light. I pour water into a basin and clean my bloody, moss-stained face. As I run the cloth over my jaw, I bite my lip from pain. My shoulders pull in at the thought of the general's hand in mine. The hundreds of eyes watching me take his help.

Chains drag on stones. "You look terrible."

My eyes dart briefly to the Shen, his thin face a worn statue exposed to the elements. Beneath the grime and lack of nutrition he could be handsome. If that's even possible for a Shen. "I look far better than you." I squeeze the cloth into the basin. Rust-colored water swirls against the white.

"Your *general*," he says the word like you could insert the word imposter in its stead, "is some piece of work. Pitting you against a man who looked like he had a field plow for shoulders."

I pull a jacket over my shirt and face him. "Maybe he thought I could handle it."

The Shen laughs sourly. "He did not."

I lean in, knees up, hands tight. "Maybe he wanted me to learn something."

"Wrong again."

Anger curls around my chest like a feather snake. I breathe in, push the feeling aside and it recedes, wedging behind my heart with the others. "It doesn't matter what you think. You're just a dirty Shen," I growl. "I don't know why I'm even talking to you."

He does that thing again. That lopsided smile, cheek pushed up. "Yes, why would you talk to me? Since I'm just a dirty Shen. I'm not worth a second glance, let alone your words." His words edge double meaning.

I fold my arms over my chest. "Exactly."

Shuffling back onto my bed, I blow out the candle, turning away from the Shen boy and forcing my eyes closed.

"This dirty Shen's name is Ash, by the way," he says with quiet pride to my back. "Ash Ki Koh."

I don't respond.

My name must be paid for and he's got nothing I want.

31
SHEN LYE LI

I'm a hungry mouse searching for a small, easily missed way in. I watch my brother, head down, shoulders looking more bone than flesh with every passing day. They're starving him. They'd be beating him for information, but he has none to offer. He knows nothing of Shen strategy. Like the rest of the Shen army, Ash is unaware of the extent of our horrible plan. When we are reunited, I will tell him my deepest shame. Even if it causes him look at me with disgust and distrust.

I press my hand to my heart. I will tell him. I will. I will.

My side is healing, but slowly. I slap it hard. I am deserving of the sharp pain.

I creep through the low ferns, getting as close as is safe, and press my fingers to my lips, waiting. Just as the general shouts, I let out a low whistle. Blue-crested birds flutter from their perches and Ash looks up. He hears me, expression a mix of hope and disappointment. Because I know he half wishes he didn't hear me. That I'd flown far from this place.

But I am here, brother.

Most of me, anyway.

32
CHAR LUNA

I'm the last banana no one wants. Thrown back and forth until it's bruised and brown and fed to the pigs. My back is so damaged I can't lean into my chair. Days of sparring with no conclusion, no victory nor loss. Every time I get close to winning, the fight is abruptly ended.

The general marches to the front of the crowded hall and clears his throat. The room grows quiet.

"These soldiers deserve honorable mention for their extraordinary skills over the last five days. They have proven themselves to be excellent hand-to-hand fighters." Sun is on the list. My heart itches, an uncomfortable feeling—a shadow of dread. Being great at hand to hand means he'll likely be on the frontline.

As Fah strides around the dining hall, his eyes drop to the Yan family. He passes our table only to turn around. "Luna." He says my name like it's a pity. He moves to put his hand over mine and I quickly place it under the table. "How are you coping?"

My brothers collectively sit upright and lean away. If this were home, I would bite. If my heart were real, I would flush with anger and embarrassment. The hickory keeps me logical.

Fah is walnut and rigidity, brows pulled to the sides of his eyes like brackets. His mouth is set grimly in one corner and up in the other. These are signals of caring. An impression of caring anyway. I tilt my head, address the lines and angles. "I'm coping fine, General Fah. I would like further opportunities to prove myself."

Irritation flashes like lightning and then is gone, a new mask in its place. Fah's wooden jaw clicks as he encroaches, eyes on each brother. "Your sister is quite forceful, no?"

They must answer. They don't want to answer. Joka runs a hand over his bamboo neck with discomfort. "She's always been a force of nature, if that's what you mean, General." The room is silent. Just the musical thrum of accidental Calls as people brush the table or a wooden bowl with their matching timber limbs. "And she's always kept us in line."

Fah pulls back, shoots out a snapped laugh like he's choking on a peanut cracker. "Ha! You speak well of your sister. Sounds as if she was very skilled at running the Yan household." He slaps Joka on the back and I wish my brother wouldn't fold like a broken table. The general leaves. Sharp flat footsteps on the floor.

Life returns to the dining hall once Fah has left the building. Beneath the thrum of conversation, creeping low like a bird flying beneath a storm cloud, Joka turns to me. "That's not what I meant, little sister. I didn't mean you make a good housekeeper."

I pat his hand. "I know. I'm not offended."

Perhaps this is how having a hickory heart makes me a better soldier. Fah can say what he likes. It won't affect me. It slides off my skin like water. The only problem will be if the water rises too high.

THE SHEN boy, Ash, lifts his head as we walk to across the square. Strange, almond shaped but not almond colored eyes staring at Joka's neck. His mouth puckers like he finds the sight disgusting. I steer Joka away. I pretend he's a cautionary statue. An example of what not to be.

We curve around the monastery walls to a large lawn area dotted with targets and take our place among other eager soldiers. Ben Ni picks up a bow and twangs the string mindlessly. "I wonder whether I could..." His hand runs down the tight thread, building some contraption in his mind.

I snatch the bow and punch him lightly in the side. "Sh! Not now little brother." He bites his lip and straightens.

My slippers suck dew from the grass, toes numbing. Joka swings nervously, and I try to smile reassuringly. Again, he looks at me with suspicion. I check my collar. Joka opens his mouth to speak but is cut off by a stern, deep voice.

A short, round man wanders onto the grass, clears his throat, and says, "You're all telling yourselves that archery is the lesser of the skills you must learn to become a good soldier. You've been led to believe that if you're not good at hand to hand, then this is the back up." He paces, his hands behind his back. "You think the archers are the weak ones." Men hang their heads. My eyes stay up. "Listen."

He cups his hand to his ear dramatically. I hear the shriek of murder birds in the distance, the slight whisper of wind brushing the inside of my ear. A sea breeze to a shell.

Confusion settles over the group, weighting their shoulders, heads swaying like willow branches as they search.

I focus on the trainer, smiling devilish as he shouts, "Captain Ipok!" Everyone turns their attention back to him. "Remember that name. Remember everything I say, and you will find yourselves on higher ground. You will not think yourselves weak. Your arrows will be like the wind. Finding their way around obstacles when the ground fighter can only push into them. You will be like the sun, chasing away the shadows to illuminate the target."

His arms flail with enthusiasm and I'm entranced.

Ipok claps his hands. "Right! Take a bow and a sleeve of arrows and let's separate the rice from the stalks."

Sun, all thick muscle and clout, handles the weapons inelegantly compared to Joka and I, who carefully weigh the bows in our hands, assuring they're comfortable to hold. *Stalks meet Rice.*

33

SHEN LYE LI

I collect water from wet leaves and drip it into my flask. My eyes fix on the dew, single droplets joining others and swelling to a small stream. Depending on who leads, there is power in joining together.

I am filthy but the thought of washing, of wandering too far from my shelter, is terrifying. Here, I'm close enough to see Ash. Fruit dangles from trees. I have water. The sun lights the branches in gold. I have what I need.

This ghost life suits me. The guilt flaps through my body as if I am mist. I wish to stay like this for a while. A long while. Without the chancellor's hand to squeeze my arm and force me to action, without Ash to light the way, perhaps I am mist.

My mind drifts. The quiet of the forest punctuated by men's voices.

I tie my robe tightly and sneak from the chamber. I've been living in the palace for two years, but I don't think I'll ever get used to the grandness, the gold on gold on gold with red velvet draped between.

I miss Ash. He sleeps with the other soldiers now.

The Keeper must sleep alone.

Archways hang like wedding boughs. In this low light, they rise up like spirits holding their breath, ready to scream. I move faster. Barefoot on the hand-woven carpet. Elements represented in hand-knotted silk and dyed wool. I imagine the hundreds of hours, the sore and blistered fingers that made this carpet and shiver with pride. It's an honor to have your work hung on the palace walls.

And me, I know my purpose. I know I'm important. But I don't feel like I belong here like our emperor does. He deserves the best of everything. He must be honored. It's his birthright.

The light of the kitchen shines up the stairs. And I follow it.

What is my birthright? To serve the emperor. To help young people name their element and unleash it. It's as important to our people as the crops we grow. The gold we mine. That's what we've always been told. And it protects us well. From the murderous, savage tribes of the Char.

A solid thump and a cry of pain distract me from my quest for food and I turn away from the kitchen.

The sounds increase and I pick up my pace. The man seems to be in so, so much pain.

I know I can help.

I'm in a part of the palace I've not been before. It's bleaker with dark iron on the doors and no decoration. Another scream and then a curse. A muffled cry. A child. A weeping child.

I run down another set of stairs and hear voices. One I have known my whole life, the other I don't recognize. I press myself to the wall, listening and watching their shadows. Their heads close together.

The chancellor's voice is pecked and irritated. "The emperor grows impatient with your lack of progress."

The other man bows his head. "I have managed to separate limb from man, but once separated both always die. Always."

The chancellor, whose shadow I would recognize anywhere for its diamond cut pointiness, spits, "What good is that? The emperor wishes to possess this magic for our people. Without it, how can the Shen spread their power over the islands and beyond?"

"The emperor must be patient. This isn't science. It's something else entirely."

A woman screams. Is she being ripped apart?

"What of the Char child? Have you learned what makes it possible for them to host Carvress magic?" The chancellor's fingers spread wide, ready to grab the man by the neck.

Shadows move away from view and I crane around the corner. A man in a leather apron hangs a carved leg from a hook. Gray, petrified wood tinged with blood. The Carvress's mark fades on the blanched surface. Other limbs swing from the rack and some sit on a table in various stages of dissection. My mouth falls open in horror.

The whimpering of a child wraps itself around my throat and tightens like a chain.

"I need to wait until he's well enough to draw more blood, Chancellor. Otherwise he won't survive another procedure."

The chancellor waves his arms like there's smoke in his eyes. His words steal my breath. My heart shrinks in my chest. "Never mind that. Just do it! We have plenty of children. And if we run out, we'll just burn another village and get more." He laughs soullessly. "I know you've told me their brains aren't wooden." I cringe. "But you'd think they'd check the bodies. Make sure everyone is accounted for. But of course, typical Char and their outdated ways. All burned villages are left untouched." I sense him rolling his eyes. "Shrines to the fallen and all that nonsense."

They're torturing Char children. Children. I gasp, cover my mouth, but it's too late.

The men swing around to see me slip behind the wall. The chancellor sighs, annoyed, and storms toward me. Shouting back to the other man, "Remember what I said. The emperor is impatient. And when he's impatient, well, let's just say he's not at his most merciful."

His sharp shadow catches me and digs into my flesh. Then his hand snatches at my skin. Through dry, charcoal-stained lips he utters, "You should not be here, Keeper girl."

He shakes me hard, and as he drags me back to my room, he threatens everything my heart may have touched since birth. Every person I care about or even knew. Ash he leaves till last, naming all the terrible things he will do to my brother if I speak about what

I just saw. I crack and crumble, my shoulders shaking, my eyes stinging with tears. I am powerless. I am...

"Besides, Keeper, they're only Char. They're barely human. And you must do your duty to the emperor and to the Shen people."

I am... a slave.

34
CHAR LUNA

My limbs ache from pulling back the bow hundreds of times. But it's a good ache. I showed promise. I learned. I smile slowly at the memory of my last couple of shots. It's something I have to make myself do, touching my lips to make sure it's framed right. I came close to the bull's eye. Closer than most. And as the days of training run closer to their end, this seems all the more important. The fuse is nearing the barrel. Just two more weeks.

"What are you smiling about?" the Shen boy asks. He's fast becoming a bunch of bones bound by rags.

I ignore him and turn to the wall to change. I trace my sternum. My heart makes strange noises hopefully only I can hear. Like the lid of a treasure box opening and closing. The Shen boy's eyes on me are a threatening brand. Like a hot iron approaching.

"Char girl. Luna," he pesters. "Girl with a back as purple as plum wine."

I tense. Shiver. I shrug on my shirt and turn just slightly. "How did you learn my name?"

His chains shuffle. "I heard that puppet with the wooden neck call you by name. Luna. Like the moon," he muses. His mouth needs water. His face needs slapping.

I take a breath. Let my heart do its calming job. I count the beats, listen to the blood draining from one chamber to the next. "Puppet?" I turn fully, crossing my legs. "You mean my brother, Joka."

He ignores my words, like naming the "puppet" offends him somehow. "Well, at least *you're* not a puppet." He stretches his neck, trying to find something. "You couldn't hide much from me." His eyes darken. "I know the curve of every rib on your back."

I frown. "Do you think you're funny, Shen boy? Do you think I enjoy sharing this cramped space with you?" Forcing calm becomes difficult. Chambers slide. Blood comes. There is no way to slow it. "What gives you the right to talk to me this way? I don't point out your wasted limbs or missing hair."

He runs a hand through his light-brown hair and gives a half smile that twists to pain when he brushes over his injured scalp. "It's not like there's much else to look at in this room."

"Boredom is no excuse for being a scoundrel."

Chains tighten as his whole body stiffens with offense. He closes his eyes, a crinkle forming as he turns over a thought. "Yet being a Char seems to be a good enough excuse to be *unfeeling*. I am no scoundrel. You know nothing of my honor. Or what I've been through."

The words strike at my heart. Though he doesn't realize what he's said. I lean against the wall and stare at the yellow circle of candlelight that wobbles with the slightest disturbance of the air. I sigh hard, expelling the small anger my hickory heart allows. "I don't think this *sister of a puppet* feels like she should have to talk to you any longer."

He sweeps a loose hair from his forehead with an unsteady hand. He's a checkerboard of scratches and cuts. Some healing. Some new. He bows sadly and rubs his forehead. Trying to iron out the wrinkles his frown has caused. "Ugh! I'm sorry. I only want to live. For…" His lips close over bright teeth as he holds words in. "Getting to know you seems like my best option."

I appraise him doubtfully. He is… surprising. "If I'm your best option then you're…"

His face is drawn. *Can you be resigned and hopeful at the same time?* "Just let me unlearn. There's nothing else I can do."

My curiosity sparks and I lean forward. "What do you mean, *unlearn*?"

He taps his foot nervously. Thinking. Choosing what to share. "Imagine that from birth you were only fed, er, fish guts."

My mouth screws up and he smiles, warm amusement sparkling in his sunken eyes. "Yuck! Why would anyone feed you fish guts?"

"Stay with me. If you were fed fish guts from birth, and were always told it was delicious, you would believe it, wouldn't you? You wouldn't know any better. You'd think fish guts were the standard by which deliciousness was defined."

"I suppose so," I say slowly.

"Well, I've been fed fish guts my whole life. We were taught that the Char were animals. Savage and murderous and only after one thing: the death of all Shen."

I untie my long brown hair. The crimped tresses fall over my shoulders. History is not only learned. It runs in blood. I'm not sure it's possible to "unlearn" what has been born into you. "The Char want nothing from the Shen except to be left alone. Left to live."

He sighs. "I'm unlearning much about the Char. But I'm also learning what they will do to get their freedom. Your people are not above cruelty, Luna. Sadly, no one is."

Something bubbles inside me. Like fermented fruit juice has been poured through my ribs. Burning acid eats at my beliefs.

His knees pull up. A bony resting place for his elbows. He awaits a response. I swallow. I rely on my heart, keep my voice and thoughts even. "We must do what is necessary to win this war."

He huffs. A sharpness to his movements. "I guess some things can't be unlearned."

His disappointment in me translates to a bitter taste. I rub it from my teeth with my tongue. His opinion should mean nothing. The air cools, *I* cool, and stare at the starving Shen boy, his eyes hopeful when they shouldn't be. There is no hope for him.

"Ash." His name spins a tenuous, dangerous attachment, delicate as spider's silk. "They'll never let you go."

"No," he agrees. "Not willingly."

MY ARROW plunges deep into the red ring around the bullseye. I exhale, relieved, and pick up another arrow. Joka pokes me in the back, and I turn to see Captain Ipok strolling across the field as arrows fly to their targets—brave or stupid, I'm not sure. He observes with keen, dark eyes. I stand up straight. Joka steps behind me. My other brothers fire off shots further down the line. Ben Ni's lands in the grass. Sun is improving. Unaccustomed to being unsuccessful, he puts extra effort into getting it right.

"You." Ipok swirls his finger, searching for a name.

"Char Luna Yan," I offer, and he raises an interested eyebrow.

"Luna Yan." He says the name slowly like he's committing it to memory. "Step forward."

I ready for insults. The *not bad for a girl* speech. But instead he beckons me closer and puts his hand up to the rest of the group. "Everybody stop!" he shouts. The wind disturbs his carefully raked hair. Four strands doing nothing to cover his baldness. The group holds, except for one arrow that flies over Captain Ipok's head and lands in a tree behind him.

I bite my rosehip lip, begging it not to be one of my brothers. "Sun Yan!" Ipok shouts infuriated. "I said stop!" To himself he mutters, "We don't have time for this."

Sun bows low, the concentration in his eyes turning to shame. "Sorry, Captain."

Ipok's chin wobbles. "Sit there!" he growls, pointing to the target in front of me. "You're lucky your sister is a talented archer. It elevates the Yan family name you just sullied with your incompetence." Sun is mortified. "It also means you may not lose your head."

A hum of surprise rustles over the group of soldiers as Ipok orders them to observe my "superior" technique, ordering me to shoot an arrow just above my brother's head.

Sun scrunches his eyes as I pull back the string. His shoulders force downward, straining not to embarrass himself further. Disturbingly, I don't share his worry. I don't feel pride or confidence at being singled out. I merely feel the tautness of the string, the flick of the feathered tail in my fingers, and the slight breeze that may send my shot off course.

I release the arrow and the group gasps.

Sun gives an infinitesimal flinch as the arrow wizzes over his head, hands clasped viselike in his lap. A quick breath assuring he's alive and then he stands, bowing sharply to me and the captain. "Nice shot, sister."

The group laughs until Ipok claps forcefully and shouts, "Get back in line!" He pats my back and I join the others. "If you're struggling, I suggest you seek advice from Luna. She has a natural talent, though I'm guessing it's not hereditary." His eyes slide to Sun as the laughter grows.

For the first time, I'm being treated like an equal. A soldier that has something to contribute.

35

SHEN LYE LI

I touch my growing hair with torn fingers. It feels like the fur of one of the rakka possums I've been sharing my tree with at night. At first shy, they've been creeping closer, claws white against the grey bark of the fig tree. Eyes full as the moon. Their striped tails hang over my face as I sleep, and I've become used to their crackly purring.

"Rrrrakkkaaa," I whisper, laughing quietly to myself. All this time alone in the jungle is affecting my mind. This misty version of Lye must settle and reform.

A guilty cloud floats behind my ears. I've allowed my hair to grow, which is against Keeper tradition. I've abandoned my people. My position. Then the guilt pushes into me with force. I had to abandon them. There should be no place for the emperor's brand of cruelty in this world. It is only through deep twists and turns that I managed to grow out from under that shadow. Find a better place to take root. My soul ran deep with the same cruelty. I was almost lost to it.

The razor makes scraping noises as it is keened over my head gently. Po Shu smiles softly, watching me in the mirror as she carefully shaves every last hair on my head.

"I wish for your eyes, Keeper," she whispers. "Blue as the sky, deep as the sea. They are beautiful. With eyes like yours, maybe I could catch a soldier's eye."

I blink slowly and frown. "The Keeper cares not for beauty. It is a vain and ultimately pointless pursuit." I clasp my hands in my lap, saying what is expected. Po Shu is slight, with pleasant skin. Her rose cheeks are natural. Her watermelon seed eyes are perfectly spaced in her face. She is also sweet and gentle. I have no doubt a man would want her for a wife.

Po Shu clucks her tongue. "Well, it is easy for you to say when you have those eyes. No matter how your skin sags, or your breasts," she giggles, "your eyes will remain the same." She shoos the guard standing in the doorway. "The Keeper must change shortly." She closes the door and my body relaxes. I allow a brief smile. If Po Shu does make a match, I will be sad to see her go. She is my... the words are difficult to bring to the front of my mind. Friend.

She cleans the blade and grips my shoulders. I revel in the close touch. "Po, you will find a husband. Just make sure he's the right husband."

She laughs. "You make it sound as if I could be so picky." She lifts the blade to my head to makes sure it is clean behind my ears.

"You can be. You deserve..." I turn to the window. Men twirl and train in the red square. She could have her pick of any—

A slicing pain above my ear. She lets out a small squeak. She has cut the Keeper. Without thinking, Po Shu presses her finger to the cut. Skin to skin contact. It is fast and merciless. My pain translates to power and it surges through my skin and into hers. A snap freeze. Her watermelon seed eyes turn glassy as her body shakes. Her heart is frozen. She can't even scream.

Blood trickles from my ear, winding like a lost stream down my neck.

No one touches the Keeper.

The door bursts open. Two guards flank the chancellor.

"What happened?" he asks, looking down on Po Shu with dis-taste as she shudders on the floor. His eyes snap to me. "Did this maid cut you?"

I fall to her side, shaking my head. "No. I mean, yes, but she didn't mean to. It was my fault. I moved. It was an accident." My words tumble out. All sounding like excuses. And whether valid or not, he does not want to hear them.

I reach out to touch her. Heal her with warmth. Perhaps spark her heart with a quick shock of electricity, but the chancellor stomps his foot. "This maid cut the Keeper. She should know better than to touch you." The guards watch Po Shu buck and shiver slower and slower. She is dying. They are sympathetic, hearts reaching for the young girl, but they will not move. "No one touch-es the Keeper!"

I ready my warmth and the chancellor kicks my hand away with his boot. "And the Keeper touches no one unless it's for Awakening." He flicks his hand and the guards yank her from my reach. "Get off the floor." I do as I am told as my heart breaks like cracking ice. Po stops shivering, her eyes staring vacant at the window from which I was about to choose her a husband.

My hands fall to my sides. "You killed her." Voice cracking.

The chancellor snorts. "I did nothing. Her incompetence led her to touch you, and your incompetence and your lack of control led to her death."

My knees wobble and I wish to crumble. I wish to grieve. I wish none of this had happened. My friend is dead.

I swipe at the blood and it stains my fingertips.

Being close to the Keeper only brings death.

I run a hand over my scars. Single strokes mark every Shen I changed. It looks uneven and I toy with the thimble in my pocket, wanting to press it into my skin. But then I think of Ash and resist.

My ribs have healed to a scab. It stretches and breaks when I breathe. I stand on the highest branch that will bear my weight and look over the archipelago of Char territory. I count the lumps of land poking out of the sea.

I wipe the sweat brewing on my brow. Soon the next part of the plan will be set in motion. Two sets of hands turn the wheel and guide the ships of destruction. And I gave them the map.

I've been flattened. I know my will is as weak and transparent as a dragonfly's wing. Another day of awakenings. Another day of the chancellor pinching, spitting, pressing on my neck. I flop onto my bed of silk and plush cushions. A bed he has made me quite aware I do not deserve.

A demanding knock on my door announces the chancellor before he enters. Always impatient. Impossible to please. If I could please him and earn his favor, it would be like the sun warming my cheeks after bitter winter. It could break me from his torture. I want to believe I'm doing this for the children. It will end their torture also. But how to identify my motives has become blurred like looking through a dirty window. The keeper's first duty is to the emperor. I bow my head as he enters.

When the emperor steps in behind him, I tumble to the floor. Knees digging into stone. Palms flat.

The chancellor clears his throat and mutters, "Get up!" through his stained teeth.

The emperor looks upon me as a jewel in his collection. A possession. A prize. And even though a part of me knows this is wrong, I still crave his approval. I need it.

I rise to my feet and bow again. "Emperor. I apologize. I did not know you would be entering my chambers."

The emperor tilts his head at me peculiarly. Like hearing me speak has reminded him that I am human. "Well, when the chancellor mentioned that you had an idea to end the fighting, I just had to hear it."

I am flustered. Unprepared. I thought it would just be him. I thought we would come up with a plan and present it. Not that I would be ambushed in my chambers. The chancellor eyes me distrustfully. Maybe this is a bad idea. Maybe I will be punished.

He takes a threatening step toward me and I tremble. "Speak, Keeper. The emperor wishes to know your idea."

I feel like a child. I need to stand straighter. Be sure. Perhaps then they will treat me differently. I swallow drily, hands behind my back then hands knotted in my front. I think of Ash marching to-

ward battle against those brutes and I fill halfway with confidence. The other half, fear.

It's enough.

The chancellor kicks my foot and I stumble. Then I straighten.

The emperor looks displeased. It creates a burning in my chest.

"The only way to defeat the Char once and for all is to have our own Carvress," I say.

The chancellor arches an eyebrow. "They're not like cheap silk. We cannot simply get our own at the market. The carvresses are well protected and very well hidden."

The chancellor looks doubtful, but the emperor's face has opened like storm break. His atmosphere reading like a growing whirlpool. The water spinning powerfully, pulling, pulling in. His interest is addictive. His grace will protect me. And Ash. He opens his hand. "Explain."

"They are well protected and well hidden, yes. But if we could lure the soldiers away from Black Sail, for even a few days..."

The emperor claps his hands. "We could tear the city apart. We have the numbers."

"We only need one. And once we have her, the Char will lose any advantage they had. Our soldiers will have both Char and Shen powers at their disposal. I think it will be enough to force a handover."

The chancellor lights up too, though it's a far less pleasant glow to bathe in. He extends an arm as if to touch the emperor. He wouldn't dare. But he ushers him out of my room before I have a chance to say any more.

"Let us retire to the smoke room, Emperor. Although this may be an interesting idea, it requires finessing, planning."

I'm left with an empty feeling. Like I caught a star only to have it grow too big for my hands to hold. Now I don't know where it will go and what it will shine its light on.

I sway on my branch, feeling nauseous at all the death I've caused. From servant to soldier to foe across the sea. And there is still much suffering to come.

36

CHAR LUNA

Teeth-itching clatter as blades clash and drag against each other. My brothers and I stand around the circle with other soldiers, watching our young instructor swoosh and slide in combat with General Fah. The mood is changing. No longer are we jostling and elbowing each other, eager to learn and to fight. The downward press of time running out is causing every soldier to stand straighter. As they try to hold up the heavy sky.

This is where we get closer to our enemy. This is when our faces are pressed right to death. It seems appropriate that this is our last lesson.

He jabs and Fah swerves out of reach. They push against each other and spring apart. It builds to a frenzy of smashing steel. The opponents gnashing at each other. Eyes focused. Each striving for the upper hand. They use memories of battles past. When skin ripped and blood flowed.

The young captain moves his sword in a circular motion, forcing Fah's wrist backward so he drops his sword. The point is at Fah's throat. "Ha! Do you concede?" he asks with a broad grin. His wooden elbow gleams ebony-black in the sun. The hinges move smoothly. Tiny brass suns inlaid around the point of the joint.

Fah bows his head. "I concede." The soldiers around me gasp as the general picks up his sword and places it in a bin with the others. His smile is tight. "Don't be shocked. We each have our talents. Where I could flatten Captain Halong with a sliding kick and swift fist, he almost always bests me at sword fighting." He waggles his finger at the proud-looking Halong. "Almost."

Captain Halong bows sharply, revealing a large bun with a streak of white through it like a sand skunk. "General." General Fah nods, moving to the side to sit on a low stonewall to observe.

Halong tests the flexibility of his ebony elbow a few times, then stomps his foot. "Take a sword."

We lean toward the wooden bin stabbed with sharp, metal weapons. Men pull out swords, turning them in the light. They smile like it's a special thing. I reach for a blade, feel the weight, but don't revel in it like some of the others. I understand this is an instrument for great harm.

Captain Halong's laughter, spitting like rain, causes everyone to freeze in their positions. "You are babies! Do we give babies real swords?"

Joka starts to answer and I jab him, producing a cough.

Halong's eyes are blinds closed to slits. His knees bend and he slaps one with his hand. "No! We don't give babies real swords." He points to a different barrel, full of roughly carved bamboo swords. "I don't intend to have half my army maimed or killed before they even reach the battlefield."

We take a wooden sword and line up. Me at the front, my three brothers behind. The bamboo is filled with some kind of plaster to mock the heaviness of a real sword.

A ring like struck crystal that softens into a whistle. A Call. Joka's sword rests easily against his neck. He smiles that smile I've seen on every face when their wooden part meets its matched timber. Peace, pure and destined.

Before Halong begins, he presses his hands together, looks to the sky, and bows briefly. His quick eyes bounce through the lines. "The Char way is to always go for the quickest, most painless kill. We do *not* torture our enemies. We also don't give them hope of recovery. We are swift. Efficient. Never cruel. Bow to your brothers." I quirk an eyebrow. "You must always honor those that came before you."

Captain Halong leads us in a simple stabbing motion done with swift force frontwards. The group grunts in unison and it's quite beautiful. Somewhat choral. We move together. We learn together. I thrust my sword, lunging. Feeling like part of a larger machine. My heart counts the movements. Keeps time like a clapper through a dance.

Fah stands abruptly and strolls to the front. His eyes stay on me as I stab with my wooden sword again. My balance is improving. I'm in sync with the others. *Maybe he's starting to appreciate my progress.*

Halong reminds us of the consequence of the action. Describing disembowelment in detail. We nod with sweat and twisted stomachs.

The soldier beside me spits on the ground and mutters, "*Merah, merah, parut.*" Red, red, scar.

The twist in our stomachs is not new, it's part of our anatomy. Changed from the moment our eyes blinked open to a screaming mother and an away at war father. We know death lies at the tip of our blades. We live it. We hear it in our parents' nightmare screams. See it in the ragged scars running from knee to hip, rib to rib. We're Char. Children of war.

My arm quivers and the sword sags when I block. I grit my teeth. I'm building strength. Even if my arm burns, I won't stop. My brothers shout in unison every time they lift their swords to the air. "Hua!" I breathe. Warm mist swirls around me. My heart, ever unchanged, is strong. Beats the time like a clock. Reminds me I need to keep up.

General Fah shouts, "Halt!" and claps like cymbals.

The group stands to attention. Heels together, backs straight, swords pointed to the center of the earth. He strides toward me, eyes framed in kindness. His jaw is loose, and he gives me a straight-edged smile, wooden teeth glistening. I bow low. "General Fah."

He holds out his hand. "Luna, give me your sword."

Confused, I grip it tightly. The group begins to murmur. "Have I done something wrong, General?" I ask.

His eyes crinkle, and he waves his hand. "No. No. You just seem to be, er, struggling with the weight."

Captain Halong interrupts him. "General, each soldier must learn to use the same size and weight of sword. We don't tailor swords to individuals."

Fah shoots the captain a scorched to ash look. Halong retreats.

His palm is still open waiting and I have no choice but to hand him my sword. He snatches it. Holding it over his head with ease, he brings it down hard against the edge of the wall. It smashes in half with a puff of opium white dust.

When he returns it, boys around me snicker. I stare down at the stump. It feels even heavier now. Heavy with humiliation brewing in my chest. I bow to the general and he pats my head. "There. You'll find that much easier."

Head still bowed, I say to the ground, "With respect, sir, I don't want a lighter sword. I must learn to bear the weight like everyone else. Unless you're to give me a smaller steel sword also."

He looks at me blankly, as if my words have merely wafted over his head like smoke. Though his nostrils flare like the smell of the smoke has at least registered. "That's a thought…"

That's not what I meant.

He stalks away before I can protest further. The man next to me whispers, "A little sword for a little girl," disgusted.

I sigh, holding the smaller sword over my head longer, putting more effort behind my thrust. Lunging lower. If he takes away what makes me equal, I am determined to compensate.

Ben Ni touches my back with his weighted pole. "Don't give up, sister."

His words almost reach my heart. They nestle between my ribs like scripture not yet read.

CAPTAIN HALONG displays a small dagger. "This is your lifesaver. Your first resort when a Shen warrior charges." It's shaped like the beak of a crow. The black leather handle rests comfortably in his hand. "Distance is our first defense. You should avoid getting close to a Shen at all costs."

This is where his ebony elbow really shows its power. Pulling back until his forearm touches his bicep, his elbow clicks like a winding drawbridge. The throw is too fast for my eyes, and the dagger lands hilt deep in the dummy's neck.

Sun places his chin on the top of my head, grinding my skull as he talks. "Well, he has an unfair advantage, now doesn't he?"

I roll my eyes. "We all have an unfair advantage in one way or another, do we not?"

Joka cracks his neck. "But not you and Ben Ni, right, little sister?" He's casting a fishing line but I'm not biting.

Calmly, I nod. There's no flush to my cheeks, no heart pounding or stuttering to give me away. Those reactions are lost to me. "Yes, of course, Joka. I meant the rest of you." I gesture to the soldiers as they pick up daggers.

Halong shouts again, an urgency to his instructions. "Remember, distance. Distance! Avoiding coming within arm's reach of a Shen should be foremost in your mind." Then he chuckles darkly. "It helps not to be too close to their ugly faces as they bleed out as well!"

Sun collects a handful and distributes them. Ben Ni stares down at the knife in his palm like it's a bird about to take flight.

"Ben Ni, are you all right?" I ask, tapping his shoulder.

He startles and grips the dagger. "What? Yes. I'm just—"

"Line up, single file across the four dummies. Today we use *real* knives. Your opponent is the dummy. Shen wear minimal armor. They rely on skin to skin contact to do harm. So, you're aiming for the commonly uncovered, vulnerable parts." He taps his neck, forearm, and face. It's a gruesome but necessary tactic. "Again, remember, we strive to kill cleanly. We're not trying to maim."

We line up in front of canvas sacks shaped like men, with drawn down mouths and black slash eyes. Each with a Shen tattoo, Water, Air, Fire, Earth and Blood. I pull Ben Ni to the back of the line next to mine, giving him time to wake up from whatever haze he's in.

My older brothers take their turns. Joka approaches it intellectually, brow furrowed, eyes concentrated. I picture the cogs turning in his head, calculating the wind, the angle, the force needed. He makes a few practice movements and releases the dagger. It lands halfway in the dummy's face. A macabre sight, but I'm satisfied with his effort. Captain Halong nods in agreement and pulls the knife from the face, placing it in a basket.

Sun is the opposite of Joka, all muscle memory and intuition. He doesn't think, he just throws. He lands a solid throw in the forearm. If the dummy were real, its veins would tear open and drain the Shen's blood in moments.

I have to kick Ben Ni's ankle to get him to throw. His dream state is hard to rattle today.

The dagger lands hilt first against the dummy's stomach, bouncing to the ground. "Disappointing, soldier. Try again," Halong orders somewhat patiently but with an anxious tap to his foot.

"Concentrate this time," I hiss as the captain approaches Ben Ni with the retrieved weapon.

Another dagger already in his hand, Ben Ni mutters, "Huh? Oh, yes sister." He throws.

Halong is oblivious, staring down at his hand, as the crescent knife plunges deep in his shoulder. Blood sprays across the white cloth dummy, giving it a far too realistic appearance. Ben Ni stands dumb, mouth agape in horror.

I rush to the captain, who's fallen to his knees. Daggers whiz past my ears. "Stop throwing!" I shout, hands up.

Metal clatters to the ground.

Captain Halong's eyes are fired with fury and pain. He pulls the dagger from his shoulder with a groan, a red dipped moon, and I place my hands over the wound.

Ben Ni steps forward.

Take the blame.

Think of something fast.

Before Ben Ni can speak, I blurt, "I'm so sorry, Captain, it was my fault. I grabbed my brother's arm as he threw the…"

Halong's brown eyes hold mine, searching for the truth. But my hickory heart makes me an excellent liar.

He grabs my collar, preventing me from holding the wound. Without pressure, blood pours down the front of his uniform, but he doesn't seem to notice. He lifts me from the ground with his uninjured arm and shakes my body, ebony elbow creaking and cracking. "You will be severely punished for this, soldier."

I don't know where to look—the blood-soaked shirt, the disappointed men, or my aghast younger brother. "Yes, Captain. Of course. I'm sorry," I mumble.

He drops me like a hot plate, my forehead grazing the stone. His hand applies pressure to his wound. Others rush to his aid but he's a difficult patient, shirking them away and snapping his teeth like an injured animal.

Ben Ni's voice sails over the growing mutter of disapproval. "Wait, Captain! It wasn't Luna's fault. I wasn't concentrating. I didn't check the field before I threw."

Joka and Sun are stunned to silence as their younger siblings volunteer for punishment. They know it was Ben Ni, but to call me out now would only make my penalty more severe.

Halong turns around, mouth twisted in pain, tanned face blanched like dead coral. "Both of you are to be escorted to your quarters immediately. No food, only water. I will send for you in the morning."

I bow my head, and we are marched to our rooms.

37

SHEN LYE LI

I wade through wet ferns that hide my approach.

Dusky light turns the world a faded gray like my robe. It serves me well and I melt into the surroundings. I place a hand on the wall, eyeing my skin. *Maybe not as well as I used to.* My skin was once pale from lack of light, lack of joy. Now it's returned to the color of my childhood, golden brown, small dark freckles dotting my arm like tiny constellations telling of a better time. But it's from lazing in a tree for too many days instead of acting. Letting the past sit over me like a lantern. Dulling my light.

I force myself from mist to solid. It is time to act.

They always take Ash to the back and turn left. They're gone forty-seven seconds before they come out again, which means his cell must be close to that corner. Climbing the wall, I open my ears to any threat. Light pours from a large building at the opposite end of the compound. The music of men laughing and talking flows through the yard. It burrows into my chest, leaving a guilty wound I must deal with later. Right now, I need to find where they're keeping my brother.

I wait for the patrolling guards to change direction and sprint for the darkened archway. With my robe trailing and whipped by the wind, I hit the wall of the walkway with a thud. My breath comes in short, stifled bursts. My side blares painfully. I reach under my shirt, pushing cool, calming water through my veins, and start to breathe more easily. I'm a shadow in form and soul, reaching for a sense of my brother's atmosphere. It will be defiant but worried. Lost in a way, like a drying puddle that used to be part of a river. Running out of time, I tread from door to door, pressing my hands against thick timber.

Empty. Empty. Empty.

Man dreaming about steamed dumplings bobbing up and down in soup.

Empty...

I pause. This one feels lost. Anxious like a stream searching for the sea. Footsteps approach. I take a chance. Grasp the handle and push.

"Joka, leave me be." A voice caught between a sigh and groan. "I don't want to hear about the academics of pain avoidance."

I think about backing out slowly before the owner of the voice strikes a match but the footsteps outside grow louder. If he gets too close, I'll put him to sleep. Hopefully he will think me a dream. I swallow the scoff that rounds my tongue. *I'm more of a nightmare than a dream.*

The voice reaches out in the dark. "Sun, I know you think this will make me stronger but..."

A lightning spark and light spreads across the room. The boy draws in a startled breath and holds it. He doesn't move, remaining on the edge of his bed, hands clasped tightly.

"Please," I whisper. "I don't want to hurt you."

His eyes are like golden oil after frying. I tilt my head. Together we say, "It's you." The boy who gave me his pack, Ben Ni.

He starts to stand, and I brace, every bone stacking straight and locking. Hands up, burnished eyes compassionate, he says, "I would never hurt you."

It's laughable. Suddenly, another weight drops onto my shoulders. *A Char boy showing me kindness.* But then, he doesn't know who I am.

He takes a step and I lean against the door. "I'm looking for food," I lie, clutching my stomach.

The boy's head falls. "I have none," young voice cracking, he offers a hand, which I dare not take. I look into a face full of innocence and heart. He's everything I'm not and it kills me to even look at him. "I'm Ben Ni."

My lips form the words before I can stop myself. "I know. My name is Lye Li."

He speaks my name gently. Carefully. Marking it to memory. "Lye Li. How are your injuries?"

My hand goes to my side. "Healing."

I need to leave before I expose myself and Ash. "I have so many questions," he says, eagerly approaching. His atmosphere is rain falling on thirsty plants.

The truth inches up my throat like a slug. Head down, sliming its path to my lips. I swallow, forcing it to slip down. If I tell him, then Ash is dead. If I tell him, those eyes will burn with hate instead of glow with compassion and this curious need to know me. *If I tell him...* I shake my cowardly head. "I have no answers."

He sighs, disappointed. "Oh. I guess I understand." His smile is one of wonder. "This is a strange situation we're in. But I promise I won't tell a soul I saw you." His hope is an illness to which I fear I'm immune. "Just tell me one small thing, please."

His sweetness tries to knead my heart into something softer. I nod. "One small thing."

"Why don't you have a tattoo above your eye like your brother?" he asks earnestly, shocking me dumb. *How could he know Ash and I are siblings?* His head tilts, gaze burning. I trace the soft, purplish skin beneath my eye. *Our eyes.* Changing blue like the sea.

I gulp, turning the handle on the door. I don't know what to say and have no answers. My words are not my own. They come from the cruel mouth of the chancellor who kept me pinned beneath his foot for too long. "Because I am everything and I am nothing," I whisper.

His expression is pain, reflecting my own. As if he could, and would, willingly reach inside my heart and take some of the darkness.

"You could never be nothing," he whispers to my back.

I slip outside, lungs constricting in panic. Not risking staying a minute longer, I am devastated and empty. My brother remains chained and I exposed our identities to the young soldier, Ben Ni.

As I leap over the wall and press myself to the damp earth, I hate myself even more because I let fear take over. In that sparse Char room, clouds of guilt and shame closed in. I fled from his kindness when I should have warned him.

Why didn't I warn him?

"You would send so many of our own soldiers to their deaths, when it is not needed? When there's another way? Why not simply lure the Char away with false information?"

The chancellor's eyes are blank. Not even hateful. Just calculated. "Why would I collect all the rats in a sack if I did not plan to drown every last one? Besides, I send the Mogui."

The demons. Our worst and most murderous soldiers. Sloppy, angry, and hellbent on one thing: death to all Char. They have a high kill count, but their methods are to tear and maim for the end result. They use Elemental power as much as weapons and blows. It is... barbaric.

I shake like a dried flower in a bottle. I try to sound strong, but my voice is a husk. "I will not support your plan. You are slaughtering for sport."

He laughs then. It's a despicable sound. Like something dredged from a pond. "Yes, it will be good sport, but taking Crow's Nest is also strategic. It will make a useful base as we strip the other islands down, plank by plank." His smile is reptilian. "And I don't need your support. You're a servant. A slave. Nothing! Don't for one second think you have any influence over the emperor."

My voice falters. "But... but it was my idea."

At this he turns away, pours a large goblet of plum wine and drinks it in composed, delicate sips. While I stand there, dutiful and bound by his control, wishing I could break free of his hold. My fingers ache to end him but are frozen at the same time.

He turns. "Yes, it was your idea. You set the Shen on this path. I shaped it into a more elegant and failsafe plan. But your hand is as deep in this pool of blood as mine. Don't dare try to shake the responsibility from it now. You should be proud."

Proud. There is no pride in murder.

There is no power in my argument either.

He will never listen to me.

He is right, I am nothing.

38
CHAR LUNA

Waiting for punishment is almost worse than punishment itself. I sit on the bed, stomach rumbling, small fingers intertwined, going over the events of the day. Ben Ni has always been absent-minded, distracted, but this seemed worse than normal. He's not one for keeping secrets but I recognize signs of hiding in him. Familiar because I'm well practiced at deception.

I tap my chin, wondering what it will be. Lashings? Or cleaning urinal troughs? *I'd rather be lashed.* My heart allows me to sort through various possibilities without much alarm.

My older brothers beg to be let in, but the guards tell them no. Joka's voice fades as they're ushered away. "Ben Ni's all right, little Luna."

Little Luna.

I sip water slowly, conserving it for the night ahead.

Ash is shoved roughly into the room flanked by two guards. They pinch his arms as they drag his thin body across the floor and throw him with a rattling thud against the wall. I look up from contemplating my lap as they kick him. He doesn't cry out.

"Maybe if you told us something then we wouldn't have to treat you so poorly, Shen boy," the larger guard rumbles. He has a half-wooden skull, so his long dark hair only grows on one side. I tilt my head, staring, having never seen such a Char before.

"Did they give you wooden brains with the skull or would that have been redundant?" Ash mutters from his curled position on the floor. He spits blood as they clap shackles around his ankles.

The heavy-set guard starts toward him threateningly and the other one holds him back. "Stop. We need him alive... for now." He throws Ash a wicked smile, holding up five birchwood fingers, stained red. "See you tomorrow for round two, eh?"

Ash straightens and gives him the thumbs up along with a grimace. "Can't wait."

I'm treated like a forgotten picture hanging crooked and dusty on the wall.

As they leave, Ash shouts, "Tell your general I'll tell him everything if he promises to let me go."

They laugh, disbelieving, as the door closes.

Ash scoops water from a bowl and washes. When the cloth covers his face, I say, "You should never insult a Char's wooden part."

He blinks, tiny droplets of water framing strange, ocean eyes. "Why shouldn't I? Seems to me he's owed some insults. I mean, I see why some of you choose hands, arms, legs, but why would you choose half your head? He must not be *all there* to start with." He taps his temple.

I shuffle to the edge of my mattress. "You assume too much, Shen boy. What happened to unlearning?"

His lips press together, displeased. "Ash. My name is Ash."

"Fine, Ash. Most times we choose, but sometimes the choice is made for us. There's a woman in our village with wooden breasts. This wasn't her choice."

Ash snorts. "Yeah, I bet her husband wasn't too pleased either."

My heart flares and cracks at the top where it connects to my flesh artery. I smack his arm, withdrawing fast, shocked at my outburst. He rubs the place where I struck him, eyes turning from bright blue-green to choppy gray. "Seems excessive to hit a man who's already beaten," he mutters angrily.

Composing myself, I say, "Her husband thanks the Carvress for saving his wife's life. For freezing the cancer before it spread."

His attitude shifts, eyes rolling as he considers. "So that man who just kicked me in the guts, what? He had a broken skull or something?"

I nod. "Or something…"

He shrugs. "Yes, well, I'm not sure that means he gets a free pass to be cruel and sadistic."

He has a point there.

I frown. "I'm just giving you some advice, so you can avoid another unnecessary beating."

Crossing his legs awkwardly, chains clanking against each other, he cranes back to see the stars from our high window. "So, you care whether I'm beaten or not?"

I sigh loudly and turn away.

I couldn't care less.

A SCREAM wakes blue-crested parrots nesting in the cherry tree by our window. Disturbed blossoms float through the night air light as a wish.

"Lye!" he shouts. "Lye, stop! Please, Lye, don't!"

His body is scrunched into a ball. A film of sweat glistens on his high cheekbones like strips of stolen moonlight. Even with his eyes closed, grief blooms from his expression like a full sail.

He shouts again. "Lye!"

I light the candle and creep on hands and knees. I'm reluctant to touch him, but I don't want the guard running in either. I don't need more trouble. Steady beats push me closer.

As my hand hovers over his face, Ash unscrunches, hands and legs flailing wildly. "Not like this. Not like this…"

I grab his shoulder and shake hard. "Ash," I hiss. "Wake up, you idiot. You're going to get another beating for waking the whole monastery."

His eyes open, but they're lost at sea. Looking straight through me, he clutches my throat with more strength than I would have thought possible. My skin turns icy. His fingers dig deeper, deeper into my skin and my veins freeze. Tiny splinters of ice stream over my chest, spreading like roots through my lungs. A stillness rakes over my body.

He's not here. There's no control to his actions. No thought. "Ash," I manage with what little breath I have. My heart can't help me here. I scrabble at his chest, grab his shirt and pull. "Let go." My voice is a narrow pipe of what it should be as my airway ices over.

Suddenly he releases me. Eyes melting back to where the forest meets the sea. "Sorry," he says, shocked at himself. His body slumps, hands shaking. "I didn't mean to hurt you." My throat still feels tight. Not thawing fast enough. He reaches for me and I scramble back, drawing a blanket around my shoulders while I shiver. "Luna, come back. I can fix it." Expression hurt. Ashamed.

"I-I-I'm not letting you touch me again," I say between chattering teeth.

"I'm sorry," he repeats, voice reedy as he tries to pierce the veil between nightmare and waking.

I ignore his apology, clutching the blanket high under my chin. My throat begins to warm gradually. "S-s-so that's what it feels like to be t-touched by a Shen."

His breath is ragged, torn to shreds by whatever he was dreaming. "No. I didn't *touch* you. I forced ice into your veins. If I'd *touched* you with thought," his voice drops low, heated, "with *care*... I doubt ice would feature very much at all."

I purse my shivering lips. "You won't get another ch-ch-ance."

He sighs, flattened by the last few minutes, but then says, "I don't believe that to be true, Char Luna."

My jaw tightens and I ignore the way his voice slips over my skin like silk. How a heart should flutter with excitement or flash white hot with indignation, but mine doesn't. It does *nothing*. The silk slips and falls to the floor and I'm acutely aware of one feeling. A sense that this lack may be wrong.

"What is Lye?" I ask carefully, climbing back into bed, body still spasming.

"Lye is my sister, Luna. Lye is my family." He sounds like his heart is in the process of breaking slowly, stitch by stitch.

I never thought of Shen as having families. Sisters, brothers… It's a strange thought because it pulls them into my world. Into a place of commonality, which I'm not sure I want.

39

CHAR LUNA

Milky orange light filters through the window. I dress quickly. When the guards take Ash from his shackles and drag him outside, his eyes stay on me. A dark stare. A challenge.

I'm ordered to follow.

Fine mist wets my face. They attach Ash to his post and direct me to a nearby weight-lifting station. *So, it's to be cleaning and polishing. That's not so bad.* Ben Ni comes from the men's barracks and I wave. His frown gauzed by fog.

"Sit," they snap. And we sit on a bench, heads bowed as the rain increases and the sun rises, murky pink like a fresh scar.

"Luna, you shouldn't have taken the blame," Ben Ni says, placing a large hand on my childlike one. "You're too brave for your own good."

I squeeze his hand. "I will always, *always* do what I can to protect you, little brother."

His head drops, neck elastic. "Oh Luna, I know. And I know you do it out of love, but I can clean up my own messes."

"I know you can, youngest brother. I just don't think you should have to." I blink, struggling to see.

Love. I tap my chest. I know I love them, but I don't quite *feel* it. It's like the end of a runaway ribbon. I catch the end and then it's slipping, slipping through my fingers. But it's better this way. I will look for love after the war. When my brothers are finally safe.

"Besides, looks like the punishment won't be so bad after all. It will be fine." I pat his leg as terror mice jump over weights and dart between my feet. Their sharp ears and pulled back expression make them look permanently frightened. One pauses on my toes, head switching left to right. *Great. I can't even intimidate a mouse.*

"Maybe if I told them the truth, that it was nothing to do with you…" he says with little conviction. We both know exposing me as a liar would be worse than both taking the blame.

I nudge his muscular shoulder. "It's too late now. We're in this together."

He smiles briefly, the sunrise throwing a hazy glow over his young but masculine face. "Whatever it is, we'll get it done in half the time together."

Curiosity sparks like a wane flame. It should be fanned with concern but that's harder to uncover. "Ben." I look to the wet jungle, branches whirring and slapping each other like they're fighting for space.

He lifts a weary chin, in a dream space. A clear space, away from here. "Yes, little Luna?"

"You were so determined to come here, but something has changed. I see it in your eyes, the way you approach your tasks. Tell me, brother, is there something bothering you?"

He blows air slowly through dark lips. Even his breath seems reluctant. I know something's not right, but the way into his feelings is unclear. An abandoned path I can't find the energy to clear.

"It's just…" he starts. Doesn't finish.

I guess. "It's just harder than you thought it would be, right?"

A sigh that reaches the rising sun. "Yes. That's it. It's much harder than I thought it would be…" There are questions and answers in his eyes. My heart rattles in my chest, knocks against my ribs. *Leave him to brood*, it says.

We're both shivering uncontrollably by the time Captain Halong strides toward us. Ben Ni again stares at the trees, water dripping from his straight nose. The captain's shoulder is bound tightly with bandages and he moves like a puppet, disjointed and in pain.

"I admire your loyalty to each other. But the standard punishment for injuring a fellow soldier is seven lashes. I argued your case with the general, as I do feel this was an innocent mistake, but this is the rule. Our tradition. Every soldier before you suffered the same punishment for injuring a comrade."

My misted eyes widen with surprise, then wander to Ash, listening intently. He wears a strange mask of worry and anger. "The only change will be, er, Luna, because of your, er, because you're female, you will be permitted to wear a shirt."

Ben Ni's hands shake, and I try to hold him steady. It's natural to be afraid. I know it is, but I struggle to find the appropriate emotion. It's like sorting through a laundry basket full of odd socks. Nothing matches.

The captain seems impressed by my stoic reaction, reaching out to pat my shoulder awkwardly. "Don't worry. I suffered a lash or two during my training. It builds resilience."

I highly doubt it, but there's nothing to be done. If this is what happens to every soldier, then this is the way it must be.

"After breakfast, they'll assemble the corp. Prepare yourself. Cement your insides. You don't want to cry in front of your fellow soldiers."

Once he's out of earshot, I curse so much Ben Ni blushes and Ash snorts.

40
SHEN LYE LI

Smashing through dense green undergrowth, I move further and further from the monastery. Slipping and skidding down the muddy hillside, I hear the ocean calling. I need distance from my hiding post. I need to think of a plan that doesn't end with my brother being killed or me being used as a weapon.

I pull up plants as I go, not thinking about the path I'm making. Signs I'm leaving. *Will the boy, Ben Ni, keep his promise or expose me?*

Tears. I taste them in the corners of my mouth. They're frustration. They're anger. Because even though I'm free of the chancellor, I'm still imprisoned. I have few choices and none of them are good.

I slosh through mud, rain drenched. Leaves catch water, fill to breaking, and dump onto my cold, fuzzy head.

I am everything and I am nothing.

I have all the elements at my disposal, all the information on what the Shen are planning, and I don't know what to do with it.

If I surrender, they would think it a trick. *The Keeper willingly surrenders.* It's a joke.

If I try to break Ash out, I'd have to hurt, maybe kill, many men. *If* I succeed. If I don't succeed, I'll have killed us both.

But I could have warned Ben Ni. My cowardly selfishness is a weight around my neck.

"Ugh!" I shout, but the birds are too wet and miserable to react.

I trip, the steepness of the hill turning to a cliff. Rain flows down the mountainside in waterfalls and I become part of one, sliding until I'm mud and soaked rags tumbling, tumbling down.

I grasp onto ferns but only halfheartedly. *Maybe it would be better if I just fell into the sea. Drowned and ended the Shen powers for at least one cycle.*

Sticks stab me, and I'm so, so cold.

I gasp and gulp like I'm already under water.

And then I hit the beach. A short, barely-deserves-the-title kind of beach. I get a face full of sand, and a wave crashes over my head.

My hands dig in and pull me to where beach meets jungle. My body is a flattened leaf. Yet still fights for life.

Why?

It would be easier to die. I wrestle with the thought, slipping in and out like a diving bird. But nothing is easy. My fight to live is tangled in a hopeless need to make up for what I've done. A need to stop living on the ghost side, the mist side, of this life. The drag of guilt is strong. Each Pulse I've found, every element I've awoken, is a stone tied to my ankles. Each lie wraps a layer of rope around my wrists.

I must decide whether to cut the ties or let them drown me.

41
CHAR LUNA

The clouds have decided to add insult to injury, pouring a month's worth of water on the monastery. I shiver in my shirt and soaked padded jacket. My bones feel soggy. I'm so cold, maybe I won't feel the lick of the lash. Maybe my skin will be numbed, and the leather will feel like a brush on my back.

I can only hope.

All the captains are present. General Fah at the front. His eyes, glistening with water, seem regretful, maybe even concerned. Or it's just the rain.

He reads out our crimes and the prescribed punishment. Ben Ni and I stand before the others, washed of worry. We know what we did and now we must accept our sentence. I swallow. Ben Ni focuses on the trees whipping violently like horse's manes.

I want to go first.

I don't want to witness them hurting my little brother.

We're ordered to stand at a single post. The man holding the whip looks to the general, confused.

He groans impatiently. "You'll have to lash one then the other." He points to each of us with a hard finger.

I step forward. Maybe if I volunteer to go first, he'll be tired by the time he gets to Ben Ni. "I'd like to go first, General Fah."

His eyebrows rise and I think he'll say no, but then he smiles, walnut jaw lengthening. "Of course, ladies first." He gestures with an open palm.

My brothers' anxious expressions puncture the curtain of rain. Sun on the balls of his feet, ready to intervene. But this will only lead to more lashings, more punishment and shame. I wave a flat hand, urging him to stay put. Joka's pallor has turned a sick green, but he forces himself to watch. They'll see no fear in my expression. No trembling nor embarrassment. I think this punishment through logically. It will appease the general. Maybe get him off my back. It *will* hurt but not forever.

I march to the post and a soldier places a short length of bamboo in my palm. "Hold it tight for the pain," he whispers, quiet as a feather landing on a pillow, and I notice he has wooden ears. He looks sorry to be here. He'll hear the screams far louder than the rest of us.

"Whenever you're ready, Chun Ah," General Fah orders.

I breathe in, water entering my nose. *It won't be as bad as I think. It will only hurt for a while. It will...*

The crack is simultaneous with pain. Although my heart means I do not fear it, I feel every torn nerve fiber as it sings in collective agony. I cry out before I can censor myself. My mouth to the sky, collecting rain. I grip the bamboo as my flesh burns. Rain pouring down my back feels like acid pooling in the five distinct claw marks dragged through my skin.

Knuckles white over bamboo. I brace myself for the next lash.

I wait.

"Switch places!" Fah shouts through a thundering waterfall.

I will have to watch after all. We are to swap, lash for lash.

I release the stick and stagger to the side. Feeling like there is nowhere to turn, no way to ever be comfortable again. Blood drips from the end of my shirt, making pink puddles at my feet. I try to smooth my hair back and the movement makes me squeak in pain. Ash stares at his feet. Muttering quietly to himself as if none of this is happening. I turn my back to him, and he makes a sound like he has a pinecone wedged in his throat.

Now, my little brother must take his turn.

Ben Ni wraps his arms around the post and grips the wood as I did. Shirtless, water hitting his bare skin. His back muscles tense in anticipation. I feel it before it even hits his skin. And when the five tendrils spread and break his hide, I think my throat might close. I wish for my heart to stop beating. Because this is wrong. I *feel* it. But not in the right way. When the tendrils drag down my brother's back and he groans, body shuddering with shock, I only feel it in relation to myself. A mirror of my own pain.

I can't empathize.

I swallow a large lump of dread the size of a cane ball. *I've made a terrible mistake.*

"Switch!" General Fah shouts.

Again, I take my place, grip the bamboo, and await the lick of the whip. There's no build up. No locked teeth and tense muscles. My mind is on other matters. My heart does its steady thing and I hate it. But there's no undoing it. The Carvress's work is permanent.

A crack and I scream. Tears blend with rain. My wounds open like a stream widening to a flooded creek. The sting is a thousand furious wasps.

I sink to my knees. The soldier who handed me the bamboo lifts me from the post and pulls me to the side and Ben Ni takes another lash, face calm. Eyes unfocused and cloud-bound until the moment it connects with his skin. My little brother is becoming a man while dark blood pours from his wounds.

His dream dies when he sees me. Pure compassion in its place. He suffers for me. I should be suffering too. As we switch, I whisper, "Together, brother. *Always.*" Words I want to mean.

My heart is a curse in my chest as I rewind events and realize how stupid I've been. How quick I was to destroy perhaps the best part of me.

I brace. I wish for magic to change me. I wish for the whip to render me unconscious. *I wish, I wish, I wish…*

"Stop!" The general's voice is loud and impassioned.

I wait a breath and turn to face the crowd and my stricken brothers. I recognize the emotion, but I don't share it. I want my heart to twist with emotion, but it does nothing. Nothing. I *need* to share their pain and I can't.

"What are you doing?" Captain Halong asks, stepping closer to the general.

He waves his hands fast in front of him. "I don't think Luna can take another lick. I think we should pity her slighter constitution and end her lashings at two."

Ben Ni and I bow low. "Thank you, General," I say, my back screaming murder. "I think we've both learned our lesson. I—"

"You misunderstand me, young lady. I said *you* should be granted leniency. Not your brother." He makes a show of pinching Ben Ni's shoulder and smiling. "He can take it. He's a strong Char *man*." He pumps his fist and the other soldiers raise their fists too, cheering Ben Ni on.

"Please, sister," Ben Ni begs. "Let this go."

Flabbergasted, I shake my head slowly. "But I can take it just as well as anyone." I don't want another lashing. Who in their right mind would? But this isn't right. And it makes no sense when the general pushed for the punishment in the first place.

Fah pats my shoulder and regards me like a lost little girl. Someone in need of rescuing. "No, my dear. You can't." He hooks my arm and pulls me to stand next to him so I can watch with painful clarity as my brother is lashed five more times than me.

Each one pushes me deeper. Sets my determination further.

Learn around your heart, the Carvress said.

Even now, my soul presses against it, scraping memory lines on the walls of hickory wood.

I will learn. I will teach it.

First lesson: *Anger.*

42
SHEN LYE LI

Smoke brushes the stars. My bare feet dig into sand warmed by the fire. A simple pleasure. It's gritty between my toes. It's exactly as I imagined it would be except for Ash's absence. His feet buried too. Knocking my shoulder and watching for a jumping dolphin trying to match the sunset, color for color.

I fan my hand to absorb the heat. The nights are colder. The rain will keep coming. I won't be able to stay here forever.

But for now, I can.

I stab at yellow roots roasting in the coals, thick skins blackening.

At least my farming past means I can survive out here.

I imagine the emperor thrown into the wilderness, hitching up his long, embroidered skirts, and digging at the base of a tree for tubers. I snort. He would die within a week. The chancellor would fare similarly. He's forgotten his roots. Or buried them deep.

"It's a great honor, Lye Li Koh. You will live in the palace. Your brother will be well cared for. It's a better life," Uncle says, patting my head. "And besides, you have family there. You won't be alone."

Family is not the word I would use for that man.

I bow. "Yes, Uncle." It's all I can say, though there are many other thoughts streaming through my head like stripped bark. What if I'm not what they say? I could fail the emperor, the Shen people. And if I am, I will never see my home again.

The other children stare at me with envy green as new bamboo. To them, I have won the fate lottery. My brother and I will be plucked from our muddy village and dropped onto silk sheets and duck down pillows. We won't have to share our food with ten other hungry mouths.

They're hurt because I didn't insist all of them come with me. I didn't because they never would have agreed. Ash had to come with me.

We don't know how to be apart.

Since our parents died it has always been Ash and Lye.

Lye and Ash...

My eyes flash open, a streak of lightning snapping across the sky. My head scrapes against the gritty beach. I'm moving. Dragged toward the sea. I reach for something to hold but my fingers clutch insubstantial sand.

I sit up. My ankle is caught in a trap of teeth. White light opens the world for moments at a time and I almost wish it didn't. A horned lizard the size of a cow is slowly ambling backward, my foot between its jaws. Its white eyes give it a possessed, ghostlike appearance, but its grip on my leg is very real. The edge of the water laps closer, and the creature keeps dragging. Enormous jaws clamped ever so carefully. It doesn't break the skin, just holds me like a vice.

Another flash, this time inside me. Reluctant heat crackles through my fingers. *Fire.*

It growls, guttural, as its back legs touch the cool water. I search for anything to hold onto or a stick to hit it with, but this narrow stretch of beach is empty. Pasted with fine sand.

Sand. I scoop some up and throw it at the creature's eyes. It twists its head, biting down a little harder. I scream and it grunts, disinterested, keeping its steady descent into the sea. It seems single-mindedly determined to pull me into the water. It's lumpy black hide shudders like the crust on a crispy rice dish.

Fire burns inside my chest. Dangerous. *Murderous.*

It blinks dim, white marble eyes, fat body swaying from side to side. It appears so gentle and yet, whether it means to or not, it's going to drown me.

I fuel my flames. It takes me over like fire always does, devouring, devouring. Traveling across my inner landscape until it reaches my fingers. I feel heat, hunger, at the same time as water seeps down my cheeks.

"I'm sorry," I whisper as I press two fingers to the side of the lizard's face. "I'm sorry," I say even as my body and soul craves the power it gives me. The feel of a life in my hands is sickening and invigorating. Warmth and the depths of freezing. And I can't control it.

Fire moves from me to the creature in an instant, crossing the divide and burning everything in its path. The lizard squeals like a pig and releases its grip. I scurry backward as it shuffles into the sea, desperate for relief from the fire raging in its veins. It shrieks in agony as it rolls in the tiny waves. But it will find no respite. The fire will burn inside until there's nothing left.

I scrunch sand in my hands as I watch it die. "I'm sorry," I whisper over and over again. To myself and to the creature.

No more death, I'd said. But it follows me wherever I go.

43

CHAR LUNA

My shirt feels woven with razor blades as I pull it over my head. I make a strange sound somewhere between dying and drowning and slump facing the wall. Candlelight pulses like a heartbeat on the peeling, white-washed walls.

"Luna," Ash whispers, voice always punctuated by the clang of chains.

Pain. All I feel is pain. Water squeezes from my eyes, salty and never-ending. I try again to change, but lifting my arms sears my flesh like it's being opened again. My arms fall to my sides, helpless.

Carefully, I lay on my side, still facing the wall. My honor has been stripped. My heart is gone and all I'll have to show for it are lash scars that should have been wider. Maybe the general was right. This agony is so complete, perhaps I wouldn't have survived the full seven.

Ben Ni did though. I scrunch my eyes against the memory of his flesh tearing. The detached feeling it gave me like carrion watching a bloody battle from the sky.

Those *feelings* poke their way in again.

I wish I'd asked more questions of the Carvress.

I wish a lot of things.

A shudder wracks my aching body. A huge mistake as my skin ripples and pulls apart. Anguish comes in every whistling sigh. I can't stop it. I can't be brave or stoic or anything.

I'm a ball of pathetic suffering. I whimper, gripping the sheets. *It will pass. It will pass.*

Chains drag over the floor, coming as near as they permit. "*Luna.*" Voice grave-deep with concern. "Let me help you."

I turn, crying out as I move. I hope Ben Ni is being cared for by his brothers.

Ash stretches, ankles bloody from the cutting manacles, but he can't reach me. When I meet his eyes with my red-rimmed ones, there's no humor or lightness in them. No mask of bravado. He looks wounded. Almost frightened at the sight of me.

Hands out, he repeats with soft sternness, "Let me *help* you."

I sniff, tears pooling on the bedclothes before soaking in. "How can *you* help *me*?"

He tilts his head, one cheek lifted higher than the other. His fingers drum on the dirty floor, tap, tap, tap like persistent rain. "I can *touch* you."

I tense. A very bad idea and I start crying again. I remember how it felt when he touched me. A slow, slow, frozen death. "No. I said I'd never let you touch me again. You nearly killed me last time."

That warm tanned cheek falls, and he stares at the floor.

Drip. Drip. Drip. Rain runs off the roof and onto the window ledge. "I was caught in a nightmare. I wasn't in control. I can do this if you let me. Luna." He says my name in a sigh and a plea. "Let me help you. I promise, you can trust me."

Trust a Shen. The idea is laughable. Ridiculous. I purse my lips and try to think straight but pain overrides everything. I'm trapped behind a wall of flames.

"If you want… me… to trust you," I say between held breaths and tiny whimpers. "Then you need to give me a reason to."

He tucks his light brown hair behind his ear and breathes softness into his voice, warm and sweet. Like he would do anything. Like he wants everything. "What can I say?"

My lips feel cracked as sandblasted driftwood. I've lost too much blood and tears. But the idea of drinking makes my stomach roil. My hands clutch the edge of the straw mattress. I'm rocking on a sea of red and regret. "Tell me the truth of why you're here in Char territory."

He bites his lip, running his teeth back and forth, thinking. And as he tells me the truth, I focus on his words, not on my back, though it rages and reminds me of its devastation every few seconds.

"My sister is the Keeper, er, was the Keeper." He speaks with deep sorrow, counting cracks in the floor. "She, um… she tried to hurt herself…" He stumbles over his words. There is shame in the tenor, but also a sense of responsibility. He takes a deep breath. "No, I won't make light of it. Not hurt herself. She tried to *kill* herself. She was weary of the death and violence surrounding her. She was tired of being a slave to the chancellor and emperor's will." When he says the two titles there's a distinct change in his voice. Chancellor is punctuated by disgust, tense anger to the tone. Emperor is said with a kind of forced reverence. Some things are hard to shake.

But the most important word is Keeper. The Keeper. *The* Keeper. We'd always been told the Keeper was the highest order of the Shen, above even their emperor. Not a slave. A goddess. "I helped her escape. I couldn't let… I had to get her away from there." His mouth presses hard, barely letting words escape. "I just wish I'd known the extent of her pain, then maybe I could have…" He scrapes hair from his brow. Can't continue.

"But…" I start. "How can… I mean… Where is she now?"

He shakes his head, pulling back. "She *was* close, but I haven't had a sign from her in days. She'll stay near, though. She won't desert me." In this he seems rigidly convinced. I understand that kind of bond.

My mouth has formed a permanent "O" as I try to fathom this information, but as soon as Ash stops talking my brain returns to torn nerve endings and my face contorts.

"Will that do?" he asks, watching my face, pain reflected back at me. "Have I earned your trust?"

I take a deep breath and nod. "For now, yes."

His eyes are thrashed seaweed under high tide. "And can I trust you to keep this information to yourself?"

That, I cannot promise. Again, I say, "For now, yes."

"*For now...*" He slides the words to the side, beckoning with his hands. "Come closer so I can see what they've done to you."

Carefully I sit up, feeling like someone has placed molten rods of iron against my skin. "You promise you won't hurt me?"

"I promise," he says solemnly, eyes earnest. And I believe him. Even if his story about the Keeper is a lie. His voice, his eyes, the language of his body lead me to trust him.

I edge from bed and onto my knees, bridging the short gap between us with a lot of panting and grimacing. I kneel in front of him awkwardly, placing the candle on the ground. "So, what now?"

He smiles, kindness and tenderness smack together between white teeth. *This strange Shen boy.* "Turn around." I turn around, wincing at every movement. He exhales loudly. "Oh Luna."

"Will you warn me," I start. "I don't want to be unprepared for the…" He reaches under the end of my shirt, fingers creeping light as spider legs until he finds the tail of one of the lash marks. Stepping to the right, he presses two fingers between my ribs and suddenly the flames are extinguished. It starts at the point where he pressed and spreads like an overflowing glacial stream. Cooling and numbing as it travels under my skin. I gasp. I now understand what he meant when he said touching me with purpose would be a different experience. The connection brushes over my chest, flickers in my heart. Crystal cold, it almost burns, but in a good way. I feel… *I feel.*

"Good," he says, satisfied. Sunlight in his voice, ice in his fingers. "It won't last forever, but it will get you through tonight."

I can't believe how instant the relief is. I could almost cry for happiness. I fall over my knees. I hold the feeling of closeness against my skin. Worry it. Examine it.

He clucks his tongue. "Your shirt is stuck to your skin. I need to remove it to wash these wounds. Is that all right?"

Not thinking, I say, "Yes." My head is numbed too, a cloudy cold feeling swamping my brain. I let him pull the shirt over my head, the ripping sound nauseating. He hands it to me over my shoulder, so I can cover my chest, and uses a cloth dipped in water to carefully dab at the wounds. He makes a lot of sharp sighing noises as he cleans.

"There," he whispers. "Done."

I spin to face him, thankful but anxious to return to my side of the room. "Thank you." I bow with a ghost of a blush.

When I lift my head, he's staring at my chest. At the part I haven't covered well enough in my haste. I look down at the Carvress's mark glinting in candlelight. My wooden sternum, the small brass spikes of the sun. I lift the shirt higher to hide it, but it's too late.

"Oh no." My hickory heart beats like a clock, blood in, blood out. But something pulses on the outside. Something that causes a flutter in my stomach and a flush to my cheeks.

Ash doesn't move. He doesn't look at me disgusted or angry or anything really. He just tips his head to the side and says, "Looks like I'm not the only one with a big secret."

SLEEP DOESN'T come easy even though the pain is dulled. An icy layer slipped under my skin like the crust of a frozen lake. The revelations, the secrets, are stacking high on my shoulders. Soon I shall bend and break.

"Luna," Ash whispers. "Are you awake?"

I scratch at the peeling paint with my fingernail and whisper, "Yes."

"I want assurance that you won't tell the general about Lye," he says, a whistling panic in his voice. "I shouldn't have told you. But I wanted to help you. I *needed* to. That must count for something, right?" Metal scrapes. "Luna, what will you do?"

Scratch, scratch. Roll it between my fingers, flick it down between the bed and the wall. "I don't know."

He sighs heavily, barrels of frustration. "I helped you and you'd still betray me?"

I don't face him. He will see the conflict in my features. I tear around the new feelings growing in my chest and seek the calm, steady beat of hickory. "I. Don't. Know," I repeat.

"You realize he despises you, pities you. He thinks you're a weak, pathetic little girl who should go home to her family."

I bite my lip, dark stone showing through parts of the whitewash. "I know."

I know. I know. I know.

I know what is right and what is wrong. There should be no doubt. If I have information of the Keeper, I should share it.

"Please, Luna." Soft metal clinks. "She is my only family."

Eyes on the wall. The dark hole in the paint gets bigger. "Even if I keep your secret, it won't change anything. I was telling the truth when I said they'll never let you go."

Now it's his turn to say, "I know. I know it's unlikely." Voices grow small and desperate when hope is slipping through cracks in the floor. "Does that *thing* in your chest make you unfeeling? Does it rob you of your compassion?"

At least I can give him honesty. "In a way, yes."

His chains shift. A frustrated groan. "I don't believe it."

"You don't *want* to believe it. There's a difference," I whisper, deader than the air around us.

I scrunch my eyes closed, feeling a tear born from real emotion run down my cheek. I don't know what I believe.

We are rich with secrets, yet we are the poorest people on this mountain.

Bitter silence stretches between us.

44

CHAR LUNA

The moment light taps the windowsill, I leave my room, Ash, and all that's passed between us during the night.

I think I may be a terrible person. The fact that I'm not sure makes it worse.

I want to see Ben Ni.

I push the dining hall door. My back aches but I ignore it. Men glance up from their bowls of pork floss and porridge and I ignore that too. I find Sun and Joka forming a protective pen around Ben Ni. Like whales to their calves. He's pale, leather vest hanging open untidily.

I swallow. Try to walk slowly.

They greet me solemnly. Sun has swapped his usual staunch composure for an uneasy, thin-lipped grimace. It doesn't suit him.

Joka shuffles over so I can sit between him and Ben Ni. I place a hand on his greenish skin. "Did you get any sleep?" I ask.

He moves gingerly, wincing as he reaches for his cup. "I tried to. But sleep doesn't come easy to a guilty conscience, little Luna."

The table in front of Ben Ni is laden with pork crackling, rolled sweet cookies, dried plums. A soldier passes and places a small handful of clawnuts on the table. It's a show of respect and admiration. He's about to spit at my feet when Sun stands suddenly, giving him a look that means *walk away*.

It's nothing less than I deserve. I frown. "Guilty? You're the one who suffered seven lashes. I only had to endure two. I should be the one feeling guilty!"

Sun's eyebrow rises, surprised. Joka coughs and smiles at me kindly. "You misunderstand, little sister."

Arms folded over my chest, I mutter, "I do?"

Ben Ni exhales uncomfortably, scooping food into his mouth and talking around it. "I feel guilty about our unequal treatment." He shakes his head. "I can't believe the general's actions."

Joka clears his throat sharply. "Sh! He's coming this way."

The general approaches, two men with silver trays flanking him. Steam rises from teapots, and the smell of sweet smoked meat makes my mouth water. A satisfied smile stretches across Fah's wooden jaw.

He stops at our table. His hand goes to my shoulder and I shrink away. "How are you feeling this morning, Luna?" he asks, looking genuinely concerned. I don't know what to make of it.

I bow, wounds catching on my shirt. "I'm well, General." I will not let him see me suffer.

Placing a finger under my chin, he stares into my eyes. Picking out dark circles, grayness from lack of sleep. "I think you should be put on light duties for the next two days. No training, just observation. Perhaps a light walk around the grounds."

He doesn't say anything to Ben Ni but eyes the treasures before my little brother with hawkish eyes.

My brothers stare, incredulous.

General Fah addresses the whole room. Sweeping his arms grandly, he shouts, "A gift from the traders of Sand Otter Island, who feel indebted to you for protecting their families while they trade in foreign seas."

The men clap as teapots and cups are placed on all the tables and trays of meat are set in the center. "Caw fee and fat-streaked pork brought from the dark west."

Eagerly, men pour liquid the color of squid ink into their mugs and grasp handfuls of the thin, fat-ribboned meat.

My brothers pour me a cup. It smells delicious but I'm too distracted to drink, and the meat rippled with uncooked white fat turns my stomach. *Light duties. Two lashes as opposed to seven. The half sword. Breaking up my sparring rounds.* I stand abruptly and follow the general, disregarding my brothers' whispered protests.

I fly out the door. "General, wait!"

He spins, irritated, though his expression changes to something else at the sight of me. Like he's standing high in a tower and can barely see me, scurrying around like an ant on the ground.

"Luna," he snaps and squints. "What do you want?"

I stand to attention, try to look like a soldier. "I want to speak with you about my treatment since I arrived here, sir."

His jaw works slowly like he trying to pick something from his teeth with his tongue. "Your treatment?"

I bow sharply. "Yes sir. I want to ask you why you treat me so differently. So... unfairly."

His eyes darken. He looks left to right and stomps his foot. "My quarters. Now!"

THE GENERAL paces his quarters, his sword bouncing on his hip punctuating his agitation. "I have done nothing but assist since you arrived. I gave you a second chance. I protected you. I granted you leniency. And you dare complain about your treatment!" he spits. "What do you want me to do, give you my room? Let *you* give the orders?"

He genuinely believes he's helping. I take a breath. Ready my answer. Hearing my preparations, he stops suddenly.

Standing opposite the general, I feel small. *Smaller.* His eyes narrow and I finally understand exactly what he's done. What he's still trying to do. Whether he realizes it or not.

Words are easier than expected. "General, sir. I've always been called small. By my brothers, my parents, by most people in the village. I've always been little sister. *Little* Luna." He's frozen, eyeing me with curiosity. "But I was never made to *feel* small. Not once. Not until I came here." There's no anger to my voice. My words are clear. Strong. "You treat me differently because I'm a girl and you wish to make me small."

He looks me up and down. "But you are small. You are smaller and weaker. And like you said, you're a girl. Girls do not belong in the army." There's no recognition in his voice. No consideration at all.

"Then why allow me in at all?"

He points at my chest. "Your father and I are old friends. I was humoring him. And I thought there could be a chance the wooden heart would make up for your physical shortcomings. But my initial judgment was correct."

"You never allowed me to prove myself. How could I make up for anything when you never let me finish a fight? When you stripped me of honor at every turn?"

He waves a hand dismissively. "It doesn't matter. We will be leaving soon. And I don't have the time nor the inclination to train you up to the level of the rest of the soldiers."

Leaving? It's too soon.

"But if you'd just let me learn like the rest, I could get there."

He turns his back to me, shuffling papers on his desk. "*Little* Luna. It suits you well. If I'm being honest, I was never going to let you come. My plan was to allow you to train and then send you home to your father to take your proper place. It sets a good example to the men of Char women's place." He shakes his head, muttering, "Though who would marry such a headstrong girl is beyond me."

Dread drapes my shoulders. My back roars with pain but I can ignore it. Something stronger is pushing up from behind my heart.

Heat. Fire. Anger.

"You were *never* going to let me fight alongside my brothers?"

He laughs. It wraps around my ribs and pulls. "Of course not."

I step forward, hands knotted like burls. "But there have been women in the army before. Several from my village."

He snorts. "Yes, and I made sure I put a stop to the bloody practice when I was promoted. I protect Char women. I make sure they are safe. That they never have to fight."

Something breaks open inside my chest. A flood of light and heat. It surges up my throat and I shout, "I've worked just as hard as the others. My archery is better than most of the soldiers here. You look at me and you see a little girl. I look at you and I see a man blinded by his own prejudice."

He barely acknowledges me, just moves his head slightly so I'm in the corner of his vision. Always making me small. "You may stay the night. But I want you gone by morning. You will not train today. You are restricted to your quarters."

The fire pulls back inside. My heart opened for a moment and is now closing, smothering my angry feelings.

My fists slowly relax to splinters. Emotion is flattened. I failed.

I grip his door, pulling it open a crack and then pause. "Why are you leaving so soon? I thought we had two more weeks."

He sighs, seeing no harm in telling a little girl his plans. "Spies informed us the Shen army is planning to take Crow's Nest Island. They travel slowly, ships overburdened with the weight of five thousand soldiers. We're leaving as soon as possible and will complete training on the island. If we're lucky, we will have some time before they attack."

"But more than half the soldiers are new. They're not ready and they are outnumbered."

His chin falls. "It matters not. The Char are very accustomed to being outnumbered and we must do what we can to slow them down. To stop them taking the island and spreading beyond. It is an honor to defend the Char. An honor to seek justice for those we have lost." His sigh is burdened.

I close the door and stalk to my room.

He's sending my brothers to a massacre. And I must stay behind. Weaponless. Useless.

Plans form and break like the tide. There must be a way.

I'm not going home.

45

SHEN LYE LI

Water laps against the huge body of the beast. Birds peck at its back and at my conscience. Sighs seem like wasted breath. Hollow and meaningless. I take out my pointed thimble, press it into my forearm and pierce the skin, dragging it upward a few millimeters. A mark for one more death I have caused. Blood fills the shallow cut but doesn't spill, dried fast by sea air.

I drag myself further down the beach, coming to the cave where Ash and I were separated. How long ago? I'm not sure. *It must be weeks if not a month.* I climb a sharp black rock close to the entrance. Its surface cuts my skin like a spear head. Vanity bats screech in the cavern. They don't want me. I look like something that's washed up on the beach from thousands of miles away. A lump of dirty cloth and fuzzy hair.

Knees to chest, I watch the waves, opening my mouth to taste the spray. I don't even remember when I last tasted fresh water.

I blink, thinking I see ships on the horizon. Blink again and realize it's nothing but rocky islands popping into view when the swell falls.

Spies have been fed information. They'll wait until they see the Char army on the move to confirm they've taken the bait.

I sigh. I wonder if they'll take Ash with them. They beat an empty barrel. He has no information to share. I should have told him. Then maybe this could have come undone. But fear gagged me. Shame tied it tightly. My hands are soaked in blood as he said, but they can still open and offer. They can surrender and take their punishment. I sway dangerously, faint from lack of water and food. My fingers grip the rock, not ready to let go. Not just yet. I can change the course. I am not powerless.

My teeth grind; my head turns to the mouth of the cave. I have fallen to the bottom of the mountain, in more ways than one. It's time to climb back up.

46
CHAR LUNA

My brothers knock on my door. I bid them enter.

Joka comes first carrying a plate, followed by Sun holding a teapot. Ben Ni limps in last, movements tight and awkward. Steam rises from the strange long pot and my stomach gurgles at the meat, sandwiched between thin crepes.

Each brother throws a glance at the chains on the wall, the rough blanket only fit for a donkey's back , and Ash's water bucket. Protective.

"He was never going to allow you to fight," Joka states, observantly. "And what was this in aid of?" He sweeps his hand around the room. "Just another way for you to feel different. To feel inferior." He grunts, a strange sound coming from my refined brother's mouth. "Making you sleep with a prisoner. A *Shen*. Oh, little Luna, we should have done better. Should have challenged Fah."

I shake my head. "It would have made things worse."

"But now we must separate," he continues, dragging a hand down his face slowly.

Sun rakes his hair back, uncomfortable. He's not good at this kind of thing. He holds out the steaming pot. "I stole this from the kitchen for you, sister. It's fresh. And try the bacon." Glum faces for everyone.

He pours a cup and I hold it under my nose. "Thank you, brother, it smells delicious."

I take a sip. It's rich and earthy. I bite the crepe, the crispiness of the meat surprising me with familiar smokiness I can't place. Ben Ni sits beside me, the mattress tilting. "We're meant to stay together," he mutters unhappily.

Warmth travels down my throat. I lick my lips and take another bite of the bacon filled crepe.

"The westerners do something special to the meat," Sun says, trying to distract us from our misery. "They, uh, smoke it." He chuckles. "I can't believe they waste a good timber like hickory to add flavor to their food."

Hickory.

I cough, spit and sputter. Joka pats my back. "You all right, sister?"

I wait for a Call, but nothing happens.

I tap my chest, fingers splayed protectively. "I'm fine." I tell myself. "So, is there any chance of talking you into leaving with me, little brother?" I dig my fingers into hope that's being dragged out with the tide.

Ben Ni's eyes are rounded, hollowed. "I must stay with my brothers," he says rather woodenly. It was a stupid question.

Sun knocks his shoulder proudly. Joka pulls his fear back. Folding and pressing it down.

Love grows. I can almost get a hold of it now. My heart is softening or maybe I'm softening around it. Whatever it is, love is there, as is the desperate fear of losing it.

We talk for a while. About Papa and Mama, how the village is faring. How all the islands must feel scraped of youth. My brothers look forward to meeting the other soldiers at Crow's Nest Island. They wish to show what they've learned.

As Joka scolds Sun for asking me to pass on a love message to one of the girls in the village, a hum begins. It bubbles under my shirt, growing to a clear and beautiful chime. My brothers' mouths fall open like trapdoors.

Ben Ni murmurs, "No," staring at my chest.

Joka is unsurprised. I find his eyes. "You knew?"

He points a finger to the ceiling. His idea formed to fact. "I suspected."

Ben Ni is hurt, eyes hooked with fishing line, dragging down, down. "Why didn't you tell me, little Luna?" he asks.

I should have. I really should have.

"I'm sorry. The general forbid me. I wanted to tell you."

Ben Ni shifts away, betrayed. "You have seemed different. Not quite... yourself. At least now we know why."

I am sorry. I feel it. The connection between my head and heart strengthening. "I thought it would make me a better soldier. But I was wrong. I realize now that it would make me a better killer but not a better soldier. And they're not the same thing."

Ben Ni presses his lips together in a hard line. "No, they're not, but it can't be undone. You have taken away the thing that makes you *you*."

Joka puts his hand over mine. Shoots Ben Ni a warning glance. "Leave her be. If I know Luna, she's punishing herself enough without us adding to it. Do Mama and Papa know?"

I nod.

Sun kneels down in front of me. "Does it hurt? Does it stop you from feeling all together?" He shows emotion so infrequently, and it sends splinters through my chest.

"Don't worry about me. The Carvress told me to learn around it, and I'm trying. It makes me stronger in a lot of ways. And the emotion, the love, it's still there. I just have pull it out." *I think.*

Ben Ni sighs, unconvinced. I move nearer and touch his young, smooth face. "Don't be angry with me, little brother. Don't leave it this way."

Something in him relaxes and he leans his head on my shoulder. Both our backs are on fire, but a stronger pain takes over.

Separation.

"Don't lie to us again, sister," he warns. And in his eyes, in all their eyes, are the words they cannot speak. *Don't leave us, sister.*

The boys lean in and we embrace, my heart still humming as the hickory swirls through my blood. Providing background music to the saddest goodbye.

"I promise. I won't lie to you again," I lie.

47

SHEN LYE LI

The growing screech of vanity bats is terrifying as they swirl around the canopy, fighting with each other over scraps of fabric and human hair.

Our boat clunks repeatedly against the rocks with every surging wave.

I play my plan over in my head as I climb toward the hole Ash was plucked from. I'll find the Char boy, Ben Ni, and offer information in exchange for Ash's release. I can't just walk in. Then they'll have us both and there will be no need to negotiate. I shake my head. No. I have to play this smart. I won't give them anything until I know Ash is free.

If they refuse, I'll find a way to break him out with minimal casualty. And somehow, I'll still find a way to warn them of the chancellor's plan.

Something swoops, stealing the air next to my head. I hold my breath, trying not to make any sudden movements. I snatch a glance at the dim circle of light. Even though I know I shouldn't, I quicken my pace because the last thing I want is to be trapped in here after dark. Moving fluidly, I attempt to match the shadow I am on the inside.

The opening mocks the sun, eclipsing to darkness. Just a crescent of pinkish light showing. I bite my lip and keep moving, strength disappearing fast. I need sustenance.

I pat my hands over the grassy dirt above, rising from the hole like the undead from a new grave. And it's kind of how I feel. Like I'm rising from a dead place. A place of darkness. I'm finally doing *something*.

I pull myself onto the earth, flipping my hood back. The last of the sun lays a small, pink kiss on my forehead.

The peace is brief as thousands of bats pour from the hole. I fall to the ground, arms over my head as disgusting leathery wings flap against my skin. But they pay me no mind. I'm as plain as the dirt I kneel on.

I'm reminded, however, that this place is dangerous, and it's not just Shen and Char soldiers wishing to take me down.

48
SHEN LYE LI

By the time Ash's thin, starved body is thrown in the corner, smashing against the stones like a bag of cockle shells, I know what must be done.

The guards spit at his feet, kicking his wasting legs. One locks Ash's shackles and places the key back on his belt. The other one raps his wooden skull with his knuckles. "You ask me that question again and you'll find yourself hanging headfirst down the well," he threatens, slamming the door and leaving us alone.

Ash looks up, eyebrows raised cheekily. Where he finds the energy for amusement is beyond me. "What?" he asks. His eyes are sinking into their sockets faster than the sun. Weariness is ingrained across his forehead. "I merely asked him if his brain got splinters when he thought too hard." He gives me a quarter of a smile. Unconvincing.

I pour water into my cup and bring it to him. "That wasn't very clever."

He drinks a large gulp and hands it back suspiciously. "Why this sudden kindness, Char girl? Girl with the *wooden* heart?" His sea-green eyes reach for me. Close the distance between us.

I frown, shuffle back a few feet. "Hickory."

His cheek pushes up, eyes brighter than they should be. "Huh?"

I tap my sternum. My heart responds with its steady, mechanical beat. "Hickory heart."

A frown grows in the corner of his mouth like air bubbles from a hiding giraffe seal. Its telescopic neck tucked down as it runs out of breath. I know he fights between revulsion and fascination when it comes to our traditions. "Oh right, sorry. Girl with the hickory heart." He points at my chest. "Why the sudden kindness?"

I unwrap the food my brothers brought. Sticky rice balls rolled in sesame seeds. Mangoes. Dried fish. I dump it on a plate and push it toward him. "You need to eat," I order.

Again, his eyebrow rises. "Why?"

There's nothing soft or doubtful about my tone when I say, "Because you're going to need strength for our escape."

HE CHEWS annoyingly slow as I explain my plan, giving nothing away about whether or not he thinks it will work. When I'm finished, he swallows the last wedge of mango, picks up the rind and runs his teeth over it to get the last of the purple flesh. He licks his lips and watches me bending over like a fisherman inspecting his net, anxious for an answer.

"And why would you do all of this for me?" he asks, wiping sticky fingers on his dirt-crusted shirt.

Leaning back, eyes wide, I'm surprised he doesn't know. "I'm not doing this for you. My brothers are leaving. And I need to be with them. I need to fight beside them." I cross my arms over a heart beating a soldier's march. "And if the general won't let me do that as a Char soldier then I'll do it in secret. As a Shen warrior."

His eyes soften. We've shared a room long enough for him to know that all I want is to stand with my brothers. "You are surprising, Luna. Braver than most."

"I am?" I'm not sure. My heart only shows me glimpses of true character. Like the thinner than thin layers of coconut jam between stacks of pandan pancakes. I don't feel brave. This plan just makes the most sense.

"So, will you train me?" I ask.

He smiles, this time broadly, a warm memory crosses his features. Sun and blue skies. "No." A hint of disappointment pierces my wooden walls.

"Then I won't help you escape."

"I won't train you because only one person can make you a Shen warrior." He rattles his chains.

His thoughts are obvious. "The Keeper?"

"My sister."

ONE OF Ash's guards marches down the walkway, keys jangling at his side. I wait until he passes and then run to Ash, positioning myself by his side.

My wounds ache pressed against the hard stone floor, and new blood wets my shirt. "Like this?" I ask, grasping Ash's forearm as he presses it lightly to my neck. His skin is warm, nothing but wasted muscle and bone.

His face, inches from mine, his long golden-brown hair flopping over my eyes, as he whispers, "Perfect."

Squirming a little, I practice, and Ash presses his lips together. "You're a terrible actress."

I narrow my eyes. "You ready?" He nods. We wait a few breaths and then I scream as loud as I can. Dig my nails into Ash's arm. He winces and I have to remind myself I'm not actually supposed to hurt him. "Help!" I push fear into my voice, when really, I feel confusingly safe.

It doesn't take long for the guard to barrel into the room, shirt unfastened, and hair half-plaited. His wooden calf is freshly oiled and shines slick in the moonlight.

When he sees me pinned under Ash, he rushes forward, grabbing my shoulder. Ash releases me and begins his work.

He's as fast as a plummeting raindrop. Fingers move across the soldier's collar bone, find the point and press. "Flood," Ash whispers, and the guard's eyes glaze over. He grasps at his throat and falls to the side, gurgling. Ash's eyes are the sea on a blazing hot day all reflection and harsh, white light.

"Ash," I whisper. His fingers push harder into the soldier's collarbone, even as the man kicks frantically against an imaginary current. "Ash!" He doesn't hear me, and I shove him violently. "Stop! You'll kill him."

Pulled back from the edge, Ash blinks and withdraws. Mouth open, drawing air in fast and reluctant.

I search the soldier's clothes for the key. "It's not here," I announce, wondering when alarm or panic might start to wrap around the outside of my heart.

The beating stays steady. Calms me.

Ash is less composed, breathing hard, pressed against the wall. "What do we do now?"

Blood pumps strong and full. Thoughts are quick and decisive. "I'll go to his room. It can't be far. He came half-dressed and very quickly." I bite my lip, thinking out loud. "Everyone else must still be at dinner. But it won't be long till they're out. I'd say we have five minutes at best."

Ash stands, chains straining and pulling him down. "Hurry then. Go!"

Dashing from our room, I search for an open door. Noise spills from the dining hall, a strangely timed warning siren.

Blood swarms my ears and I run toward the guard's room. Men approach, jostling, laughing. I duck in and shut the door. There are eight beds in this tiny room, meaning there are seven men heading right for me.

Where is the key?

I think of the lashings I'll receive for this or worse, and my stomach turns over on itself. My skin will open, exposing nerves and raw, red flesh. My death would be a scar on the Yan family name that would never fade. But the death of my brothers would be a far worse consequence. I have to find the keys.

There's nothing but clothes, shoes, and keepsakes. A collection of jade carvings lined up neatly on a silk cloth on top of a trunk. I yank the cloth away and open the lid. Relief pools in the loose spaces around my heart like liquid silver. The keys ring like bells as I lift them from the trunk.

Tucking them into my waistband, I replace the jade figures and exit, colliding with a tall, lean soldier, who smiles lewdly. He slides a hand down my arm slowly, breath stinking of wine. A last celebration before the troops leave. I tense.

"Ai! Have you been *entertaining* Jen Ka?" he asks, eyes hooded. "Don't go yet." His finger trails across my shoulder blade to my throat. A touch like a pointed blade. I swallow, disgust rising acidic in my mouth. "Stay and *entertain* me."

Maybe if I had a heart I would know how to play along. Maybe I could pretend to be attracted to this drunk, slurring man who's looking at me like I'm a Year's End suckling pig.

Maybe not.

I grab his hand, twisting it, and it cracks nicely. "I wouldn't *entertain* you if you were the last man on the island," I spit, adding pressure to my grip.

He cries out as I shove him into the room. Just as I slam the door in his face, his muffled words come through. "Should have known the girl soldier wasn't interested in men." He's not a man. Not a good one. Good men don't force their way. They don't need to.

I run.

The sea of retiring soldiers edges closer like a lazy tide. Soon we'll be under water and there'll be nowhere to hide.

49
CHAR LUNA

Shredded of strength from weeks of starvation, Ash slows our progress. Burdened by two packs, I wrap my arm around his waist and hold him up as we stagger across the square. Teeth sinking deep into my lip every time he grips my whipped back too tightly. But we have no time to stop and think of wounds. I hoist him unceremoniously over the wall, and he lands on the ground with a thump.

They haven't discovered Jen Ka, unconscious in our room. My hope is they won't find him immediately. It's a pointless, ball-shaped hope that will come bouncing back to hit my face.

I help Ash to his feet and propel him forward. Heavy-footed, he tramps through the undergrowth like an ill elephant.

"You're very strong, little Luna," Ash manages through panting.

I grimace. "Don't call me that."

He half laughs, half coughs. Though I'm struggling to see any humor in what's just transpired. "Okay. Sorry. How about Hickory Heart?"

I grunt under the strain of his weight. "Can we leave the nicknames until after we make it out alive?" I ask, trying to urge him forward. "Although, I know what yours would be."

He stumbles over a tree root. Ferns slap my face. "Oh yes, what's that?"

"Useless!"

He goes quiet, a tenseness to his body as he tries to move more carefully over the terrain. "Sorry. I'm far weaker than I realized. Taking down that huge guard used a lot of my strength. Pulling back did too," he mutters.

I grip his waist tighter. "Just be quiet and conserve your energy."

The ground dips, becoming so steep I barely keep my feet. I skate over wet leaves and dodge trees that seem to sprout out of nowhere.

An arrow whistles past my ear and I slam Ash to the ground. Lying on top of him, my heart against his ribs, I feel every breath, every human heartbeat. My hands trace the curve of his sharpened shoulder blades as his muffled voice whispers, "Stay down."

Another arrow coasts past us, embedding in a tree. They're shooting blind.

Voices rise, men confused, shouting orders.

We crawl along the forest floor, hands searching, hip to hip, ice to heat. Dependence bandaging us in the dark. Torches line up along the monastery wall. A search party readies. The general can be heard above the rest.

"Don't waste your arrows on that Shen boy. And as for the girl, she won't get far." Men protest. My brothers may be among them. "If we don't find her, it matters not. When she comes slinking back to her parents, her shame will be punishment enough."

Ash curses, his hand finding mine and squeezing. "He underestimates us both."

I withdraw, tugging on Ash's arm. The torches are still a fair distance away; we have a little time. "We have to run."

Ash takes a deep breath, slings an arm over my shoulder and I summon all my strength—every lashing I would have borne, every fight I could have finished, every argument I should have won—and keep moving.

TORCHLIGHT SPREADS wide across the mountain top and most of it heads downward to Black Sail City. They expect me to take the easy way. *They don't know me at all.*

A few men advance slowly. Checking every fallen tree, every curved rock. My arms burn. My back wet with sweat and blood, lash wounds weeping. Ash is a warm force beside me, moving as fast as he can, ribs pressed into mine. Flesh heart knocking against my wooden one, trying to revive it. Breathless, he doesn't waste air on talking. We travel down. To the sea.

Men press on like an approaching barge, sluggish. Like they know they'll find us and it's only a matter of time.

I drag Ash, head on a swivel. I step wide, I step fast. I don't see the lagoon until I'm neck deep in water and Ash is sinking like a lump of lead.

Tears blink, pain and pink water surround me as my wounds fill with cold, dirty water. They heard the splash. Orange torch lights bob up and down like giant fire moths, getting brighter.

I grasp at Ash's shirt, kicking hard. Pulling him above the surface, I thump his chest to produce a cough. He sputters and I cup a hand over his mouth. Letting him rest against my chest, I swim backward into the reeds. Our packs float in the water and I throw them into the bushes. Floating orange lights get closer and closer.

"Get ready to hold your breath," I whisper, lips brushing his ear.

He nods and I release my hand.

The torchlight nears the edge of the lagoon. We inhale deeply and dip below. Eyes open beneath the surface, we watch orange flames sweep the opposite edge of the water, hovering like three ominous suns. My heart pumps slower. My lungs burn. Soon, I will run out of oxygen. Ash will run out first. He thrashes beside me. I clasp his hand. He bucks once but holds steady.

Just a few more seconds.

Gradually the fire moves away. As controlled as I can, though my mouth is desperate for air, I rise, keeping my other hand on Ash's head to stop him from bursting through.

We break the surface and draw long, ragged breaths of air.

"They could be under the water."

"If they're in that lagoon, they're as good as dead anyway."

A spongy paw wraps around my leg and pulls.

50
SHEN LYE LI

My feet sink ankle deep in the wet mud. It was much easier falling down the mountain than climbing back up. I pull my foot out, the suctioning sound mocking my feelings, almost like my soul is being slowly peeled from my body. I waver between strength and weakness. But I think of Ash in the center of the courtyard, the way his head hung lower every time I saw him. Life slipping away by millimeters. I think about the fifteen hundred Shen warriors sailing to Crow's Nest Island meeting a thousand Char. I think of the three and a half thousand Shen sailing to Black Sail City, one task on their minds: Find a Carvress. They will take the city apart stone by stone, pole by pole until they find one, killing every Char that gets in their way.

I continue to push against the slope. Just as the slope pushes against me.

I lift my head from where it's been staring at soggy slippers to dancing dots of light, weaving through the trees. Shrinking like winter suns. *Eyes up. Ears open.*

He shouts a name. It didn't sound like my name, but the care behind it makes me think maybe it was my name. Either way, I hear my brother. And I hear water.

Trying not to crash through the undergrowth but feeling like I can't get there fast enough, I grasp trees and fling myself toward the sound. Hands buzzing with electricity, storms growing between my fingers. He calls me. My brother needs me.

I sense an atmosphere of denial. Ice plates pushed over the edge of a stream, shattering. I hear Ash again. "No. No. No. Luna!" he whispers and shouts. Voice laced with fear. Luna. A name that eclipses my own.

I hoist myself over the edge of the sharp rock funnel to find Ash, standing knee deep in a rock pool, plunging his hands down over and over again.

He links his hands together behind his head and curses. "What did I do?" he asks the star-punctured sky. "Where did she go? Luna!"

I touch him and he spins. Eyes lit by moonlight, the color of a funeral. "Ash," I whisper, one eye still on the orange lights moving steadily away from us.

"Lye?" He's confused, blinking fast. Then he steps forward, grasps my hands, recognition clear. "Lye!"

He pulls me into the lagoon, and I think he's going to hug me, but he shoves my hands to the murky water. "Something pulled her down. Lye, you have to help her. Can you sense it?"

I reach out to Earth and Blood, powers fuzzy, pushing to the muddy bottom. The shape of two wrestling figures, one human or at least part human, the other not. It's long segmented tail and toothless mouth make me shudder. "There," I point. "A ghost gecko."

Ash's eyes widen with horror and he goes to dive. I stop him. "You can't swim well, brother." Whoever's trapped in the ghost gecko's grip means a great deal to him. I sense their connection like trees that wind their roots around each other when earth is scarce. I grit my teeth against jealousy, knowing I could never forge such a fast friendship. I must save this person.

I roll my memory back to fleeting pleasant days in the palace. The pool tiled with jade and ivory. Learning to swim with second and third concubine. The emperor's mother watching from above. I take a deep breath, concentrate on the shapes twirling on the floor of the lagoon and dive. Eyes close as cold, cold water soaks me through.

I sense the elements surrounding the struggling duo. Water displaced, Earth disturbed, and bleeding into the lagoon. Blood. *Old* blood.

The gecko and the human are one and the same. The large lizard's arms and legs wrapped tightly around the person. I push both hands at its large puppet-like jaws as it opens and snaps with toothless gums. When its mouth closes over my fist, I open my hand and release Earth, creating a mudslide that thickens its blood. The gecko spasms once, releasing a small *girl*, plaits waving like riverweed, floating toward me lifeless. Arms extended as if to embrace me. But there's no energy in her. Her atmosphere reads *nothing*. The gecko sinks like a rock, lungs filled with mud.

It's strange to be the only living thing in this water when I feel so close to death. Like Ash forged a friendship with this girl. I have a similar relationship with death. It's a comfort. A way out if things become too difficult to overcome.

Lungs bursting, I pull the slack body to me, and paddle for the surface. Ash and I drag her onto land. Face blue. Small body flopping like a waterlogged ragdoll.

Stricken, Ash shakes her violently.

He looks to me. "Please, sister, do something." I don't know what to do. But his eyes, atmosphere, and whole body read of desperation. They say, *If we don't fix this, something permanent and dark will take up residence inside me.* I cannot allow him to sink to my level.

Lightly, I run a hand over her soaked body. If there's water in her lungs, the only thing I can think to do is to beat it out of her. I roll her onto her side and thump her back. It makes a horrible, hollow sound.

I repeat the motion. This time adding a little warming fire to my touch. Darkness blooms over her shirt and I stare at a blood-stained hand, feeling like *I'm* sinking. The girl's heart slows and her limbs grow colder. I breathe harder. Ash makes awful, painful, regretful sounds that dig chisels into my cracked heart.

I look outward. Not wanting to see the wounds on her back. I try one last thump.

And then...she coughs.

She coughs and moves and doubles over, spewing water and other things into the reeds.

Ash embraces her shaking body and I move to her other side, taking her hand and pushing just the slightest heat into her veins.

A small cry comes from her lips. Something like defeat. "This is too hard. There are soldiers chasing us, animals trying to eat us, you're too weak and I'm not strong enough. We'll never make it," she whispers, bent over.

Ash brings his cheek close to hers, smile lengthening. "We can't give up that easily." The girl touches her chest like a reminder and turns. Her eyes run over my bald head, to my dirty slippers. "Look! We found my sister without even trying."

Taking a deep, long overdue breath, the girl nods and says, "Thank you, Lye Li. You saved my life." She almost bows, but stops halfway, conflicted.

Ash throws his arms over our shoulders. "Sister, this is Luna. The girl with the hickory heart."

I gasp in shock. Ash has escaped with a Char girl.

I just saved a Char girl's life.

My hands drop limply to my sides. Conflicted also. When one is beaten over the head with the scroll of hate and disgust for as long as me, it is hard to smooth over the dents.

My brother's eyes tell a different story. A different scroll. One I believe I must commit to memory.

51
CHAR LUNA

We have no time to gasp and gulp and be surprised. I stand, a little wobbly, blood weirdly warm, like soup coming off the boil. "We need to keep moving. Ash said you have a boat?" I aim my words at the Keeper, a slight, fuzzy haired girl with Ash's eyes and a miserable expression. She's not what I expected, but then none of this is.

Her expression hardens and she steps toward the monastery. Ash glances back and forth between us. I give him a shove. "What's she doing?"

He regains composure. "Lye, what *are* you doing?"

Eyes ahead, hands fisted at her sides she says, "I must warn them."

"Warn them about what?" he asks, catching her robe and holding it tight in his fist.

The Keeper's mouth is clamped tight, as are her fists. Her gaze falls to her feet and then she begins speaking fast like she's trying to cram everything into a dying breath. "It's all a trap, Ash. Only fifteen hundred Shen are heading to Crow's Nest." She says this as if it is the worst news possible.

"This seems like good news to me. At least this way, we will be more evenly matched." I don't understand why she sounds so desperate, so urgent to warn the Char. They will be pleased with this information.

She shakes her head, looking devastated and ashamed. "The rest of the five thousand will attack Black Sail City. They will tear the island apart to find what they want. And if they don't find it, they'll attack every island until they do."

Find what they want. Tear the island apart. Attack every island. The words are punches delivered to the weakest parts of my body. Black Sail City will fall, unprotected.

Lye continues, "And don't be fooled into thinking it will be a more even fight. He's sending the Mogui."

No! I know of the Mogui. Papa's face turned a green algae color when he told the tales of facing them. They are selected for one trait only. Not intelligence, not even skill. They are prized for being the most bloodthirsty and most ruthless. Killing Char is their life's purpose.

"But they're not all Mogui? That many…"

Lye's face is stone and ash. "It is an army of Mogui."

My ribs turn to chalk. Fifteen hundred Mogui. My heart tick-tocks like a clock when it should be bursting from my chest.

"What is the purpose of this, sister?" he asks through scuttled fingers.

I reach out to stop her too, almost touching, but the warning in her eyes is like blackest clouds, heavy with lightning. I retreat. My voice is as dark and skating as these clouds. "What do they *want*, Keeper?"

She half turns, her whole being set on the monastery and her own destruction. "They want a Carvress. And they won't stop until they find one. Please listen. The emperor's plans are far bigger than this one battle." Her arms stretch wide, trying to gather the sky between them. "He means to build an unbeatable army. Then the Char islands will finally be his."

I want to laugh. I want to cry.

Shock paints Ash's features. "What? How do you even know this?" He jerks her backward, unwilling to let go.

Her eyes are brimful of shame and secrets. "Because it was my idea." He draws in a shocked breath and she bows her head under the responsibility. "I regret it more than I can say." She begins scratching at her arms. Opening old wounds on her wrists. "Before I said no more, I did terrible things. I *was* a terrible thing. I regret so much, brother. I couldn't admit to you what I had become. How far I had fallen."

I don't know what to think. This feather thin girl doesn't look like some sort of master of war. But I don't know her. I feel like I don't know anything.

He shakes his head, anger building, but when he looks upon her bleeding forearms, the mortar holding it together crumbles over concern for his sister. He swallows. Shoving it down. "Lye, stop! You should have told me. You never give me the benefit of doubt. I am not a child. I understand impossible choices. I understand torture and what it can do to someone's soul. But now it's too late. The Char won't hear you. They'll kill you before you reach the square." He is right. None of us will be able to get close without being shot.

The Keeper's voice is flat and low, a ribbon pressed into dirt. "But I must. I must do something to redeem myself."

Ash forces her to face him. They stare into each other's eyes for a breath, and then he says, "We'll find another way. Death is not *always* the answer." It feels like a repeated pattern. Like he fights for her life more than she does.

She bows her head.

My heart helps me push my anger and fear aside. "We have to move," I insist. This plan, this ambush on Black Sail, must wait until we are safe.

Finally, she concedes with a slump like her spine has been yanked from her body. I retrieve our soggy packs from the bushes, and then the Keeper and I gather Ash and begin our descent.

As we run down the mountain, one question burns through my efforts to concentrate simply on escape. "What did she mean by *before she said no more*?"

Ash turns to his sister who nods softly, eyes fixed forward. "There is much to tell you. But for now, understand she is not who she once was. *Before* was when she was the Keeper and a controlled, powerful slave. But she broke her shackles. It means no more Shen will have their elements awakened. It also means we will forever be fugitives."

MORNING BRUSHES our shoulders. "I'm not going in there again," Ash states, hand going to his bald patch. "My hair is already decorating those bats nests." He shudders.

The Keeper sighs. "It's the quickest way to the boat."

He crosses his arms over his chest, swaying a little so his show of strength is undermined. I could push him over with my finger.

Watching this display of sibling conflict is so familiar and yet foreign. My disconnection to my brothers is like a sore spot I enjoy aggravating. My worry for them increases by the minute as I picture this army of murderous Shen. Warriors who relish death.

"The Keeper is right," I say, glancing at the dirty girl to my right. "We need to get off this island now."

Ash takes a piece of my hair between his fingers, sliding down slowly. "Your silky brown hair… They'll want to peck your scalp clean." He stares for longer than necessary and I pull away from his touch. A reminder lives in my chest but it's still so hard to get to. *Am I supposed to be embarrassed? Flattered?* I can't tell.

The Keeper looks between us like there's something floating there we can't see and says, "Please stop calling me *Keeper*. Lye is fine. Lye was my name before, so it's my name now."

Hands on hips, I nod. She's like a willow branch, thin and weepy, yet there's something strong about her. Strong and reluctant. "Fine, Lye. I don't fancy having my hair pulled from my head either. What do you suggest?"

With a slight smile, just the hint of a breeze through those willow branches, she scoops up a handful of mud and slaps it on top of Ash's head. It drips down the sides of his face and onto his chest.

"You need to make yourself as ugly as me," she states with no vanity or self-pity.

We slap mud over our heads, faces and arms, looking and smelling like river rats. Ash braces himself at the entrance. "You sure this will work?"

Lye shrugs. "Hopefully."

We descend into the silty mouthed cave. A gray dawn fills in the world with pencil details. I huff as I land loudly on a rocky ledge, nearly spilling over the edge. Lye catches my shirt, careful not to touch my skin.

Above us, the sound of thousands of fanged, leather-winged creatures presses down. We follow Lye, clinging to the shadows, keeping our heads bowed, muddy water dripping into our eyes. The brother and sister weave through the rocks like they know where they're going, and I bump and scrape into every protruding out-crop. The smell is damp and heavy with bat droppings, and I take my breath in small, shot-like bursts.

The rush of saltwater calls to me. I clamber over a rock the shape of a large tooth and sea spray hits my face, delicious and fa-miliar. Salt air enters my lungs, washing away some of the stress of the last few weeks. It lasts seconds as the siblings climb into a small boat and Ash calls me down.

I take an oar and Lye wrestles the other one from Ash. We row out of the cave and into a coloring sea. Char islands poke from the water, some like frozen waves, others like the curve of a turtle's shell. All beautiful and defiant.

We bob in the choppy water; the siblings with eyes like the sea seem to know little of it and look lost. "I know where we can go," I say, pointing at a small group of islands. Shouting above the wind and waves, "Glass Shard Island. It's uninhabited." They trust my direction.

Glass Shard Island is wedged between the Widow's Hands. Two great fans of rock like cupped hands, holding a shard of glass. "It's said that the Widow holds the glass shard while contemplating suicide so she can join her warrior husband." I cup my hands to demonstrate.

Ash, sitting in the bow of the boat, scrubbing mud from his face with seawater, mutters, "How romantic," and rolls his eyes.

Lye rows beside me, mouth set flat and harboring secrets. Ash guides us, eyes on the island.

"Pay him no mind. Shen territories are not named creatively. They're orderly and easy to remember. Our village was called Third Marshland," she says fondly.

Ash sits up a little straighter, eyes falling to a dreamy, tropical sea. "A humble but beautiful little village, though, wasn't it, Lye?"

She nods, teeth gritted as she puts her energy into rowing. "Yes, it was."

As I watch and listen to this, I feel confused. Lies we've been told about the Shen and their way of life. The idea that we all ache for our villages sits strangely in my chest.

I frown, digging the oar in and pulling it deep through the water, eyes landing ever so briefly on the marks running up Lye's arm. Neat scores like accounting marks on a page.

There are stories ingrained in these scars, just like the dents and scratches on a Char's wooden part. Whether I will have time to learn them is unknown. Whether I *want to* learn them is also a question mark. I put my energy into rowing. Let my heart take over. *Right now, I just need to get to the island.*

52
SHEN LYE LI

I feel unfinished. A sketch that needs ink. The purpose that sent me up the mountain rose like a morning fog and met the clouds before I had a chance to do what I wanted. *Needed.*

The boat hull grinds against the beach and we are still.

I step one foot onto the beach just as Luna warns, "Careful!" hands flapping. But it's too late. Fragments of glass pierce my slipper and I jump back into the boat. Apparently, there's more than one reason for the name Glass Shard Island.

Luna sighs heavily and throws an oar onto the beach, balancing like a circus performer. "The beach gets struck by lightning constantly. It's why it's uninhabited." She plucks driftwood from the water's edge and throws it at us. We lay it on the beach like a bridge and tightrope walk our way to the forest line. "It's also why we get this…" she says, tying a rope to a large piece of glass that sits up in the sand like a frozen splash of water. "The lightning turns the sand to glass."

A flash of light. A crack like a leather whip on skin. We quickly help Ash, the bag of bones masquerading as my brother, to a safe place. Deciding to make camp close to the beach, we begin the lookout for Char or Shen ships. Luna throws the packs at us and orders, "Make a fire," pointing to the trees behind us. "I see a lemon lychee tree up there." She holds a long knife and a length of twine in her hands. "There's enough water in the skins for today. But we'll have to find more." Her eyes are the color of crystallized ginger. Purposeful and yet unclear.

Ash watches her wind twine around her hand. "Where are *you* going?"

She smiles strangely, like a person mirroring another. A mask. "I'm going fishing."

She stomps away. Small, strange Char girl.

As soon as she's out of sight, I turn to my brother trying to light a small pile of wood and leaves with wet matches. He looks up with tired eyes. "Can you help me?"

I hold the matches between my palms, centering hot winds like the ones that come off the Northern Desert in summer. With my eyes closed, I almost feel the sting of red sand as it gallops down the center of the village. Covering everything in paprika dust. Thinking of home brings a calmness, which allows me to use my powers this way. It's rare. And soon enough I will return to elements flying from my fingers without bidding.

I hand him the drier matches. "Thank you, sister."

With a look of concentration, lip between teeth, brow furrowed, he strikes the match and claps when flames crackle the leaves.

"Are you going to tell me how we come to be traveling with a little Char girl with, what did you say? A hickory heart?"

His eyes flick to me briefly. "She doesn't like to be called *little*." Around us, waxy green leaves lean in. The smell of burning glass mixes with fruit sweetness and smoke.

I exhale loudly. "Ash, talk to me. Do you have some kind of feelings for this girl?"

He stands, searching for lemon lychees. I wait, used to my brother's long, studied silences. He picks a handful and returns. "Yes, I have feelings! Feelings of frustration, irritation, confusion. Not the kind of feelings you hint at, Lye." He takes a large sip of water from the skin and frowns.

I crack open the lemon lychee, my mouth watering at the citrus smell. "Okay, fine then. She annoys you. That seems like a strange reason to bring her along."

He peels the lychee with bone-thin fingers. I'm glad to see him eating. "You're mistaken, sister. I didn't bring her along with me. She brought *me* along with *her*. She broke me out, Lye. She helped me escape."

The fruit bursts in my mouth, sugary and refreshing. Talking with my mouth full, I ask, "But why would she do it? A friendship between a Char and Shen seems, well, impossible."

He tenses, throwing the skin of the fruit into the fire. It spits and sizzles and smells like candied peel. "Unlikely but not impossible." His jaw works like I offended him. "Besides, she did it because we made a deal."

My skin prickles. Lumps appearing like a pickled cucumber. My heart thumps loudly, drumming a frightening beat in my ears. In my experience, deals are made to manipulate. To dominate. They are also easy to go back on. "What could you possibly have to offer her?" One hand reaches into my pocket, rolling the pointed thimble between my fingers. I slip it over my thumb.

Ash takes my other hand. It sparks with electricity and he recoils. This is what I do. I hurt people. Whether on purpose or by accident, contact with me always ends the same way. With pain. Beneath folds of heavy cloth, I dig the point of the thimble into my hip.

"She has three brothers, Lye."

The fire grows, searching for fuel, always hungry, always destroying. Everything. Embracing this heat is what I've been taught. They never bothered to show me how to extinguish the flames. I had to teach that to myself. "And I have one brother. What does that have to do with anything?"

"All I wanted was to get back to you, Lye, and to make sure my sister, my family, was safe. That's all Luna wants. She wants to keep her brothers safe." He says this with endearing respect. I'm not sure whether he's lying to me or to himself when he says he has no feelings for her. Because it's written all over him. Scribbled up his bat bitten arms. Dipped between his bony shoulders. But I let it go. For now.

"So, what? You promised to help keep her family safe in exchange for breaking you out?" My voice as sharp as a murder bird's tail feathers.

He drinks, chews casually, and then cuts me a sideways glance. "No. I promised *you* would help her." His cheeks are heated red. The food is doing him good. But I can speed up the process.

"And what can *I* do?" I ask, hands shaking. Dread creeping up my throat. Because I can do much. None of it good.

He coughs, trying to push the food down, and takes another sip of water. Then he gives me his *I think you know* eyes. The thick canopy of wide, overlapping leaves above us moves with the breeze. A dizzying dance.

I shake my head. "No. It's…" I shake my head harder, my neck hurting. "Just. No."

"I gave her my word, sister. Will you make a liar out of me? A cheat?"

Anger hisses, fire licking up the cage of my ribs like they're made of bamboo scaffolding. "It was not your word to give. Besides, I don't even know if it's possible." Memories of the palace and the experiments flash through my mind. They were about to force me to turn a Char after failing to change a Shen. I was supposed to awaken their Element. But turning a Char was dangerous because the turning would have to be twofold. Awakening an element and forcing their allegiance to the Shen. The former would be almost impossible to achieve. The new plan of finding a Carvress proved more tempting. I sigh loudly. It's why I thought of it.

He stands, wobbles a little and grasps a tree.

"Let me help you," I say, coaxing him closer. He doubts yet always trusts, no matter how many times I've shocked him, burned him, or almost drowned him.

I put my hand on his chest and concentrate on a sail filling wind. One that pushes the blood around his body faster. He breathes in, feeling the healing power for a moment and then brushes my hand away. "That will do. I don't want my veins to balloon with too much air and pop." He laughs half-heartedly because we both know it's possible.

I lean back, drying my slippers. My face scrunches. "See! You know how dangerous I can be, yet you would have me turn and train a Char girl." I roll my eyes. "I'm no shifu, Ash. So many things could go wrong."

His hair swings over his thin face. "That's the risk with almost everything we do. But it doesn't mean we shouldn't try. I know you want to atone. You seek redemption. I see it all over your face." Then he points to my arms, to the wounds he usually tries to ignore. "I see it all over your *arms*. You withdraw to a dark place and then punish yourself over and over. But this could be your chance to make something right. To bring some light back."

Waves wash over the glassy beach with a sound like marbles clinking against each other. Our boat hull is getting a good scrub. Somewhere out there, the Shen are coming.

"Redemption." I run my hand over the many small ridges. The cuts are not big enough to fill my carved out heart. "I'm not sure I deserve redemption. There's too much to make up for. I wouldn't even know where to start."

I flick the thimble from my thumb and clasp my hands tightly, guilt hardening my insides.

Ash leans his head on my shoulder as he whispers, "Start here. With Luna." He stabs at the ground with his finger.

My head hangs between my knees. A tear soaking into the dirt. "You think training a Char girl will help me redeem myself?" I'm unsure of my heart.

He knocks my knee with his. "Do you see any other opportunities presenting themselves? This is all you have before you. I think it's a start. All you need to do is choose. Help her or sit there with your hands in your pockets, playing with a thimble that can't bring you any peace. Only more pain."

I gasp at his bluntness.

For someone so small, she creates big noise. Luna crashes through the dark green ferns, stamping down ones that catch her clothes. She waves three fresh fish, tied with a string. "Please, Lye. My brothers, Sun, Joka and Ben Ni, need my help."

Ben Ni.

My eyes lift to Luna's face. Her expression is at war with itself. Flickers of concern and love for her family shine out at me. But then a curtain of blankness and practicality drops over her eyes. Eyes that look familiar. Amber gold.

Ben Ni. The boy who helped me, *twice*, is her brother.

It seems like a sign. A wavering mirage of a sign, but with them staring at me like I hold the key to their happiness, I simply nod.

"Is that a yes?" Ash asks, eyes alight. Too excited for what could be a disaster.

I hold up a hand. "We'll try. It may not work, but we'll try."

53

CHAR LUNA

I flinch when Lye reaches for me and my shoulders shoot up around my ears. "What are you going to do?" I ask, leaning away. Letting a Shen touch my bare skin still feels wrong. I'm reminded of how it felt when Ash crept his fingers over my back, a rush, a relief. But my body was out of my control and in his. Trust brokered that encounter. Can I trust the Keeper?

I focus on my heart. The ins and outs of its mechanical movements. *This is a means to an end. That's all.*

Lightning cracks on the beach jolt us. Night is falling. Soon the sky will turn white and electric.

Unlike Ash, who gave me no warning, Lye talks me through it. With two fingers extended like she's about to take my pulse, she murmurs, "I'm searching your atmosphere and looking for your Pulse." She says these words in a way that suggests they have double meaning.

Ash stares like I'm something peculiar to be studied. An unidentified blob washed up on the beach that you poke with a stick. Lye looks around my head but not directly at it. Following an invisible tell.

"Will it hurt?" I ask.

Picking fish bones from his teeth, Ash mumbles, "This is a first, Luna. We don't know. And the…" He points at my chest.

"Hickory heart?"

"Yes… That may complicate things."

Lye blows an imaginary hair from her forehead and gives her brother an icy glare. "I don't usually do this with commentary, brother. Please let me concentrate."

Her eyes roll and fix on a point through the trees. My ears catch the scratch of a rakka possum, collecting fallen fruit in its curled claws. It's very loud, as if it's right next to me.

"What?" I ask, peering through thickly threaded tree trunks, trying to see what she sees.

"Huh," she manages, still staring.

Ash gathers his hair, tying it with twine. He looks ten times better than he did this morning. Skin glowing. Shen must heal fast. "What does she read as?" he asks.

So many words that don't mean what I think they mean.

Lye's attention is on her fingers and then me. "Luna," she quirks an eyebrow, "you read very strongly of Blood."

Ash laughs. "That *is* a surprise!"

I scowl, feeling like they're speaking a different language. But my heart allows calm. Tells me to simply ask, "Why do you laugh?"

Lye exhales. "Blood is uncommon. It comes to those who are exceptionally warm and caring. People with a great deal of empathy. I myself have little Blood power."

I touch my heart. Feel the slip and cut of the valves. Somehow, the person I was is still in there. She still breathes. Can show herself through layers of hickory and brass.

Eyebrows rise. "Now what?"

Three strikes of lightning crack close together. Glass smashes. The smell of coal as it melts.

Lye taps my temple, scanning my neck. "Now I find your Pulse." She tilts my head the other way, frowning when she doesn't find what she's after. She lifts my chin. "Look to the sky."

I do as she asks, trying not to shrink away from her touch. Trying to find trust, folded between layers of history and hurt.

Quick clouds sweep across the tiny island. Lye huffs. Gasps. And I have no idea what's happening.

"There you are," she whispers with affection like she's just found a puppy hiding from thunder under the bed. And before I can prepare myself, she presses two fingers to my chest. To the thin flesh stretched over bone just above my wooden heart.

I breathe in and forget to breathe out. My eyes are on the stars peeking through the glaze of storm clouds. My mind and body are flooded with images of blood pumping through veins, warm and nourishing. Animal paws pressing leaves underfoot. Imprints of spidery threads woven in the dirt. Welcome sun on thick fur. Strong limbs shaking trees for fruit. It's everything all at once, and it fills me until I think it must be streaming from my fingers, eyes and mouth.

She releases me.

Ash comes closer as Lye shuffles back, chest heaving, exhausted. "Did it hurt?" He inspects me carefully. Nose a breath from mine. Breezy summer voice.

I finally remember to breathe. My heart feels warmer than before, his eyes on me causing conflict. A tug of war between what has been placed inside and what was already there. I frown. Focus on the steady beat. The feeling of connection just at my fingertips.

"No. It didn't hurt. It was just… a lot."

His eyes slide to Lye, who looks pale. "Did it work?"

She nods.

He's a little worried. A little excited. "You've just created the first Shen-Char hybrid!"

Lye straightens, proudness in the way she stacks her bones. "Let's wait and see if she can use the power I've awakened." She sounds doubtful. I'm not. *This has to work.*

THE FIRE has crumbled to ash. Light spreads over the beach, close to the color of the fire pit, freckled gray and white. I yawn loudly. Every time I closed my eyes last night, a whip-like crack forced them open.

Lye sleeps like she's entombed. Legs straight, feet pointing up, one arm crossed over her chest, the other in the folds of her robe. Ash snorts and rolls over, legs twisted in his blanket. Feathery pieces of ash float between us and my eyes go to the sea. Thoughts on family.

I stand and stretch, careful not to step on the glassy beach and nudge Ash in the side with my foot. "Wake up!"

His eyes shoot open and Lye springs up like a spirit separating from a body. I shudder.

Char ships cut through the current, great oars pulling hard. I blink. The sails are down, just a slit of brightest red visible. The black lacquered sides glint like a nightmare in the dawn.

My brothers are aboard one of those ships.

I picture them gripping the sides, dragonhead cannons sliding across the deck with every swell, chains tightening and slackening. They must wonder where I am and why I ran away with the Shen prisoner.

"I did it for you, brothers." I bow my head. A secret prayer on my lips. They would know I had a good reason.

Ash stands beside me, eyes narrowed on the ships. There's something unspoken, lagging on the edge of his mouth, but he pulls it between his teeth. "They head straight for Crow's Nest Island."

I nod.

As they disappear over the endless horizon, something slips inside my chest. I'm starting to recognize it as the shift between wooden heart and real emotion. I catch it before it gets away, but it only causes me pain. It's an ache. I miss them so much already. And I'm deathly afraid for them. They're not ready for battle. Like most of the new soldiers, they're fresh as seedlings. They've not had time to harden and strengthen into true warriors.

I turn to Ash, eyes eager, and he leans away from my enthusiasm. "I'm ready to train. When do we start?"

He smiles with one side of his face. Like the rest of his smile is a secret he's not yet willing to share. "We start with breakfast."

54
SHEN LYE LI

This scrappy girl with a wooden heart and Blood powers of a strength I've never seen is to be my redemption. I watch her doubtfully. Mouth pursed. She stares back, defiant.

"Did you just swallow some sour fruit, Keeper?" She says *Keeper* with distaste. "Lemon lychee too lemony for you?" Her smile is grim.

"Lye," I remind her.

"Lye," she repeats, but I know she thinks Keeper. We have an uneasy alliance and I'm not sure who needs to prove what to whom. But without trust, I can't train her.

"You're small," I observe. A half foot shorter than me but well-muscled.

She kicks another log out of the way, flattening dirt with her feet. The fight circle is rough, but it will do. "I may be small, but I'm fast. Fast and fit." She ties her two plaits together with twine at the base of her neck and puts her fists up. My brother watches her with equal parts captivation and bemusement.

I perch on a log like a bird. "You misunderstand. Being small isn't a disadvantage. In fact, it can be very useful to a Shen warrior.

It means you can get to places others can't. The Shen are taught to use differing sizes and strengths to their advantage."

Luna stalls her attitude, ears tuned to my voice. I direct Ash to stand before me and climb down from my seat.

"Now before we start, I need assurance that you're going to listen to everything I have to say and take instruction, both without question." I walk in a circle around Ash.

Luna frowns. "I've never taken anyone's instruction without question."

Ash snorts and I press a finger to his shoulder, giving him a sharp zap. He flinches. Arms tensing. Eyes narrowed.

"So how do we come to a place of trust?" I ask both of them. It's a laughable question when so much of my training came from a place of fear. But the trainer who had a lasting effect balanced trust on the end of his fighting pole—shifu Che Lu. My lip curls briefly. I will never forget his kindness.

Luna sighs. Ash shifts from foot to foot.

"You ask me to trust the person who hatched a plan to destroy my people?"

I nod. I don't know how to prove that I'm not that person anymore. "I do. It is the only way."

Then Ash faces Luna. "Do you trust *me*?" he asks. The question is weighted. Unspoken desires flatten between the words.

She studies his face, scrunches her eyes and taps her heart. "I guess." Their eyes connect and she tips her head, seeming confused by the lure. "Yes. Yes, I do trust you."

"Well then." He claps his hands together loudly and birds tangle wings as they rise from their nests. Luna's eyes clip to the noise. Her awareness of living creatures is heightening. "I trust my sister completely. So, if you trust me then you must trust her. Settled." He crosses his arms over his chest, satisfied. His logic can be so linear.

"It's not that simple." Luna chews on her lip, wary.

"I think I know how," I murmur. "The swiftest and most effective way to kill a Shen is by attacking their Pulse. And in my case, it is one of the only ways to defeat me."

Ash shakes his head. "Lye, no. Not even I know where your Pulse is."

I bow my head talking to the earth. "I know, brother." I shake at the idea of this secret that reveals my true vulnerability. But I lift my head and beckon Luna closer. She leans in until her ear almost touches my lips. I whisper the location of my Pulse.

She pulls away. Eyes serious and appreciative. I have given her the key to my death. Luna takes a fighting stance, legs parted, fists up. "Okay, so let's get to it."

My brother and I laugh. It hurts like I've regurgitated a large bubble.

I put a hand to my forehead. "First you must learn entry points. Elemental fighting is half anatomy, half opportunity."

She arches an eyebrow, listening. Ash opens his big mouth. "Yes. It's finesse fighting. Not like the Char, clubbing things with wooden appendages and hoping for the best."

Luna sweeps out her leg swiftly, knocking him off his feet. He lands on his back with a hard thump. His hand reaches for her ankle in retaliation and I choke back a giggle. "No talking." I loom over my brother. "You might as well stay there now. You can be my dummy."

"It suits him," Luna mutters as we kneel beside Ash.

Overhead, blue spiker birds listen intently, spiny crests nodding along to my instruction. As Luna's mind opens to her Element, to the blood pumping through every living creature, the birds shuffle closer, claw over claw.

I instruct, demonstrate, and correct as she quickly absorbs the information. It comes far too easily, like it's her birthright. Not some idea she had just days earlier.

"Okay, show me the heart path," I ask. Ash crosses his legs casually and folds his hands under his head, an unborn smirk growing.

Instantly, she points to the two pulse points on either side of Ash's neck.

"The stomach path?"

She points to a place just left of his navel.

"Legs? Kidneys?"

She points to spots on each hip. And then eases him to the side so she can climb his ribs and press in the right place for kidneys.

"And lungs?"

With a bored sigh, she points that out correctly too. "I feel like I'm back at school."

Ash shuffles to his elbows. "Looks like she's got it. Can we get to the fun part now?"

I nod, reluctant. It's dangerous, but we don't have much time.

Luna offers a hand to Ash, helping him up. "What do I do?" she asks.

I wave a finger at them. "You can't get distracted."

I place Ash's wrist in Luna's fingers.

"Close your eyes." She closes them, Ash watching intently. "Think of your Element, however it comes to you. It can be any animal, even a worm and any part of that animal, claws, feathers, or slimy skin." She screws up her mouth at that. Ash smiles adoringly at her reaction and I worry.

"An animal." She cocks her head. "Um... a heart bird. The wings of a heart bird."

"Okay, good. Now picture that wing fanning out and each individual feather stretching from the tips of your fingers and into Ash's veins." Ash's arm tenses.

"I can feel it," she whispers with a serene expression.

Ash's arm jerks suddenly and he chuckles. Pulling away from Luna, he rubs his skin. "Oh, that tickles."

"What happened?" I ask both of them.

Luna answers first. "I did what you said, I pictured the wings spreading open and feathers clogging up his veins. I pushed them through. I was trying to control them but..."

Ash calms and says, "It was more like being brushed with a petal."

I frown. "You have to have some control, of course. But these are elements. You have to let go. Let nature take over."

Luna looks down at her hands and back up at me. "Let go?"

I nod. "Yes. Let go of your emotions and the element will work through you."

We try again.

And again.

Ash gets slapped for laughing and we try again.

This inability makes no sense. I saw the size of Luna's power. She should be able to send strangling spider's webs straight to his heart with ease.

She glances at her chest, small brass spokes poking out just below her collar. "It's my heart."

I nod. Understanding passing between us. Because I know what it is to shut off your emotions. I also understand the fear of turning that wheel, opening the floodgates, and drowning.

55

CHAR LUNA

Our first day was frustrating. My heart is a foal learning everything for the first time. Stumbling. Galloping ahead. Falling.

I rub my sternum; the polished wood feels warm to the touch. It's a part of me. It may be the worst part. But no one misses their old part. No one. I think of Joka with his bamboo neck. The way he'd calm himself just by touching it. I don't feel that way. I touch it because every time I can't quite name the feeling, every time I feel like something is off, I remind myself why.

I ache for my heart.

I ache for something that doesn't exist.

"What are you thinking about, Luna?" Lye asks, head tipped to the side curiously as we collect firewood and fruit.

I pluck a lychee and smile sadly. "My brothers. Joka's the smart one. Smart but fearful. I worry he'll get into trouble by panicking at the sight of danger. Sun will be okay if the fight is clean and simple. But he won't foresee an unorthodox attack." I rub my arms, a sickening feeling crawling over my skin when I think of them in battle. How quickly it could all be over.

Lye smiles wistfully. "Ash is the opposite. He only thinks *outside* of what he's been taught. It can be a strength, but it also makes him take unnecessary risks."

I can see that.

"Oh, and Ben Ni. He's so young. So naive. He's the dreamer. One day, he'll invent something that will change the world. But in battle this is a liability. Compassion will get him killed." Something hurts, a splinter driven outward from heart to skin. "I wish they could be everything. Not just one strength each and so many weaknesses."

I wish I were with them now. Together maybe we'd stand half a chance.

"We get one gift, one strength, if we're lucky. To ask for more is greedy." Her expression wavers from serene to anger swiftly like the flap of a wing. She lifts her chin to the sky. "And compassion is never a bad thing."

Her words stab at the place where my heart once was. It can't pierce it. Which may be the saddest truth of all.

We walk the path to camp, Lye floating like a ghost and me trudging heavier than a troll. "And you, Luna. Where do you fit into your family?"

Me. "I used to be the one who kept them all together. I could usually tell when one was upset or struggling, and I would do what I could to help."

Lye turns, eyes crystal-like. "You were the heart."

I nod. "And now I am nothing."

Lye frowns at this. "Look. I don't claim to understand much about the way Char magic works, but I do understand a little of how the heart works."

She's only a year or two older but seems ancient. Worn in places but wise.

"Your heart and your head are inextricably linked. Your heart doesn't do all the feeling for you. It sends emotional signals to your brain and vice versa. One reinforces the other. Say you're frightened. Your heart beats fast and painful in your chest from adrenalin. It works with your brain to come to that emotion." Her eyes wander. "It's just a theory, but I'm guessing your feelings, your heart of hearts, is still in there. You just have to learn how to feel around the wooden part. You also have to allow it."

I smile a broken smile. "The Carvress said something very similar to me."

"Wise woman."

Ash is building a shelter with umbrella plants. He looks sturdier, healthier. Fire bronzes his already dark skin. Things peel back around my heart. A window opening, letting in the slightest sea breeze. "I'm scared it will make me weaker. That letting go could be a mistake."

Lye's eyes are on Ash. "Or it could make you stronger. Love does that. It makes you capable of things you never thought possible."

I tense. "My priority is my brothers." That is where my heart of hearts must lie.

"Hm." She tips her chin and steps into the firelight. "I can help you if you let me."

LIGHTNING MIRRORS the inside of my head as I contemplate what Lye said about what I must try to do. The opposite of what I've been doing. Whenever I've felt an opening, an emotion pushing its way out, I stamped on it. Unless it served me.

Letting go means releasing everything, and I fear there's a huge pile of crushed-flat emotions just waiting to be set free. The blood warm connection to creatures around me, to life, flows through my senses and wishes to take me over. And I want to let it. I *need* to.

Flashes of the brother and sister huddled together through the night make me miss my family. The drawbridge winds up over emotion but instead of letting it close, I jam my foot in the gap. I let feelings of separation and loss swirl around my brain. I clutch my ears. It hurts. And I want, *I want, I want,* to let the bridge slam shut. But I grit my teeth and keep it open.

A real tear born of feeling, not physical pain, runs down my cheek. Then another. I hold my throat. It feels scraped raw and I make a choking sound. Lightning cracks. One. Two. Three. Four. Tears in the fabric of the sky.

A hand takes mine. Warm and blistered.

I should pull away. Instead, I let him bring me closer.

His eyes show no mockery. They crinkle in a small, tender smile of understanding. He knows this pain. I heard him cry out. I shuddered at his emotion, repulsed. I shudder now in shame of my judgment.

It builds like a dam just aching to break. Tears roll on tears, my heart hiccups in my chest and an exquisite white-hot ache sits just below my throat.

I cry out for the unfairness of it all. For the battle we're about to face. For not having enough time to learn what must be learned. For my brothers, sailing to Crow's Nest, brave and nervous and wondering where I am.

Ash smooths my hair from my face. Cradles me in arms that were chained and weak. Barely thicker than my own. But I feel comforted. I feel safe.

I feel.

As the sun rises in his eyes, I understand this isn't weakness.

My heart protests. Thumping like persistent wind against sails.

This can't be weakness. Because love, comfort, family, and safety are strengths. They are what we fight for.

56
SHEN LYE LI

Wick spiders busily re-build their hive. They poke their pearl white heads out of holes in the thickly layered web, blink at the sun, and disappear. Their hive drips like wax down the trunk of the palm tree. They're careful, frightful little creatures. But determined. The rain fills their nest at night; they bail it out every morning and rebuild the broken parts. It's a pattern they're stuck in. A stubborn hope. That one day it will stop raining.

I roll my shoulders and breathe hollow, cool breaths. Back no longer warmed by my kin. I heard her heaving sobs. I woke Ash and told him to go to her. He whispered comfort to her confused mutterings. She was like a firework that couldn't quite explode. Lighting. Dying. Lighting. Dying. But once he embraced her, the fuse lit.

My shoulders tense and I roll them again. The responsibility for her suffering weighs heavily on my heart.

BALANCED ON the log, I watch the Shen boy and Char girl dance around each other, feet digging in the dirt. Reactions fast but aimless. I slap a frustrated hand on my thigh. "Ash! You must remember. Now, you're fighting Shen power against Shen power. It's not what you've trained for. Luna. Take it slow. Think of simple things that can conquer water. It will do you no good to fight a murder bird against a river."

She stops all motion, hands at her sides, frowning like a child who wants her turn. "But how will I know what he's chosen?"

Ash smacks her hands. "Hands up! Don't lower your defenses while you're thinking about what to do next," he says through pants. He bounces from foot to foot, careful of her space, holding back.

She fakes a punch and slides her foot under his, tripping him. He lands on his bottom with a thud when he shouldn't. "And you, brother, need to stop treating her like she'll break. She's far more skilled than you give her credit for." For this to work she must be pushed. *Push her to the limit!* The chancellor's voice rings in my ears as I remember the tip of his staff punching my stomach over and over. I suck my lip between my teeth. I will not step over that line.

Luna hovers over his rising and falling chest, awaiting instruction. Spiker birds crow shrilly, hurting my ears. Like metal drilling into rock. "The only way to know what he's chosen is to touch him. The tattoo is your first clue. You'll know whether they're Water, Fire, Earth, Air, or Blood. Shen power is instinctual and reactionary. You'll need many defenses in your repertoire." I urge her to touch him.

Gingerly, she reaches for his neck with two fingers. She blinks. Fights for air and falls to the side. Ash releases her shoulder, expression resonating loudly with alarm. He curses and cups her face. "Luna?" He directs anger my way, for telling him not to hold back.

"What did you do?" I ask, not fearful. Curious.

"Snap freeze. Up her shoulder and into her head."

She rolls to her side and jumps up. Recovering impressively fast. Fists up, a tiny mongrel, she murmurs low and dark, "That gave me a slight headache." Her scrunched eyes tell me it was more than slight. I'm impressed by her stoicism.

Ash tips his head to the side and grins. "Slight?" I know my brother. He'll take it as a challenge. And I'm starting to understand Luna. She meant it as one.

I clap my hands. "Again!"

There's no way to learn elementals without trial and error. To some, it will come naturally. To others, it takes years of practice. Luna is the former. Ash, the latter.

They match now. But she will overtake him.

Right now, Luna's only reacting, not attacking. Leaves smack together in a misting rain. An audience for a first in our history. And, I hope, a last. I step off the log and pace around them. I tap Ash's shoulder. "Ash, announce your plan of attack. And Luna, I want to hear your planned response."

They draw circles in the mud. Ash lunges, tapping her elbow. "Hailstorm," he whispers.

Luna's arm jiggles as small balls of ice travel up her veins. She grits her teeth and grabs his wrist, yanking him forward. Touching his temple, she says, "Er, turtle shell...?"

"That *shields* you," I say, hands behind my back. Their atmosphere is a cloudy mix of warmth and tension, brewing like a tropical storm. "What *stops* him?"

They spar comfortably, hands jutting out to slap and send waves of elements through each other's bodies. "Narwhal cut," she whispers as she presses her palm to his heart. The hail bounces off the back of the whale and the horn, designed to cut through ice, breaks open his attack. His body goes rigid and she pulls back.

Moving his hands in a circular motion, he stumbles slightly, takes a deep strengthening breath and runs at her, slipping a hand to her hip as he passes. "Flood."

Her legs turn to jelly and her knees buckle, then she straightens, lunges, and whispers, "Bee stings," touching his stomach.

I reach between them but I'm too late. She mixed bees with flood, drowning her insects and sending them scraping up her own veins, stinging as they go. She cries out and Ash has the sense to retreat before it gets worse.

She falls heavily. I drop to my knees and touch her cheek, shaking my head at my pitiful teaching, but I'm trying to do this with gentle encouragement, not with violence and threat. It is unfamiliar. I push embers into her veins, burning the bees and evaporating the water.

She coughs hard and sits up. "That felt like I'd swallowed a cupful of tacks." She pounds her chest.

Ash rubs her back soothingly. Their atmosphere changes like a sun trying to warm the shady side of a planet. It always turns away from the heat. Wanting the light but fighting against it at the same time.

"Sometimes the combination of elements can prove dangerous to both. It's a delicate balance." *Like a Char and a Shen building a relationship.*

She crosses her arms over her chest. "It's nonsensical." But she lets Ash help her up and they take position. She's determined to learn. I need to feed off her enthusiasm and be more determined to teach.

The sun arcs over our heads as the partners scratch a strange love story in the dirt. Atmospheres clash like pressure systems. I look to the sky for some relief, as I watch my brother falling in love with Luna, and Luna trying to love him halfway and failing.

57
CHAR LUNA

A wooden limb is something you can see. Something you can feel. It doesn't change shape or leave your body in waves or claws. It's simple *I miss simple.*

We tramp toward the training circle again, wet grass lashing our legs. My slippers are soggy and smelly. All of me is soggy and smelly. I huff with aching joints and a new ache I barely understand. From days of having my body filled with ice, water, hail. My veins are stretched and thin. At least my heart pumps strong and steady, no matter what Ash throws at me, *into* me. I touch my chest. He's relentless in his attacks. But there's a new twist to his regard. A twist of bright blue in his eyes that wasn't there before. A warmth spreads in my chest. Something opening. Unfolding. Something foreign.

Ash lifts a branch and lets me pass under the arch of his arm. "Why do you always do that?"

My hand falls. "Do what?"

He places his hand over his flesh heart and a small, jealous spike splinters from my wooden one. "Put your hand over your heart."

Shrugging, I turn inward. "I think it's because I need reminding. I need to remind myself that it's there and to feel around it." I rub my arms, a sudden chill giving me goosebumps.

"And why would you need to remind yourself right now?" he asks, turning to face me, sweet lemon-scented breath mixing with mine.

I step back, squelching the mud, aware of Lye just ahead. I blush like the underside of a sunset cloud.

Still close, broad shoulders hiding me from Lye's view, he leans down and whispers, lips dusting my ear, "Blood and Water are the hardest foes. You know why?"

I feel even smaller than I am, like the ground is sinking into stairs below my feet to the earth's core. "Why?" I whisper, soft as the lamb's ear weeds I've just crushed under my slipper.

"Blood *needs* water." He strolls away, whistling.

Blood needs water. Blood is made of water.

Lye shouts, impatient. "C'mon you two."

LYE SWAYS like a languid slip of water reed. A plant easily misjudged as weak, but is instead strong, flexible, and very hard to break.

Her brow creases, a strange swap for her usually serene expression. "Now, bear with me, it's been a while since I've sparred."

Ash cups his hands around his mouth and shouts, "Go easy on her, sister."

I blow a stray hair from my forehead and take up stance. "*Don't* go easy on me, Lye. Shen warriors won't."

She nods and breathes in like she's filling her lungs with all the air. Composing all the bad things she's going to do to me. Then she stills. No stance, no fists up, or legs back. She stands straight and tall. She looks…at peace.

I blink to conjure up the image of a strangling python and aim my touch at her stomach. The moment I touch her, my python's mouth is full of oil fire flames. It bucks, curling and fading to gray.

"Fire," she says calmly, "is the most common element in the Shen army. It's what you'll face more than any other. Sending animals sensitive to fire won't work."

I purse my lips. *Aren't all animals sensitive to fire?*

She twirls in a graceful arc, one arm up, the other across her middle.

I run through possibilities and come at her with octopus tentacles, poisoned and thick. Many arms reaching to suffocate. She snuffs them out. Roasting with oven fire, the tentacles become rubbery and useless. Then she's cutting through the air in a dance that's as distracting as it is beautiful. One hand to the sky, the other on her hip. Her foot pressed into her upper thigh. She sighs and it sounds like a black crane's wings warming up to flight. "Try again."

Kicking, I try to knock her off balance. She barely moves. I come close and slap at her leg, sending a plague of locusts through her calf. She wobbles but her power is precise and soon the locusts are dust. "That would've worked on a less experienced Shen. You must think and fight clever. Don't put physical energy into your attack. Put all of your energy into thought." She taps the side of her head.

Bouncing back, I jump from foot to foot, stalling. I kick her leg hard and she falls forward. Grasping her head, I push fire ants into her throat. They burn and bite instantly and it surprises her enough to push her off balance. They're so small that even when she aims fireballs at them, she misses. They start to take over.

She holds her throat and I pull back. Scared I've hurt her.

Her gaze dips to her feet and then lifts. A smile, wide and bright as a half-moon. She laughs, placing a hand on my shoulder. It stings briefly but then it's like fresh air pulsing into my skin.

Ash quiets, an expression somewhere between pride and shock.

"She beat you," he says in disbelief.

Lye laughs louder, a tinker like brass cowbells. "She most certainly did!" Her face is light with mirth, but her stance prepares. "Let's see if she can do it again." A veil of toughness draws over us. In bout after bout, I learn my responses to fire. I learn that I know them before I even think them.

The location of her Pulse remains a secret I will never use against her. It is wrapped in the furs and feathers she gifted me.

She has earned my trust. She has taught me well.

58
CHAR LUNA

Two full moons have passed over Coalstone Village. I miss the creak and the crack of home. Papa's oak hand, heavy on my shoulder. Kitchen steam carrying scents of salty pork and sweet dough. I stare down at my filthy clothes. The only thing I smell right now is my own stench.

The moon hits the water and skittles across in whites and navy blues. I stand abruptly, startling the siblings. "I'm going for a swim," I announce.

Lye's mouth pulls down, grim. "It's too dangerous."

I lift my arms, releasing more stink. "So are my armpits."

They both let out a short laugh, Ash's longer than Lye's. She nods. Though I don't know when she became the captain of this trio. "Fine, but Ash will go with you."

Something unfamiliar bounces in my chest and I try to not let it slip away like an untied anchor. "But I, uh, want to bathe."

Ash jumps up next to me as smoke glides over the fire and into our eyes. He points to the surf. "I promise I won't look." His dark, unreadable eyes mirror the night.

I groan. "Lye, you can swim." I point. "Why don't you come with me?"

"I'm very tired, Luna." Her voice wavers between steel and feather.

"Fine."

We hug the jungle, pass the broken glass beach, and climb over some rocky outcrops to a small, sheltered bay. The moment I see real sand, I throw my slippers from my feet and jump down, toes sinking deliciously into the mud.

A bubble of breath escapes as I release some of my aching.

Ash chuckles, a heart-deep sound. "If I'd known all you needed was a bath to improve your mood, I would have suggested it days ago."

Standing on the outcrop, he's just a shadow against the midnight-blue sky. "To be honest, Shen boy, I'm just thankful to have a mood at all." I knock my chest with my fist, the sound like rapping knuckles on a door. "It means I'm making progress."

He lands solidly on the sand. These weeks on the island have been good to him. With food, water, and exercise, his tone is returning.

My eyes fall to my feet. "Turn around."

He crosses his arms and turns. "This reminds me of our time in the monastery. Turning around while you undressed." I strip down to my underclothes and pull my hair free of its bands. It's crimped like tidemarks, rippling down my shoulders to my waist. Cheekily he adds, "And I promise I never peeked.... Well, maybe once."

I shove his back. We are not Air, but stormy electricity crackles between us. The cool air ruffling my bare skin invigorates me. Excites me. Lightning flashes on the glass beach behind the rocks, and Ash tenses, ducking. I have the urge to trace the dip between his shoulder blades, softly undulating like unbroken waves. I reach out. Pull back. "Count to ten and then turn around," I order.

I run for the water with the truest smile.

"Are you sure this beach is safe?" he shouts. Another two cracks.

"Do you see any glass?" The waves smack my legs as I wade in, warm water pulling the dirt away gratefully. I plunge my clothes into the salt water.

"...eight—No, I guess not—nine, ten." Ash turns to the sea and I sink below water level, just my head and neck showing, hair pooling around my shoulders like an oil spill.

He searches for me, running to the edge of the water. "Luna!" he calls. I wave and he relaxes.

I point to a rock, loving the sound of water swishing over my arms. "Climb up there."

He shuffles nervously into ankle-deep water, and I giggle as he climbs quickly up the mound of rock. Acting like the sea burns his skin.

I swim towards him, kicking frog-like. Lightning adds slices of light to our night and I see Ash's expression in pieces as I approach. His eyebrows arch, a contemplative smile. Squatting like an old fisherman but not looking as comfortable as one. "Maybe one day you could teach me how to swim." He looks beyond the bay. We live in words like *maybe*. With war closing in on us from every side, *maybe* is the closest we come to a promise.

I hold the edge of rock, moving with the swell. "Maybe."

Scrubbing my clothes with sand until they're clean, I throw them on the rock. They slap loudly and Ash jumps, slipping. His panic is adorable. Fingers spread wide, clinging.

I can just touch the bottom, but I prefer to bring my legs to my chest and float like a barrel. I lay my head back and let my hair spread like crow's wings. Ash speaks but my ears are full of water.

I lift my head, the weight of my hair pulling me down. "What did you say?"

He presses his hands to the rock on either side, gingerly stretching his legs and letting them dip into the water. "Nothing. I didn't say anything."

I narrow my eyes and sink, bubbles of air coming from my mouth. When I pop back up, I splash him. He reacts offended and shocked as if I've thrown horse dung at him. I laugh harder. It feels good.

I offer him my hands. "You don't need to be afraid." I point a toe to the sand, checking. "If I can touch the bottom, the water will only be up to your chest."

The lightning is only seconds apart, painting a disjointed picture. He's doubtful, feet bobbing with the waves. But there's something else in his expression, his gaze blanketing me in sunlight.

He takes my hands and enters the water, making all sorts of ridiculous noises about it being cold. His fingers dig into my forearms and as the lightning flashes again, I try to catch his eyes to calm him. "I've got you," I say slowly, and the words mean more than they should. His face relaxes, a deep breath swelling his chest.

I pull him with me. "No!" His fingernails scratch my skin. "No. No. No."

I roll my eyes. "Put your feet down." He does as I instruct, but his grip is tight. He pulls my elbows into his hands and strokes my skin. When a wave rises, he pinches me. The water makes him uncomfortable and unsure. "How can a Water Shen be afraid of the water?"

"I'm not afraid. I'm giving it the respect it deserves." He grumbles but only half means it. He releases one of my elbows but keeps a tight hold on the other, pulling his shirt over his head with a sharp tug. White light flashes over his torso for a moment, and though my heart struggles to feel, it doesn't shy away from appreciating the line of his frame. I blink and look away. Uncertain of how I'm supposed to feel and how I should behave.

He drops his shirt and as he goes to retrieve it, my hickory heart scrapes against his chest. I know he felt it. Laughing awkwardly, he pulls back, staring at my sternum, the brass spokes of the Carvress's mark catching the lightning. "Sorry. I don't think I've got my sea legs yet."

"That's for being on a ship." I smirk. His eyes rest on my chest. He reaches for me, palm out. I freeze. "What are you...?"

Water laps and lightning sparks. Light spreads over the waves. "Can I?" he asks, eyes lifting.

I breathe in and hold. Nodding. Not sure why I'm nodding.

Ash's hand lands on my chest light as a moth. Tentatively at first, but when I don't jerk away, his fingers trace the wood that spreads to the beginnings of my ribs. They run around the circle sun of the Carvress's mark. He barely breathes himself. This moment feels held in itself. Separate from time and space. My heart beats steady when it shouldn't. Warmth spreads everywhere else. I bite my lip. We are inches apart.

He lingers, skin on brass and water between. "Does it rust?"

I shake my head.

"Does is hurt?"

I nod. "Sometimes."

"What's it doing now?" His hand moves upward, leaving the hickory and caressing my neck, coming to rest at my jaw. His eyes are storm clouds over water.

I swallow. Feeling the moment shift and try to slip beyond my reach. I catch it. *Hold* it. I dig my toes into the sand and step closer. Heat growing, white and painful. Soft and breaking.

I place both hands on his shoulders. A thousand heartbeats pulsing at my fingertips. I am a hickory heart and learning feelings. Fangs and fur. Blood and bone.

Rising to my tiptoes, I press my lips to his. His breath draws in. His mouth is salty, rough and careful. His hands move to my back as the water rises, lifting me from my feet. We crash together. Hurt each other. Want each other.

I open to the possibility of him. Scramble and hold. Push and pull.

Reluctantly, our lips part while white light shatters across the water. I lean back. Watch his chest expand with deep breaths. I almost hear the beat of his heart. His real heart.

This would be the time to stop.

He catches himself. Tries to slow. But his arms are hungry for my skin. His fingers beat rhythms over my back. "Why do you hesitate?" he asks, concerned.

Because my heart does nothing. It should be racing. My body fights it. Tingling warmth extends over my limbs. But my heart. *My heart.* It beats out the same tired song. My head falls. My eyes close.

I'm worried this won't feel real.

I drag my hands down his chest to the beating chambers nestled between his lungs. A need to be closer blooms in my stomach. I'll borrow his heart. Just for one night.

It may not feel real, but it will feel good.

Ash strokes my cheek and I lean into his palm. "Luna?"

I answer him by pressing closer. By letting my underclothes float gently to the ocean bed like cut seaweed. Wood scrapes on skin. Heart steady. Breath held.

Eyes full, his hands run from shoulder to hip. His lip between his teeth. He seems... blessed by the sight of me.

The water nudges me into him. I kiss him stronger. Drowning in the goodness of physical feeling. Ignoring the pain.

He takes me at my actions and lifts me up.

The water hides us. Holds us. If this is love, I don't know it. But I like being this close to him. I like the heat of his skin, the strength of his grasp.

I surrender to it.

As we move closer to being one, I throw my head back to take in the cool, sweet air and connect with the endless stars. Char legends frozen in burning light. They tell of love. Of tradition. Of hearts that move and change.

Something cracks: A fissure opens and hurts.

"Stop." I push against his chest. His confusion, his devastation, would be heartbreaking if I had a heart that could break.

The lapping water against our naked skin is as loud as thunder.

"Did I do something wrong?" he asks, too close. Too open and bare.

"No. I did," I whisper.

Clasping my undergarments to my chest, I run from the water. Leaving him wondering. Waiting for an answer, a reason.

The reason: He deserves better.

And, so do I.

Ash catches my arm as I shrug on my shirt. Dripping wet with a lost look. I hurt him.

"Please." I try to pull away, but he gently holds tight. "Please. This isn't the way. Can we just put this aside? Forget it happened..."

His mouth flattens. "I can't do that."

My eyes scream all the things I can't say: Give me more time. When this happens, I want to be completely in it. I want to *feel* all of it. I think I could love you, but I'm not there yet.

He releases me suddenly. "You think I ruined you," he states.

I hold my stupid heart. "I was already ruined."

It's what I'm trying to repair.

59
SHEN LYE LI

Time ticks down to battle. We've sheltered on this lightning charred island long enough. Days have slid past recognition easily these last few weeks, but my heart tells me it's close. I picture Shen ships parting ways like the split end of a hair. The sea cuts under their bows, sending ripples out to every Char island.

I turn away from my sleeping companions and press the thimble into my arm. Five punctures for five boats. Dots of blood bubble like sap on grazed bark. It comforts me in a sick way. A dark way. When one has no control, they snatch it up where they can.

Ash yawns, stretches, and I spin around. Our eyes connect. I don't need to say it. He begins packing our things.

"What's happening?" Luna asks as she rolls from her bed and threads her fingers through her hair to plait it.

Ash looks upon her tiny frame with longing and a new expression. Like it hurts him to want her. "If we're to get there before the battle begins, we need to leave now."

"What about training?" Luna asks. "There's still so much to learn." Her red, watery eyes bug out with desperate enthusiasm.

Probably only a year or two between us but I feel half a century older.

I laugh like the wind catching a leaf, loose and shaky. "We'll continue on the boat and when we get there." Though I feel she's already well on her way. Like me, she's naturally gifted. It is a curse as much as a strength.

She springs up like a tight coil. Hair like seaweed and briny with salt. Ash's eyes float on a sea of affection and my heart hurts for his choice. "It's a day's hard rowing at least. We should collect food."

She stomps past me and I catch her sleeve. "Wait." She stops still, slight fear rising in her atmosphere like a wolf's ruff. I try arranging my features to look less stern, attempt a smile. Ash laughs and I shoot him a warning look. "Luna, let me show you a trick."

I accompany her into the forest. We've picked the lemon lychee tree near camp clean. I place my hand on its trunk and she does the same. "What're we doing?" she mumbles.

We face each other, the slip and the spring. "What eats lemon lychees exclusively?"

Brows knotted, she replies, "Spiker birds... but..." and then, "Oh!"

"Can you feel their energy? They have a signature. You can use it to find more of the same."

Her pursed lips and the way she grips the trunk concerns me. Knuckles white, arm shaking. My mouth falls open as a flock of spiker birds fight for space in the branches of the tree, eyes bright and waiting.

"Luna!"

Her eyes snap open and the birds startle, flapping away as fast as they arrived. They cloud the sky and return to the forest about a hundred feet away.

She gazes at me innocently. "What? Did I do something wrong?"

I wave my hand. Full of wonder and trepidation. She is not like me. She is something else entirely, and I shudder to think what the chancellor and the emperor would do if they got their manicured hands on her. "No. Not at all. You just looked a little stressed."

She releases the tree and points north. "Oh. I sense a flock of spiker birds. They're pecking at the skins of lemon lychees a hundred paces away." She frowns at her new power. "We better hurry before they're all gone."

THE WIND off the water is cold. It bounces from island to island loudly. Calling out like a lost child. My student and my brother, who looks more like himself, color rising in his cheeks like a fanned fire, face each other.

Luna swivels like a hawk and sniffs the air. "I think we can use the sails. We're coming at Crow's Nest from the opposite direction of the Char invasion."

We hoist the sails, wind catching and jerking the small boat sideways. I clutch my stomach, unused to the rise and fall of the jelly-like sea. My brother seems unfazed by the movement.

"How is it that you're not sick?"

He grins. "I'm just more adaptable than you, older sister." But then he shivers in Luna's direction. "Can you send fluffy rabbits to warm me up?" He rubs his shoulders and trembles exaggeratedly and they let out a laugh that peters to a tattered sigh.

There's shyness to their interactions now. Something has passed between them that I missed. And it makes me feel isolated and above.

"How about some fire ants? That'd warm you right up!" Luna snaps with half strength jaws.

Their humor throttles my heart. This is not a game. I know the depths to which these Shen will sink. I was right there with them. I'm not even part way to clawing my way out. I twist the rudder suddenly, the boat turning half a circle.

"Don't joke!" My voice cracks a little. "What we're doing is dangerous." The wind moans unhappily in my ears, and I pull my hood over my thinly covered head. I've done this too many times. Each awakening, each "training" session with the chancellor pulled a little more from me. A small sliver of rib. A fragment of scapula. Scraping by scraping until I felt like I was held together by a lattice of honeycomb bone. In the past, my reaction to any insubordination would have been a sharp crack of lightning to the throat. Or a wind that felt like it was sucking the skin from your body. This needs to be different.

I take a deep breath and push patience into my tone. "Luna. Think about disarming Ash."

Ash glares out to sea. "That wouldn't be hard."

I continue, "Say he's holding a knife and you want him to release it. What could you do?"

The boat rocks sickeningly, hugging the water and rising with the swell.

Ash puts his hand up. "Um. Am I allowed to fight back today or am I just a guinea pig to be prodded, bitten, and scratched?"

My mouth twists, a bite of humor in my words. "Definitely guinea pig."

"Seems about right," he mutters, but he takes a knife-wielding position. Luna smacks his wrist hard. His hand splays open. "Ouch!"

I chuckle. "Well, that's one way to do it. What if you're facing a much larger, less starved opponent? His grip won't loosen so easily. And the Shen will have their defenses up. They'll shock you or burn you the moment you touch them if you haven't got your element prepared."

Luna nods. Tries again. She finds his ulnar pulse and presses lightly. She withdraws quickly when his arm goes leaden and drops to his side. Ash cries out.

She shuffles back, hitting the side of the boat. "What did you do?" I ask calmly.

She gazes at her hands. "I, uh, I thought of a termite, how it works its way into a building and weakens it from the inside, making the beams hollow and unsupportive."

Ash shakes his arm and it responds loosely. "Well, it certainly felt like that. Like my bones were disintegrating."

Luna taps her chest, swallows and scrunches her face with effort. "I didn't know I could make that kind of impact," she says, perplexed. "Will he be all right?" Her eyes buzz like bees reluctant to alight.

I cluck my tongue. "He'll be fine. It's temporary unless you hold for longer. The longer you hold, the more deadly your power becomes."

"How long is too long?" Luna asks eagerly, but also with apprehension. It is good that she cares to know the difference.

"It depends on your opponent, their strength. It's really something you can only sense when in the fight. With Ash, well..." I tap my chin.

Ash coughs. "Ahem! I know I'm just the guinea pig today but I'm still here. You can't just speak for me like I'm not here."

Luna glances at Ash, brief color swimming across her cheeks like a swarm of blood fish. "I'm sorry." She bows low.

He sweeps a hand through his hair, eyes brimful of things I don't understand. *May never understand.* "That much I know, Luna."

Salt air crusts my lungs. I don't know how I feel about the connection between them. I'm not sure I get to have an opinion on it anyway. Maybe this is what war does—speeds things up, pushes bridges to be built in half the time because they're at risk to be destroyed. Time is running out. Love is the seconds by which it's counted.

I right the rudder. The sails billow, red as robins' breasts, and we thread through the water like silk through a dancer's hands.

Ash plunges his hands in the water and Luna looks at the sky. One born of the sea and one made of it. They both say the foreboding word at the same time.

"Storm."

60
CHAR LUNA

I'm a hundred-foot scroll rolled the wrong way. I must take time to unroll carefully and roll up the right way. I was learning to crush my emotions. Now I must unlearn. Un-crush. Undo.

Lye is a strange teacher. She doesn't bark and intimidate like Fah or the other captains. Her very presence is enough. She suggests and coaxes but she also shrewdly observes. It is hard to think of her as the "before" creature. The person who thought to steal a Carvress. I know I should fear her, but I sense nothing but regret and redemption. Although her eyes do splash between me and Ash like she's half a second away from intervening. If she finds out what I did, perhaps the ruthless, terrible Keeper will emerge and spark me to dust.

And Ash. Ash is making it hard to roll the scroll the right way. He steps on it, sends ruffles through it that twist and tangle the paper. He makes me want to speed through a slow task.

Ash is impossible.

Ash is too much.

Ash is becoming a need in the back of my head. A hot coal hidden under grey powder. Mistaken for dead, it will burn to touch.

His eyes scald me with a curtained, bewildered stare. His mouth threatens to undo me with the unfinished-ness waiting there.

Lye grips the side, turning green.

Clouds reel in, blotting the sun. The islands darken to shadows. We're midway to Crow's Nest. The sails flap violently as the wind changes its mind. I bite my lip. Heavy rain pelts the sea and begins filling the boat. I sit beside Ash and we try to row against the changing current.

Ash faces me, water turning his hair to thick ropes hanging over his forehead. "What do we do, captain?" He smiles but it's more of a grimace as he pulls the oar through choppy water and it doesn't cut.

The boom swings in the wild wind. I duck but it grazes the back of my neck. I cry out in pain, grabbing my head. Locking the oar in place, Ash lunges, eyes full of worry. He grasps the wayward sail, holding it with both hands as it fights against him like a fish straining against a line. Waterfalls pour down our faces as he murmurs, "Are you hurt?" Heat and heart in his voice.

I inspect my hand—no blood. I shake my head. "I'm fine."

We battle the sail and get it down. His hand touches mine. Not in an *I'll heal you* way, or an *I'll comfort you* way. It's more of a belonging way. Which frightens me more than anything.

With wind screaming, rain ripping at my skin, I wonder how Ash managed to create a small, warm moment in this chaos, and how I'm allowing myself to get sucked into it. His head tilts, water sliding over his lips, and leans forward. I'm just stuck, frozen under a simulated sun in a storm. Because I want it and I don't.

I need time.

I let out a protest gasp. He stands suddenly, the hull rocking. "Where's Lye?"

Caught in our sunlight moment, we didn't realize the boom knocked Lye from the boat. I pull Ash down before he falls too and remove my shoes and outer garments. I keep my eye on her bobbing bald head as it floats further and further away. The swell rises like a surging mountain and she disappears from view. Ash tears at his chest, screaming, "Lye!" He swings to me. "What are *you* doing? Luna, stop!"

I ignore his pleas and dive into the water. I'm a strong swimmer when there's not a ghost gecko pinning me. I head for where I last saw her. Ash's shouts fade like they've been sucked up into the ether. I tread water for a moment, dragging over the swell. I spot her, face impassive, paddling sluggishly and not really getting anywhere. Not really trying to.

She sees me. Eyes like unburied coffins. Her face reads regret. She mouths, *Let me go*. And she sinks.

I plunge down, grabbing at water and hoping to find an arm, a piece of cloth, *anything*. My eyes are open, but it's murky. Shadows could be the clouds above or creatures waiting to snap a quick meal. Fear seizes me. Hope surrounds me. Emotions wrap around my heart and push me to keep looking, keep trying. They tell me there's more to this girl. A layer of marked skin, the tally of repentance, is only the first page to a longer story. *She needs to finish her story*.

She's my teacher and also my friend. I close my eyes and remember her lessons. I reach for living things. I cast my power like a net, sensing what's water and what not.

A few feet behind me, a hanging shape curls around my mind. I'm aware of the lack of water, the slowest pulse, the last drumbeat. I grasp her. Swimming up, up, up. Bursting like a dolphin breaching, I hold Lye against my chest.

She breathes. Relief makes me buoyant and I kick harder, searching for the mast of the boat, for an anxious Ash pacing the deck.

"Let me go," she murmurs with little energy, hardly any fight, and I know I was not mistaken before.

"No, Lye," I say, squeezing her middle and heading for the boat that's just popped into view on the crest of a wave. "I won't let you go."

Ash's arms reach for us. I make sure he hauls his sister over the edge first. Then he takes my hand and yanks me upward so violently my shoulder clicks.

Lye lays on the floor like a caught fish. Ash glances at her and then throws his arms around me. I think he's going to scold me. It's what my father would have done. But all he says is, "Thank you." Releasing me just as ferociously as he sinks to his sister's side.

She looks past her brother to me, a plea in her eyes. I nod minutely. We have a secret now. Ash can never know she was willing to drown. That she almost *wanted* to.

The more I learn about the Keeper, the Shen and their ways, the less I understand about anything.

WAVES PICK us up and tumble us down as we huddle in the hull. There's nothing to do except wait it out. Ash wraps an arm around his sister and holds her shaking, nauseous body. I sit on a board above, watching the islands we must reach get smaller.

Lye's eyes close, exhausted from near drowning and unending seasickness. Ash's hand finds mine and he squeezes. I let him hold it. I can start here. I smile softly.

He tips his chin, that cheek pushing upward as he shows me a slit of teeth. "What are you smiling about?"

I touch my heart. I'd almost forgotten it was there. It nestles more comfortably against my flesh now. "Nothing really. I was just thinking it's your turn to drown. We started with you, then me. Now Lye. It's back to you again."

Our hands mesh together. Carved from necessity and something else I can't quite pin down. "Well, we both know that wouldn't be difficult." A hardness to his laugh. "I could drown in a bathtub."

The rain eases, just a spray giving us a sparkle and shine as the sun hacks at the clouds to make itself known again.

"Why is that? Shouldn't you be all things aquatic?"

He presses his lips together. Withdrawing his hand from mine and tapping his mouth. My hand feels lost without it and I clench my fist.

"Are you all things fur and claws?" he asks.

I roll my eyes. "No, I suppose not."

"I was raised in marshlands. We were never taught to swim. I can wade in knee-deep water but that's it. Before we broke from the Shen, Lye and I had never even seen the sea. We knew our village and then the palace. Nothing else."

I experience a sharp pang in my chest at the idea of being without the sea. The thought of not hearing the rush and wail, feeling the salt spray on my face, hurts me. "I can't imagine that. For Char, the sea is family. It's part of everything we do—it's who we are."

He lifts Lye's head from his lap and places it gently on a rolled-up jacket. It oozes water as her weight sinks in, but she doesn't wake. He nudges my shoulder gingerly, vulnerability in his voice. "Will we ever speak of what happened?"

My cheeks redden. My heart feels punctured and overwhelmed. "I can't. Not yet. Please, Ash, let's just start simple."

I sense his pulse quicken; his shoulders slacken. But he tries. For me. "So, what else makes a Char? I always thought of them as brutish and barreling. Lacking elegance. Clubbing their women and dragging them by the hair."

My eyes lift to his, grateful for the subject change. "We are those things," I say proudly. "Aside from the clubbing women part. Char are brutes, fierce and strong. But they're also gentle and kind. Family is the most important thing. We value our way of life. We have humble desires." My heart thumps like an oak fist on the table. "It doesn't take much to make a Char happy."

Our hips touch. He turns toward me, light shining from those deep-sea eyes, and asks, "And what makes a Char happy?"

I purse my lips, contemplating. And he waits.

I think of my parents, happily intertwined by the fire. Hot food on the table. A sturdy, noise-filled home. I know what makes a Char happy. "To be left alone to live our lives free from the fear of attack. We don't want much. We just want to feel safe."

He shifts infinitesimally, so there's a breath of longing air between us, and sighs cavernous as the roots of the islands. "You know what? I wish that too."

Lye's eyelashes flutter. "It does no good to wish it, brother. We're at war. Safety is a luxury." She pulls herself to sitting. There's darkness in her eyes that wasn't there before. Like she scooped some of the seafloor with her as she rose from the water. "How far have we drifted?"

I scan the horizon. "Without a charmed wind, we won't reach the island by nightfall."

We drink water, tapping our feet. Panic rising as we drift further and further off course. "Couldn't you use your Water powers to summon a current?" I ask Ash, swooshing my hands around like a magician. He laughs sourly at this. "Water isn't sentient. I can't ask it to do my bidding." His gaze flicks to Lye, whose head is in her hands, studying the grain of wood in the deck. "Sister?"

She huffs. "My powers are spread over five elements, making each less powerful on their own. Besides, only an extremely powerful Blood elemental can summon creatures to her." She stares at me.

I look over my shoulder. "Me?"

"Her?" Ash asks incredulously.

Lye nods. Like this says it all.

I'm not powerful. I'm little Luna. I can scrap enough to not be crushed by my brothers in a tousle. I can help out in a fight. But I'm not the powerful one. "No. Not me."

Ash nods along slowly. Lye points. "You're far more powerful than you realize." She lowers her gaze. "If the Emperor found out about you…" She swallows the rest of her sentence.

Bewildered, I protest, "But I am Blood. I sense animals, heartbeats. I have no influence over the sea."

Rising sibling smiles. *I can sense animals.* I blanch. "What do you want me to do, ride a whale to the island?"

Ash smirks. "Could we? I mean, can she do that?" he asks Lye. She shrugs and I feel like I'm hovering over my dream self, watching the most absurd scene play out.

Lye is a twig with a furry, almond-colored head. Her robes are filthy and wet. Her eyes are impossibly sad and purpled. But when she speaks, you listen. When she says you can summon a dolphin or two to drag your boat to the island, you believe it.

"Just try," she urges, nodding her head toward the water.

I gulp. "What if I accidentally call a shark?" An image of rows of razor teeth in red gums flashes in my mind and I bite my tongue.

She holds up a finger. "Avoid thinking of sharp teeth."

I roll my eyes. "Gee, thanks."

I dip my hand in the water. The Shen siblings watching me with eager, almost hungry, eyes. I close mine and spread my fingers. Mind searching for warm blood pumped by strong, playful hearts. I hold the shape of the snub-nose dolphin in my thoughts and breathe deeply, letting my fingers waft with the beat of the water. *Soft sunset skin. Rounded faces and kind, intelligent eyes. A double dorsal like two half-moons chasing each other.*

Something nudges my palm and I want to jerk away but I will myself to stay still. The siblings draw in shocked breaths and I open my eyes. The streaked skin of a snub-nose dolphin, round head bobbing up and down in the waves, caresses my palm. I pat it gently and it nudges me again, happy, trusting.

My mouth hangs open and could stay open forever as two more dolphins emerge. They bellow joyfully at the sight of me. Lye's expression has gone from almost defeated to bursting with pride.

The dolphins look to me expectantly like soldiers awaiting orders with beautiful muzzles focused on my hands as I gesture madly. "What on earth do I do now?"

Ash holds up a rope with a terse grin.

61
SHEN LYE LI

It wasn't that I wanted to die, exactly. I didn't throw myself from the bow. I was knocked. But once the waves dragged me away, I had a thought. A single thought. *I don't want to die, but I don't know if I want to live either.* And that was all it took. He always told me I was everything and nothing. I gave into the *nothing*. My feet stopped kicking and I let myself sink.

It was a moment of weakness. One of many. But hopefully one of the last. I've had to shake years of Shen brainwashing from my mind. But pieces of it cling to the sides of my head like vanity bats refusing to give up treasures. These pieces whisper in my ear and tell me I'm wrong. The emperor is right, and I am wrong.

But hearing Luna speak of the Char, of their simple wish to be safe, chased the bats into the sky. The Char don't want anything from the Shen. They just want to live in peace.

I know now that I'm not a deserter. I'm a defector.

I choose the *everything*,

And I'll *do* everything in my power to help Luna save her family. Once balancing on the fence, I've jumped solidly onto the other side.

The sea breeze washes over my tufts of hair, soft as goose down, as we race across the ocean towed by three pink-and-orange striped dolphins. I put a hand on Ash's shoulder, and he nods knowingly. *This girl*, the girl with the hickory heart, has more power than I've ever witnessed. She's dangerous. I swallow my dread. If the emperor discovered Luna, he would have to possess her. He would make her a slave like he did me.

For this and so many other reasons, he must be stopped.

"Unclench your fists, sister," Ash whispers, placing a hand over mine. Fire burns inside my closed fingers. Anger roars. The memory of the emperor and chancellor, holding lives over my head, binding me with threats that may as well have been heavy chains. Their greedy eyes shining like oil on water.

Luna, similar to me, is in quiet contemplation, though she doesn't look tense or angry. More impassive, and I wonder if her heart has taken over.

"It must be nice to switch off your emotions for a while," I remark, startling her from her reverie.

Her chin sticks out, eyes narrowing. "Maybe, if I had any control over when and where that happened. At the moment, I'm a clock that can't tell time." She glances at Ash and mutters, "Always out of sync."

My mouth clamps shut. I know what it's like to lack control. We all have battles raging inside. Each different. Each uniquely devastating.

Ash hangs from the mast, hair blasted by the wind, and shouts, "Land!"

Black rocks jut out of the water like broken wafers. The dolphins, giddy and frolicking, will swim out of the way, but the boat will plow right into them. Luna awaits my instruction, billowing with panic.

"Just do what you did before, Luna. Only instead of asking them to swim to the island, ask them to come to you. To slow down."

"You know I don't actually speak dolphin, right?" A blanket of irritation falls over her face briefly but then she swallows, nods, and dips her hand in the water. Ash and I watch with fascination and apprehension. Black rocks are rising up to bite us like grungy teeth.

Water slaps the boat as she closes her eyes, hand making a pocket. "We've arrived," she whispers. "Thank you."

Three heads approach, blue eyes curious and cheerful. They nuzzle Luna's hand as she lifts the ropes from their necks. The look of unease as she touches them doesn't go unnoticed.

We've arrived on the western side of the island. Scraped straight cliffs that no shrub can root to stand fifty yards in from a beach deserted of people but lush with plants. We stare up at the seemingly impenetrable bluffs that wrap around all of what we can see of Crow's Nest Island.

"Are we meant to climb over that thing?" Ash asks, agape.

Luna snorts. "Unless you expect me to summon a thousand birds to lift us into the crater on the other side?" He gives her a look like that's a possibility, and she smacks his arm. "I'm not doing that." Her eyes roll to the sky. "I wasn't even supposed to do that." She points at the dolphins surfing the waves.

Ash grabs an oar. "Seems to me you did exactly what was needed."

She takes the other oar and I guide the rudder. "I'm Char," she snaps with foundling anger. "Don't forget that. I'm learning Shen ways to protect my brothers. It doesn't mean I want to be a Shen." Wrestling with an already torn identity.

Before they begin arguing about who's better, Char or Shen, I stomp my foot. "Row!"

We weave and knock toward the shore. Shen boats will approach from the north. Char have probably set up camp in the crater to train and wait.

Soon this basin will fill with blood.

62
CHAR LUNA

Power sits uneasily beneath my skin, battling with my Char heart. I place a hand over my chest. The steady beat, the slide of the chambers. This is who I am. Yet I'm split in two. Now I must open myself to a power that could easily overrun me. The force of it tugs at my insides. Snapping the elastic that has kept me together. If I give in completely, I lose what makes me Char. If I don't embrace it, I could lose my brothers. It's an unsteady balance. Like hopping across boats crammed in the inlet of the bay. It would be so easy to fall between the cracks and be trapped under the hulls. I lean into my heart, but I heed the Carvress's advice to not let it rule me.

The boat scrapes the short shell beach with a noise like grinding bones. We tie it under a mangrove tree. We strap what we can to our bodies. Soon the sun will slip away and trade places with the moon.

The siblings look to me as if I should know the way to proceed, but I've never been to Crow's Nest. I bite my lip and plunge through ferns reaching my middle. "I think we should locate the Char camp."

Ash bites into some fruit, spitting peel onto the ground. "Don't you think we should make camp and leave at first light?"

I shake my head. "No. We're too vulnerable out here. If a scout comes upon us, this will all be for nothing." I grasp one of the small trees springing up around us. Giant grass and dwarf trees. This place has fun with proportions. I sense the pulse of scratching rodents. The network of insect palaces beneath my feet.

The cliffs look impossible. *How do the people of Crow's Nest travel between the islands so easily if they must climb this every day?* Papa's voice floats in mind, a song dancing through the leaves. A whistle and a hum.

Beware the crow's nest, so high
To climb it would be to touch the sky.
No one can touch the sky but the birds.
The only way through is the way heard.
Listen, listen to ocean's song.
Careful, careful you don't get it wrong.
The cliffs can be climbed but not by man
You must pass between them fast as you can.
There's no monster, no beast to cut short your years.
No, your undoing will be by your ears.
Listen, listen to the ocean's song.
Careful, careful you don't get it wrong.

Lye and Ash stare. Ash with admiration. Lye with suspicion. "What was that?" Ash asks, holding a branch in his hand. "It was beautiful."

"A beautiful warning," Lye mutters, eyes on the menacing walls of the crater.

I shrug. "It's just a lullaby. A song my father would sing."

Ash lets me pass and falls in behind. "But what does it mean?" His finger pecks my back. Icy shivers from his Element or my own reaction, I'm not sure.

Flat round rocks like giant dinner plates lie in our path. The cliff teeters and towers over us like a stack of coins. "I guess we're about to find out," Lye says between gritted teeth, because what looked like cliffs from a distance are actually thin, stacked columns packed so closely together there's barely enough room for one of us to squeeze through. Ash whistles.

I touch the rock. It feels unsteady, leaning into the wind. "Looks like we don't go over the cliffs. We go through."

The two siblings look at me with dread. Neither wants to go in. Not in the dark. Not like this.

"I don't think this is a good idea, Luna, it's too dark. Too, er..."

I take a step in, the sound of the sea disappearing almost instantly. I take another step, listening, feeling my way. When I come to a fork in the path, I choose left. The sound of the sea rushes back, water crashing, wind howling.

"Lu... na!" Ash's worried shouts come to me in snippets. I follow his voice back to the fork and try the right. The sea sounds disappear again.

I tap my chin. "Huh."

I turn around, colliding with Ash's chest, heartbeats out of sync. I gaze into his smooth, tanned face. Eyes that crinkle in the corner at my touch. I put a hand on his chest. *I want his heart.* It races beneath my palm. *I want it in more ways than one.*

Lye clears her throat and we bounce apart. "What have you discovered?"

I show them the way sound changes on different paths. "I think we follow the path that leads away from the sea. The silent path."

Light touches the tops of the towers. Coming in at a window slant, moving away from us. We don't have very much time.

"Listen, listen to the ocean's song. Careful, careful, you don't get it wrong," I whisper under my breath, padding into the labyrinth of stacked stones and tomb-like quietness.

Lye pokes me in the back. "Careful *you* don't get it wrong."

ASH LAUGHS when he's nervous. When he's happy. Or to mark any change in emotion. But when he laughs among these stony monoliths, it bounces from rock to rock sounding like a thousand Ashes are laughing. I slap his arm, sending a flurry of teething puppy jaws to his throat. He coughs and scrapes his skin, glaring at me.

"Stop laughing," I order. "We need to lsten."

The path widens around the corner, revealing a long, silent corridor. I relax a little and walk ahead, picturing my brothers crouched around the opening to a tent. Elbowing each other and trying to keep their minds off the coming battle. Joka will rationalize. Sun will appear bloodthirsty on the surface, but he won't want to kill unless he must. Ben Ni. I wonder whether he's even capable of hurting someone. Faced with a choice between his brothers and a Shen warrior, I have faith he'll choose to defend himself and the others. My hope is I'll be able to step in before that happens.

Back to back with my brothers is where I need to be. *Where I will be.*

Sunlight scrubs up the cliffs as the bright bulb leaves us. Maybe the Yan boys gaze at the same giant star, soon to leave us in darkness. We need to move faster. At the end of the corridor, I dig my feet in and march, twisting and turning without thought. I listen for sea sounds, and turn back when the squawk of a gull or the beat of a wave flurries about my head. I'm searching for silence.

I pause, ears straining. I hear nothing. Nothing.

I smile, so brief it may as well have been a blink.

Because I hear nothing. No sounds of the sea but also no voices. No hushed whispers between siblings. No scuff of slippers on the hard-packed dirt. Just nothing.

I turn around, dread-full.

I *see* nothing.

I sprint to where I think Ash and Lye were, and sound beats against my body like a solid thing. Wind. Waves. Water crashing on the shells and sand.

Spinning in circles, I backtrack, thread my path over and under itself until I'm tied in a knot.

I'm lost. And even if they're calling, there's no way I'd hear them.

63

SHEN LYE LI

I grab my brother's arm. A cyclone of worry passes through my fingers and he lurches away, dizzy. "Where's Luna?"

"I don't know." Every word is drenched in terror.

Ash runs forward and is about to round the corner when I shout, "Stop!" He freezes and I catch him. "We can't leave each other's sight, brother. I don't want to lose you too."

Ash laughs, a weak, powdery sound with no real mirth. A sound I've become horribly familiar with. "We haven't lost her. She must be just around the corner." He cups his hands around his mouth and shouts, "Luna!"

We wait.

Silence.

The sun clings to the very tips of the stone like a fledgling bird scared to launch from its nest. We scan the path, hoping her small body is just hidden in the unfriendly shadows. But there's nothing.

"I can't believe she stormed ahead like that," he says, exasperated. "She doesn't think…"

I pat his hand. "Yes, brother. Like someone else I know." I feel his dread. Though not in the same way. His is born of higher love. But I do care for Luna. I think she may even be... my friend. The thought makes me want to laugh hysterically. Because I don't have any experience of what that is. *A friend.* If she's my friend, she's the first.

We stay together. "There's nothing to do except keep walking," he says tensely.

"And hope," I add.

He doesn't respond.

Following silence is a strange journey. It presses around us, sucking thoughts away, leaving only nail-biting worry. He shouts her name into the maze, hoping it will wind around a corner, shoot down a narrow gap and find her ears. *But if she's lost the trail...*

I squeeze Ash's shoulder, focusing on calm seas and warm sun. He resists me and they lose none of their tenseness. "Ash, if she's lost, she won't hear us. The sea sounds will swallow any noise we make."

His eyes are rimmed hard as china. I press my lips together and sigh. His feelings are as clear as if they were carved into the rock. He cups his hands again, stubbornly screaming into the shadows, "Luna!" voice growing hoarser with every deep-pitted shout.

Our feet grow heavy as hope disappears with the light. I stop and force a water bottle under Ash's nose. He snorts and pushes me away. "We shouldn't have let her guide us. We should've stayed at the beach until morning," he blurts angrily.

"Sit, brother." I point to a stack of stone discs, conveniently shaped into a seat. He tries to push on, but I exert my strength, forcing him to rest. "Only for a moment. We'll find her, Ash." Eyes averted, I whisper, "We'll find the girl you... love."

He sweeps a hand through his hair, freezing midway when he hears my muttered words. "I don't lo..." I stare him down with matching eyes. Though his are like a hurricane, and mine are just the beginnings of a storm. His hand drops. "Oh, I don't know how I feel about her. I do know she doesn't love *me*."

I perch beside him like one of the gnarled carvings on the tiled roof of the palace. Like them, I guard. "You love her," I state, sighing deeply. But not because I don't want him to love her. I sigh from the depths of my soul for how hard this will be for him, and for her. I sigh mostly because none of that matters. They are lucky to find love. I wish I were that lucky.

He gives a sad, punched-of-all-the-air laugh. "If you're right, I love a girl with no heart." He clasps his hands, head bowed in what could be prayer. "It's an impossible situation."

I place a hand over his. Smaller, thinner, softer. I push back the elements. I want it to just be us. Brother and sister. No magic. No Keeper. "She has a heart. She has a hickory heart." I've seen the change in Luna. The moment she stopped fighting it, her emotions began to emerge. She's new though. Love is a winter-bitten bud in her chest. It needs time to grow. "You say she doesn't love you, but my guess is she struggles to identify what love is. She needs time to find it."

Ash's expression is pain and heart. Love and loss. These are all good things. They're human things. "Perhaps."

I tap my mouth, trying to stop my smile bursting into a laugh. "Oh Ash! Only you would fall in love with a girl with a wooden heart."

He laughs too, shaking off a little tension like molting feathers. They fall to the floor while sprinter lizards dart across the rock corridor, trying to catch the last glimmers of sun on their golden-brown skin. The laugh dies quietly.

Deep breath in and Ash asks, "Do you think we have a chance? Do you think she can ever love me back?"

I don't hesitate. Because I know she can. In her way. "I do, Ash."

He stands and offers his hand. "Thanks, Lye."

I take it. "For what?"

"For not warning me away. For letting me love who I want to love."

I laugh again, a giggle that rises to the sky like star blossoms on the wind. "I know you well enough to know that warning you away would only make you want her more."

My giggle comes to rest on a ledge only a spotted eagle could reach, leaving us in the cold. Luna's still missing, lost inside the sound of sea. We sweep every crack, every change in the rock. A passage runs at a right angle to our path. If we go left, the sea sounds are deafening. Silence dominates the right.

We take a risk. We bet on finding Luna instead of a way out. We turn left.

64

CHAR LUNA

I allow panic to drip down my throat and flood my chest, wetting my hickory heart and causing it to expand. My feet make patterns in the dirt as I run through each corridor searching for quiet. I call out but can't even hear my own voice.

Stop. Stop searching, Luna. The further I go, the more lost I become.

I press my back to the stone. Cold ices my back, which is scabby and scarred. Digging fingernails into the earth, I watch the sun rip from the very tops of the towers and am left in darkness. I sink to the ground. This can't be how it ends. Lost in a labyrinth, listening to the ceaseless battering of sea against the land. The most abusive relationship.

Sound washes over me. I grasp for a thread of comfort. Of home.

I wonder if my parents know what I did. Are they living under a chipped roof of shame? Perhaps I'll be disowned. Removed permanently from the Yan family. Nameless. Homeless. Maybe I deserve it. Maybe all of this was stupid and foolish and just the kind of thing Mama worried would happen when I chose the hickory heart. I swipe my face. Bitter tears crawl down my cheeks. I ball up to make myself part of the rock. A cold little lump. Little Luna, turned to stone.

If I had any thoughts of getting up and fighting, they're stripped away by the relentless noise. I swallow drily. I'll indulge in weakness and wait for morning.

THE SEA plays tricks. Creating wobbly mirages of islands within reach. Images of beautiful women lounging on rocks with luminous tails and seductive eyes. Illusions stretch toward desperate minds causing shipwrecks. It has an insatiable hunger. The sea speaks your name in a voice you crave, beckoning you into its dark depths. I hear it now. I hear *Luna* in a voice I desire, carried on the wind. A dangling hope that will be snatched away.

I dare not open my eyes. My head hangs between my knees, listening to the seagull squawk and the devil whispering, *Luna.*

Luna.

"Luna!" Ash's voice is strong and rough.

"There she is!" Lye's is painted in opal tones.

It's a trick. This sea is maddening. And cruel. And not to be trusted.

A hand on my shoulder, shaking. "Luna, are you all right?" There's affection in that voice, coming to me in broken pieces. *The sea doesn't feel affection.* A spark of electricity runs from shoulder to sternum to shoulder and my head lifts like I don't have a choice.

The Shen siblings are lit by the scarce light of a burning torch. Worried. Relieved. Emotions knotted together. Voices stolen by the wind.

Lye clutches her ears and shouts, "Well, this must be the wrong way. It sounds like we're in the midst of a hurricane."

Ash's clutches my arms, eyes cutting through the noise. Warm, green sea and foamy bubbles. He runs his hands up and down. I stare blankly. Feeling his touch. Not *feeling* his touch. I'm stuck in the storm, not sure what is real.

Our noses touch. Hot breath on my skin, he says, "I was so scared we'd lost you."

Shakily, I reach for his cheek, fingers moving into his hair. He leans into them. He feels real. Sun warm and sure. I withdraw. We're caught between wanting and the consequence of desire. His face falls, disappointed. Lye stands against the dark like a ghost fighting for form. She lives comfortably in the shadows. Darkness becomes her. She smiles briefly.

I search for words. I swim up and against the current of madness sweeping through me like a gale. "Well, you've found me. But we're still lost."

The thread of silence is gone. The way through this maze with it.

Lye dumps an armful of twigs between us and touches her torch to it. Because of the strength of the noise, we expect it to be blown out. The volume of the sea is deafening, but there's no force of wind. The twigs spark and grow to a small fire. We huddle around it.

"I'm sorry," I shout, eyes downcast. "This is my fault. I raced ahead and now we've lost the silence."

Ash puts a hand on mine and I let it rest there for a moment. "We'll find it again."

It hopeless. We're losing time. I look to Lye. "How long before the ships arrive?"

Her slumped demeanor answers my question before she speaks. "It can't be long now. A day or two at most."

I kick the dirt, sending small orange sparks to kiss the stones. They die before they reach the sky. "We might be too late then." I close my eyes, picturing the battlefield already planted with bodies. "Crow's Nest is a huge crater. Even if we make it through, it may take a long time to find the Char camp."

Lye nods. Ash frowns.

"And what do you plan to do when you find them, Luna?" he asks, a new intensity in his eyes. "Even with your new powers, it's dangerous. They'll hang you for what you've done. If that general gets wind of your…"

My chin falls. The punishment for desertion is a harsh one. But I'm willing to take the risk so I can be with my family. I'd die fighting next to my brothers. I'd die if it meant they would live.

Lye interrupts, placing a calming hand on his leg. "She knows this, Ash. She's always known. But we promised we'd help her. *You* convinced me it was the right thing to do." All words are shouted over the squalling racket.

He stands, suddenly frustrated and confused. "Well, maybe I've changed my mind. Maybe I'm realizing just how dangerous it is." Even as he says it, I sense doubt.

"You're letting your feelings for Luna cloud what you know is right... You're..."

My eyes connect with Lye's and I put my hand up to stop her. Ash glares at the wall of stacked stones, arms crossed with an unresolute expression. I approach, let our arms graze like cherry branches.

"I was always going to fight, Ash," I say. "You don't have to join me. But I won't leave my brothers to face the Shen alone."

Teeth gritted, his jaw works. I intertwine my fingers with his. *It hurts.* It hurts and heals at the same time.

"You drown and come back to life. You feel and then you pull away. I keep finding you and losing you. I don't want you to stay lost forever, Luna." He pulls my hand up to his chest, laying a small kiss on our joined fingers. "But you know I'll fight by your side."

I didn't know. But now I do.

Lye jumps up from the fire. "This is all very nice, but it won't matter if we miss the battle." We spin around, separate and meet her in the center of this strange, noise-filled corridor. "You two have given me an idea."

Our hands, now parted, hang at our sides, but she grasps them, small fire sparks coming from her fingertips. She mashes our palms together with a look of black mischief.

"What are you doing?" I shout.

Ash's eyebrows rise, puzzled.

She grins. "This may not work, but I think you two may be perfect for such an experiment." Her eyes glaze over like a bad memory crossed her consciousness.

Ash yanks his hand away, but she snatches it back. "Lye, what are you up to?"

Gulls shriek in our ears. A boat hull creaks and smacks down over waves.

"Luna, you told me that a large river runs right through the center of the island."

I nod, not sure where this is going. "Yes. I also told you Crow's Nest is the only place where white marron is found. What of it?" My mouth waters at the thought of the delicious, paper-thin shellfish.

Lye nods vigorously. "Exactly!" she exclaims, eyes dancing in the firelight. Ash's expression dawns like the sun with understanding that's lost to me.

He shakes his head. "I'm not that powerful, Lye, and you don't have the reach."

Lye's body takes stronger form, a fade-in from ghost. "Yes, this is true. You're not powerful enough on your own. And my multi-elemental powers are too entwined and weak to work long range. But…" She holds up a finger excitedly.

"But what?" They're speaking a secret Shen sibling shorthand I don't understand and it's starting to irritate me.

Still holding our hands together, Lye shakes them vigorously. "You two may be powerful enough… together."

Ash smiles broadly. "You want us to pool our powers. But can she…?" He points at my chest disparagingly, and I feel like I've been struck with the flat side of a sword. "I mean, can she do it with her, you know…"

I glance between the siblings. I'm just a traveler through their world. I'm also about to be the guinea pig to Lye's experiment. Again. Lye shrugs, yelling through howling wind, "We have to try."

We face southward, in the vague direction of the center of the crater. "I've only seen this done once before. It needs a strong connection of great power. A willingness to bend to one another. To open your hearts completely to one another." She says the last part quietly, but I hear it. So does Ash because his eyes find mine and light like fire over water.

"I don't understand," I say. "How can blood and water mix?"

Lye's laugh tinkers on hysterical as it often does. "How can they not!"

Ash's expression is somber. Unruffled. He squeezes my hand and I try not to be afraid of what's next.

"Don't let go, Luna," he tells me.

And it could be simple. He could be inviting me to take a stroll along the boardwalk. It could be the beginning of courtship. But it's not. This carries weight. Like flecks of lead in Lye's reverent, hopeful eyes.

Lye steps back. "Before you attempt this, remember, you're *combining* your elements, not fighting them. Think of the ways blood and water need each other, feel them coexisting, depending on each other and then, instead of pushing your power into each other, spread it outward. Reach for the river. Reach for the marron."

I close my eyes, thinking of a parched deer, scratching and searching for a spring running deep in the earth. Of dolphins twisting in the sea, drawing patterns with air bubbles, reveling in it, loving it. I think of every way in which blood needs the water. Every way in which they must work together to survive.

It hits me like a flood. Then sweetens to the first fresh taste of rain. Life giving. Our connection is a missed heartbeat, a splinter, a way home I've never thought of before. It's everything coming together into one single bright light, sending a jolt through my body and fur, fangs, and feathers from my fingertips.

He crushes my hand and I feel the same jolt running through his body. We share lungs and heart, breath and beat. I squeeze my eyes shut, scared to witness what we've become. Like maybe we've cracked open in this rocky corridor, water and blood spilling everywhere.

I feel the water. But I'm not drowning. I can breathe. I can move in it. See through it. And I know without him telling me that Ash feels water through gills, rippling against scales. He senses animals scurrying through fissures in the rock around us.

"Open your eyes," Lye says loudly. We open our eyes. Lye pumps her hands gently. "Don't let go."

I bite my lip hard, the power overwhelming. I'm not sure I could let go even if I wanted to. Ash makes a strained sound and I turn. His neck muscles are taut, body tense as if he bears a great weight. "Luna needs to let go…just a little," he says through teeth clenched with exertion. "She's too strong for me."

Alarmed, I concentrate on peeling back. Evening up the power so we're in balance. I read his expression closely. Adjusting until he looks like he breathes more easily. And when we hit that balance, it's like summer springs forth in my chest. Everything is warm, bright, and perfect. We've captured a season in the cage of our ribs.

I take a deep breath and exhale a thousand painful breaths in one.

There's a rightness to this I didn't expect.

Lye walks backward in front of us. "Okay, now comes the hard part." Ash and I exchange glances. Heat and understanding. We're part of each other now, like fins and waves. Thirst and quench. The "hard part" will be *breaking* this connection.

We march in our own tiny army. "Now what, sister?"

Lye beckons, teasing out the power. "Reach for the river. Like when you found the lychee grove, Luna. But this is more difficult. You must burrow your senses through layers of rock. Work together. Marron and river. River and marron."

Ash squeezes my hand again and we reach for the marron scuttling across the undulating riverbed, thick with fluffy algae. Breathing muddy water into our lungs, running riverweed through our claws. Swishing and swaying with the current.

We walk.

Every step wraps another band around our combined strength, binding us. Even though his heart is flesh and mine hickory, they beat together in an exhilarating and terrifying harmony. Ash and I can find the way. It's as clear as the river cutting like a knife wound through the base of the crater and as crisp and clean as the pearl shell of the white marron.

And I'm not sure whether to be thankful or fearful.

65

SHEN LYE LI

We reclaim silence a few steps from the end of the towering maze. The sounds of the sea cut off like a lid closing on a barrel full of shrieking gulls. It's a humble quiet as my brother and Luna come together in the most incredible way. They started out awestruck, but now it's almost like this is always where they were supposed end up. My part in it brings satisfaction but also a heavy sense of loneliness.

On one hand, Lye Li wishes for connection. Rightness like she sees in Ash and Luna. While the Keeper shakes her head. *This can never be.* Ever at odds. My two selves.

Our feet sink into mossy earth. The sound of chirping crickets surrounds us. The location of the Char army is immediately obvious. Fires burn bright and gruff, rough voices echoing across the immense crater. They're but a few miles away, camped on the higher, more defensible side of the riverbank.

We duck down instinctually, even though it's dark.

Creeping toward the tree line, I search for a place to rest. Ash and Luna remain pinned against the crater wall, crouching down.

"What are you doing?" I whisper. "Now that we know where they are, shouldn't we find a place to camp for the night?"

They stare down at their clam-shelled hands. "We don't know how to break our connection." Ash's voice edges into uneasiness.

I squat, touching their hands, glued together like an uncracked walnut shell. I stretch them apart as if I'm opening an animal trap. As their fingers untwine, Luna moans like I'm tearing her skin. "Ah!"

Their atmospheres mingle like a fast cloud catching a slower one. There's weather brewing in their collision. It's hard to tell if it's good or bad.

Caught in each other, Ash half laughs, half quivers. "That was...well, I don't really know what that was." His head sways, spellbound.

Luna dusts her hands on her pants. "It was...illuminating," she muses, and I die a little at the hope sparking in my brother's eyes. Perhaps I am too damaged to see clearly. Or perhaps I am just damaged enough. But I fear this love will bring as much pain as it will joy. I know my brother, though; he will always think the pain worth it. It is our biggest difference.

Shaking off her trance, Luna scans the trees, landing on the camp. Ash stands beside her, no longer afraid to be near. I take my place at my brother's side. "They're so close," Luna whispers, fists clenching.

"Now we await the Shen," Ash says. Taller than both of us, yet seeming the same height.

And I await something I've hidden from them both.

Someone.

HE GRADUALLY feeds the emperor poison. A snake with endless venom dripping from its fangs. It's so slow the emperor is unaware of its progress. In a way, he almost wants it. Has come to need it.

"She will do what I say. We have an understanding. And of course, a special connection." The way the chancellor hisses the word "special" causes my stomach to ripple with nausea.

The chancellor paces the room while I sit in a plush velvet chair whittled from ebony. I trace the carvings, sharply withdrawing when I realize they're thousands of tiny screaming skulls.

The emperor, young and handsome but drained of anything good, sneers and pokes me with the tip of his sword. "And what connection is that? That you're both orphans?" His eyes narrow as he sizes me up. "Yes, the role of the Keeper is a sacred one and she has served me well thus far. This new challenge will not be beyond her obligations. She serves me first. Above all. You'll make sure of that, won't you, Chancellor Shek Ki Koh." He points a warning finger, encrusted with jeweled rings.

My apprehension peaks. What new challenge? I have fulfilled my duty as Keeper. I have awakened more elements in my time here than any Keeper before me. I bow my head. I am buried to my neck with doubt. Everything has twisted. Twisted beyond recognition. Duty resembling something far more like crime.

The chancellor nods with a disdainful look. Blue-green eyes like an impure emerald. He resents the reminder of where he came from. I certainly don't want to be reminded. "You deserve a worthy empire. With this new army, the Shen could spread their influence over the Char islands and then the globe..."

A guard hoists me from my crumpled position as the chancellor waves me away. The emperor's eyes are red and gold with greed.

As I'm escorted to my chambers, I whisper to the guard, "This isn't what I thought it would be. It's changed." I've changed. What was sacred has become a curse.

He grunts and spits on the red, tasseled carpet running the length of the great hallway. He has Air in him, but it's a stepped-on cyclone trying to lift from the ground. He says what we all say, what we must. "It is an honor to serve the emperor. You should be grateful."

Right then, it occurs to me in a very small, fleeting kind of way that perhaps the emperor should be grateful to me instead. And the chancellor owes much to my family.

I feel a small hate burning behind my eyes. A fire not of elements but of my own heart. If I don't find a way to suppress the flames, they could be dangerous to everyone.

66

CHAR LUNA

"Do you fear the battle?" I ask, eyes refusing to close. Lye sleeps curled in a ball; face scrunched in an unpleasant dream. I'd wake her but she needs rest. Perhaps more than she'll ever get. Rubbing the frown from my forehead, I feel our scales are balanced now. Though I'm sure she would disagree, we are even in my mind.

"Yes, of course. I'd be foolish not to. It will be my first," Ash replies, staring at the cupped stars that could pour into the crater like sand. "Aren't you?"

I tap my heart. "Not as much as I should be."

Pursing smile ready lips, his eyes flit over the brass and wood that I've given up trying to hide. "Oh yes. The hickory heart, I almost forgot."

In truth, so had I. *Almost.*

"So, you weren't involved in the attack on the Char barracks?" I ask, warily.

He shakes his head, saddened. "No. And I'd like to think I would have opposed it but..." His sea foam eyes cross the distance between us, earnest. "The emperor's influence is strong. Loyalty flows deep within Shen blood."

I gaze down at Lye then back to Ash. My heart warms, like timber by the fire. "I understand. Char don't question a command unless forced to, and we do what we must to survive. Shen and Char follow orders. We have that much in common."

He clasps his hands, resting them on his knees. "I'm not sure I want to be Shen anymore. I know my sister doesn't." He pauses, hesitant of his next words. "Do you think we could be Char?" I'm taken aback by this question and I don't hide it very well. Ash flaps his hands, embarrassed. "Sorry. Forget it. I don't know what I'm saying."

Could a Shen become Char? Only a Carvress could answer that question. "It's possible, I guess. Could you see yourself as a...what did you used to say?" I tap my chin playfully. "A puppet?"

His face falls as he mutters to the ground, "I could, Luna. I would take a wooden arm, leg, or whatever, if it meant we could be together."

It creeps up my throat. Heat and charged particles. I smile. "That's not what's standing in our way." My heart beats steadily, reminding me there are still things to learn. Things I *want* to learn. "Besides, if you decide to make the change, it needs to be for yourself. Not for me."

Lye snorts in her sleep. Her brother looks upon her with affection and worry. "I think she would trade just about anything to change to a Char."

I regard her, knees up, tense, like she's been punched in the stomach. She's always seemed uncomfortable in her own skin. "Maybe. Or maybe she just needs to change something."

He nods. "There is much she feels she must make up for."

"You don't agree?" I shuffle closer.

Ash sighs. "In war, people are forced to do things they don't want to. Many see that as a good enough excuse to ignore their conscience. Lye's different. I think the very fact that she feels this burning need to redeem herself is pretty close to redemption."

I touch the earth, feel tunneling creatures beneath the surface. One eyed moles lazily loop their long white nails into the dirt. This

Blood sense is becoming frighteningly natural. "For my sake, I'm glad she decided to take it further."

His eyes coast over his sister's curled-up form. "Yes, she has honored the Koh name," he says proudly.

The cross-hatched skin on her forearm looks like a messy tattoo in the thinning light. "I've noticed she's left her arm alone for a while now. It's a good sign, right?"

His head grows heavy, the burden of his sister's peace of mind weighing him down. "I hope so…"

The enormity of what we are yet to face seems unreal amidst this peaceful setting. The stars, the lush grass, and the sounds of the river clash with the idea that we're on the edge of bringing death.

I steel myself. Cage my chest and prepare. "I think I'm ready."

"No one's ever ready."

HEAT CRAWLS and pulls at my eyelids. I yawn and kick off the blanket, sweaty and sore. Whatever coolness the crater harbored overnight has been sucked out and replaced with a suffocating, all-of-a-sudden summer.

Lye keeps watch while Ash scoops water from the river. Angry words float to me, rising in tenor and temper. I hurry to warn them to be quiet.

I stare up from the crater base. It's like the bottom of a kettle. The clouds swarming the edges are a closing lid, sealing heat inside.

"You can't stop me, brother!" Lye snaps.

Ash, knee deep in shallows, pours water over his head and shakes his hair. "I will tie you to a tree if I have to."

Lye's eyes glint wicked. "You'd have to disable me first." She takes a fighting stance and pieces of mud crumble into the water from her position on the bank. Ash sighs, hollow and tired.

I duck, pulling Lye to the ground. "Will you at least try and stay hidden from view," I hiss.

Lye snorts. "They can't see us from here, Luna. They don't have hawk eyes."

I raise my eyebrows as if to say, *Well, they kind of do.*

"Really? Hawk eyes?" Ash sloshes forward, more alert.

Reaching to the water, I sense the heartbeats of a dozen fish, panicked and pounding every time Ash shifts his feet. "No, not hawk eyes exactly but a wooden eye sees for miles."

Lye taps her precipice-like cheekbone. "Now that would be useful."

Ash rolls his eyes and they land on me, a softening and strengthening happening at the same time. "She wants to fight with us, Luna. Tell her she can't. It's too risky."

Lye flutters her lashes, bottom lip protruding. I laugh out loud and quickly cover my mouth. "Even if I had a heart that sulky face would never work on me. And Ash is right. It's too dangerous for you to be seen. The moment the Shen recognize you, you'll be taken. And in their hands, you're a huge threat to all of us."

Her shoulders sag. A dark lick of oil lacquers her voice. "I'm not a possession, Luna. I'm not a weapon to be used at *his* will."

I place a hand on her angular shoulder, tight as a warrior's bow. "I know. But if you were captured, you would be."

Ash clambers up the riverbank, three water skins slung from his shoulder. "See, sister, Luna agrees. Please listen."

She turns to the far-off camp. A thousand soldiers awaiting the Shen and their fates. "But I can help." Her voice shrinks.

Behind the camp, the evacuated village is built into and over the crater wall. "You've already helped." Char cling to mountains. Build in a way that sits lightly on the environment. We like to fit in our place, find harmony and balance. "So much."

Ash is less sympathetic. Throwing words at Lye like metal stars. "If they caught you, they won't kill you sister. You wouldn't have the release of the death you so crave. Your life would be caged once again. Until the next Keeper was born, you would be drained dry like a cup of wine. I won't let that happen to you." His fist is high and threatening.

Her face falls, conceding, even as something brews behind her expression.

67
SHEN LYE LI

I sweep my brow of moisture and squint through the trees. Tiny men twirl and kick, black robes like charred leaves blown by an indecisive wind. Their lives are just as delicate. One touch of fire and they'll spark and disintegrate.

Luna lets the branches fall back into place and we crawl away soundlessly. Small animals trail us, and she flicks her Blood influence casually. Sweeping her fingers and bidding them to return home. Her power nestles comfortably within. Not second nature, just nature.

I frown. I haven't found comfort in my power in an age. Sadly, the only time I recall not being at war with myself was when I embraced cruelty. Acceptance of who I am is steps ahead of forgiveness for my sins, and the staircase feels endless. My fingers dig into the dirt as I wonder if I will ever be done climbing. The cool, cakey soil gets under my nails and stains the lifelines on my palms. I smile. At least I'm ascending and not standing still.

A sigh pulls from deep in her chest and she taps her heart. "I wish there were a way to get word to my brothers. Let them know I'm here."

The northern side of the crater looks like a bite has been taken from it. "They'll know soon enough."

Luna follows my line of vision. "Do you think it will be soon?"

I shrug unconvincingly. "Yes. But exactly when is impossible to tell. We just have to wait."

"Seems strange to just sit here and wait for an attack."

It certainly does.

Once at a safe distance, we dust the mud from our elbows and knees and walk to our camp.

Ash sits on the ground, sharpening knives. The sound makes my teeth hurt and my body cringe. I think of the Shen man wearing a butcher's apron, sliding a long knife down a leather strap. Chisels lined up on the table dipped in blood.

Luna slaps Ash's shoulder. Ease grows between them. Slow and fragile, like the first few strands of a web. But it will strengthen as they add more silk, more ties.

"We should get in one last spar before…" She can't finish her sentence. This forced lightness is just that. Forced. None can focus with the press of battle sinking lower and lower like the sun. It's a weight and a blindfold.

I kick Ash in the side with my foot. He glances up. "Why am I to always be kicked and slapped like an abused doll?"

Luna grins and teases. "Well, you're just so pretty."

He puffs out his chest. "Can't argue with that."

We laugh. It feels rare as a black diamond. I wish we could catch the laughter and store it for later. These sounds are precious and may not be repeated.

Luna and Ash flatten the earth with their feet. Today we center on small things. We try not to let thoughts of an inevitable nightmare dent our courage.

Ash and Luna take position on opposite edges of the clearing. I clap softly. "Begin."

They sweep around each other in a dance. Mirroring movements almost perfectly. Luna strikes and Ash knows exactly where her hand will land, ducking out of the way. When Ash kicks low, Luna jumps like his leg is a fallen log in her path.

They're concentrating, lips pressed together, sweat drenching their clothes. But they cannot for the life of them land a blow. I realize what I'm watching well before they do and can't help but giggle.

Ash's snaps to me with irritation. "What are you laughing about?"

Luna seizes the advantage and tries for a quick punch to the face, but even distracted, Ash still moves out of the way before she can connect. She lets out a loud groan and shuffles back, wiping her face with her shirt.

"It's just. This won't work." I gesture at them. "Since combining your powers, you're sort of in each other's heads. It's why you can't land a blow." They look at each other in a way that simultaneously excludes me and warms my heart.

"So, what do we do then?" Luna asks, bouncing from foot to foot with nervous energy.

I walk between them, parting the sea of feeling. "You'll both fight me."

Luna's eyebrows rise. "At the same time?"

I nod. "In battle, you won't get to choose one foe. You may have one, two, or even more coming at you at once. Though lacking finesse, the Mogui will use each other to maximize their number of kills." I bend my knee and prepare. "Let me show you how I defend against multiple opponents."

Luna brushes her fingers across my stomach and whispers, "Bear claw." I feel the tear, veins shredding, but I push back with a forceful wind, knocking the bear from his feet. At the same time, Ash crashes down on my forearm, sending ice upward. Easily enough, I melt the ice with fire, chuckling as he withdraws his hand and shakes it.

I'm a spinning wheel of elements that no one can touch or predict. This is my power. I'm light as air as I dance across the dirt in a joyful dance, caught in my elements, which spill from my fingertips like a fountain overflowing. It is the first time in a long time that I remember my Keeper power feeling like a good thing and not a curse.

I'm swift and unbeatable. Icy claws and weather patterns. Flames and mudslides. I laugh, giddy. *I am everything and I am stronger for it.*

I only stop when I hear Ash wheezing and Luna retreating.

Hand up, doubled over, Ash says, "We give up. You win."

I win. My mouth twists in the corner. Almost smiles but loses momentum.

I win?

What do I win?

Joy falls like discarded armor.

Luna rubs her arms where I've sent licks of fire and beaded hail. "That was amazing." She's awed and envious. Then she looks to Ash who shakes his head like he knows what she's going to ask. "We could disguise her," she starts.

"No," he says flat as bay water.

I calm and bow. I allowed Ash to forbid me from battle because I was afraid of my power consuming me. Afraid of hurting people. But I can't sit back and let them fight alone. "I shouldn't have let you tell me I couldn't fight. It was foolish and weak to let you make that decision for me." He sighs, resigned. "It was never up to you."

I reach for my thimble. Brush my fingers over the point and then release it.

Ash opens his mouth to speak and then shuts it, storming away. Atmosphere brimming like a dam about to break. He doesn't understand that protecting me hurts me. How can he expect me to hide in the bushes while my little brother goes to battle? No. I need to be there. With him. Even if it's against his wishes.

Luna goes to follow but I catch her arm. Defensively, she sends a spray of spider webs through my skin. It catches me by surprise and my grip slackens, gummed up. "That's a good one. Keep that in your armory."

She watches Ash sulkily moving through the trees toward the stone towers. "He won't go far," she says, mostly to herself.

I sit on a log bordering the sparring circle and she collapses heavily beside me. She is ungraceful. Effective, but heavy handed. "What else have you got? You should have strong favorites that are easy to call upon. One for every element you may face."

She stares at her feet for a while, gripping the log. Beetles crawl in and out of the holes in the wood, responding to her unwitting call. "Spider webs for Earth. Shark tooth for Water." She scrunches her hands, breaking off a piece of bark and crumbling it in her fingers. "Bird beak for wind. And Blood. Well, Blood is hard."

"You will not need a response to Blood," I say, recalling the long line of soldiers I was forced to awaken before we fled. So much fire, some water, air and earth. Never Blood.

She turns and stares. "What? Why?"

I point to the bugs teeming around her dirty slippers. She lifts them. Urging them away, but careful not to squash their delicate bodies. They sprinkle and dash. "You're the only one."

She laughs. And the laugh turns to a gasp. "No. I can't be."

"Trust me, it's true. You are rare, Luna. And being rare is dangerous," I warn. "I know what it is to be the *only* one. People will either want what you have or seek to control you." *And they will do unspeakable things in the name of that pursuit.*

She bites her lip, deep in thought.

I elbow her, attempting to lighten the mood. "So, what's going on between you and my brother, eh?"

At this she straightens. "I don't know."

The sky is darkening. Clouds stack on top of one another, creating charged humidity. "What don't you know?"

"I don't know my heart. Often, it still feels like a foreign object in my chest. Doesn't he deserve someone with a true heart? Someone who can be sure?"

I smile. "This group is always trying to make decisions for one another. Luna, you don't get to decide what he deserves. He chose you. All you have to decide is whether you want to choose him."

She clasps her hands in front of her. "I. Don't. Know."

I tap her hands. The gentlest drum. "Then you don't know."

"That's it? You're not going to try and convince me he's a good man and that I'd be lucky to have him?"

I don't know much of love. I've never really had a chance to know it. Surrounded by lush, tapestry-covered walls that may as well have been prison bars, I was always secluded. Excluded. Separated from everyone. There was no way to make a connection, let alone grow one.

"We both know he's a good man. I don't need to convince you of that. But I'm not going to tell you how to feel." I add in as a sisterly warning, "Just don't make him wait too long, all right?"

She bows her head. "All right."

I make my way to Ash, who's muttering to himself and staring at the growing clouds. "Stop sulking, brother."

Deafening thunder rolls around the inside of the crater like a giant marble. Suffocating heat and electricity trapped. We look up at the sky.

I don't need to be of Water to know rain is coming.

68

CHAR LUNA

Brothers, I ache to see you, but I wish it were under better cir-cumstances... My shoulders wish for your nudges. My ears hope for the sound of your laughter. My prayers are filled with the desire for your safety. Soon, brothers. Soon this will be over.

"Is it terrible that I kind of wish they'd just come already?" I ask, jittery. Eyes to the north. The sky thrums with captured energy. Almost like it anticipates battle.

Lye tosses her head back, squints to find a star through the heavy clouds. "You could wish them not to come at all, but we know that wish will be unfulfilled. So no, I don't think it's terrible."

Ash pulls one leg up and sinks deeper into the crumbling bark of a cork tree. "I do. Why would you want to bring the battle forward? The longer we stay safe, the better."

We're three points of a triangle spinning without direction. My heart beats steady as a march. My Blood sense feels the uneven bulge and pump of theirs. "It's coming either way. At the moment, our fates are stretched out before us, getting thinner and thinner. Besides, the safety you speak of is false."

He grunts a response and I let him have his anger. We all have ways of dealing with this uncertainty.

I kick at the scraps of clothes in front of us. No armor. Just loose shirts and tunics. The gray clothes of the Keeper are pushed to the side, leaving Shen Water blues and Char black.

Lye sighs, disappointed, poking at the clothes with a stick. "This won't make much of a disguise."

Tearing a black shirt in half, I lay it over her head, tying it at the back. "At least we can cover your fuzzy head." She blinks, a girl playing dress up. Big anticipative eyes and wheat fluff hair.

Ash huffs, restless. I know he feels the atmosphere changing. The crater is spilling over with nervous sparks.

Heart birds preen their feathers in branches, shivering at the electricity coursing through the air. I scrape at volcanic soil, adding a splash of water to make a dark, gray paste.

"What are you doing?" the siblings ask as I sharpen a stick with my knife and dip it in the crude paint.

I take Lye's chin in my hand. She concentrates, only shocking me gently, like eager hands touching a hot pot without protection. Squinting, her eyes burn painful pictures of need and belonging. "Hold still," I order, painting the Carvress's mark on her cheek and smudging black under and over her eyes like a mask. She stares serenely ahead, floating on a baited sea. I sit back on my heels and survey my artwork. It might confuse the Shen and hopefully show the Char she's on their side.

Lye goes to touch her face and I stop her. "What did you do?" Trust isn't easy for someone who's been shown nothing but hurt and hate.

"I've given you a Carvress mark," I say. "Today you're an honorary Char."

She grins proudly and stands, gathering clothes in her arms. "I'm going to change."

"Don't go far," Ash warns, and she nods. He sinks back into the tree.

I shuffle to him on my knees, mud and stick in hand. "Your turn." I lift the stick to his face, but he grabs my wrist before I touch mud to skin.

"Stop," he whispers, eyes dark, watered reflections in the murky moonlight. Something stutters in my chest. *Or maybe I imagined it.* My brain and heart knock in and out of unison and I feel exhausted by the wondering and the questioning of every heartbeat, every feeling.

There's nothing light about his movements. Everything is dusky and intense as he pulls me to him. Fast and hard so our chests collide. He's scared. I *feel* it. Not just in his heartbeat but because of our connection. We may have separated our powers, but it lingers like a healed scar. He wraps his arms around me tightly, crushing me against him.

And as we embrace, I just wish I could feel as scared as him.

It's no good to go into battle without fear or compassion. Without contemplation of what I could lose. I know that now. Chest to chest, hickory to heart, I realize one truth: I must not only battle the Mogui Shen, I must fight my heart.

Lye stomps loudly toward camp wearing strips of black and internal armor, and Ash releases me a little, still silent. There are too many words held back on his tongue. She bends down and wraps her arms around us. Small sparks of lightning travel up my spine, tingling and locking my bones.

"It will be all right, you two." Then she tips her head, garnering messages from the sky. She listens and shrugs. "Or it won't."

This finally breaks Ash's stoniness and he lets out a cough, mortar and pestled with a laugh. "You're a strange one, sister."

We huddle together, faces and thoughts inward.

Wishing, hoping, praying.

ME EYES droop and I snap them open. It's my turn on watch. The siblings sleep in fits and bursts, twisting in their positions, agitated. I must watch the northern side for lantern lights or changes in the darkness. Signs like rocks sliding. *I must...*

Papa sweeps crumbs from the table. The Call, a gentle thrum like harp strings, fading to awed silence as he's only touching his little finger to the oak.

Crumbs fall to the floor and Mama slaps the back of his head gently. "Ai ya! Even when you're helping, you're not really helping!"

He chuckles and grasps her waist, pulling her into his arms and spinning her around the tiny kitchen. Bumping into the furniture that can't accommodate his large form.

Sun presses against the wall, pride in his chin, ready for playful punches. Always.

Joka emerges from his room, a book in his palm. He sees our parents and smiles. Bamboo neck stretching, eyes downcast again. He planes a finger over text to find his place. Ben Ni, leaning back in his chair, hums a tune. His look is dreamy and romantic, giving accompaniment to the awkward, confined dance. His eyes, just like mine but sweeter, more innocent, soak in the love between his parents.

Joka rests his book on Ben Ni's head and our little brother does his best to sing while keeping it balanced. He is the foundation of this family and always reminds us what is important.

It is fair that we love him more.

Papa swings Mama out and she clucks her tongue, not coming back to him. The swell of white teeth and laughter affects even her mood, but she quickly finds clothes to fold, busying herself as Papa lifts me from my chair to stand on his toes.

A smile emerges from his broad, war-creased face just for me.

Ben Ni starts tapping a rhythm on the table.

Tap. Tap. Tap.

Taptap

Taptaptap

Eyes shoot open and I gasp. Heart pulses fast and out of time, building and building, peaking and trough-ing. *But it can't be.* It's a staccato drumbeat, the boom of an explosion, all squashed together in one horrible mess of noise, pounding, pounding through my head and every vein in my body. And it's getting louder and closer.

I spring up. It's not me. It's not *my* heart. It's a huge number of hearts, pumping oceans of blood. I'm caught in the current of over a thousand excited Shen as they march toward the edge of the crater.

"They're here!" I say far too loudly.
The Mogui are here.

69

SHEN LYE LI

Squinting through a narrow dawn, we search the north for signs of Shen. Luna clutches her heart, panting needlessly, unable to disconnect from the thousands of hearts pumping millions of liters of blood around soldier's bodies.

"Luna, let them go," I urge, scanning her bulging eyes. I grasp her shoulders and send a wave of cold water through her body like a slap. She finally blinks, mind reclaimed.

Misty rain throws a veil over the vast valley.

We stare at the cliffs, willing and unwilling colored Shen robes to appear.

Ash shields his eyes, pointing straight and sure. "There."

Winding down the side of the cliff are Shen in battle dress—blue, orange, white, and brown. Moving unpredictably. We step to the edge of the tree line, knives clutched in anxious hands. Three in line, all focused on the color spreading over the north like paints poured onto a page. I tighten the black cloth around my head and grind my teeth. We await a sign. A sound. A clear *Go*.

Ash spins at the rustle of leaves behind us. "Move," he hisses, slapping palms on our backs and shoving.

Orange glides through the jungle. The sound of cloth smacking against wet leaves doesn't seem like a war cry. But it is. Shen are also approaching from the south, closing in like they're herding cattle. Broad arms and broader swords. Colors crystalize into warriors.

We bend low and sprint for the river, tumbling down the bank of high curved rock, rising like a wave that will never break. Unlike everything else in this valley.

"We didn't come here to hide," Luna whispers harshly, shooting Ash an irritated glance. Her body is battle hungry and her atmosphere of hot blood, ram hooves scraping the dirt, is ready to charge.

His fingers wrap around his knife, knuckle white. "We didn't come here to die either." His lips barely move when he utters, "We need to find our moment."

Poking our heads over the riverbank, we watch the Shen side-shuffle like crabs across the sand. The Mogui move clumsily. Knocking shoulders in their excitement to begin.

Rain thickens from mist to droplets, soaking our clothes. Mud paint drips down my face.

Luna's eyes burn fiercely in the direction of the Char camp. "Look." With knowing and affection, she whispers, "Listen."

A black cloud stretches over the lip of the riverbank. Char move fluidly, separating into clusters like starlings, bamboo ladders protruding from each group. *A sound breaks forth like a split in the sky.* It is unlike any sound I've ever heard. The Char are as still as lava stone, but it comes from them. A golden, tuneful hum floods the crater with a bursting heat that could almost evaporate the rain. Each note has its own tenor, its own flavor, yet they each melt together into a thunderous, harmonious, proclamation. Announcing the Char.

Luna's face is longing to join in as Ash and I try to understand what we're hearing. "It's the Call."

She pats her shirt and pulls a small lump from her pocket, holding it like it's new and frightening. She places it flat over her hickory heart and a hum emits from her chest. A rippling, flowing music, which lifts thick in the air and joins the song that's filling the crater and rocking the earth. Her serene face glows with a sense of belonging I envy.

The Mogui stall, muddled. Colors clashing. But then I hear a familiar voice. A cruel dark, hungry for blood voice. "Attack!"

Ladders fall across the river, bridges from peace to war.

We run alongside the river, getting closer and closer to the action.

This is where beauty ends, and horror begins.

70

CHAR LUNA

The Call captures me. I finally feel that sense of *meant to be*, like I'm one important drop of water in a surging river. I'm ready to leap into the fight, but I don't know how. How am I supposed to join them?

My heart beats strong and true. Flushing every vein with new blood. The Call ends and the shouting begins. Every corner of the crater seems packed with yelling men and feet pounding the dirt. When in reality it's a square mile of grass on the low side of the river and we're just on the edge of it.

From beneath the sheltered bank, we see black collide with color. Beautiful and bleak. And from then on, it's absolute sickening chaos.

We're not watching men and women fight with skill. We're watching the Mogui scramble for death and the Char scramble for life. There's no consideration. No method. This is reactionary fighting, no strategy, no anticipation just each move existing in a bubble without a greater plan. It feels like throwing bodies at bodies and counting how many are left at the end. plan

My fingers grip the bank edge like it's the lip of a boat that's sinking. Knowing the moment I leap, I'll be swallowed by a sea of clashing swords and elemental storms.

With Ash and Lye by my side, we have a chance. Small but definite like the sharp prick of a pin. Ash's muscles tense, feet pumping. Lye's battling expression is a complicated mask. They're watching their people killing and dying. It cannot be easy.

Out of sight, I move along the river. Scanning windmills of black cloth striking colored robes. My eyes hop from face to face, limb to limb. I'm searching for a balsa foot, a bamboo neck, a boy in the clouds. Flesh tears and opens in the wrong places. Skin and muscle hangs from a man's cheekbone, flapping like smoked meat. I gag. I swallow. I rely on my heart to keep me calm, but this isn't the Char way. Blows are unconsidered and hapless. Causing pain and maiming. Injury rather than swift death.

A piece of rock breaks above me and an orange whirl drops heavily onto my shoulders. Fire sparks over my skin as the Shen warrior and I land in the fast-rising river. I don't have time to shout out. I don't have time for anything except instinct. *Survive.* We grapple. Fingers pinching, climbing ribs. Water splashes and I grasp for my knife, which lies useless on the beach, knocked from my hand.

Fire grows, singeing my insides. I roll onto the sand and on top of the Shen man, whose eye is captioned with a tattoo flame. Burning with hatred and disgust, he grabs my wrist and sends a shot of wood fire through me with a devilish smile.

Breathe. Think. You are powerful. Little Luna.

I retaliate. "Cockroach," I whisper. Sending bugs crawling and chewing under his skin, they withstand the heat and eat him alive. He releases me, eyes wide with surprise at the Char girl who just used Shen power against him. I hold as long as is necessary to disable him. Screaming and scratching deep into his arm, he stumbles backward into the river. I watch, horrified as he opens his veins with his dagger, reaching his fingers to scoop bugs from his body. Blood spurts fountain-like from the wound. I stare at my fingers, buzzing with Shen magic.

This power. It is deathly and it comes too easily.

I sense the Shen's pulse slow to a drip. His eyes roll back, white and lifeless, and he floats away like driftwood. My first kill feels as empty and lonely as the river beach. Ash and Lye are gone.

Without pausing, I scramble up the side of the river bank and dive into the sea of violence. I search for my friends and family. Engulfed by a battle that sends screams to the heavens. As I wind through the fight, smashing and striking out, I sense blood spilling and seeping into the earth. So many hearts straining to beat one last time. The color of the landscape is changing in the worst possible way. And I'm the painter, swiping my blood-dipped fingers across the canvas with detached, terrifying precision.

It is necessary. It is worth my soul slipping from my body like a torn dress. Because it will save them.

Every life I take is one less life that can harm my brothers, Lye, and Ash.

ASH BATS at a Mogui, using every ounce of strength just to get close to her. Focused with his lip between his teeth, he lashes out and connects with her forearm. Her eyes water at his touch but she recovers fast. She's wearing blue, a water droplet stamped near her eye. This is a fight of strength of power, not opposing power.

They tap and sweep, move in a death dance while others dance in partners and groups around them. I gulp, the bitter lump refusing to travel down my throat.

I start towards Ash as his opponent draws back her blade. Feet trip, arms fly out to grab but I duck and weave, using my size to my advantage. I reach for the Shen woman who has nothing but Ash's death in her eyes.

He's losing. He will lose. He's going to…

Lye spins, graceful as a crane, fast and effortless. It is both horrible and helpful that death suits her. Her calm allows it to be swift and effective. Her water glazed knife flashes briefly before slashing across the Shen woman's middle. Her foe's skin splitting open like a sack of rice. The sound and smell is that of hell. Her eyes roll grim and she falls.

Lye stands over the body, whispers something to the sky and grabs her brother's arm. They nod and separate. Moving deeper into the field as rain pours and mud thickens. *Reddens.*

I wrestle with men who can't match me. It's too easy. Words tumble through my head. Warnings and reassurances. *For them*, it says. *Do it for your brothers. This is the way you don't lose yourself.* I hold fast to these words as my death tally threatens to consume me. And Ash...*Dear Shen boy...*I thread the memory of his touch, the understanding in his gaze, between my ribs, hoping it will stave off darkness.

Faces I know—faces I *knew*—lie partially submerged in volcanic mud. Mogui laughter floats over the bodies. Their relish in killing is clear.

Swallowing, I raise an arm as a Water Shen crashes down on me. I hear it break before I feel it. A snap, two breaths, and then searing hot pain. I scream, bloody and fragmented. Withdrawing it against my side, I switch my blade to the other hand. The Water Shen's battle cry is incensed. Fingers darting at my body like a cornered serpent searching for any skin. Greedily, he goes straight for the heart. Pressing two fingers, he tries and fails, realizing he's gone right for my wooden part.

I grip his hand and send shark teeth through his fingers. He tries to pull away and I clutch it harder against my heart. Shark teeth snap and slice everything inside like razors. Tearing his veins until his insides match the warzone outside. His face pulls into gruesome disbelief and he collapses. My heart beats steady but my brain, my soul, sinks. Something is being taken from me. Innocence I will never recover. It beats its wings and lifts to clouds, shrieking a farewell caw.

I stare at the lifeless face for just a moment. It's all I get because the next warrior is upon me.

Lye whirls from view and Ash is swallowed by colored cloth. I jump into the fray, pulling Shen from him. Nursing my arm but ignoring the pain. *There'll be time for pain later.* I try to keep my feet, but it's as if I'm balancing on the end of a pole. The world spins out of control. *The world has changed.* I'm swimming against the current. Throwing Blood at everything that touches me. I need an anchor. A grounding.

I hear the steady shout of young men. Courageous and sure. Voices I know like the first heart bird song of the morning. My brothers.

I find Ash flat on his back, fallen Shen warriors groaning in the dirt like toppled skittles. I pull him up. Men stagger around us, some fall, some press hands to gushing, gaping wounds and I'm not sure if I inflicted them or not. Their laughter is dying as they are. Ash's arm drips with blood but he moves. He breathes. My relief is bigger than the sun.

"Where's Lye?" I ask, following the Yan family voices. Peering through color and mud.

"I don't know," he replies, pained. "I lost her."

There are more soldiers lying on the ground or limping to the edges than are fighting. I quickly count. Shen still outnumber us. Orange dances around black like tribal fires.

Joka's voice carries through the crowd. Clear and direct. It's a lasso around my waist calling me home. I run. I run until my lungs feel like they're bleeding. Until I see two brothers back to back, surrounded. In trouble. Ash nods, our connection still strong, and we sprint to join them. Rolling under an Earth Shen, I kick his feet out, grasp his ankle and send murder bird feathers up his leg. He buckles, limbs spliced and bulging.

When my back hits Sun's, I am home.

"Luna!" Sun exclaims, jaw tense, eyes on the next foe. An Air Shen lunges with a sword and he deflects. I twist around the blade and touch the Shen on the knee, sending a hibernating hoarder bear up his thigh. He sways with sudden fatigue and Sun elbows him in the side of the head, knocking him out.

Ash hurdles the body and slots in by my side, startling my brothers. Sun reacts swift and brutal, pressing his sword to Ash's throat.

"I'm on your side," Ash manages against the blade, jugular pulse bulging. Joka trains his arrow on Ash's heart.

"Sun, Joka, no!" I shout. There's no time for long explanations. I act fast with palms to their shoulders, simultaneously giving them a taste of a mauler claw, a hiss of acid. Shocked, they relax their weapons.

Joka looks relieved, like he finally understands why I freed Ash. Sun fires his fury outward. He nods sharply to Ash, sweat sheen bronzing his face. Forehead creased in concentration. "For now, I will fight with you, Shen deserter."

Joka shouts a warning as several Mogui come at us. They seem inhuman. Mouths open, blood dripping from wounds, and yet they still come. My brother's bamboo neck is splashed with dried blood from a cut above his ear.

When a Fire warrior attacks me, I move like a Shen and press two fingers to his neck, wrapping spider webs around his throat and strangling him.

"You've changed, little Luna," Joka manages through panted breaths, blocking a blow and reaching for an arrow. He shoots, bolt landing in the neck of his foe. Death is fast. My father's words come back to me through my older brother. "Was it a good change?" He looks from Ash to me.

I don't know. "Later, brother."

"Yes, later," Sun remarks darkly. "Let's win *this* battle before we enter another."

"Where's Ben Ni?" I ask, deathly frightened of the answer. Imagining my youngest brother face down in the mud with so many others.

Sun kicks an Air Shen in the chest with his balsa foot, answering between exhausted breaths. "Safe. He's not fighting."

A lantern of relief exits my chest but floats nearby, not enough hot air for it to truly escape. I won't rest until I *know* he's safe.

Joka groans, spent. But we move in unison. We're surrounded, weary and bleeding. But we'll fight until flames burn our veins or lightning shocks our systems.

Fists up, knives out.

Our Char war cry may be the last sound we make, but we will make it together.

71

SHEN LYE LI

He screams commands across the crater. Black oil voice spraying Shen faces. It pierces my heart like an arrow on a line, pulling me to him with threads of loathing and revenge. Reminding me of every barked order, every icicle he pressed into my head, and every time I fought against the heavy stomp of his foot over my mind only to be crushed.

I'm conveying death and devastation with every touch. Mogui Shen attack, their atmospheres empty except for destruction. I open my wings, whip around and knock them over like feathers. Barely halting my stride as I push to the back line. To where the coward stands on a rocky platform behind the action.

His expression is shrewd irritation, like this is taking too long. Like the Char should have the decency to die quickly and conveniently so he can get on with his day.

I bend and scoop mud, smearing it over my face. War paint for an assassination. It could end here. My suffering and theirs.

Crouching low, I curl around the platform. I incapacitate anyone in my path to the soulless music of *his* stomps.

From on high, standing safely above battle, the chancellor shouts to his archers, "Fire!" Lifting his arm and lowering it, the movement sends sprays of arrows into the field. Hitting Shen and Char alike. Men make horrific noises when hit by an arrow. A wet cough and an airless wheeze doused in surrender.

Clutching my knife, I climb behind *him* just as he raises his arm to order another assault of arrows.

His thin legs sway in blue silk. A Water Shen like his brother. *He is nothing like his brother.* I pad, like the ghost I am, and bring the blade to the chancellor's throat. He reacts only slightly, hand touching my arm. He is arrogance and charm. Cruelty and calm. He doesn't send anything through my skin. He whispers, "Hello, Keeper," like a crocodile stalking prey.

I press the knife in harder. "My name is Lye Li Koh."

His shoulders tense like frostbite. "I could call you sister."

Sister. "You could but that word has no meaning to me. It is a chalk title, older brother. Nothing more."

Black days and nights swirl around me. Points of knives aimed at children's throats. Threat on threat on threat pressing down like the heavy, bleeding stones that make the palace. An ill mother who couldn't survive the cruelty of her eldest son. A son who was a shame and was ashamed of his humble beginnings. A father who left us, hands up in surrender. The chancellor and my older brother are one and the same. But I only see an empty darkness. The blood between us turned rancid years ago.

He is nothing but greed and evil.

He will torture me no longer.

I want to make him bleed. Watch his life slip away.

I want *revenge*.

I ready the knife to pull across his throat when a voice slices through the darkness. A tear in the nightmare, small light finding its way through.

"Stop!"

Luna's younger brother, the Char boy with hazel eyes and a golden heart approaches me, hands out.

"He deserves to die," I hiss, becoming serpent-like in my anger.

Ben Ni nods. Kindness filled with dreams. "He does. That is true. But you should not be the one to execute him." He tips his head, reading blackness, hatred, and the extreme need for blood swirling in the sea of my eyes. "I see it in you, Lye." He breathes my name like it's precious. Like he's been waiting to say it. "If you kill your brother, you'll disappear. Everything good about you will die with him."

I am shamed. Ben Ni now knows another secret. "You heard that?"

Sensing my grip on revenge slipping, the chancellor, my brother, sends water attacks up my arms. I deflect them easily. They're birds pecking an apple. Nothing. *He is nothing.*

"He called you sister. Is that the truth?" I confide in the boy with a golden heart that matches his golden eyes and nod confirmation. Ben Ni approaches, looking between us. "I see little resemblance." He regards the chancellor with distaste. "Please, let me take him to our general. He'll know what to do."

I shake my head, unable to let go, gesturing around the field with my other hand. "Look at what he's done. Why on earth would you try to save him?"

Ben Ni is foolishly hopeful. Among all this death and violence, he has faith. "I'm not trying to save him, Lye Li, I'm trying to save *you.*"

Kill. A voice whispers in my ear. *Kill him.*

It will be easy. It will be delicious. It will be over.

But I focus on Ben Ni's compassionate eyes. I let him approach, let him pierce my dark oil bubble until he has hold of the knife and is gently prying it from my tense hand. I sink to my knees, feeling a cloud lift from my heart. But it leaves a void. Without revenge, I am empty and directionless. Palms flat on the stones, my stomach heaves, though nothing comes out.

Holding the knife in a threateningly, voice wavering with youth and uncertainty, Ben Ni says, "Chancellor Koh, you are under arrest..."

The chancellor springs like a panther, ankle dagger in hand. A flap of blue silk. A sound I will hear over and over for the rest of my life. Ben Ni falls backward limp, blood flowing from his stomach.

Luna's scream could end a battle. Flatten men with its sheer agony and power.

She flies up the stacked stones, collapsing at her brother's side.

The chancellor scrambles to escape but Ash throws him to the ground. A man with a face drained of all color except the white of pure grief and a wooden foot stands on my sneering older brother's chest.

Ash stares at me, stricken.

I'm shrinking, becoming vaporous and insubstantial.

Let me float away like a mist. Dissolve to nothing.

What have I done?

72

CHAR LUNA

o. No. No.

Blood bubbles between my fingers like a horrible, horrible fountain. *Not him. Not Ben Ni.* Rain makes pink pools around us. *He is the best of us.*

I press on the wound with both hands. The pain of the break is nothing compared to this. I pull the blood-drenched, shredded edges of his tunic together, so I don't have to see what lies beneath. Lifting my tear-filled eyes to the rain, I pray to every deity and god I can think of. Every spirit I don't believe in. *I'll believe in you. I'll give my life to you, if you just save him. Spare him. Please.*

Joka kneels beside me, intelligent eyes assessing Ben Ni's injuries. He begins to shake his head and I grab his chin with bloodstained fingers. "Don't," I threaten. "Don't say it. Joka, please." My voice is pinched to nothing. I shrug from my jacket, ball it up and place it over the wound. I never knew blood could run like water. I thought it was thick and slow like honey. But this is thin and flooding and too much. Too, too much.

My throat burns like I've swallowed hundreds of fire ants. "Please," I beg anyone who'll listen, head swinging, frantic. "Please, please, please. Help him."

Ben Ni coughs gently, his whole countenance crushed and disappearing. *He's disappearing.* He reaches for my face. I lean down. I can't let go. I can't stop.

Stroking Ben Ni's hair, Joka looks into his youngest brother's eyes, which are turning from warm hazel to rotted wood. "Luna," Joka whispers, but I don't want to hear him. I don't want to look at him. I just can't.

"Don't go, little brother, stay here with me," I plead. "I still need to beat you at cards. I still need to teach you how to talk to girls. I…" You're the best of us and you've still so much to give.

Sun wraps his big arms around me.

"Little Luna," they say.

"Sister," they say.

Their voices are ocean deep in grief. They already grieve because they've let him go.

Pushing against my will, I move my chin inch by inch. Forcing myself to look at Ben Ni. "It's all right, little brother," I murmur, patting his cold chest. I try to smile, to give him some comfort as his spirit pulls from his bones. "Think of the sea, the warm lap of waves. Stars reflecting over the water."

He takes small panicked breaths because he knows what's coming. And he's not ready. Every single breath kills me. My brother's arms squeeze tighter.

Joka speaks low and hushed, heart breaking apart with every word. "You can go home now, little brother. Mama's just put crystal buns in the warmer. Papa's readying his pipe. He'll do a dragon, your favorite. Brother, they're waiting for you."

Ben Ni tries to speak, but his last breath takes his last words with it. The dreamer is finally in the clouds.

With my hands scrunched around my blood-crusted jacket, I still apply pressure on his empty wound. My brothers pry my fingers away.

Youngest brother is dead. I couldn't protect him. I failed.

My head blooms with an unbearable pain, so cutting, so deep I can't escape it. It crawls over my skin, biting and tearing. My breath draws in and in and in, beaded with broken glass. I can't, I can't, I can't...

My heart beats steadily. Mechanically.

As certain as murder birds will dive and fight over blood-covered carcasses, I know what must be done. If I am to survive this, what was built must be dismantled. The emotions I strived so hard to reclaim cannot remain.

I let my hickory heart rule. And it happens with swift and efficient relief.

I tilt my head. A door is closing. Warmth recedes. The tide won't beat on this shore. It will freeze. I tap youngest brother's chest. "He should close his eyes," I state. "Or murder birds will peck them from their sockets."

Shocked breaths suck the air around us. "*Luna!*" is said with a deserted sigh.

My brothers whisper Char death chants into the sky. But I don't join them. I stay at Ben Ni's side. No sword nor Element will move me from this place. I shall stay here and keep the body safe from beaks and beady eyes.

Mogui cling to the edges of the rock platform. Death hunger hangs from their lips, but they won't move while we have the chancellor captive.

"Bring the Shen Chancellor to me," I whisper as rain eases and sun pours reality upon us. My limbs are on strings. I am the puppet Ash named me. Disconnected. Logical. Everything Ben Ni lacked that led to his death.

I straighten his clothes. I retreat to an unreachable hideout behind skin, bone and hickory.

Ash throws the bound chancellor to my brothers. What's left of my brothers. I swallow. Three now two.

I grip my knife, hands sticky with blood. Ash and Lye stand back. Equal expressions of horror. Lye shakes, a leaf in the wind while Ash poises, ready to strike. He steps out of the way and gives me this honor.

Sun kicks the chancellor down. The fiend's bony knees strike the stones, and he winces. The pink water of Ben Ni's diluted blood soaks into his fine silk robes. They're ruined. It's a shame to ruin such nice clothes.

But then killing him will do that also. I hold the point of the knife to his chest. "Luna." Joka leans forward but I put up a hand to stop him.

I twist the blade, silk gathering into a rose. The chancellor glares, head tipped to the side, fascinated in a way that should make me cringe, but I feel... I *don't* feel.

"A wooden heart," he observes.

I push in. A small cut. His heartbeat quickens. "Yes. It means I'll have no regret in ending your life."

His eyes, a bitter green like dying coral, narrow. "Perhaps. But I don't think that's what you'll do."

Ash steps forward. Lye steps back.

The chancellor is right. It would not be wise to kill him. He is worth more to the Char alive. For the moment. "Surrender," I order. The tip of the knife craves flesh. I bury it shallowly. He seizes in pain.

I gesture around the field. "You're not going to win. Call surrender and stop the bloodshed."

He shrugs. "We have more soldiers."

The knife clatters to the floor, a triangle of red at its point. I press two fingers to his throat. Pain is what I need to inflict to get what I want. The kind of pain found in spider bites, snake venom, poison that racks your body and twists your nervous system until you pray for death. Pain feels fitting. Pain fits me.

He writhes, body bucking. Mouth stunned flat.

I ease off, still holding power over him. "Call surrender or you'll die slowly. Excruciatingly. I'll make it last for days." His shocked eyes read my unwavering expression and he nods.

The boys untie him at the point of their swords, and he pulls a red flag from his breast. With one long, thin arm, he waves it three times.

It takes several minutes for word to carry across the field, but slowly the battle noise dies. Weapons are lowered. The Mogui fall to their knees and howl to the sky like animals.

It's over.

Merah, merah, parut.

Youngest brother is dead.

I take Ben Ni's cold hand in mine. There is nothing in him. No blood. No love. Nothing.

I wonder... I claw at my chest, scratching at the skin that meets the hickory until it bleeds. I do it slowly. Mindlessly.

Ash grabs my hand and tries to stop me. I send fangs at him. I send hurt and broken skin and blood. "Leave me," I manage in a bereft-of-anything-good voice.

He retreats but sits nearby. As do my brothers.

I won't leave him. I am anchored to this place.

Someone needs to watch over the body.

This I can do.

73
SHEN LYE LI

The sky should be dark and heavy with electric clouds. It seems wrong that the sun sends bars of light down on this shattering scene.

Soldiers drag other soldiers. Surrendering Shen are bound and lined up. The battle has ended, but the next part is just as challenging. Just as devastating. There's movement all around us. Even the river swells and changes. It bulges out in places like a snake that's swallowed an egg.

Everything moves except the girl with the hickory heart.

She seems caught. Stripped of something fundamental. And I'm the one who caused it.

I want to fall at her knees and beg for forgiveness, but all I can do is stare as arms of guilt stretch out to throttle me.

The atmosphere is all Luna. Clouds of grief billow and bounce against her but can't get in. Birds build circles in the sky over her head. Bugs crawl from hiding places and run in lines to her feet. Her power stretches out like an indomitable fog.

I gasp and hold the breath, tight and painful in my chest. I've never seen anything like it. Then I hang my head in shame. While others hang their heads in sorrow.

A soft growl lifts everyone's eyes except Luna's. Slowly, the boys back away from the body of Ben Ni. *The body.* That word wedges between my ribs like a sharp rock. A lava lion snakes down the cliff side. Orange eyes on Luna. It's stone-colored fur bristles when the boys put hands on daggers and swords. Bows pulled tight.

I manage one step forward. Palms up, I say, "Stop. It's not here to hurt us."

It's shiny tail, luminescent gray like the volcanic stones it lives amongst, flicks as it hovers several feet above Luna and her youngest brother.

The group breathes in. Holding. Awe and sadness collide in that one breath.

The lava lion leaps gracefully to the ground, surveys the terrain and turns its angular, cut-from-stone face left and right. Then it sinks in submission to its belly, crawling until its head is under Luna's hand.

She doesn't flinch.

The brothers mutter between themselves, not understanding this scene because they don't know this version of Luna. Blood Shen warrior with a hickory heart and power beyond even her comprehension.

But I know this Luna. I created her. The responsibility lies like a crown of feathers on my head, easily disturbed and destroyed. I fear any creation of mine will be a flawed one.

The Char with a bamboo neck steps forward, arrow poised to shoot.

And then we hear an otherworldly, out of place sound. The creature rubs its face into Luna's palm and purrs.

CHAR SOLDIERS escort our brother, the chancellor into custody. He walks as if protected. *Above everything.* His cause and foul intentions are still intact. But I have no doubt the Char will change that. With our help.

Ash watches him go with an expression of disgust. He doesn't know the truth. I learned ways to suppress his memory to shelter his mind and innocence. I always felt knowing would cause harm. Perhaps now, the truth will die with Ben Ni.

I roll my thimble between my fingers and draw it out. This death should feel like the straw that breaks my sanity. It should be the one that destroys my body and mind. But his eyes, his kind, gentle eyes linger with me. His need to protect me, to stop my descent into darkness, means I am obligated to stay in the light.

Snapping the ties that hold me to the earth, I walk forward. Ash tries to stop me, but the moment he touches my shoulder, he feels the bite of a ghost gecko, gummy but tough. A warning.

When I sit on Luna's other side, the lion hisses. Luna sighs while her mouth moves around whispers I can't hear.

Words will not be enough, but I say them anyway. "Luna, I'm sorry. This is my fault."

The lava lion scratches its paws into the rock, the sound like metal on china.

"We saw you but couldn't get there in time," she says coolly. "Soon you can tell me about my brother's last words. Though I think I can guess what they would have been." Her fingers spread deep in the lion's fur. "You'll tell me he saved you. That he *died* to save you." Her mouth curls around the word *died* like she can't quite grasp it.

My mouth dries to a desert. My debt heavy and growing heavier. "He did. He died to save me. Please forgive me. If I could take his place, I would," I babble, desperate to make it right though I know I can't.

She waves her free hand, sweeping air that's thick with suffering, and frowns deep as foundation cracks. "No."

Of course, no. How could she possibly forgive me? I killed her brother. It deserves a cut from wrist to shoulder. It deserves nothing I have.

She lifts her eyes, un-cried tears dead on her cheeks. "If Ben Ni saved you then he must have believed you worth saving." Her words are rational. Unemotional.

She takes my hand. A swirl of heartbeats and blood pulsing through hundreds of creatures hits me all at once. "Be worthy," she says firmly, releasing me and turning back to her brother. She smooths his clothes with an odd expression. And I worry what this death has done to her. I fear what peg has been removed to set this wheel in motion And where it shall turn.

Carefully, she buttons Ben Ni's shirt and arranges his hands over his chest. She taps the lion's head and it rises, arching its back and yawning enormous jaws. It pounces up the cliff gracefully. Swinging its tail from a nearby perch, it keeps watch with flame-like eyes.

I hesitate, then place the thimble on Ben Ni's breast. It will mark the time when I decided to stop punishing myself with small cuts and meaningless pain and leaned the blade of justice toward those that deserve it.

Be worthy.

The words are a mantra and a mantel. They will sink deep into my bones from now until they sit with comfort upon my shoulders.

74
CHAR LUNA

Ribbons of black linen trail over rocks like shadow spirits. I watch, detached, as my brothers bind Ben Ni in the traditional way. At least now the birds won't get to him. I sense their hunger.

Ash keeps me caged in his arms. And it truly feels like a cage. A cage around my heart. Around my failings. My arms tense and I shake him off, marching into the haunted battlefield. Mud splashes my clothes, covering the blood. *Ben Ni's blood.*

I pass wounded and dead, and the scene blurs together like the crater has actually erupted. The volcano brought to life by this violence and anger. Flesh is twisted. The piles of mangled bodies and tangled organs look inhuman. The sight causes my soul to retreat further. Emotions snuffed out like an eclipse to a bright hot sun. My need to care has disappeared. Their wounds and their pain have no effect on me.

I slam into someone living. Limping but living. I ready my defenses, but a walnut jaw works above me. Stepping back from General Fah, I bow low.

"Char Luna Yan," he states.

I should run. I should press something heavy and sleepy into his chest and run. But my legs are stone. My whole being is exhausted and can't muster the energy. "There was…" I start. He could strike me down. It is his right. "There was…a reason."

Fah's eyes lift to the back of the crater to where the wind teases black cloth into a long and miserable flag. "My men have told me of your heroism. You risked much to fight in this battle. And your brother Ben Ni… what he did…" Sorrow caps his eyebrows.

He died. That's what he *did*. He gave up his breath and blood. He foolishly thought he could change the world. And the world answered with a resounding no.

My eyes meet his and there's something I never thought I'd see. It's not a favor. Not pity. I tilt my head, examining his features. It's respect. "Ben Ni did what I would expect him to, sir," I manage. Fah surveys me curiously. But a blank expression can look just like grief and that is what he takes it for.

Fah's arm hangs limply, sword slipping from his grasp. He sways and reaches for my shoulder. I bear his weight, fortifying my broken bone with silkworm thread. Closing my eyes briefly, I conjure small amounts of milk spider venom to numb his pain so he can get on with the business of ending this battle. His eyes widen and he bows short in gratitude.

"It seems to me the Yan family saved hundreds of lives today," he says as we walk toward the Char camp. "*Every* member of the Yan family," he emphasizes. Then he straightens, loses his balance, and uses me for support.

"And what of the chancellor?" I ask, minimally curious. "What happens to him now?"

General Fah closes his eyes, counts seconds under his breath. "He will be *questioned* for information."

My lips feel like mortar. Dry and hard. "He will not give it willingly."

Fah sighs, dark and disembodied. "No. He will not."

I tap my heart. It's coated in cinder and soot. It's the perfect tool. "I will question him," I announce. I don't ask.

By the time we've reached camp, the general agrees.

IT FEELS crowded in the tent with Ash, Lye, General Fah, and my brothers. Crowded and yet empty like a basket full of hollow eggs. Ben Ni leaves a ghostly shadow. We make room for him in his absence. Our table at home will have an unfilled seat. I blink. *Perhaps it will be more comfortable with no elbows in my sides.*

These words fight within me. I know it is an odd thought to have.

I step forward, addressing the general. His gaze is level as I say, "The Shen emperor means to steal a Carvress. He lured our forces to Crow's Nest Island to deplete our army and leave the Carvresses unprotected. He sends more than twice as many soldiers as we faced to Black Sail City. If they don't find one there, they will go to the next island, and the next, until they're successful."

Fah's eyebrows rise in surprise. "He would risk losing so many in an even battle?"

"The Shen have far greater numbers than the Char. These deaths are a small drop of water compared to the ocean of lives they still have at their disposal."

My brothers stare like they don't recognize me. *I* don't recognize me. Joka puts a hand on my shoulder and gives a forced, heartbroken smile. "There's logic and then there is callousness, sister."

My eyes skate to Sun. He twists uncomfortably and then his head falls. "Many died today, Luna."

I nod. "Yes. Many died. Youngest brother is dead. Being careful with our words won't change that."

Lye's voice grates on me for its emotion and weight. "The empire is obsessed with developing a Shen warrior with Char strengths. They will do whatever it takes."

Whatever it takes.

And what will we do?

"How much time do we have?" Fah asks, hands already grasping at paper and ink.

Lye frowns decisively. "None. We are out of time. We cannot reach the city before it's attacked. As we speak, they are likely crawling over the mountain like termites under cover of night." She approaches the general and he flinches, moving away like she's diseased.

A strange smile creeps over his features. A secret in his eyes. "They won't discover the Carvress of Black Sail City in her workshop," he says, tapping his leg, thoughts rustling underneath a plain exterior. "They will not find the Carvresses in their usual places. Though whether that's good news, I'm not sure."

There's only one reason for the Carvresses not to be in their workshops. Joka says it before me in hushed awe, "The Concord."

Lye and Ash exchange confused glances and I nod to the general. That the Carvresses are all together could either be a fantastic stroke of luck or the easiest kidnapping in history.

"What's the Concord?" Ash asks, closing distance between Shen and Char. The general eyes him suspiciously but trust is necessary. Even if it feels elastic.

I answer. "Once every three years the Carvresses gather for the Concord. They take turns hosting. The time and place is always secret until the last minute."

Fah stands tall, proud. "A secret from the general public. High commanders are informed. Just in case."

Just in case.

"Well, this is that *just in case* moment, General." Lye speaks with authority. A calm influence over growing discord. "Where and when is this Concord being held?"

Eyes down, he mutters, "Coalstone Island. Right now."

My brothers shift. Hearts beating wings for home. "My village," I say to Lye. Her puzzling expression doesn't reflect the hopelessness of the rest of the group.

Lye runs a hand over her peach fuzz head and blinks sea-green eyes. "Perfect."

"Perfect?" The general inspects her face for a tattoo. "Is it true you're the Keeper?"

Lye nods. "I *was* the Keeper. Now I'm a Shen defector seeking refuge and offering my assistance." Fah stares at her, then laughs hysterically. She keeps going. "If you let me, I can help. I can negotiate with Shen prisoners and help plan your next move. I have knowledge no one else does. I even know how we can send warning to the Carvresses." Her eyes slide to me, though I have no clue as to why.

Fah swallows his shock and weighs the facts. He takes several seconds to answer, surprising me when he says, "We've lost many men. *Too* many," with a deep, accountable sadness. "I'm not so proud that I would not accept aid when it's offered. Especially when the situation is dire and the action might save Char lives." Then he turns to me. A thousand degrees of change in that one movement. "Can she be trusted?"

He seeks my counsel. *My* counsel. It's beyond belief. But perhaps all this needless death challenges beliefs. It either turns people toward hope or hopelessness. I choose the state of nothing that hovers between the two. General Fah chooses hope. I nod once. "Yes, General. You can trust her."

Lye beckons. I come to her empty of emotion and ready to do what is asked. "Luna, I need your help." Her voice is strong, decisive. "Only you can you save the Carvresses."

Lye's expression drops like a waterfall, a pause while sadness washes over her features. I'm not sure she deserves this feeling of grief – a grief I can no longer feel. "Since Ben… since the battle, your Blood powers have surpassed anything I've ever seen. I think there's something we can try. A way to send a message. If you're willing?"

I bow my head. "I am willing."

75
CHAR LUNA

"What are we looking for?" Ash asks as we trudge through soggy jungle, palms folding around us. The plants mute the sounds of rounding up of prisoners and the completion of the battle. These final moments are like tying off the end of the rope to prevent fraying.

My heart beats like a monotonous, music-less drum. It should hurt like it's on fire. I shrug. *This is what I am now.*

Lye plans with the general, slipping into the role with disturbing ease. She listened when I said be worthy. I see it in her seaweed eyes as she braces for her future purpose.

I tap tree trunks as I search, reaching for life, for blood flowing through every creature, though the one I seek has its own signature. A fast beat. A flutter. A tiny heart doing a lot of work and working for another.

Ash holds a pouch containing a message written in tiny letters.

"I'll know it when I feel it," I reply, moving deeper into the trees.

We walk side by side, a wall between us. Ash brushes my shoulder and I jerk away. He sighs sadly but doesn't challenge me.

I don't know how to be around him, around anyone, right now. I grasp a thin trunk bending in the breeze. A sense of heat and small, frightened peppercorn eyes flicker through my fingertips. I pause.

"It's all right. You're safe," I whisper, lying easily. I extend my hand. A pair of heart birds bounce down branches and land on my palm. Their chests press together to make a heart shape, faded red in failing light. "I need your help." They blink, heads switching side to side as birds do. They don't understand me. They just... *feel* me. What I want. What I need. Tiny soldiers in my vast army.

Ash sucks in an awed breath and moves delicately. Fingers brushing my skin as he ties the message to the leg of one bird. I feel the restless sea through his touch and the tide pulling away, dragging sand and debris with it.

With great concentration, I place a vision of home in the birds' minds. Our humble wooden hut, waving on stilts, smoke piping from the chimney. Mama and Papa waiting for their children to return home. I hold it strong. I don't let it upset me.

It saps my energy until my brain feels squeezed like a sponge. I sway and Ash catches me. I carefully step away, shrug from his arms like I'm a loose sheet. The birds flutter their wings, cool air on my skin, and they're gone. "I do not envy your devotion. It will only cause you pain." The sky looks pricked by a pin as two red birds fly over the lip of the crater. Droplets of blood that will always come back to each other. Until death.

Ash's head dips. Sorrow surrounds him. He's losing.

He's already lost.

He takes my hand. Heat flickers and dies between our palms. "Come back to me, Luna." He searches my eyes for a sign of hope.

Hope is a wish. And like Papa said, wishes are a waste.

I press his hand to the wooden cage I now live in, my hickory heart. "I'm right here."

Breaking connection, I head to the light of camp. To the burning of bodies. The tang of blood and metal. "You're nowhere," he mutters under his breath.

We stop at the thick, canvas tent that feels as solid as palace walls.

Feet pointed toward each other, I fear our arrows will miss in the dark.

One heart beats with love. The other doesn't recognize it.

I grasp the heavy cloth, turning away and Ash grabs my shoulder. He is desperate seas and life rafts. "Don't go in there," he urges. His fingers are gentle. He could squeeze harder. "Don't do this."

"It's too late," I say, voice wooden and as it should be.

Head swaying, he won't let go. Refusing to accept what was always going to happen. "No. She's in there." He points at my chest, to the dead thing that can't be changed. "The Luna I love is still in there."

I shake my head like the pendulum of a clock. Seconds are dependable. They make no time for heartache. My foot dips into the light from the tent. "You're wrong, Ash. She's gone." Pain surfaces and I sweep it away. "I need her to be gone."

He shivers like I've forced the air around us to turn cold. But there's a fight on his lips. He will not give in that easily.

I turn my back to him and enter.

76
CHAR LUNA

The chancellor glances up from his bound hands and smiles maliciously. "The Char girl with Shen powers. How fitting that it be you." He intends to unnerve me. *There is nothing to unnerve.*

I bring a candle closer to his chair. "Good evening, Chancellor Koh. I am here to ask you some questions." My body sits straight and logical. Bones stacked and connected.

"I will tell you nothing." His voice is falsely noble. Confident. I tilt my head. Parts of him seem familiar. Like a poisoned, polluted version of the Shen siblings, Lye and Ash.

"Let's start with numbers. Precisely how many Shen soldiers have you sent to Black Sail City?"

"Your brother died a coward," he snarls with black teeth, spitting on the ground. I stare at the phlegm, wobbling in the mud and run my tongue over my teeth, loosening a seed that's been stuck there.

I close my eyes and stretch my fingers.

Tusk rats with long, curved teeth like sabers lift the hem of the tent and scurry to his silk-covered feet. Violet eyes blink, awaiting command.

They will be perfect for what I have planned.

His eyes are the color of sea-sickness. He searches my face for signs of sympathy, mercy, or even anger. He will find none.

I sense his heartbeat. His blood is thin, not unlike his soul. It pumps erratic, vibrating with dread. Swelling with hate.

Teeth and claws are ready.

"This is going to hurt, Chancellor." I flick my hand.

It will not hurt me.

Nor will it heal me.

77

CHAR YAN

SETSU

Sleep does not come easily to Setsu Yan and his wife, Ki Anah. Not since the children left. The house is a rotting pumpkin, hollows of missing are scraped from every corner. Sound and life have been sucked from their home like a waterspout. The children left chairs askew, crumbs on the floor, and teacups stained. Setting them right feels wrong.

It was their duty to leave, but there's little comfort in it. Not when fates are unknown. Their lives like fishing line are taut and hopeful, but easily severed.

Ki Anah strokes Setsu's shoulder, stretching her small arms to cage his broad chest. A way to keep him whole. During the night they take turns holding each other together like worn bandages. She cries quietly when she thinks he's sleeping. But salt stains scratch down the sleeping bench. They may evaporate but they leave a stain. He won't cause her shame by calling attention to it.

Setsu rolls from bed like a barrel down a gangplank and takes the three steps to the kitchen window. His heart is set on seeing the red-winged sails and carved ebony stern of a Char boat, a white victory flag flying exultant. It's a reckless, wasteful wish. It will only hurt him. But his children's absence leaves a cavernous space in his chest. He fills it with dreams of homecoming.

Tapping his sternum with a steady oak hand, he thinks of little Luna and her hickory heart. Sighs float like steam from a cooling teapot. Her bravery and fierceness carve a name in the mountain. Her decision changes her life in ways she doesn't understand yet. But he's proud of his daughter. Setsu shakes his head and grumbles. He was always proud of her.

Filling a pot, the Char father stokes the fire, brewing whisper tea. It will calm his nerves and maybe he'll find sleep somewhere between dawn and morning. Setsu has new respect for Ki Anah and what she suffered every time he left to fight. It's a special kind of loneliness, an ache for ghosts to become real. A fear that ghosts will be all that returns.

He jumps at a sudden thud and the house rattles. A red-breasted bird smashes against the glass and falls to the ground outside. Bright as a blood sun. He's known dimwitted blue crests to fly into windows, charging their own reflection, but heart birds aren't usually that stupid. He cocks a dark eyebrow. It's also nighttime.

Tap, tap, tap. A second heart bird, the mate, pecks the glass. Setsu stares at the anxious creature, hopping about on the window ledge.

Ki Anah rises from the hearth, clutching a blanket to her chest. Dimpled and chipped teething beads from three sons and one daughter fall from beneath her pillow with a clack. "Apa ini! What is it?"

Dipping the wick of a candle to the fire, she comes to his side, cherry wood hip cracking. The heart bird, eyes bright and desperate, continues to tap. Its mate lies stunned on its back, legs spasming. The bird should be guarding its love, not pecking a deranged beat at his kitchen window. Ki Anah lowers the candle to light the ledge and draws back in a shocked gasp.

"Setsu," she whispers, voice as grave as a Char burial. "Open the window."

KI ANAH

Holding Setsu's magnifying glass to the tiny letters, they read it twice under dull yellow light. They embrace hard, Setsu lifting Ki Anah from the ground, her legs swinging from wooden joints that need oil.

Then they run.

Setsu to his neighbor, who has the fastest boat. It's unlikely he will reach Black Sail City before the Shen arrive, but he shall be close upon their slippered heels. Retired Char warriors know to stand to arms when the army is away. They're older but have experience. There are plans in place for this. The Shen think them unprotected, but they're very wrong. They will defend the city and its people to their last breath.

Ki Anah watches her husband glide from the dock as she has so many times before. His eyes set firmly on the city across the channel. As he nears, he will hear the beginnings of a battle she prays he can win. Her heart beats strong and proud in her chest. She knows her husband. He will survive to carry the weight of the city. Lift it up. Save it.

She doesn't watch for long. She has her own task. Pulling her cloak tight around her waist, she puts her cherrywood hips to good use, climbing the Coalstones in leaps and easy bounds. With every step, she thinks of her children and her people.

She will not let this happen.

Ki Anah never thought she would save the world. Not that she thought herself incapable of heroism. The need just never arose. She reveled in her simple life with joy found in small pleasures. The clatter of plates in the sink after a good meal. The sound of her family's laughter, pushing to the corners of their home until it felt like it would burst with happiness. Catching pieces of her youngest son's dreams and keeping them like fabric scraps in a chest by her heart.

She locks it now, bites her lip, and moves swiftly against howling wind.

Some would slip in the watery weather. Rocks shine slick and plants grease the path. But she's single-minded in her focus. Her hips are made for more than bearing children and standing long hours over a stove.

When Ki Anah reaches the entrance to the Carvress's workshop, she swings down without pause. There's no time for ceremony. Hours if they are lucky. She stomps loudly through tunnels, weaving past wooden chimes singing in dis-chorus. They snap at her dodging shoulders, music high pitched like a warning horn. They know danger approaches.

Ki Anah is unafraid. She has the strength of a mother. It's wired to her bones like a second skeleton. It's the beat of five hearts with her own. Sacrifice is second nature. Fierceness pumps her blood.

The music of female voices is a song she must end abruptly. She doesn't knock but intrudes on a sacred ritual, knowing she would cut through every Char tradition with sewing scissors and cleavers to do what is needed. The door swings open and nine exquisitely carved faces stare. Mouths open mid laugh, mid chant. Eyes different but the same. Swirling tones of timber.

The Coalstone Carvress drifts forward and Ki Anah bows low. "Forgive me, Carvress but we must leave. Immediately! The Shen are coming." She sweeps her arms around the cave. "For all of you."

The Carvress takes Ki Anah's hands and their eyes connect. Truth passes between them. Urgency sparks like a firework.

KI ANAH becomes the warrior. The protector. Perhaps she was always these things but on a smaller scale. Nine pairs of unruffled, stunning eyes blink at her through stripping rain as they sail from Coalstone Village in the Yan family boat. Hands clasped neatly in their laps. Grace and poise. Magic and ritual. Trust between these women is a given. Now all of Char past, present, and future bobs up and down at the mercy of the sea.

She steers the boat northwest. A path set out before her. The ocean is on her side today, pushing wind into the sails. The ship soars forward.

She will not fail her children or her people.

"Where are you taking us?" the Carvress of Black Sail City asks with a look of water brushed steel.

Saltwater runs through Ki Anah's veins. She feels it move beneath them, solid and reassuring. She knows the way. It's tattooed under her skin. A map etched in timber and bone. Brass and blood. She holds the rudder steady. Heart steady. Head steady.

They sail to her children. To safety.

Above the squall, she shouts, "To Crow's Nest Island."

ACKNOWLEDGEMENTS

The Girl with the Hickory Heart was born from a newfound confidence to write characters with my specific background. This somewhat scary-to-start-with feeling that maybe I could put all of me on the page was inspired by the movement of diverse reads and own voices. Hearing that books by authors from different cultures and races was both needed and called for gave me the push to go all in with a fantasy drawing upon all my Asian ethnicities: Chinese, Thai, Indonesian and Malaysian. So, I wish to thank the thousands of contributors to these movements. You made me feel like mine was a story worth writing.

To the team at Owl Hollow Press, Emma, Hannah and my editor Olivia; you gave Hickory Heart a home. You nurtured and nudged this story along until it was at its absolute best. I am so grateful that you gave it a chance.

A huge thanks to my amazing street team. They are the first readers of all my books and have never failed to give me both encouragement and constructive criticism when I needed it. Loudest cheerleading and consistent involvement credit goes to Amie Kalleske, Chevon Strawbridge, Cayla Quinton, Doris Evans Marcantel, Cheer Stephenson-Papworth, Jennifer Dailey-Houston, Tamara Hank Graham and Bel Sheperd.

My three children, Lennox, Rosalie and Emaline, just thank you for being you. I could write ten books based simply on everything we've experienced and overcome together. There are little pieces of each of you in every story I write. I love that you're discovering them now you're old enough to read YA.

And then there's my husband Michael, who has always replied to my question of, 'should I go get a real job?' with 'you already have a job, you're a writer.' Your unwavering belief in me, keeps me writing when I doubt. You give me all the inspiration I need to write any love story. I'd say I'm lucky but we both know luck had nothing to do with it. We chose each other. We work to keep choosing each other.

Finally, I'd like to thank my Nana, the strongest Asian influence in my life. So much of this story came from my life with you. You taught me to swear in Chinese. You valued creative pursuits equally with academic achievements. You were fierce and proud and musical. You smothered me with affection and delicious food. And even though I wish you could have stuck around a little longer, I am so very grateful for all the life and love you crammed into the twenty years I had with you.

LAUREN NICOLLE TAYLOR is the bestselling author of The Woodlands series and the award-winning YA novel *Nora & Kettle* (Gold Medal Winner for Multicultural fiction, Independent Publishers Book Awards), which is the first book in the acclaimed Paper Stars series.

She has a Health Science degree and an honors degree in Obstetrics and Gynecology. A full time writer and artist, Lauren recently moved from Australia to Canada with her husband and three children for a new adventure. She is a proud hapa and draws on her multicultural background in all of her novels.

Lauren is represented by Golden Wheat Literary.

Find Lauren at http://www.laurennicolletaylor.com.

#HickoryHeart
#TheGirlwiththeHickoryHeart

facebook.com/TheWoodlandSeries
twitter.com/LaurenNicolleT
instagram.com/laurennicolletaylor

CPSIA information can be obtained
at www.ICGtesting.com
Printed in the USA
FSHW011112270721
83551FS